DARK COMEDY

MARK L. WILLIAMS

Copyright ©2024 by Mark L. Williams.

ISBN 978-1-964097-83-1 (softcover)
ISBN 978-1-964097-84-8 (ebook)

All rights reserved. No part of this book may be reproduced or transmitted in any form or by any means, electronic or mechanical, including photocopying, recording, or by any information storage and retrieval system without express written permission from the author, except in the case of brief quotations embodied in critical reviews and certain other non-commercial uses permitted by copyright law.

This book is a work of fiction. Names, characters, places, and incidents are the product of the author's imagination or are used fictitiously. Any resemblance to actual locales, events, or persons, living or dead, is purely coincidental.

Printed in the United States of America.

INK START MEDIA
265 Eastchester Dr Ste 133 #102
High Point NC 27262

DARK
COMEDY

*satis magnum alter alteri
theatrum sumus*

MARK L. WILLIAMS

*In Memory of
David*

*Director, actor, mentor, business manager,
friend
and in memory of our many
Tuesday evening colloquies
at those many and wonderful Greek restaurants*

Dark Comedy

VILLAGE LIFE

The village of D_____ is small and inconspicuous enough that few people sharing the Alsace region of France were aware of it's existence. There were no grandiose monuments, impressive churches or scenic attractions to lure either visitors or tourists. Agriculture remains the cornerstone of the local economy. The farmers, dairymen, and their families are satisfied to live and work off the "beaten track." Occasional forays into Strasbourg or Metz might create a stir among the populous. Such adventurers might be labeled "snooty" or "uppity." Those few bold enough to spend a week in Paris would be "politely shunned" by their neighbors upon their return, until they "renewed" their rural-village credentials.

In the settlement, there were few merchants beyond those vital to an agricultural community. One such was Bernard Schortmann, a burly man of chiseled features and stellar character. He inherited his dry goods business from his father. His honesty and charisma earned him many friends. Indeed, he was not known to have a single enemy. He had a reputation for fairness, was admired for his honesty, and worshiped for his extension of credit to anyone caught in dire straits.

Bernard married Paulette, a farmer's daughter who was virtuous, respected. and admired. What she lacked in beauty was more than compensated for by her loyalty, energy, and an indefatigable spirit. If a villager suffered an injury or illness, that person could expect a visit by Paulette Schortmann; she would appear with home remedies and nourishing, health-restoring, and palatable sustenances.

The Schortmann family included two daughters. This was unexpected as both husband and wife came from ancestries which, hitherto, produced males by a wide margin.

Yvette, the eldest by three years, inherited her father's honesty and work ethic. Vet, the name she wore around the familial hearth, enjoyed her mother's good looks and – under *mater's* tutelage – became a talented cook and baker. Though a good student, she was hardly a scholar.

Yvonne Schortmann, however, constituted an amalgam of anomalies. Beyond the obvious, she, alone of any family member in living memory had jet black hair. Her eyes were – in the estimation of a professional – "celeste," a blue so delicate, penetrating and hypnotic that citizens with superstitious tendencies avoided her whenever possible. Further, in a family of "normal sized" people, Yvonne was tall – tall for her age, certainly, but as a young girl, it was feared she'd reach two meters. Her growth spurt, however, ended at the age of thirteen when it ceased, leaving her a shade above a meter and three-quarters. At such a tender age, she was horrified at being the tallest among the local females.

Yvonne ("Yve" to her friends and "Vovo" to her sister) was frequently called "the rake handle." When her upward growth ceased, however, she began to fill out. She showed signs of intelligence and possessed uncanny perception from an early age. Similarly, she was bilingual. The villagers spoke French, but the family lived so near the (post-war) border that Yve picked up German vocabulary and syntax as easily as a new suit gathers lint. Because she was born two and a half decades after World War II, she became aware that local attitudes toward Germans – any Germans – were notably saturnine.

The population of the village of D_____ is overwhelmingly Catholic. Most were Sunday-Mass Catholics. The remainder were nonsectarian. A notable exception, predictably, was Yve. She was frequently in and around the church, researching or discussing with the learned concerning scriptures and the lives of the saints.

Yve possessed a curiosity that qualified as an obsession. It wasn't enough to know, for example, that birds flew; she *had* to understand the "how." Similarly, it was not enough to know the scriptures and the Catholic rituals, Yve drove everyone – including local clerics – to exhausting tolerances. Unlike her fellow citizens, she *wanted* to *know* – even if she couldn't understand.

Especially, if she didn't understand.

Because Bernard Schortmann was highly respected, he served as mayor in rotation with two other similarly revered men. One of the most public and important duties of the mayor was organizing the Armistice Day observance. The mayor's duty was to read the "sacred list" of those villagers who marched off to war, never to return. There were fifty-eight villagers who fell during that tragedy. Their deaths depleted the youth of the village by nearly a third.

On her first participation in the annual observance, Yve shivered in a dress and coat she and her mother made. It was overcast and threatened rain. Mayor Schortmann stood boldly before an antique microphone to read the names of the deceased. The mayor's retinue remained poised to erect a protective structure should rain commence during the ceremony which, once the reading of the list began, could not (by "sacred" tradition") be curtailed or postponed.

Standing near the mayor was his wife. Next to her was their eldest daughter, Yvette. The precocious Vovo was expected to be shoulder-to-shoulder (more correctly, shoulder-to-head) with "Vet." However, Yvonne seldom observed traditions she didn't understand. She wanted to stand, proudly, next to Papa as he executed this important duty.

That evening, after the dinner dishes were washed, dried, and returned to their proper places, young Yve knelt beside her father, deep in some historical treatise. She respected silence for only so long.

"Papa?"

He read, silently, to the end of a paragraph.

"What are you after now?"

He was not impatient. However, he knew when Yvonne interrupted him, she was seeking information that, to her, was most important.

"The list of the dead," she announced in a soft, reverent tone.

"What about it?"

"The names. I counted them. There were six French names. The rest were all German."

"And?"

"Weren't the French and the Germans trying to kill each other? That bothers me."

"Those young men came from this village. We remember them. We honor them because they were sent off to be destroyed in the biggest mistake since Pharaoh hardened his heart. They were born here – in this place. We honor their memory. The uniform they wore isn't important."

She sat silently. She was processing.

"In case you never noticed, *Schortmann* is a German name," he reminded.

She continued her ruminations. After a respectful time, her father resumed his reading.

Eventually, Yvonne got to her feet and sat on a chair nearer mother. She did nothing. She said nothing. She was, however, struggling to make sense of confusion.

Stoicism was, perhaps, Yvonne's most noticeable quality. She was never intentionally aloof, but certain matters required rumination. It was best to ponder and contemplate when left with one's own thoughts. When, for example, Vet's breasts began to bud, Vovo was aloof and morose for days. She was "cautiously envious;" that is, she was pleased for her sister's sake, but breasts are for nursing. Nursing required babies. This made Yvonne jealous. Jealousy was a sin. Regardless, she didn't want to share her sister with anyone.

When in doubt, send forth an Our Father.

Yvonne invested considerable time on her knees while struggling with her selfishness and petty emotions.

Dark Comedy

Many people found it difficult to accept Yvette and Yvonne as siblings. They talked, played, acted, and conversed as if they were best of friends. Neither Mater nor Pater recalled an instance when their offspring engaged in childhood combat or, even, harsh words. This anomaly was predicated, in large part, on Yvonne's proclivity for accommodation.

Vovo was the youngest. Her duty was to respect and obey her elders. She would defer at the proverbial drop of the hat. Similarly, she accepted as a duty (perhaps a "sacred" duty) to placate. She hated arguing; she hated raised voices. For her, being an agent of peace was far more than a sacrifice, it was her duty.

Many were the times when the spontaneous Yvette grabbed a toy from her sister's hand for no other reason than she wanted to have it – temporarily, at least. Yonne never protested. Her lower lip might initiate a momentary pout, but she would not demand restitution or familial justice. No matter what pain or aggravation her sister visited upon her, Yvonne remained the dutiful little sister.

It came as no surprise that Yvonne, at the age of eight, announced her desire to become a nun – a sister of mercy, an instrument of charity, a friend of the poor and the needy. This would please God.

Perhaps, it would. Her parents and her sibling, however, remained cool to the idea. There were other ways to serve God. Yvonne's personality and demeanor were both a joy to the village and a shinning example to its people. As a planter or a harvest hand, Yvonne would stand out as a good and faithful servant of both her God and her community.

Yvonne wasn't convinced. There were several, serious-minded people who considered the girl with the evil and hypnotic eyes as less than angelic. Were the young girl to feed the entire village on two fish and a loaf of bread, no few would dismiss it as a demonic feat rather than a holy miracle.

Moreover, if Yvonne took the vows, she might leave the village forever. That, her family and no few of the citizens, would consider a calamity.

Yve's earliest memory was watching her five-year old sister making crepes for breakfast. She stood, barefoot, on a stool and labored over a kitchen counter and the gas stove. Mama was keeping a sharp eye, but Yvette was doing all the labor. Subconsciously, Vovo thought "I can do that." It was some months before she attempted to emulate the scene. It earned her a sharp smack on the butt from Mama.

Clearly, cooking was Yvette's domain.

Some weeks later, Yvonne cuddled up to Mama who was engaged in much-needed darling. After watching for some while, Vovo picked up a needle and attempted to "load it" with thread. Eventually, she succeeded and began copying Mama. Her work was, as expected, childish and clumsy. Mama was forced to undo the child's "mending" before redoing the chore to her own exacting standards. When Yvette attempted to thread a needle, she got a sharp smack on the butt from Mama.

Clearly, needlework was Yvonne's domain.

As the siblings sharpened their skills, their expertise earned them a place in the family economy. Vet was tasked with preparing the evening meals twice a week – to include shopping. Similarly, Vovo was expected to handle any stitching not requiring exactitude. The children not only accepted their separate employments, they also aimed for perfection. Any plaudit from Mater, no matter how mundane, constituted a cherished reward.

During her formative years, Yvonne cultivated a dislike for the human toe. Some children were revolted by the mere sight of a snake or regurgitation. Not so, Yvonne; she was remarkably unmoved by creatures, both wild and domestic, as well as their leavings. However, she cringed at the sight of her own toes. She cringed whenever she saw anyone barefoot – she would blush and turn her head like some Victorian aristocrat at the sight of something "unseemly." Vovo wore bed socks and, except when necessary, refused to look at toes – her own or anyone else's.

Dark Comedy

Vovo tended her fingernails and cuticles with exactitude, even as a child. However, Mama had to trim Yvonne's toenails. During "surgery," the child would have her nose in a book or cover her eyes. Bathing, of course, created problems. Her feet must be cleaned. She employed the Braille method. However, no matter her precautions, Yvonne, inevitably, got a glimpse of her "disgusting" appendages.

One of the great pleasures of Yvonne's early life was Papa's back rubs. It mattered not what (childish) trauma plagued her, Papa's bedtime back rub provided bliss and reconstitution.

Then, one night …

After providing her backrub, Papa pulled back the covers of Vovo's bed. He did not tuck her in. Instead – he "petted." Yvonne wasn't comfortable, but she trusted Papa whose soothing, whispered words allayed her reluctance. It wasn't unpleasant. In fact, it – "tickled." That wasn't even near correct, but the sensation she felt was warm and exciting.

He didn't "pet" her every night. She never asked for a "pet," but she enjoyed one when it was administered. One night, Yvonne became so excited, she wet herself. Papa was not angry. He lovingly washed her. While she stood in a pajama top and her bed socks, he cleaned her bed and changed the sheets. He gently lowered her onto the clean linen, tucked her in, kissed her on the cheek, and wished her good night.

The one moment of sibling envy emerged with Yvette's budding breasts. She confided in her mother who offered sage advice and gently tamped down Vovo's resentment. Even at her tender age, the child realized that Yvette was blameless and unable to curb her development just to please an implacable sister. Nevertheless, Yvonne's attitude and outlook was decidedly green for days.

Confiding in Mama was both wise and rewarding. Sharing her thoughts with Papa was, perhaps, not a felicitous decision.

"I know how to promote growth," he reported.

For months after – and quite against her will – Yvonne scolded herself. Whenever she saw a "well endowed" woman, particularly a stranger, she would think "Her father must have been very good to her." No sooner would that childish though flash through her brain than her face turned scarlet. Her shame was unbounded.

Two days after Yvette finished school, she was off the business school in Nancy. Yvonne felt alone and, for a time, helpless. She was responsible for the family darning and making her own school clothes. However, there existed a huge void in the two days when Vet was responsible for the evening meal. Vovo attempted to fill the position, but her cooking skills were seriously remiss. It was decided that the family would enjoy two "snack nights" a week. Yvonne could, and did, make quality bread and certain "confections." She was encouraged to confine her culinary activities to those specific activities.

Yvonne lobbied hard and persistently for a billet in a convent school. She continued to entertain notions of becoming a nun. Toward that end, a stint at "Our Lady of Terror" would provide a firm foundation for acceptance as a postulant. For months the family searched for an institution that would accept Yvonne. There weren't many. The next step was to determine which schools would be best for "our sainted daughter."

Ultimately, the family decided upon a religious order based a few kilometers from Clervaux in Luxembourg. Papa was enthusiastic because he conjured images of St. Bernard (who, Yvonne knew, was from Dijon). Mama was concerned because the school was in the German-speaking area of the country. Yvonne was concerned over the bureaucratic nightmare of copious forms to be filled in and submitted, plus the documents and passports and visa stamps required.

Despite monumental second-thoughts, Yvonne Schortmann left her village with a single suitcase and two books. She trained to the nearest hub and boarded another train that would deliver her to a life-changing (or a life-making) experience.

FRESH START

Bernard Schortmann remained a leading citizen, a loving husband, and a wise and fair disciplinarian of his children. However, Yvonne experienced relief when she left her father behind to begin a new life. The purpose of the nocturnal "back rubs" was to prepare his daughter for proper connubial felicity. After the "petting sessions," he trained her in other "activities;" activities which generated – or required – detached ambivalence. Eventually, she asked to be "excused," but Papa insisted.

Finally, Papa introduced her to farm-animal behavior. He coaxed her into abeyance, but Yvonne's ambivalence graduated to full-fledged revulsion. She lay quietly on her side and watched Papa divest himself of his "bag of seeds" preparatory to disposal.

Twice or three times a week, she enjoyed the comfort of his legitimate back rubs. Once or twice a month, however, it was time for "lessons." She grew more and more anxious. The lessons were – in the early days – rather jolly, in an admittedly perverse sense. Over time, however, Yvonne became more and more reticent. Several times, she attempted to explain that she was becoming increasingly uncomfortable with her lessons and hinted, as subtly as she was able, that the "lessons" were sinful. Papa, however, was the master of the house. It was her duty to obey.

Yvonne was not one to shirk duty, but she wasn't strong enough to obey. Leaving home was, perhaps defiant and cowardly, but she could not endure any further.

Immediately upon arrival at her new school, Yvonne felt both relieved and mortified. She had fled from her problems rather than facing them. If that was not a sin, it would serve well enough. She prayed that God would excuse her cowardice. She prayed for the strength to confront her fears rather than run from them. She prayed, also, that she would be a credit to herself and her family in her new environment.

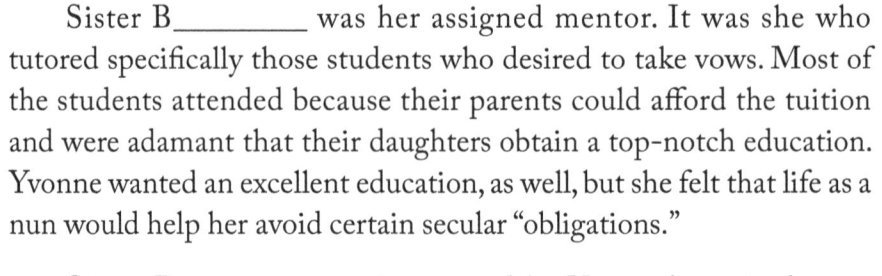

Sister B_____ was her assigned mentor. It was she who tutored specifically those students who desired to take vows. Most of the students attended because their parents could afford the tuition and were adamant that their daughters obtain a top-notch education. Yvonne wanted an excellent education, as well, but she felt that life as a nun would help her avoid certain secular "obligations."

Sister B_____ was impressed by Yvonne's aptitude as a seamstress and the marks she collected from her village school. She tested her over the course of her first week. Based on the test results, Yvonne was situated in the top-tier in every subject save one. In Latin, Yvonne would be assigned to the novice (a.k.a.: "beginner") level. Latin was taught by Sister R_____, whose reputation as a stickler was – as Yvonne was to discover – well deserved.

Every student had a roommate. To encourage "proper social atmosphere," rooms and roommates were rotated every month, on Saturdays to avoid conflict with class time or Sunday Mass and afternoon religious study and training. Within eight weeks, Yvonne was known as "Magic Needle" and a willing tutor for those struggling with math or secular literature. If any girl needed clothing repairs, Yvonne provided succor in exchange for a few coins or, alternatively, aiding her with Latin.

Classes were taxing. Study time was a valued commodity. It was a disgrace to be sent home for poor performance. The omniscient and omnipotent sisters were ever ready to pounce upon the indolent with memorable vocal and physical punishments. Few students were willing to risk the ire of their mentors. Similarly, room inspections were conducted daily. Sloppiness and filthiness were not tolerated.

Once a week, there were physical activities over and above physical education classes. These were held outdoors, weather permitting, and the girls were free to run and jump and squawk and tumble for ninety minutes. Even in winter, the girls would spill out on the activity field and chase one another or, authority permitting, instigate snowball battles.

Yvonne Schortmann was a valuable person to know. Though she cultivated no close friendships, she became a beacon of succor and wisdom. Many – if not most – of her fellow students relied upon her for quality clothing repair and sage advice on matters best described as cosmopolitan. Most of the girls were brought up in the school's cloistered environment and housed with their parents only during the four, week-long breaks a year. Yve, as a visitor from planet Earth, was a celebrity. Her tales of life beyond-the-walls were eagerly attended.

Though she refused to advertise, the student body knew of Yvonne's desire to become a Sister of Mercy. Because no other student lusted after that Spartan existence, Yve was respected by all but venerated by a select few. Those with personal problems constantly called upon Yve to supply the best advice. The few with spiritual difficulties turned to her when the holy sisters failed to satisfy their needs. Then, of course, there were spiritual conundrums that were considered too fatuous or embarrassing to bring before the established order.

Supplying advice, either secular or spiritual, made Yve uncomfortable. She was neither a sage nor a sanctioned religious advisor. However, her personal code would not allow her to rebuff any plea for help. Bad or misguided advice made large problems out of small ones, but to deny a supplicant aid or support was contrary to Yve's nature.

She wrote copious letters. Any letter dispatched to D_____ addressed to Mama was a guarantee that the next missive would go to Papa. All communications would be shared. The idea including both names on her missives never entered her mind. Her letters to Yvette were chatty and detailed. The return posts from her sister were hurried and short. Yve understood, of course, that her sibling was very dedicated to her studies, but she longed to have longer and more detailed accounts.

During Christmas "break" (seven days), Vovo insisted on sharing Vet's room. They could chat themselves to sleep. It was exciting and rewarding to talk, sister-to-sister, and exchange gossip about school, schoolmates, and school adventures. Further, rooming together reduced the opportunities of Papa's "back rubs."

MENTOR AND FRIEND

Sister B_____ possessed an angelic face, unlike the beet-faced teacher nuns who administered sanctions on recalcitrant or lethargic students. Sister B_____'s office existed to monitor and aid any candidate for sisterhood. Her faith was solid and ran deep. The lines on her face and around her eyes testified to the battles, both internal and external, she'd waged in the service of God. She'd experienced great pain, but she was no stranger to joy. She loved all the girls left in her charge – particularly those who broke her heart.

Yvonne and Sister B_____ were as close as student and sage could ever be. There was no matter too great that the two of them could not discuss intelligently and without hysterics. There was no matter so inconsequential for Sister B_____ to dismiss. She did not speak in platitudes. All issues were discussed in the context of a shared faith.

During her student days, Yvonne met with Sister B_____ weekly. As Yve was the only postulate candidate in residence, she was awarded Sister B_____'s undivided attention. Their forty-minute consultations often lasted considerably longer. Without fail, each colloquy concluded in prayer. They alternated; if Sister B_____ offered a prayer, Yve knew that she would be called upon to end the subsequent meeting. These discussions and prayers forged a priceless friendship. Yvonne could, and did, meet frequently with her friend and mentor beyond their officially scheduled dyads.

How genuine was this bond? Yve frequently pondered the matter. Was her faith and trust in Sister B_____ resilient enough to bring up an issue that was of the highest concern. No matter how jealously she kept her secret, the young woman from the small French village would have to relate how seemingly innocuous back rubs turned into something – well, "satanic." The longer she held back her secret, the greater the potential tumult. Sister B_____ had yet to turn petulant or criticize her ward harshly. By delaying any discussion, she risked a breach of the precious bond between them.

After eighteen months, Yvonne decided that the "grace period" had expired. Better, she thought, to keep her concerns in darkness. As expected, her loathsome secret gnawed at her every waking moment of every day. When she woke because of haunted dreams, she lay in a cold sweat, unable to go back to sleep.

During Yvonne's two-year residence at the school, there were never more than thirty-six girls attending. This guaranteed small classes and considerable individual attention. The rules were few but strictly enforced. The school warden maintained a three-strikes and you're out policy. Once an expulsion was announced, the only avenue of appeal was through the Holy Father.

Yve was well into her final year. During a scheduled conclave, Sister B_____ made an announcement that caused Yve's face to burn and her neck hairs to prickle.

"When you arrived here," the holy sister stated frankly, "my ardor was as white hot as your own. I've noticed a change, Child. Perhaps, there's been no change. However, I'm convinced that you're troubled. If you have second thoughts about taking your vows, we need to address them."

Yvonne's eyes, driven by panic, grew round and horror-stricken.

"I've no second thoughts, Sister."

Yve was emphatic.

"Nevertheless, Child, *I* have second thoughts. They are, I assure you, both real and disturbing. Can you reassure me? I pray you can."

Yve averted her eyes. This, she realized, confirmed Sister B_____'s suspicions.

She shuddered and broke into a sweat. Her ambition to become a nun was at stake. Indeed, her prospects crumbled. This, she knew, was the result of a secret she'd foolishly protected. Her silent denial had, at last, doomed her.

The girl sank to her knees. Tears formed in her eyes. She was no longer a student in good standing, she was a penitent. All the plaudits she'd collected as a student and as a woman worthy of respect were consigned to nothingness. She was reduced to the status of a beggar. As such, she'd access the good will, good wishes, and the helping hand of the woman she loved and valued. The possibility that she, one day, might become a peer or, at least, a colleague of Sister B_____ vanished into a dark cavern. There was only one avenue open. Yve must go forward.

"I have sinned, Sister."

Her voice was calm and assertive, but the tears were flowing in earnest.

"I have lied by keeping silent. I have been with a man, Sister."

Sister B_____ had heard every tale of woe in her years as a servant of God. Yvonne's revelation created nothing more than a mild, transitory chill.

"I'm not certain this, by itself, is …"

"Often," Yve added, emphatically.

She never interrupted Sister B_____. She seldom interrupted anyone. This breach of etiquette increased the temperature considerably.

Yvonne brushed away her tears in lieu of an apology.

"My sin, Sister B_____, is not commission; it's omission. I kept this horrible thing locked away. That's a lie. The lie smolders. It's my smoldering you noticed."

"Have you confessed, Child?"

Yve did not answer for an uncomfortable while.

"I – I couldn't. I wanted to, but I was so disgusted and ashamed of myself that – not even absolution can wash this away."

"You must confess," Sister B_____ insisted. "As for absolution – to believe that you are not worthy of God's mercy and grace is beyond credulity."

"That does not alter the fact that I cannot banish my own feelings. I cannot take the vows, sister. I can't take any vows. It – they would turn into lies. I'm not worthy of trust. I'm not worthy of forgiveness."

"I will not permit you to say such things!" Sister B_____ inserted, brusquely.

"You can admonish me, Sister," Yve responded, calmly. "You cannot dispel or dismiss my feelings."

Sister B_____ took a long breath and held it momentarily.

"You must struggle alone, Child. I cannot help you. Pray to God that he will expel these demons. Pray and struggle."

Yvonne ceased crying. She gulped for air before returning to normal breathing.

"What do I do, Sister? I cannot move ahead . . ."

It was Sister B_____'s turn to interrupt.

"You *will* move ahead," she insisted. "You are an excellent student, and you have talent and skill. You are Magic Needle. It isn't only your peers who call you that. I've heard it in the cloister."

Yvonne bowed her head in shame. She'd not only betrayed herself; she betrayed Sister B_____, her teachers, and the students who – for misguided reasons – held her in high esteem. She took a deep breath and struggled to fight back a second flood of tears.

"Child, leave this horrible thing with your next confession."

Yve said nothing.

"You cannot be free of this until you confess," Sister B_____ reminded.

Silence

When the silence became oppressive, Yve spoke with a soft, squeaky voice.

"What am I? What am I to do?"

"You must confess," came the insistent reply.

Most girls trooped to confession on Friday afternoons when the (male) supervisors and administrative personnel visited and inspected. Others, including Yvonne, confessed Saturday mornings before breakfast. Likely, she would confess again Saturday morning, but she would omit her greatest burden. She must punish herself. Perhaps, one day, she'd confess as Sister B_____ urged. However, until that time, Yve would suffer. She deserved no less. Until she was satisfied she'd suffered enough, she'd keep her secret locked in her painful heart.

"What now?" she asked, at last.

"First, get off your knees, Child."

"I can't – I can't ever be a nun – not now."

"Do you think you'd become one by fraud? That door, I think, may have slammed shut. Get off your knees. We must look ahead."

"I'm not worthy to stand in your presence," she moaned.

"There's a perfectly good chair just behind you. Please, Child, get off your knees."

Slowly, she complied. Once seated, her eyes remained fixed on the floor.

"Let's avoid the issue of confession for the moment."

Yvonne appreciated the reprieve. She knew Sister B_____ would insist at every opportunity, but – for the moment – the matter was closed.

"We, a rather enclosed community, have amazing reach in the secular world. The Lord will provide. You do not have to be a holy sister to do the Lord's work."

"The Lord and I may not be on good terms, Sister."

"His will be done," Sister B_____ reminded. "He has work for you, Child. He will guide you."

"I'm so disappointed, Sister. I truly wanted to be a wise and patient mentor – like you."

"My failings and my sins are many, Child. Let's leave everything in His hands."

She didn't know that Sister B_____ was spying until Yve noticed her loitering conspicuously near the confessional. She made a point to look at Yve and cast a tacit but obvious question. Yvonne's cheeks blazed. She averted her eyes.

That, she assumed, severed their relationship, both religious and secular, forever.

Two days later, the recalcitrant schoolgirl received a note during math class. Sister B_____ rebuked Yve sharply for missing their Tuesday meeting of long standing. She *demanded* that this inexcusable rudeness be addressed following the evening meal.

What was the point? Yve would never be allowed to become a postulant. Indeed, she was amazed that she hadn't yet been expelled for mutiny. Gradually, she realized that her sins and the horror she insisted upon carrying could not scald her any more than they had. If Sister B_____ insisted upon delivering the expulsion notice, Yvonne would accept it as an act of justice. Should her humiliation come before Sister Warden, questions would be asked and answered. Yve's sins would be made public.

Sister B_____ would ask Yvonne to formally withdraw from school. Sister Warden would demand a reason. Yve could plead heresy. It would constitute yet another lie. Perhaps, Sister B_____ could propose another option – one that did not require additional sinning. The girl doubted it possible, but the resourceful Sister B_____ had proved exceptionally adroit in dealing with the impossible.

Sister B_____ was seated at the conference table when Yve arrived. Instantly, she closed the door and dropped to her knees – unclean and unworthy. Sister B_____ stood as if to do battle.

"Don't you dare!" she admonished sharply. "Grovel all you want but not around me. You have only to confess to banish this evil. I will not be a party to this sham!"

"I am unworthy," Yvonne reminded.

"And you are proud of it! You wear it like a badge of honor, but not around me. Either get off your knees or crawl back into your satanic burrow."

This was the first display of temper Yve had experienced from the one person she admired more than anyone she'd ever known. She obeyed, but she kept her head bowed.

Sister B_____ returned to her seat and, quietly, requested the student do the same.

Reluctantly, the girl complied – keeping her eyes averted.

"You have hurt me, Child – deeply. Still, I see good in you. I expect great things from you. There will come a time when you will be called upon to make great, personal sacrifices. I pray that you will face these opportunities with courage. You have courage, Child, but you are unreasonably stubborn. You will not be wearing the garment, Child, but that does not mean you cannot do the Lord's work. He has something planned for you. Whatever it may be, know that He will test you. He will test you mightily. Keep courage, Child. Do not fool yourself into thinking that willfulness is courage."

There was a prolonged and very heavy silence.

"Your confidence in a sinner humbles me," Yvonne responded.

"We are all sinners, Child. If only saints did God's work, very little would get done. You must do as He demands."

"Even if it makes no sense?"

"Especially if it makes no sense! Do not think for a moment that you know better than God. That's pride. Pride, my Child, is one of the deadly sins. The more He demands of you, the more obstacles Satan will put in your path. Keep faith. Bild."

"I hear what you say, Sister."

"Good. Think on these things. After your prayers, when you climb into bed, think about doing God's work. Arm yourself, Child. The more you are tested, the more you are humbled, the greater the task. I don't know what God has in mind, but I know he has selected you for some important thing. I will keep you in my prayers."

Mark L. Williams

INTO THE *REAL* WORLD

Six ladies completed their schooling that spring. The ceremony was small but important and well-attended. The graduates wore purple, ankle-length robes.

Yve wore pajamas under her robe. The leading scholar wore a T-shirt and shorts. The remaining scholars were trimmed in tasteful and formal finery. The parents and guests of those passing out were similarly attired.

Yvonne Schortmann would have been the leading scholar that year had it not been for Latin. The only tri-lingual student in residence that year found the numerous Latin declensions, mysteriously, just beyond her understanding. She struggled and nearly conquered, but she fell just short of "The Brain." Yvonne was not disturbed by her rival's success. They'd both obtained a top-tier education and, in a matriculating class of six, the world would little note or long remember the quiet struggle for first place.

Bernard and Paulette Schortmann were in attendance. Sadly, Yvette was hard at work for SNCF, the French rail service. She was the clerical staff assigned to a trouble-shooting team based in Rennes. These four people were constantly shunted hither and yon to deal with freight and passenger "issues." It was impossible for Yvette to know where she would be or when she might earn a little time off to attend to family matters. She was, after all, the new kid on the team and low person on the team totem pole. She did, however, send a chatty and congratulatory letter honoring her sister's first major milestone.

Vovo wept over the plaudits her sister offered from afar. She accepted, as her first act as a "former student" to reply to her sibling's heartfelt missive with one of her own. Meanwhile, the family

Dark Comedy

Schortmann (minus one) spent the afternoon in Clervaux. That evening, the enjoyed a celebratory meal at one of the finer establishments in the area.

The plan was an overnight near the Convent. The next morning, Yve would remove her paltry possessions from her room and return home with her family for a week or two. There was a chance that she could find employment in her village. Papa's business needed someone to help with orders and paperwork. Additionally, "Magic Needle" would be in high demand in a rural community.

At the "dorm," Yvonne found a note taped to her door. It was from Sister B_____ demanding an immediate audience.

She had to ask twice along the way since Sister B_____ had many duties. She caught up with her, eventually. She was instructed to return to her room and wait.

Yvonne followed orders.

She was sorting through her things. She had precious little clothing to pack. Many of her school accoutrements would be of no further use. Those items she "collected" during her two-years residence were inconsequential; these could be passed on or tossed out by the next co-inhabitant. When she'd exhausted employment, she lay back on her bunk in her "civilian clothes."

Several minutes passed before Sister B_____ appeared.

Yve spang to her feet. It wouldn't do to greet a guest while on her back. Without preamble, the holy sister thrust a folded slip of paper into the girl's hand.

"Madam Errad in Wasserbillig," Sister B_____ announced. "She needs Magic Needle – now."

Yvonne gulped.

"How – ?"

"Mana from Heaven," Sister B_____ interrupted excitedly. "One of our lay brothers knew about this woman who is in dire straits. He told someone who told someone . . . it's no matter, Child. God's mission begins in Wasserbillig. He wants you there – now!"

"And if this woman has no use for me?"

"God wants you in Wasserbillig," Sister reminded. "Trust in Him. Listen for Him. Obey Him."

Suddenly, Yvonne's doubts and inhibitions vanished. If Sister B_____ was certain that this cryptic message was a sign, then Yve had no right to be skeptical. Truth to say, she wasn't all that eager to return to her native village.

Hurriedly, she called her parents' hotel. The following morning, Papa drove his "pride and joy" to the Clervaux train station. She had a modest rucksack on her back and a small wad of paper money in her pocket. Within a few minutes, she had a ticket to Wasserbillig. An hour later, she was on a train for Luxembourg City. She'd change there.

As her train lurched out of the Clervaux station, Yvonne paused long enough to entertain the obvious question which she had, hitherto, avoided.

Where and what is Wasserbillig?

She arrived in the early afternoon.

Wasserbillig, what she'd seen of it from the window of her carriage, was considerably larger than her native village. One immediate feature attracted her attention: the streets of Wasserbillig were all paved. It would be some time before the village of D_____ would match that.

The second realization was frightening. If she threw a rock, chances were excellent that it would land in Germany. Beyond that, she was lost.

She went up to the ticket counter and asked for Mme. Errad. The agent, a bearded man of middle years with sleepy eyes, either didn't –or pretended that he didn't – hear. What few people there were in and around the station were clearly transients. They, likely, knew as little as she.

Yvonne made her way toward the Grand Rue. Wearing a t-shirt and jeans and lugging a rucksack, she was just another hippie on holiday. Summoning up her courage, she began stopping locals to ask after Mme. Errad. No one knew anything. Most were incredulous that the young woman would bother them with such trivia. Likely, they thought she'd been smoking or ingesting something.

She stepped into a café and ordered a cold coffee. Her prime mission, at that point, was to access a public toilet, but it couldn't hurt to ask.

"Madam Errad?"

"Her of the dress shop?"

That sounded hopeful.

"*Oui.*"

The young man pondered the request as he filled her order.

"I don't recall, exactly," the boy reported. "Go down one more block and cross over. There's a street going north. It will be on one of the streets running east. I don't know which one.

If you run into the Rue Des Romans, you've gone too far."

She thanked him.

She sat, sipped at her coffee, and wondered. A dress maker needed "Magic Needle." A dress maker in Wasserbillig. How good could she be? The neighboring city of Trier, in Germany, must house a hundred such establishments. What would justify a commercial enterprise in this tiny little place? Well, she'd trust in God – and Sister B_____. In truth, she had no choice.

She visited the "necessary" before renewing her quest. Once across the street and "heading north," she began stopping pedestrians again. She kept her useless paper handy. People might mistake it for the actual address and assume she'd lost her way. On her third query, she was directed to the next street.

"Turn right," she was instructed. "When you see a sign with scissors…"

Yvonne stood and wondered. Is this where God has sent me? It was as unpretentious as a business could be. The display window was small. Perhaps, the building had once been a residence. Perhaps, it was a "sweat shop" where illegals were chained to the floor and forced to

produce for pennies a day or be surrendered to the authorities.

She shuddered, took a deep breath, and forced herself to open the door. A tiny bell announced the intrusion. Before Yvonne had the opportunity to survey the scene, she found a hostile visage from behind a mannequin.

The woman had blowsy, gray hair and a scowl that would give a gorilla pause. She deduced from Yve's apparel and traps that she was *not* a customer. In one hand, she held strip of cloth with a pair of scissors dangling from her little finger.

"You have a reason for being here?" she demanded, in a guttural, heavy smoker's voice.

"You need help?"

The frightening woman paused to examine the celeste eyes. However, she was not hypnotized by them.

"Who in hell told you that?"

The demand negated a recitation of the truth. Should she suggest that God and Sister B_____ sent her from the other end of the country? The crusty, blowsy woman would cut her short and send her packing.

"I was told," Yve responded, with a warning tone of voice.

She expected to be ushered back out onto the street forthwith. However, the matron held her fire. She examined Yve carefully. She examined the celeste eyes anew and moderated her umbrage.

"I need someone with skills," she barked. "You've got a pretty face, but I'll bet you don't know a thimble from a cross-stitch."

"Try me," Yve dared.

The woman was set to bark again. She balked. She threw her head in the direction of the nearby clothes rack.

"See that mauve dress?"

"I do."

"What's wrong with it?"

Yve sauntered over to the display. These were quality dresses and gowns. They, most certainly, were not cranked out by slave labor. In her native village – if it were possible to find such items – no one could afford to buy. The rack was a veritable cornucopia of quality merchandise.

Yvonne wiped her hands carefully on her t-shirt before daring to touch the mauve dress. It was beautiful. It was more beautiful than anything she had seen in her life to that moment. She handled it as if it were fine Meissen China.

"The stitching is a mess," she concluded.

"That stitching is why one little shit don't work her anymore. I fired her sorry ass. My other employees are out sick – so they claim. I'm up to my butt in allegators. You want a job, Missy, you redo the stitching on that dress."

"May I use a machine?"

"In the back, together with everything else you might need. Ruin that dress and my next creation will be made from pretty-girl skin."

Yvonne was not frightened. If the woman came after her with a knife, or any other implement, Yve could knock her across the room with one mighty swing of her rucksack. In case of that eventuality, Vovo parked her trusty backpack within arm's length of her station.

Several minutes later, the proprietress joined her at another, nearby machine. She cast one withering glance at the interloper prior to ignoring her existence completely.

"Done!"

Yve's announcement was so bold, the walls amplified her voice.

"The bloody hell you are!" the woman replied in a heavily accented and mangled English.

She came up and around. Yve held the dress up with one hand, leaving her other hand easy access to her backpack. The woman firmly, yet delicately, removed the dress from Yvonne's grasp. She turned it outside-in to examine, in minute detail, the street vagrant's work. After her close examination, she fetched a magnifying glass and had another go.

"What's your name?"

"Yvonne Schortmann."

"German?"

"French. From the Alsace."

"What in God's name are you doing here?"

That, Yve decides, was too good to pass up. However, in her own best interests, she let the opportunity go by.

"Sister B_____ at the convent school, knew you were looking for help. She sent me here."

"You one of Zorro's friends?"

Vovo was not too sheltered to miss that allusion.

"I intended to be a nun," she announced. "It won't happen."

"Why?"

"I don't care to discuss it."

The woman's reaction made clear that she didn't care – not one bit.

"Where are you staying?"

"No where. I came straight from *la gare*."

"*Bahnhof*," the woman croaked. "You're not in Paris anymore."

She gingerly draped the dress on a special hanger and, just as carefully, hung it from a, previously, empty rack.

"I've never been to Paris," Yve said for no reason.

"You need to fill out some papers," the woman said without preface. "Once that's done, I'll start you out on a trial basis. The pay will be slim until the tax office gets it act together – then I start paying those bastards. I'll put you up at the Creepy-Crawly Hotel for the night. You can pay for the rest of the week while you look for a place."

Yve nodded. At this point, she was amiable to nearly any proposal. Somehow, she imagined that the Creepy-Crawly Hotel in Wasserbillig was not that far removed from the shared rooms she'd had at the convent school. Indeed, it might be a step up; she'd have no roommate.

"Your test isn't over, pretty girl," Mme. Errad announced. "Tomorrow, I want you to make a copy of the dress you just mended. What's your color?"

"My what?"

"Your color? What color do you look best in?"

"I – I never gave it any thought," she admitted.

"Chartreuse. I think you would look good in chartreuse."

Yve's stomach did a twirl. She had no idea how she might look in chartreuse, but the idea made her a bit nauseous.

"Why do I have to look good in chartreuse?"

"You're working for me, now Missy What's-your-name. You make this dress in chartreuse, and you will wear it. Part of your job is to model what you make. It pays extra – not that the tax office will know about that part, so it won't be that much extra."

"Do your other employees wear your wares?"

Mme. Errad laughed heartily.

"I want to sell dresses, not circus tents. You have a nice face and a nice figure. I want my clients to see you in nice clothes. Now, Missy What's-your-name, I've got another task for you."

"Missy What's-your-name does not suit me. I'd like a little more respect."

"Oh? Just who in hell are you?"

Yvonne thought for a moment. She didn't want to be demanding. It was better, she concluded, to be humble.

"Little Shit?"

Mme. Errad laughed.

"I think I like you," the proprietress announced.

"Against both my will and my judgement, I think I like you too."

A bond – a tenuous bond – was forged. If Mme. Errad was "mana from heaven," her presence would be appropriate in a desert setting. That abrasive woman would provide Yvonne shelter and sustenance until God sent her to do – whatever it was He wanted her to do.

WASSERBILLIG: THE BORDER TOWN OF OPPORTUNITIES

Yvonne did not want to waste time (or income) looking for digs. She read the local *Shop, Swap, Rent and Buy*. She used Mme. Errad's shop phone and put in a bid on a garret room, sight unseen. After work, she walked six blocks to a days-gone-by home of an affluent citizen. The house was a bit worse for wear, but there were signs of recent and continuing refurbishment. She was escorted by a matronly woman of advanced years to the gabled apartment.

Yve examined the "space." It had a single bed, a stuffed armchair with little signs of wear, a modest chest-of-drawers (with a small, oval mirror above it), a new throw rug, and a floor lamp. A bare bulb dangled from the inverted "V" of the garret. Should Yve sit up in bed, she'd have to tilt her upper body to match the tapered wall.

There was a shared WC at one end of the hall and a shared shower at the other end.

Yve shelled out a half-month's rent in advance. This left her with precious few liquid assets. However, since she expected to be a transient, her needs were simple and few. The disciples, she recalled, were sent out without provisions. Though hardly a disciple, she trusted in the Lord to provide.

For two weeks, Yve's major meal of the day was a croissant or *brotchen* and an apple or banana from a street vendor or a small shop. Not daring to incite a rodent invasion of her "room," she refrained from taking food into her domicile. On those occasions when she absolutely *must* have after-work nourishment, she'd purchase a *bratwurst* from a cart.

Little Shit did not survive her first full week. She was promoted to *Little Nun*. Eventually, Mme. Errad, uncharacteristically, christened her *Sister Yve*. Yvonne, initially, grated over the moniker. However, any effort on her part to modify her employer's locution was certain to initiate a scene.

Yve had experienced her quota of "scenes."

"That dress would look better if you wore a nice pair of sandals," the woman pontificated.

Sister Yve decided that the initiation of a scene would curtail more vociferous scenes in future.

"No sandals," she announced. "My toes are ugly! Everybody's toes are ugly! I'll quit."

"Or," Mme. Errad announced, "You will get fired."

Sister Yve glared at the boss.

"Do it!" she dared.

It was beyond endurance for Yve to wear a chartreuse gown. It was humiliating to pose in that gown for a professional photographer. It was torture to glance at the proofs. Above all, it was a intolerable that one of those photos was converted into a near life-sized display at the entrance to Mme. Errad's office. Yes, her first-ever paycheck was impressive for a woman without previous work experience. That payment was inflated by her duty as a photo model. Nevertheless, she had a terror of toes. People with irrational fears and hates are not moved by either flattery or threats.

Mme. Errad was forced to relent. Her business was predicated on quality, high-end (or, at least, *higher* end) designs and wares. In addition to Sister Yve's expertise in fabrics and needlework, the young woman was an aesthetic enhancement to any garment she wore.

Her celeste eyes were enticing and demanded people's attention. Her celeste eyes distracted from the goods she modeled. Hopefully, Mme. Errad wouldn't notice the distraction. Either way, her eyes were beyond her control.

Genevieve Saint Cyr thirsted to be a fashion designer. She entered the "big leagues" at an early age. She'd worked in Paris and Florence where she met M. Errad. Because she devoted much of her time to her husband, she was left behind by the high-pressure fashion industry. When her husband got ill, she relocated to the restorative powers of the Lahn River Valley. If, she decided, it was good enough for Russian Tsars, it was good enough for her husband. Alas, after six years of healthy food and exercise, her husband withered and died.

Mme. Errad returned to France long enough to realize that she did not want to be a little frog in a big pond. Rather than be gobbled up by the demands and pressure of the fashion elite, she sought a place where she could become a large frog in a small pond. Wasserbillig was as near a tiny pond as one can get.

She started her business in the small shop where a confused and trepidatious young Yvonne Schortmann found her decades later. She specialized in modifying and repairing clothing brought in by the locals, but she reaped a reasonable livelihood by designing and selling to the local gentry. Her clientele stretched along the Mosel to Koblenz and across Luxembourg to Liege in the north, Reims in the west, and Strasbourg to the southeast. She was *the* designer for twenty-eight society women who found Mme. Errad as good as (but far less expensive) than the "named houses."

Errad's "regulars" would place an order six months in advance. The woman would send out designs to meet the customer's specifications. When the client specified the design most desired, Errad and her team worked meticulously to produce the best product possible. To date, dissatisfied buyers were zero. There were, however, a few sharp criticisms. Whenever possible, Mme. Errad provided inventive means of redress.

Her "team," as Yvonne discovered quickly, were not togged in circus tents.

Mme. Carla (first names only in the shop) was a "pleasingly plump," rosy-cheeked widow who was trained, from a very humble beginning, by Errad herself. She was very quiet when working and a chatterbox at all other times. She was cheerful, gregarious and personable.

Mme. Claudia was in her thirty-second year as a wife and mother. She possessed thick, unhealthy-looking legs and blazing cheeks. She had skin damage. Perhaps, she was stranded during a snowstorm or something equally traumatic. Her face glowed when she imbibed coffee. However, she was congenial and the first to respond to any cry for help.

Mme. Marie was the youngest of the established staff. She was not yet thirty, but her physical attributes were minimal. She was tall, thin, and possessed a visage that a charitable people would describe as "plain." She wore a pair of pince-nez when doing detail work; the rest of the time, the glasses dangled over her vacant chest.

The fourth member of the Errad team constituted the problem. Sister Yve was the most recent of eight "menials." All Yvonne's predecessors had required remediation and careful supervision. This resulted in the slowing down of production. Sister Yve, also, required attention, but she was a blessing. She mastered special techniques very quickly. She did not require constant attention. At the conclusion of each task, Mme. Errad would inspect her work. It was a rare occasion when the novice was called upon to redo or correct a commission.

Unlike most of her predecessors, Sister Yve was congenial. She would join in most conversations but never dominated or attempted to dominate them. She frustrated her co-workers when they asked her questions about her past. Yvonne was both terse and glib.

"Why did you not become a postulant?" Marie asked one afternoon.

Every ear was turned to hear.

"I am not worthy," Yvonne responded.

She was not brusque, but her manner of response made clear her reluctance to expand upon this simple statement. Her colleagues tacitly agreed to squelch their curiosity.

Since Yvonne had no bank account, her first "paycheck" was presented in cash. This was an inconvenience, and Mme. Errad let her know in no mistaken terms. She was similarly castigated when she had to take off work to open an account. Not wishing to absent herself more than necessary, she entered the establishment closest to the shop. It was a German branch bank. In typical European fashion, she had to present her passport and fill out enough forms to keep the paper industry flush. It should have taken several minutes; she was arrested far into her lunch break.

"When I suggested you open an account," Mme. Errad scolded, "I assumed you'd find one here. Where did you go, America?"

There was no need to recount her bureaucratic nightmare. Even her impatient employer knew government regulations and the resulting paperwork were designed to keep entire legions off the welfare rolls. Further, Yve scolded herself for her uncharitable and unchristian attitude toward the entire adventure.

As time went on, however, she utilized the bank as a conduit to pay her bills. At first, she was obligated only for the rent of her "dormitory" room. Eventually, however, the bank saved her considerable time and postage as her financial world expanded.

She was paid to pose wearing Errad creations. She resented being called away from her legitimate work which increased in geometric proportion to her "modeling." Errad, however, was the boss. To keep her backlog to a minimum, she often remained for an hour or two after the others went home.

To facilitate this dedication to her work, Sister Yve was provided a key to the establishment. The young neophyte was flattered by the trust Mme. Errad had in her. Only later did she learn there were strict labor laws. Employees were limited in the hours they worked. Yvonne was a "Black Worker," a person being paid beyond her legal allotment of hours. When she discovered her *sin*, she was mortified. It wasn't enough that she'd disgraced herself in the eyes of her faith; she had graduated to the status of a criminal.

Dear God: What do You expect of me? How can I do Your work when I violate the law? What kind of example am I?

Fortunately, St. Martin was near both her residence and her workplace. She attended Sunday Mass. She discovered that Carla was also a regular attendee. Her other co-workers, Mme. Errad among them, attended sporadically. More importantly, however, she was able to confess her sins, particularly those days she worked late.

This was a conundrum. Yvonne was paid to pose while displaying Mme. Errad's creations. However, she was paid to do a day's work for Mme. Errad. She considered it a sin to *not* do her assigned work while being paid to do *special* assignments. This was not fair to her employer. It wasn't fair to her co-workers who were expected to make up her share. Doing so, however, violated the law.

She confessed as Sister B_____ would expect. She accepted and served her penance. Nevertheless, she could not know peace while continuing her sins. Was it her duty to remain loyal to the law, or to keep faith with her coworkers?

She struggled to find the answer. Finally, she decided to leave it to God. From that point on, she kept on the alert for any signs "from above." When she failed to discover a sign, she feared that she was too obtuse to recognize them. The alternative, of course, was that God had given up on her.

These juvenile ruminations were fatuous but real. Yvonne Schortmann was confused and, spiritually, in pain.

After putting down payment for her initial residence in a hotel room, and an advance on her garret (dorm) room, Yvonne spent most of the remainder of funds on underwear and socks. In her small chest in her small abode, her top drawer was reserved for underwear and socks. The second drawer contained whatever she was not wearing. Her walking shoes were in daily service. She wore one set of clothes for two days before changing into her second set for two days. She satisfied herself with rinsing out her one set after changing into the other. That allowed wet clothes two days to dry.

When her emoluments began, she bought enough inexpensive clothes to change daily. It was a misery to lug her laundry to the nearest coin-operated facility (which was not all that near) to give her items a proper wash.

Her first serious (extravagant) expenditure was in exchange for a pair of dress shoes. She selected black heels as they were most likely to go with most of the items she was expected to show off during her photo sessions.

Predictably, her choice would not go well with the chartreuse gown, but those pictures were snapped before she could afford shoes. She posed in her walking shoes; her feet were cropped out by the processor. Mme. Errad was not pleased, but the alternative would have proved worse.

Subsequently, Yvonne announced that her *colors* were shades of blue or black. The cheap heels – utilized only at work and only for photo shoots – were acceptable if not fashionable. When Mme. Errad discovered that the shoes could be "modified" during film processing, the photographs made her creations appear slightly more flattering. Unfortunately, "touch ups" required additional expenditures.

Thus, another sin was added to Sister Yve's growing collection.

In her own best interest, Mme. Errad bought two more pair specifically for Yve's modeling. This provided her with a wider range of possibilities. Simultaneously, Yvonne felt such extravagant expenditures constituted theft on her part. She was taking bread out of her employer's mouth.

Why am I here?

She pondered the question incessantly. This did not lead to questioning her faith, but she and Sister B_____ assumed she was summoned by God. It seemed that her association with Mme. Errad fell under the heading of punishment. Was that her mission? Was it her task to make her employer suffer?

Because of Sister Yve, Mme. Errad had to shell out extra money.

Luxembourg City was hosting a fashion show on behalf of the "want-to-be" crowd. The major players were denied access, as if they would stoop so low. It was a tourist draw for the city and filled a public-service requirement on behalf of the Grand Duchess. "Smaller" companies were invited to send two or three garments to be modeled by professionals.

Who thought of inviting *Errad Concepts*? Hers was not a "smaller company." Errad's was a cottage industry which filled, perhaps, two dozen major orders annually.

Mme. Errad was incensed.

"They dare to play with me?" she huffed. "Those brigands! I'm going to shove this thing right up their upturned snoots! And I'm not going to let some overpaid mannequin – all teeth and hips – marching around in *my* design. You're up, Sister Yve."

Yvonne was mortified.

"I'm not a model," she protested.

"There are two ways to view this," the boss explained in a reserved and civil tone. "Everybody is looking to make a splash – fancy duds for the rich and famous. The people who come to me are middle-class women who like to look good, *not* like they're cocktailing with the snooty crowd in *Vogue*. The people who see you, a pretty, young woman off the farm, will see a design they can wear to local soirees where people socialize – not those stuffy cretins who only attend events to show off their up-turned noses."

Yvonne was on the cusp of reminding her boss that she was not, strictly speaking, a farm girl. However, she'd been around Mme. Errad long enough to realize that the woman's armor was impenetrable whenever she was in high dudgeon.

After a respectful interlude, the young woman approached *the chief* tentatively.

"It isn't wise to send me to that fashion – *thing*. I can't afford it, and you're paying my way is nothing short stealing your money."

"It's an investment, honey."

Yve stepped back. This was the first term of endearment she'd ever experienced from her.

"I'm imagining a nice, tasteful pant suit – not flash and glitter but something the average woman can wear to an anniversary celebration or the opera without any qualms."

Yvonne took an additional step back. This was at a time when pantsuits had drifted quietly into the backwater. One hardly saw them. Pants and slacks, currently, were worn with tie-dyed tops or synthetic sweaters.

"A pantsuit?"

"Sister, you are very pretty when you're not in a pout – which is seldom. But let's say truth: are your legs so much to look at?"

"*They're* providing the models," she protested.

"And I'm providing mine – YOU! Either help me with this thing or get out of my way."

Is this why God sent me here?

Yvonne got very little sleep that night. The question mocked her. Why would she be sent on a mission among the Babylonians? What celestial purpose would be served?

A pantsuit! More specifically, a pantsuit which would accommodate her cheap, black pumps! She imagined a huge runway awash in a sea of fashion critics and photographers. Perhaps, royalty would be on hand to add to her humiliation.

Humiliation! She took that as her refuge. She could deal with humiliation. If God wanted her to do His will, she'd suffer humiliation without a second thought. It would be better if the Almighty made her privy to His plan, but –

She prayed that He would show her His purpose, but she promised to do His bidding regardless. Still, she experienced trepidation. Was this an opportunity, or was this divine punishment?

PROJECT SHOWOFF

Five women worked with fury to put Errad Concepts and Wasserbillig on the map. The woman who signed the paychecks was not out to make a splash and shake up the entire fashion industry; she'd had enough of too much of that. She wanted orders. She felt her design and her model would generate a spike in business. During every step of the design phase, she consulted with her team. She wanted smart; she wanted attractive; she wanted clean lines and sharp creases. Marie suggested lace on the collar and/or the shoulders.

"No lace!" Errad announced. "I don't want *flash*. I want the eye to take in the whole creation and not be distracted by bobs and jigger-dos."

"White blouse underneath the coat?" Carla asked.

The entire team pondered this query for several moments.

"Do we need a blouse?" Claudia asked.

"The client can answer that," Yvonne suggested, cautiously. "If the woman wants to wear a blouse, she'll wear one."

"Sister is right," Errad nodded. "The pantsuit is the star attraction. Let the buyer select the accessories."

Claudia and Marie made a soft, guttural sound. It was thoughtful and dubious at the same time.

"I picture Sister Yve wearing a choke collar with a small crest," Claudia announced.

"Or a broach – maybe on the lapel."

Errad considered these additions.

"Let me think on it," she requested. "My initial reaction is *no*. I don't want anything to pull focus from the garment, but it's monochromatic. The introduction of another color might be an enhancement."

"My shoes are black," Yvonne reminded.

"Ah, yes," Mme. Errad nodded. "Sister Yve's Daisy Duck shoes might be plenty enough."

Yve's blood pressure spiked. Perhaps, her dress shoes were not high fashion, but she resented the implication that they were ugly and bulky. She reigned her temper in and let the comment pass unchallenged.

After a few more minutes, minor alterations were made to the design. Finally, Mme. Errad held up the sketch pad and confronted Yvonne.

"You think you can wear this?" she asked.

"I'll wear whatever you tell me," Yve, the obedient slave, reported.

"I'm not asking if you can wear *whatever*. I'm asking if you can wear this?"

Yvonne crinkled her nose momentarily.

"Red?"

"Not fire-engine red, Sister."

Errad put aside the sketch pad and went to the shelves. She brought down a bolt of cloth and presented it to her recalcitrant and reluctant fashion model. Gingerly, Yve ran finger and thumb over the edge of the cloth. It was heavy but not bulky. The shade of red was fetching, not oppressive.

"I'd be pleased to wear this," she acknowledged.

"Okay," the mistress concluded. "Let's get our tired butts to work."

Most garment makers are open to "modernization." Synthetic fibers and other developments are eagerly seized upon by trendsetters. Genevieve Errad, however, was hardly beyond the toga era. Zippers, particularly the earliest ones, weren't particularly reliable. More importantly, they spoiled, in Errad's estimation, otherwise flawless designs. She advocated, mightily, for zipper banishment in both the design and production phases. The established "staff" lobbied (mightily) for inclusion. They insisted that the zipper would be made invisible by the inclusion of a button-down flap.

"That will ruin the line," she insisted.

"A line covered by the coat," Carla and Claudia reminded, in unison.

Mme. Errad examined the hitherto silent Marie.

The woman remained silent.

She, then, focused on Yvonne.

Yvonne remained silent.

"NO ZIPPER!"

End of discussion.

Later, when "radar ears" was out of range, Carla eased over the Sister Yve and nudged her none too gently.

"Why didn't you weigh in?" she whispered, hoarsely. "Madam listens to you."

"I'm not a designer," she reminded.

"You're a wearer," Carla countered. "Wouldn't a zipper be more convenient?"

"Yes," Yvonne replied instantly.

"Thanks for your support."

This dose of sarcasm kept Yvonne in a funk for the remainer of the day.

Madam Errad's single entry in the "city do" was priority number one at the shop. However, many locals relied on the establishment for more mundane matters. Repair and alterations were considered "pop-

Dark Comedy

corn money," but service was essential to Madam's reputation. Such "walk-in" trade was left to the "newbie." Though Yve could deal with most items with precision and alacrity, it absented her during much of the "production phase."

She didn't mind being left out. Errad hovered over every detail and constantly applied verbal lashings when her exacting standards did not match the efforts of her journeymen. Yve feared she would court insanity if the boss was constantly perched on her shoulder.

Belt or no belt?

A belt would "break the line." No belt necessitated elastic. Which sin was the lesser? Only Mme. Errad was allowed to make that call. Yvonne hoped the woman would agonize and decide badly.

Another sin. This one she'd leave in the confessional. She was ashamed of her base thoughts and prayed for the strength and guidance to rid herself of such pettiness.

Obtaining disposable income allowed Yvonne to improve her diet. Since leaving school, she'd existed on bratwurst, rolls, and canned fish snacks. It was no sacrifice for her to enjoy a sit-down meal at establishments where cloth napkins abounded. This was her Monday ritual – a reward of sorts for being independent. The rest of the week was divided between fast food, salads, and fish (on Fridays). On special occasions, she'd buy a couple hundred grams of smoked eel and give her taste buds a welcome treat.

Eel, especially, was a calorie bomb. So were many other items on her diet. She parted with some of her "opulence" and purchased a pair of running shoes. Since she was no longer required to participate in physical activities, she made herself jog either before or after work.

However, her lack of enthusiasm for exercise frequently outstripped her desire to remain trim. Therefore, she made believe that the Order of Our Lady of Wrath was spying on her and reporting back to Sister B_____. The result was a triumph over sloth. Yvonne "forced" herself to run every other day.

Her imagination hung around her like a dead albatross. Even when she was utterly fatigued or suffering from contagion, she would force herself to run. Strange, she was seldom plagued by any maladies when she opted to eschew running.

Assigned by Mme. Errad to be her model, Yve experienced tyranny. The moment the failed nun entered the establishment, Errad had a measuring tape and a scale at the ready. Her weight and body measurements must be within strict parameters. Two pounds more or two pounds less would "break the line." The pantsuit – (*THE* pantsuit) – was made specifically for Yvonne. Until she completed her modeling task, she was subject to constant tyranny.

When the weather turned, Yve was forced to modify her exercise regimen. On the infrequent snow days, she exercised so much caution, it is doubtful she obtained any benefit. Rather than face a stormy-faced employer, Sister Yve would reduce her ingestion to match the proportion of her athletic curtailment. This was very tricky. She didn't often succeed.

"You're pushing the envelope," Mme. Errad frowned over the scales one morning.

Yvonne said not a word, but she vowed to forgo nourishment until lunch the following day. It was so much easier than disappointing her mentor. She could ride the waves of derision and weather a storm of invective, but she could not suffer a look of disappointment or a sigh of resignation – not for the woman who took a proprietary interest in her.

"I'm not a model!"

She announced this to all and sundry. She reiterated it at varied intervals during her "grooming" period. Perhaps, she could master enough poise and technique to pass for a model – at least, for the duration of this one event. From whence cometh her tutelage? No one in the shop possessed any expertise. No known person in Wasserbillig or in neighboring Trier was conversant in the "art."

"You let the pantsuit do the work," Errad reminded. "I want you to walk and act like you know what the hell you're doing. If anyone is watching you – piss on them! If they aren't looking at the pantsuit, they're not worth thinking about."

She wanted to believe that. Yvonne was not a disciple of vanity. Nevertheless, she didn't want to be a frontier rube surrounded by swelt and swaying professionals. As in all things, she sought succor on her knees. She'd leave it in His hands and trust that He would not allow her to become a laughingstock. However, there was a very real possibility that He did, indeed, intend for her to look the fool. Not knowing His purpose haunted her. She knew He had a purpose; she only wished He would share.

PANIC

In addition to the "original" pantsuit, the Errad team produced a "spare." It wasn't easy. There was considerable *Schwartz Arbeit* in play. The team was dedicated to their mission and did not object when informed that their illegal hours would be compensated for over an as-yet-to-be determined period. It was pride rather than personal monetary gain that drove the team. They wanted to produce the best merchandise possible while maintaining their regular, work-a-day service and quality. Few, if any, of the walk-in trade were aware that a major project was afoot.

Three weeks remained before the showing. An official letter was delivered. It was composed at the behest of the Grand Duchess though, in truth, the woman (new to her job) probably had no part in its composition.

As she read, Errad's hand began to shake.

"Sister Yve!"

Yvonne was well trained. When she heard that voice, that moniker, and that tone, she instantly ceased work and rushed to the source.

"What is it?" she asked, her heart in the throat.

"The night before the show," Errad said with a squeaky voice. "There will be a reception.

At the Palace!"

Yvonne's first response casual. This is Luxembourg, not the United Kingdom. Mme. Errad's expression, however, indicated extreme trepidation.

"The Palace," Errad emphasized. "That means *formal*."

"Do I have to go?"

Dark Comedy

"We both do. This is in honor of the designers and the models. That's a very small crowd, Sister. One doesn't refuse such an invitation unless one is dead."

Yvonne felt her face glow.

"I've no gown," she gasped. "There's no time to make one."

Errad snapped her fingers.

"The chartreuse gown!"

"No!" Yvonne yelped.

"That gown with – some kind of wrap."

Yvonne closed her eyes and tried to hold back her tears. Seeing herself in that horrible color and in front of all those snooty designers and models – not to mention the royal assembly who were obligated to host their own reception.

"Couldn't I go in street clothes?"

Errad didn't bother to answer such a vapid question. The royal family of Luxembourg is small potatoes when set aside the few European monarchies remaining, but it still rated a nominal sense of propriety. Still . . .

The mysterious – even eerie – command performance was turning into a nightmare. In Yve's estimation, the chartreuse gown, with that pretentious slit up to her left thigh, was worthy of low comedy. Her black pumps would decidedly prove a fashion *faux pas*. She'd feel marginally more comfortable in a Santa suit.

She and God were in for a prolonged session that evening.

Why am I doing this? What good can come of it? Is this why Sister sent me here? How can any of this torture be of service to Him?

Emergency situations call for emergency action.

Maria was the color coordinator among the group. The following morning, she appeared with a pair of shiny, tan flats.

"Brown heels would work better," she said apologetically. "Unfortunately, this was the best I could find."

The best she could afford, no doubt.

"Flats are too informal," Yvonne protested.

"Stop it, Little Shit!" Errad piped up. "You keep insisting you are *not* a model. Think of yourself as a trend-setter. Be a little eccentric. Do you think they will throw you out of the Palace like some street urchin. The Palace is where everyone is on their best behavior. They must prove to themselves and all the witnesses that they are not petty. Grace under fire. Even if they disapprove, they won't take issue. They aren't going to send a hired assassin after you. That might happen in Paris or Montenegro, but not here."

It continued to get worse and worse. Still, if Mme. Errad could go to the Palace with her, Yve was determined to be equally brave.

That evening, after her prayers, Yvonne Schortmann experienced a revelation. Was it sent from God, or was it the product of her own ruminations? She preferred to think that her Heavenly Father was the source. It was a "game changer."

Yve realized her fears and tribulations were the product of a serious character flaw. She obsessed about inconsequential matters. An invitation to a Palace reception was an honor. Mme. Errad was correct: they would tolerate her quirks and abnormalities with grace and understanding. The alternative would be to ask her, politely, to leave. Physically removing an invited guest would reflect badly on the Palace bureaucracy. Similarly, her performance on the runway would consume two minutes, likely less. She and the pantsuit would be lost in the glitz and glam of the competition. The deportment of little Miss Nobody from Nowhere was not going to dominate any thoughts beyond her own.

"I leave it in Your hands," she muttered to her Maker. "There is only one concern outstanding: why am I doing this? What is the purpose? That's two questions. Sorry."

Within minutes, Yvonne Schortmann initiated the experience of a long, restful sleep. This marked the first such luxury in weeks.

Dark Comedy

INTO THE FRAY

Mme. Errad and Mlle. Schortmann boarded the train alone. The trio they left behind must run the business in their absence.

The gowns and the pantsuit were dispatched to their hotel by special currier. What luggage they had was confined to Errad's cosmetic case and Yve's rucksack. The young woman breathed a sigh of relief. There was one, final humiliation she refused to acknowledge.

Errad did not want any part of Yvonne's dark tresses to spill over any part of the red garment. A permanent was discussed and brushed aside. Too many bad things could happen to spoil an expensive perm. Instead, a team of four fussed over Yve's hair. They, millimeter by millimeter, snipped off that part of her hair which would, otherwise, lap over the collar of the coat. To avoid damaging Yvonne's simple but preferred style, the team used two black combs to keep her hair from touching the coat.

For the reception, she would comb out her hair to a fare-thee-well and let it fall free range to the base of her neck. The combs would be used only to keep strands off her ears and out of her face.

Prior to her "private conversation," she would have resisted such adjustments. Suddenly, the fish-out-of-water attitude dissipated. The new and improved Yvonne viewed her modeling debut as a once-in-a-lifetime, glass-slipper experience. She would play the game. She would curtsy, smile, be personable, and complete the task for which five people toiled over for several weeks. She would strut down the runway and do her "routine" as she was coached. She would return to the changing room, change into her street clothes, and catch the first pumpkin home.

Alas, the best laid plans ...

Yve's habit of dispatching copious and chatty reports home allowed *mater* and *pater* to book rooms in the same hotel. It was not a high-end hostelry since Errad's Concepts was hardly a high-end business. Regardless, they were promised services and amenities. They must eat out as there was no restaurant at the hotel. However, their reunion was more important than a gourmet meal.

Further, since Mme. Errad and Mlle. Schortmann would share a room, there was no chance of a M. Schortmann "backrub."

When they arrived, they trundled their "carry-ons" to the taxi stand and were whisked away to their hotel. It was a monument compared to the tiny shops and residences that lined the narrow avenue. They were provided a royal welcome by the family Schortmann and an employee. After hugs and kisses, the retinue accompanied the "celebrities" to the desk for check-in, then into the elevator to their floor and into their room.

There were two double beds, a bathroom with all the features, a small, round table near the drawn curtains, a writing desk and a TV. It was well lit and clean.

"This is five times the size of my room," Yvonne let slip, injudiciously.

Mme. Schortmann gasped and let forth a flood of sympathy for her "poor princess." A moment later, she was scolding her "careless daughter" for not renting a proper apartment.

M. Errad, the third wheel, quickly excused herself. She went, so she said, in search of coffee. She was anxious to absent herself from family matters. An hour later, she cracked the whip and "cleared the temple." She and Sister Yve must prepare for their royal summons.

It was the first time Yvonne had seen M. Errad in a formal gown. She had designed and made it herself, so it showcased her assets and cleverly minimized her liabilities. Yve felt the sting of envy; she'd swap her chartreuse "nightmare" for Errad's gown in a heartbeat.

Yve's "wrap" was a short, black cloak that only added to the "humor" of her despised dress.

A limo called for them.

"They sent a limo for us?" she gasped, keeping her voice down.

A limousine and chauffeur parked on the narrow street in front of the Last Chance Hotel (so called by M. Errad) was an instant tourist attraction. By the time the honored party reached the lobby, a small crowd had gathered in hopes of seeing a movie star. As the driver held the rear door open for his clients, Yve witnessed two bright flashes. Her picture had been taken. She didn't know if she should be flattered or disgusted.

There was room in the back for a pool table. She and Mme. Errad could plant a tree between them, but their mutual timorousness kept them close.

"Will you return us to the hotel after – *dismissal*?"

She was at a loss for words. It was her first encounter with royalty. Though beheading was no longer in the royal command inventory, the mere existence of a royal command was both awe inspiring and decidedly frightening. The books of etiquette – at least those to which Yvonne Schortmann had been exposed – omitted sections of proper behavior in regal establishments.

"If Madam wishes."

"She does," Mme. Errad injected.

She feared being stranded. Bus stops and taxi stands at or near royal venues might prove rare.

"May I leave my – *wrap* in the – vehicle?"

"If Madam wishes. It will be secure."

"Thank you, Sir Knight."

The driver's mirth and Errad's elbow to the ribs were simultaneously registered.

As expected, there was a circle drive. The Errad Concepts carriage was in the holding pattern.

"Do you do this often?" Yvonne asked to break the oppression of silence.

"Often enough to keep my job, Madam," he replied.

"I'm a bit frightened," she confessed.

"If it is of any worth, Madam, the royals are as petrified as you. If you commit a breach of protocol, there will be embarrassed coughs and a few chuckles. If the Grand Dutchess slips, it's in every European paper and newscast by morning."

"Thank you for saying that, Sir Knight. I'm Yvonne Schortmann by the way."

"A pleasure to serve you, Madam Schortmann."

He didn't give his name. Likely, there were security measures in place.

"You're scheduled for ninety minutes," he advised. "Occasionally, these receptions last longer, but we will begin queuing up about that time. Notice the number on the windscreen."

"Thank you. I've never been summoned to a palace before."

"I trust, this is but the first of many, Madam."

Yvonne bit her lip, closed her eyes and thought an Our Father. She didn't belong here. She had no business here. She wondered why God had brought her here. Since boarding the train, she'd dispatched several Our Fathers. She predicted that there would be several more before her mission was completed.

They showed their embossed invitation to a grim-faced security man. He nodded his head and directed him to an usher. They showed the card again and were allowed through the wide double doors. Inside were three liveried men and a woman whose symbol of office consisted of a broad, blue sash. It was a "she" who stepped forward.

"Please, help yourself to some wine. The Grand Duchess will arrive in a few moments."

It was a large reception room by Wasserbillig standards, but modest by European standards. However, the floor was polished such that the overhead illumination made it appear as though Mme. Errad and Mlle. Schortmann were walking on a carpet of light.

The wine was champagne. It was Yvonne introduction to the heady delight. She downed two glasses with unfashionable alacrity. She was about to enjoy a third when Mme. Errad took her hand.

"You will have a splitting headache tomorrow if you drink that stuff," she warned. "You've had enough."

"Yes, Mother."

Her boss could have – perhaps, should have – launched into her. This, however, was not the time or the venue to exchange sharp words.

There were, perhaps thirty people in attendance. There were designers, event organizers, promoters, and – models. Even in "civilian clothes," the models stood out like show dogs amid a pack of dingoes. They were tall and svelte and reeking of confidence and self-importance. They sipped their champagne and smiled with perfect, glistening white teeth. They were getting a king's ransom for being here.

They got paid a king's ransom for being *anywhere*!

Yvonne felt very small and very provincial.

Father, I don't belong here. May Your blessings be upon me.

Finally, the Grand Duchess entered the room. The assembly ceased breathing. She was beautiful. Her gown was beautiful. Her glittering symbols of office were impressive. She didn't need to be surrounded by an impressive array of servants (some, of course, were security people in disguise); there was no mistaking her for anyone else.

Yvonne knew that she was born in the Americas and had attended a prestigious French school – but not in France itself. She married, Yve hoped, for love. Regardless she had a passion for doing good. Because of her position, she could move a lot of horses. Reputedly, she supported several organizations that catered to unwanted and underprivileged children. This reception and the accompanying fashion program originated with her. The proceeds were earmarked. The money would go to a reputable organization that fed the underaged, hungry and poor.

Her royal subjects, for that night at any rate, queued up for formal presentation. A footman (?) – Yvonne didn't know the titles of these people – accepted the embossed cards and read out, in a resonant voice, the names and titles of the invited guests. The Grand Duchess would welcome them and say a few words. Conversations were discouraged, but if the Grand Duchess wanted to chat, there was no one brave enough to remind her of the rules.

Errad and Schortmann were properly briefed. The Palace chief of police (Who knew all the titles?) quietly and efficiently reminded every person in line about the rules: 1. Address the Grand Duchess as "Your Highness" or "Your Royal Highness." 2. Do not chat her up. 3. If she asks a question, respond briefly. No lengthy expositions. Keep your answers as close to *yes* or *no* as possible. 4. Do not ask for royal favors. 5. Do not shake hands. IF H.R.H. extends her hand, take it gently, but do not extend your hand unless she extends hers *first*.

There may have been additional rules, but Yve's nervousness blotted them out. The Palace Official made it very clear that she and the others in attendance were humble guests. The Grand Duchess was the star of the show. Don't upstage the star.

Finally, her palms moist and her knees quaking, it was her turn at bat.

"Madam Genevieve Errad and Mademoiselle Yvonne Schortmann."

The duo took two steps forward and bowed as instructed – bend slightly at the waist and point you eyes at H.R.H.'s shoe tips. Upon straightening up, something unexpected happened: the Grand Duchess extended her hand. During their tenure as spectators, Errad and Schortmann witnessed the extension of the royal hand thrice. They never expected such an honor.

"Madam Errad, thank you for your service to Luxembourg."

"It's an honor to serve, Your Highness."

"Mademoiselle Schortmann, I know of you. You may hear from me in future."

Yvonne's throat was closed. She swallowed hard as she accepted the royal appendage.

"Your Highness," she squeaked.

She was lucky to produce that anemic response.

They bowed again, stepped back and off to the side.

When they were safely out of earshot, Yvonne leaned over to her mentor.

"I guess these other people are French and German," she gulped.

"And Belgian," Errad amended.

"You – I understand. Your business is in Luxembourg. You help pay her salary. But – what was that about *hearing* from her? How did she know of me?"

Errad cleared her throat.

"If you do hear from her – and I said *if* – all will be explained. I'm certain."

What a verbal photo for the family scrap book!

"The Grand Duchess says she knows of me," she reported slowly and reverently. "She says I will hear from her – in the future."

An excited mother and father eagerly applied a congratulatory hug. While this ceremony was performed, Mme. Errad handed Sir Knight an exorbitant tip which, she hoped, was neither inflated nor grudging in the eyes of the recipient. He nodded his thank you and returned to his chariot.

Yvonne slept very little that night. The words of the Grand Duchess rattled around in her head. Was hers a polite lie, or did she need Yvonne? Why? What could she do? She didn't own a business; she wasn't a model; she had never performed any act worthy of note; she'd never accomplished anything meaningful – why would the Grand Duchess require anything from a Nobody from Nowhere?

Dear God, did You bring me here to serve that woman? Why? What have I to offer? I trust in You and I will serve You as best I can, but what is Your plan for me? What can I do for the Grand Duchess that any one of her many other subjects cannot?

Dark Comedy

FACING DOWN A NIGHTMARE

How long Yve harbored dread, quaked in the solitude of her garret room, fretted over the demands placed upon her, and shrank in horror at the very thought of performing an act for which she was not properly trained? Had she kept count, the resulting figure would be impressive. Suddenly, the oppression of fear and inadequacy was lifted. The hateful, long-dreaded fashion appearance shrank into insignificance.

The Grand Duchess had extended her hand; she – the beautiful, superbly educated, and poised Grand Duchess – said to the insignificant, failed nun, that she knew of her. That required serious effort. Many people close to Her Royal Highness must have searched high and low (mostly "low") to conjure the existence of such an inconsequential person as Yvonne Schortmann.

You may hear from me in future.

Odds were excellent that Yvonne may *not* hear from the Grand Duchess. Nevertheless, people in the publicity business seldom make vapid comments.

These thoughts merged with several others to create emotional inebriation. The realization that she would *model* in the company of highly paid professionals and in the presence of (an estimated) twelve-hundred paying customers wasn't worthy of concern. She was nervous. She did not, however, panic.

Mme. Errad helped Yvonne dress. The entrepreneur fussed over her employee for several minutes. She assured herself that the line was not broken, that Yve's hair was kept above the collar, that there were no wrinkles or blemishes on the garment. She checked and re-checked to satisfy herself that her "model" was devoid of a watch, ring, bracelet, earrings, necklace ... *anything* that might distract from the display. There was Yvonne's pretty face, but there was nothing Mme. Errad could do about that. Compared to the pros, in their makeup and loaded down with "tasteful" accessories, Mlle. Schortmann would attract very little attention.

The "model" stood immobile for nearly forty minutes. She didn't fidget. She didn't scratch. She didn't speak. Periodically, Errad fussed over the suit, plucked away invisible bits of lint, and smoothed out lapels. Yve paid not the slightest attention.

"The girls walk with long steps," Errad observed. "They all strut with one foot in front of the other."

Yvonne heard. She did not listen. If she attempted to replicate the gait of the professionals, she'd make a hash of it. She didn't swing her butt or her torso when walking and jogging through the village; she'd not begin now,

The impresarios intended to keep the show rolling – no "dead spots." They emphasized that when one girl retreated from the stage, the next would enter. Mme. Errad had other ideas. She would not allow some butt-swinging, sashaying, professional to steal a moment from her creation. When Yve stepped forward, the boss restrained her for two seconds. She did not inform her "model," so it was fortunate her action did not initiate a struggle; it might have "broken the line."

There was no runway to thrust out into the assembled masses. The traffic pattern was so simple, it was nearly idiot proof. March to the brink of stage right, pause, move to center stage, pause, execute a slow pirouette so everyone could see the display from all angles, move stage left, pause, march to up center and off.

The professionals had dressers to help shed one creation and aid in fitting them into the next. Yve had none of that. She would wear only one item. When she exited, Mme. Errad took her time removing the red pantsuit – very gingerly – and packing it away with the greatest of care. Yvonne, reduced to bra and panties, shed her natural modesty and took her time getting back into her "civilian clothes."

Dark Comedy

    The show ended with the designers joining the models on stage for a bow and a wave. Errad and Schortmann joined in this finale, but they were simply going through the motions. Their mission was completed. There was nothing to do but return to Wasserbillig and wait for orders to come in.

    This was the most brutal part of their mission: They must wait.

Mark L. Williams

FAREWELL CELEBRITY STATUS

Mme. Errad opted for a niggardly snack at the hotel after escorting the carefully protected pantsuit to the security of the room. The Schortmann elders insisted their daughter join them in a late-evening nosh. Yvonne was amenable. The monkey that had roosted on the back of her neck for weeks was gone. It was time to face life devoid of persistent, gnawing fear.

She was quite jolly. She was awash in the honor of an exchange with the Grand Duchess. Further, the young woman had made her fashion model debut without any hint of recrimination. The professionals acknowledged her participation by paying no attention to her. Had they opted to be caddy or resentful, they'd make their feelings manifest and pointedly overt. Alas, the specialists performed their functions expertly; they had neither the time nor inclination to monitor an upstart.

Gaity and Yvonne Schortmann were estranged far too long. That evening, they embraced each other anew. She laughed often during the family congress. When she wasn't laughing, she smiled. She'd been denied the opportunity to become a postulant, but the pain she experienced was receding. There was life beyond convent walls; Yvonne was ready to live it.

There was a singular moment, however. Mother, as mothers are (seemingly) obliged to do, made a comment – admittedly oblique – concerning her daughter's marital status. Paulette sprang from a family that considered an unwed daughter a family disgrace. Yvonne was out of school and in need of a husband. To her credit, the non-model model, did not respond by noting her elder sister's "continued bachelorhood." Instead, she adroitly steered the conversation in a different direction. The concept of matrimony was quickly buried.

Madam Errad tossed and fussed all night. Yvonne slept soundly for eight blissful hours. She would have enjoyed an hour or two more, but her crabby roommate made this impossible.

The hotel served a simple but welcome breakfast buffet. Yvonne enjoyed orange juice, two croissants, a slice of ham, a slice of cheese, and two cups of coffee. Her scowling tablemate opted for naked toast and coffee. Upon their departure, much of the toast remained.

There would be no chauffeured vehicle that morning. They hailed a cab and reported to the station with time to spare. The uninhibited younger woman ambled into the café for coffee and cake. Her recalcitrant companion sat on a bench and guarded her carefully packaged pantsuit. Any miscreant could have seized their luggage and made away without any word or action from the attending agent. Should a thief reach for that prized pantsuit, Mme. Errad would draw blood.

Several times, Sister Yve attempted to lift the woman's spirits to no effect. The woman was tired and morose. She'd invested a lot of money in the project and, until she saw some tangible evidence of a healthy return, she was determined to be a misery.

Upon her arrival, she reported to the shop. It was Sunday. The shop was closed on Sunday. After securing her "treasure," she sat in her office as if expecting the phone to ring. Eventually, she dozed off.

Yvonne stowed her traps in her tiny room and changed into her running clothes. She ran across the bridge into Germany and made a wide loop. There were several churches in Trier. Yve hoped to would discover one that offered afternoon or evening Mass. She saw no overt signs but didn't bother to ask anyone. Perhaps, God would forgive her. She'd have to bring it up at her next confession. She'd pray for forgiveness in the interim.

Alone, in her tiny room, she dropped to her knees and prayed. She thanked Him for His blessings and assistance during their journey. She thanked Him for His patience with her. She thanked Him for His guidance. She prayed for the Grand Duchess.

That night, she prayed again.

"Blessings upon you, Grand Duchess."

This was not appended to her prayer. It was the heartfelt blessing of a lowly, unworthy girl who discovered something in the secular world worthy of devotion. Kind words and a handshake constituted an honor she'd not soon forget.

There was excitement in the shop.

Carla reported to her boss that four orders were phoned in Saturday morning. Two customers wanted a replica of the pantsuit as worn by Yvonne. One desired a pail blue version. The last wanted a suit in "hospital white."

Mme. Errad made it a rule: never sew a stich until money is on the table. Nevertheless, this news was exciting. She was even more excited when three more orders were phoned in before lunch. The sleepy dragon of Sunday was the giddy schoolgirl on Monday.

She grabbed Yve. This was no gentle gesture. She *grabbed* Yve by the arm and pulled her, none too gently, into her office.

"Sit," she commanded.

Yve obeyed.

The boss remained standing.

"We're going to be very busy making pantsuits," she announced, proudly. "This will create problems. We, also, have an order for a conformation dress. Then, there are the customers who need a button sewn on, or a dress that needs to be let out, or a torn seam mended or – all the things that people need done. They cannot wait for days or weeks. They need service now."

Yve was confused. When Mme. Errad ceased her recitation, an eerie silence followed.

"Thank you for telling me," Yve replied tentatively. "I never knew."

Sarcasm is wasted on Errad at the best of times. In her harried state, it didn't register.

"I need a favor."

Yve gulped.

"What do you need?"

"I need you to make that conformation dress. Can you do it?"

"If we have the material and the measurements. Yes, I can do it."

"And the other things?"

Yvonne's curiosity was fully aroused.

"You know I can."

Mme. Errad was clearly uncomfortable.

"I want you to run the business while the rest of us make suits."

Yvonne didn't bat an eye.

"I'll do it," she assured.

"Sister Yve, you were a big part of making this happen. By rights, you should be a big cog in this project. I'm asking you to mop floors while the rest of us go to the ball."

"I'll do it," Yve repeated. "I will be proud to do it."

Errad rubbed her hands nervously for a several seconds.

"We will need the machines, Sister. ALL the machines."

"Understood."

"You will have to work – *after* hours for – who knows for how long?"

"If I can come in late, I'll work until midnight – if needed."

Errad sighed audibly.

"God bless you, Sister Yve."

"He already has," she concluded.

Mark L. Williams

A NEW LIFE

By the time winter's chill settled in, *Errad's Creations* was commissioned to make and ship sixty-nine pantsuits. Seven orders came in from the United Kingdom. Someone in Czechoslovakia placed and order and three more came from Denmark. Since the customer had to pay for shipping, the profit margin on sixty-nine units was considerable. The democratic creator and owner of the "Little Shop That Could" divided the profits. She made certain that every employee received the same share of the profits as the owner.

In addition to her share, Yvonne was paid for modeling, both in Luxembourg, in the shop, and for the camera. Additionally, she got a small bonus for managing the walk-in trade and another for laboring beyond the legal number of hours. She banked most of her emoluments. As a result, her savings were, for a French-village maiden, impressive.

Mme. Errad urged Sister Yve to find a proper apartment. The young woman promised to "look around." She did, but only to keep her word. Yvonne was comfortable in her "space capsule." She didn't need large lodgings. It was inconvenient to share a shower and toilet with three other tenants, but she spent two years in a convent school. She knew how to share.

Yvonne discovered that a café breakfast would carry her through a normal day. When she began working nights, she would adjourn an hour before closing time and enjoy a modest meal before resuming work. She fell into the habit of snacking at the same establishment. Depending upon the weather, she would find refuge as well as sustenance at an *Eis* which served excellent sandwiches and a tolerable *schnitzel*.

She didn't notice the young man who shared late afternoons in the same establishment. Had she, Yvonne would realize he, normally, drank coffee or a *Chino Italiano*. Periodically, he would have a sandwich.

Dark Comedy

Because Yvonne never noticed the young man, she never noticed how he studied her. With her attention riveted on a paperback book or a magazine, she never realized how intensely he watched her every move. Frustrated by his inability to invent an opening gambit, he boldly invited himself to her table.

"Excuse me," he said, not asking permission to sit down, "I notice you come here often."

She resented this interruption. She looked about to discover three unoccupied tables. Immediately, suspicious, she closed her magazine and laid it aside.

"I do," she acknowledged.

Her resentment turned into curiosity. He was rather handsome, but in Luxembourg only men of a certain "type" accosted women in a public space. Regardless, she sensed the young man was not the kind to be rude. There was plenty of time to turn brusque. If forced, she would create a scene and force the proprietor (or one of his lackies) to protect her.

"You pique my interest," he continued, softly. "You strike me as a very serious person. You have an interesting face."

She felt herself blush. She never knew how to accept compliments. In this instance, she wasn't certain it was a complement. Frankenstein, after all, has an "interesting face." Perhaps, it was the "celeste-eyes syndrome" that bothered no few while attracting others.

"At the moment, I suspect my face radiates curiosity."

"It does, and that aspect makes it even more interesting."

She cleared her throat.

"You're an expert on faces?"

"In a way," he reported, studying the cover of her magazine. "I'm studying art at university."

"Across the river?"

He nodded.

"What, exactly, do you study?"

She switched languages on him. Her German didn't get as much exercise as it once had.

"What I study and what I want are mutually exclusive."

She let the language of her visage take over. He read her accurately, which stoked her interest.

"I study the masters," he began, with the hint of a blush. "I want to make copies of their works. No, I'm not a forger. I hope to go into business making copies on demand for display, both commercial and private. I assure you, only my signature will be on my work."

This interested her.

"You must have talent," she deduced. "What does the university have to do with this?"

His face lit up. He was getting somewhere. This stoic woman was interested enough to ask questions.

"To copy a master, one must study them in detail," he informed. "I can't afford to travel all over Europe and haunt the museums. However, there are art experts at university. I take classes, of course, but my education is predicated on my talking, one-on-one with experts. You'd be amazed at the myriad of techniques a great artist employs."

"You are wrong," she replied. "I would be awed by what a great artist does to make a great work. I doubt, very much, that I would be amazed."

He smiled. He approved of her evaluation.

"My name is Blumenfeld," he announced.

German, she concluded. He did not provide his given name.

Blumenfeld. Was that a Jewish name? Yvonne was not anti-Semitic – well, not that she was aware. She was, however, Catholic.

Was she assuming too much? Perhaps, he just wanted to chat. There was no reason to believe he was actively searching for someone to be *Frau Blumenfeld* – not yet at any rate.

"Schortmann," she responded.

She followed his lead and kept her given name to herself.

"German?"

"French."

He appeared skeptical.

"Excuse," she amended. "My name is German, but my family is French. There are many German names in the Alsace."

"Ah," he replied knowingly. "I'm from Cochem. My father is a vintner."

"My father is a merchant. He was mayor of our village three or four times."

Why did she create a dead end?

"Do you paint?" she asked quickly.

"I sketch, mostly. It will be some while before I take up a brush or a knife. To realize my ambition, I will have to be skilled in both."

Silence.

"*Fraulein* Schortmann, may I show you some of my sketches."

He stifled an embarrassed laugh.

"No," he was quick to assure her. "You do not have to come into my abode. This place will do quite well."

She smiled.

"I would be interested," she nodded.

"If – ahm – this will not sound right, I know, but – may I – I mean, I would very much like to do a sketch of you."

"I'm not a model," she replied for her own amusement.

"You are wrong."

It was his turn to amuse himself. He used her very words to correct her.

"You are a very good model," he added. "Let me see what I can do from memory, and you can see how well I do."

This congress might take her down a path she didn't care to travel. Nevertheless, the young man was personable and handsome, in an ill-defined and roguish way.

"Okay," she concluded, using the Americanism that had infiltrated virtually every known language.

He smiled and left her to tend her magazine.

Strange; he told her of his university billet, but he didn't ask her what she did? Was this a point in his favor? Yvonne would have to ponder that.

It was nearly midnight when she returned to her "zone." She turned on the reading light and picked up her Bible. Bright and early, late and fatigued, Yvonne read two chapters in the morning and two more at night. It wasn't nearly as much reading as she did during the school days. She felt she was cheating herself. Had she succeeded in becoming a postulant, she'd be reading several chapters a day, likely, and praying over everyone.

She dispatched six verses and laid the book aside.

Yve was restless. She stripped down, put on her pajamas and consigned her "soiled" clothes to the hamper. It was a wicker basket with a wicker lid. She'd purchased it to segregate her old clothes from the clean ones until she had a bundle enough to hike to the coin laundry. She returned to the chair and picked up the Bible to resume. Instead, she surveyed the room.

What did the room contain that belonged to her? The clothes in the dresser, on her body, and in the wicker basket were hers. The magazine was hers, but it would soon be left in a public dust bin. She had bed linen and a change of same. The edition of the Bible she earned by completing classes in her village church was her most prized possession. She had two washcloths, two hand towels, and two bath towels. The throw rug she bought to keep her bare feet off the cold floor on chilly mornings.

That was it.

She owned a few of the tools of her trade. Those were stored in the shop. Yve didn't count those as possessions, however. He co-workers "borrowed" when in need, just as she "borrowed" from them. Therefore, these items were communal property and not, strictly speaking, her own.

Her bank account bulged. She could afford a better apartment but feared an unexpected catastrophe. If she experienced an unforeseen turn of fortunes, her money wouldn't "bulge" for long. Her dogged persistence in remaining in her tiny apartment was part of her contingency plan. She could last far longer in her current station than she could anywhere else.

She read a few more verses.

She reread three verses because thoughts of Blumenfeld distracted her.

She set aside the Bible and concentrated on the bare wall above her modest bureau. Blumenfeld no longer distracted her. The wall served as a point of focus. Her thoughts were focused upon the young student.

He was attractive – not too attractive, but he was not an ogre. He impressed her as an intelligent young man. He was assertive – he'd boldly come to her table – but he was not pompous or pushy. She wondered if he was talented enough to sketch her.

Did his trespass please her?

There's a point to ponder.

She finished reading an Old Testament chapter and prepared to tackle the next.

Yes, she enjoyed their brief conference.

She began reading.

Would she be disappointed if she did not see him again?

Yes, she concluded, she would be disappointed.

She shifted her position and forced herself to finish the chapter.

She closed the Bible, unfolded her legs and crossed herself.

"I must include this young man in my prayers," she whispered to herself.

Yvonne returned to the café three times on consecutive days.

No Blumenfeld

She told herself she'd been stood up. It was just as well. Her work awaited. The sooner she got to work, the earlier she could get home.

Home? A gabled space with a creaking floor. Somehow, the concept of home embraced substantially more.

"I haven't been avoiding you," a soft voice announced.

She looked up to find a red-faced and winded German pulling out a chair across from her. The hand not employed in providing space for himself clutched a large portfolio with wire binding.

"I was afraid you'd given up on me."

"I was a bit concerned," she replied.

"Please, forgive me. When I'm picking someone's brains or studying details of a painting, it's . . . it's like being in the Garden of Eden. One is so consumed with the sensual experience, one loses track of time."

"I know the feeling," she lied.

Remember this for your next confession, she reminded herself.

He may not have attended her. If he heard, there was no sign of her comment registering. Instead, he flipped through his portfolio until he came to the item he sought. He looked at it for several seconds before shaking his head.

"This is rubbish," he concluded.

He turned the sketch around for her edification. The face presented was extremely attractive. Yvonne was much impressed.

"That's me?" she asked, incredulously.

"Not even close," he sighed.

"Herr Blumenfeld, I am flattered. She's beautiful!"

"Perhaps, but it isn't you. I really thought I could work from memory, but – as is often the case – I'm a simpleminded fool."

Unexpectedly, she felt the urge to defend him from himself.

"I'm impressed," she insisted. "May I have it?"

"On one condition," he insisted.

Yvonne bulked. She walked right into the trap like some brainless schoolgirl.

It was her turn to sigh. She leaned back in her chair and marshalled her forces.

"What is this *condition*?"

Her voice reflected disappointment. She wasn't upset with the want-to-be artist, but she was furious with herself. Trusting people, as she had learned the hard way, could be the avenue of pain and disappointment. Amazingly, the young man either didn't or couldn't read the subtext.

"Let me sketch you now."

"Here?"

"Why not?"

Yve pondered this query for some while.

"As soon as we order," she suggested.

That night, she had two unframed sketches tacked to the slanting wall over her bureau. One was of a beautiful young woman with dancing eyes and an enigmatic expression. The other was a reasonable recreation of Yvonne Schortmann. It was accurate but disappointing.

The hastily contrived portrait featured a visage of sadness. The eyes were dull and without focus; the woman of Blumenfeld's memory possessed sparkling eyes; anticipatory eyes.

Yve's lips were thin and dispassionate; the imagined woman sported an hypnotic cupid's bow with the edges turned up, ever so slightly, as if she knew something the artist didn't.

There was no contest as to which version was the more attractive. Yvonne purposefully juxtaposed these works as a warning to herself. Yvonne Schortmann hoped to become attractive and personable, but that was a work in progress.

Dark Comedy

A DIFFERENT LIFE

The two new friends made coffee dates. Most of them were in Wasserbillig. They rotated their custom to, as Blumenfeld expressed it, "spread the wealth." On those Saturdays when Sister Yve did not help in the shop – the pantsuit subscription had reached seventy-two – they would meet in Trier at the cross in the market square. On these occasions they sipped coffee at a fast-food outlet before examining a Roman ruin or two. The young "artist" (for Yve considered him to be nothing less) shared the sketches he'd made of these landmarks. Often he would re-do or add details to his work.

Never once did Yvonne ask why a university student should stray so far from Trier to take coffee (and, occasionally, cake) in Wasserbillig. Public transport was easy, efficient, and cheap – well, reasonably so. Perhaps, she didn't want to know. Somehow, Norbert Blumenfeld had entered her life. It was comforting to think it was divine intervention. If it wasn't – well, some things are better left alone.

There was that heady, mind-numbing moment when he saw her off at the bus stop. He escorted her thither and loitered while waiting. When the bus approached, he offered his hand. She took it and lifted herself off the bench. Before she could comprehend, his warm lips were on hers.

"Sorry," he said, softly. "This may not be the right time, but –"

"Don't – apologize."

She wanted to say more – much more. However, public transportation doesn't cater to orators. The driver's job was to stop and open the door. It was Yvonne's obligation to mount the vehicle and show her pass. When she turned to wave at her "escort" he was blocked from view.

She lingered in the memory of that kiss for most of the evening. It was nice. It was very nice. However – there was danger. She wanted to pray over it, but she didn't know what she wanted, nor did she understand her own feelings. She opted to leave her feelings for Blumenfeld and his kiss with her Heavenly Father.

Their next meeting was awkward. Neither wanted to discuss that kiss; they, in fact, avoided any mention. Blumenfeld was very coy – and Schortmann was thankful for it.

"Are you free Saturday?" he asked.

"I promised to work until noon," she responded.

"Two o'clock? Haupt Markt?"

"Okay."

"I have some people I'd like you to meet."

She wasn't too pleased about that, but she feared soliciting additional information might not bode well. It was a public venue, however. If she sensed anything amiss, she'd be safe enough. Besides, she trusted him; he was no longer a stranger.

As it happened, they were in a public venue when he "popped the question." They were on the second floor of a Kaufhof, near the escalator. She was searching for simple gifts of appreciation for Mme. Errad and her coworkers.

Blumenfeld turned to descend, but her hand on his arm arrested him. She wasn't the least subtle. Yvonne stepped into him and kissed his mouth more anxiously than intended. She knew her face was scarlet when she disengaged. There was no way she could explain or insist that it was accidental. She'd made herself a fool and there was no remedy.

It was his place to do or say something. Whatever he did, whatever he said would make her humiliation unbearable. She didn't dare look at anything other than her feet. She could feel the smirks and knowing glances of the witnesses. She was certain she had sinned, but she was unable to define the nature of her sin.

"*Bis Samstag,*" he said calmly – quietly.

She nodded, her head still bowed in shame.

She took a deep breath and surveyed the scene. The young man was out of sight, and the people who had a purpose in life ignored Yvonne, the statue. She had, injudiciously, parked herself near enough to the escalator to be a hazard to navigation. The shoppers, apparently, were too civil to author admonishment. The quality of mercy was appreciated, but her shame multiplied a hundred-fold.

Quickly, she ushered herself and her acute embarrassment out of traffic. She walked to a bus stop, changed at the appropriate station, and rode home with her head pressed against the cold glass of the vehicle. She walked through the slush. Her earlier intention was to purchase either shoes or boots for walking in snow and water-laden streets. Her abomination in public erased the mission from her mind.

Catching cold would constitute a justified, if only partial, punishment for her inexcusable behavior.

Yvonne very nearly abandoned her "date." She had embarrassed and humiliated herself in front of a friend and the dozens – if not hundreds – of witnesses. Cowardice would not, however, serve. She made a promise, no matter how oblique. To break an engagement was a sin, and she'd piled up a surplus of those. Confession may be good for the soul, but it must be tedious for that poor prelate who was forced to listen to Yve prattle on about her barbarous life and behavior.

There were times when she wished she were not a Catholic. She could fall to her knees and beg God for forgiveness and be done. As a Catholic, however, there was always a process or ritual. No wonder people fell for the indulgence scam of bygone centuries.

That's another sin!

It was like an anchor around her neck. To hide in the shop or her room in Wasserbillig would constitute yet another sin. She felt that God's patience with her must be very thin. She did not want to surrender to temptation and risk divine retribution.

She went.

He was not alone. There was a young couple with him.

Witnesses?

As she approached, the young couple grew older and older. They weren't yet middle aged, but they weren't the university students she mistook them for initially. She was tall, lithe, and wore very little makeup – she didn't need to. He was taller of the pair, and he was rather handsome. He carried considerable weight, but it was not of the beer-swilling variety. This man's bulk, as his hands testified, was the result of strenuous labor.

"*Fraulein* Schortmann," Blumenfeld began as if the *Kaufhof* incident had never occurred.

"May I present *Herr* and *Frau* Schulz."

Greetings were exchanged.

"These are my landlords," Blumenfeld announced.

A chance meeting in the street? It was possible. In warm weather the Haupt Markt was tourist central. During the winter months, fewer citizens congregated there.

"I haven't nerve enough to ask you up to my apartment," Blumenfeld explained. "I opted to provide chaperones."

They all joined in a polite, if reserved, laugh.

"Did I misunderstand?" Yve asked. "I don't recall you're inviting me to your apartment."

"No misunderstanding, *Fraulein*," he began. "I didn't want to frighten you. My roommate is moving to Hamburg. I'm looking for something smaller. Meanwhile, the family Schulz is looking for a new tenant. I recommended you."

"We are pretty particular about who we take in," the attractive woman announced. "*Herr* Blumenfeld speaks very highly of you."

"Thank you, but I'm not really looking for a place at the moment," she responded. "It's a bit of a commute to my work."

"A monthly ticket isn't expensive," Blumenfeld reminded. "The bus will take you to within two blocks of your shop."

"As long as you're here," Herr Schulz added. "You can, at least, have a look. We'll buy you lunch."

That was tempting, and the offer seemed innocent enough.

Ten minutes later, Yvonne and Norbert were sitting in the back seat of a car driven by Herr Schulz. Yve avoided contact with the man seated next to her, and he reciprocated.

"We do not own the building," the driver informed. "We only own the apartment. I helped renovate the building and, in leu of payment for services, we took the apartment."

"You live in Trier?" Yvonne asked.

"Within a few blocks of the apartment," he replied. "If you have a problem with water, heat, or electricity, I can be there within twenty minutes."

She looked at the artist. He made no sign.

It was a third story walkup. The building itself was post-war for certain. Judging by the exterior, it may have been taken from blueprints of the late fifties or early sixties experiments with new materials and designs. The stairwell was well lit, and the steps were of stone or a clever imitation.

The interior, however, was not designed for efficient use. The living room featured wall-to-wall carpet to ward off the winter's chill. It was gray, unfortunately, but in good condition. The bedroom was, likewise, capacious. Both were equipped with modern radiated heat. The outside walls and windows were modern and well-insulated.

These were the major "selling points."

The kitchen was little more than one might find on a U-boat; there was no stove or oven and precious little room to place one. There was small sink below the only cabinet. Norbert bought a small fridge, inconveniently located under the sink. He'd not need it in his new digs and willed it to the family Schulz for use by any future tenants.

The bedroom was spacious but devoid of carpet. There were no built-in closets or shelves. The bathroom was modern and functional. Yvonne's heart swelled when she viewed a full-sized tub. Above the sink was a mirror and medicine cabinet combined.

Attached to the living room was a large window and glass door leading onto a small balcony. There was room enough for a chair or stool. The view was of the narrow street below.

The neighborhood was quiet, and the street bore little traffic during her visit.

"The bed in the bedroom is spoken for," her artist friend reported.

"Where do you sleep?"

He pointed to the couch.

It was well upholstered and had two, long, inviting backrests.

"You sleep on the couch?"

She couldn't help herself. Not until after the words escaped her thoughtless lips did she recognize her incredible rudeness.

Blumenfeld smiled.

"April, April!" he teased.

Despite her French upbringing, she recognized the German catch phrase for "April Fool."

He removed the backrests which were large pillows. He lifted the head of the bed which opened the recess for sheets, blankets and a pillow. Releasing the catch, he went to the foot of the bed and raised it up to show a nice storage space for whatever one wished to store. Blumenfeld used the space to store his sketch books and related materials.

Next to the window and balcony was a walk-in closet – "walk in" if one stooped or crawled. There was room for considerable pelf *and* a sturdy wooden rod for hanging clothing.

They descended to the basement. There she found two washers and driers. Neither was coin operated. There was a secure area for bike storage. It required wrestling the vehicle up a narrow set of concrete steps after exiting a solid wooden door. Three bicycles resided in a sturdy bike-rack designed for six vehicles.

Through an arched passage were storage units made of heavy wooden slats. There were seven, secure cells of thick wooden slats and large slatted doors. Each was secured with heavy-duty locks. Norbert had no further need of his lock and promised to leave it and the keys with Yve should she rent.

In Blumenfeld's unit were two boxes of seasonal clothing and a toolbox. Against the concrete wall was a wooden table with a plastic surface.

"During heavy rains, this space floods a bit," Blumenfeld informed.

The warning was unnecessary. Yve could deduce as much by looking at the lower three inches of the table legs.

The quartet returned to the apartment.

"The couch stays," Blumenfeld informed her.

Yvonne sat on the bed/couch and contemplated. She was tired of sleeping in a bread box. Here, she could spread out. She could bathe whenever the urge struck her. She could move the table from the cellar into the kitchen and buy a hotplate, offering a viable option to eating out.

"How much," she asked, thoughtlessly.

"Three eighty a month," Herr Schulz replied.

"Hot." His wife added, quickly.

Three hundred and eighty marks a month with heat and water. Plus, she'd have access to washing machines and driers. She could get a bike and increase her range. She could buy and assemble a cabinet for the kitchen and have a place to store dry and canned goods. She could buy and assemble a shrunk for the bedroom for her clothes. She could buy and assemble a bookcase for the living room. She could have books and bric-a-brac to make it more like a home.

Here was an adventure in the offing.

"I'll take it," she announced. "There are certain conditions."

Herr Schulz nodded.

"I'll need someone to help getting that table up here. I'll need someone to help assemble the furniture. I'll need someone to help hauling furniture."

"I'll help with the lifting and the assembly," Blumenfeld responded instantly.

"We have a van," the family Schulz announced in unison.

Yvonne Schortmann sat silently for several seconds. An hour before, she hadn't a thought of changing her abode. Unexpectedly, she was committed to opening a new chapter in her life.

Why, she asked herself, did she act so fatuously? What made her change the direction of her life on a whim? How could this happen in only a few minutes?

THE SHOWDOWN

There was so much to do. In addition to physical relocation, she had to struggle with mountains of bureaucratic claptrap and liters of ink. An alien was about to take up residence in the Republic of Germany. In addition to filling in and getting approval for tons of papers and questionnaires, she had to prove that she was not wanted by the authorities in other countries. She had to prove she was not carrying a deadly disease. She had to swear oaths to a series of statements, many of which were silly or archaic. She had to have her passport examined by experts and stamped.

She continued her work, leaving precious little time to keep up with the governmental merry-go-round. To satisfy the panicked Mme. Errad, she changed her mailing address to that of *Errad Creations*. Even that did not quell her employer. The woman was obsessed with the notion that Magic Needle was off to fame and fortune with some rival who was willing to pay Yvonne what she was worth.

One day, however, the tempest dissipated through one phone call.

"Sister! Phone."

Who would call Yvonne? She had no phone of her own. Everyone who desired to contact her, including Sister B_____ (whose infrequent missives lifted her spirits no little) were restricted to stamped epistles.

If there was one, absolute and unamendable rule in the shop it was that the phone line must be kept free for business. Even business calls must be brief. Yve, therefore, wasted no time getting to the office.

Errad gave her a withering glare. This better be short.

"Hello, yes?"

"Vovo?"

"Vet! I'm thrilled, but the wicked witch won't let me chat."

"I've got a commission for you."

"You want one of our pantsuits? We're up to our knees in orders."

"Not a pantsuit, please. Would you make my wedding gown?"

Suddenly, the lump in her throat and tears forming in her eyes kept her speechless.

"Vovo?"

Yve gulped.

"Yes. Congratulations. I'm – thrilled."

"Can you do it?"

Yve nodded. Moments later she realized her sister couldn't hear her nod.

"I will be so very, very proud," she announced, choking slightly. "Exceedingly proud!"

"We're thinking about June. Is that enough time?"

"It should be. I need – well you know what I need. Send it to me at the shop. I'm moving."

"Where? Will you keep your job?"

"Yes. I'll get started the minute I get the numbers. Don't forget to include any design features you want."

"No, Vovo. I'm leaving it all up to you. I have faith."

There was a pause as Yve teared up again.

"Sis? Are you there?"

"Yes. I'm in shock. I want to know all about this guy. I can't wait to get started."

The moment she hung up, she began crying in earnest. Errad, fearing a death in the family, rushed to her side. It took a few seconds to compose herself.

"What is it?"

"My sister. She wants – (gulp) – me to make – (gulp) her wedding dress."

The woman let Magic Needle compose herself.

"Who is the guy?" she asked.

"He's the guy who is going to marry the best woman ever."

If Errad, the wicked witch, had a heart, it was touched by this sentiment. However, emotions are transitory.

"Satin," Yve insisted.

"That's going to run into money," Errad reminded.

"It's my wedding gift," Sister informed. "I'll pay for it if I have to beg in the streets."

Her employer had heard such pronouncements before. She didn't believe them then; she wasn't going to start falling for one – not even from Mlle. Schortmann.

"I need a design," Yve decided. "None of that *Gone with the Wind* motif. Something simple yet elegant."

Errad sighed.

"That narrows it down."

"Make a sketch," Yve suggested. "I'll have plenty of ideas then."

"I'll work on it tonight," the woman promised.

Suffering from emotional overload, she and her German "beau" began the purchase and transfer of do-it-yourself furnishings. Not entirely, however. She bought a modest bureau. It was, she suspected, designed with a child in mind. However, it would be enough to hold her undies, socks, and a few accessories. That was put in the middle of the far wall. The shrunk, into which she'd hang all her togs, would go into a space between the door and the far wall. The door opened inward, so the item had to be just out of range. They made it with a few millimeters to spare. It looked awkward, but Yve opted for the functional over the aesthetic.

She helped where she could. Most of the assembly involved screws. To prevent her from raising a crop of blisters, Blumenfeld allowed her to use his gloves. He got the blisters.

As a "housewarming gift," Blumenfeld bought his friend a desk. When assembled, it had two cubbyholes on each side, a shelf above for pictures or bric-a-brac, and a nice, polished surface for her to write on or for Blumenfeld to rest his art pads while sketching.

They took frequent work breaks. Inevitably, these breaks were punctuated by being close and whispering to each other. Whispering led to a stolen kiss or two. A stolen kiss (or two) would gradually (or not so gradually) graduate to a demand.

Yvonne wept briefly and explained how ashamed she was over her behavior at the department store.

"That was too – forward," she insisted.

"I saw no harm," he replied. "It was an unexpected pleasure."

"I'm a fraud," she confessed. "I'm female, so I am denied refuge in the Foreign Legion. As a Catholic, however, I could become a nun. That was my goal. I succeeded in convincing myself that it was what I really wanted. Now, I openly admit, it was a lie. Being a nun was simply a substitute for the Foreign Legion."

He drew her to him and allowed her to rest her head on his shoulder.

"I ran away to a Catholic boarding school. One of the sisters saw right through me. Perhaps, they all did. Thankfully, I was confronted – exposed more like."

They remained silent for some time. His arms comforted her.

"When you hold me like this – when you kiss me – it's like – like my brain explodes, and I want nothing more than to be with you – to be a part of you."

"You sound as if that is a bad thing," he mused.

"It isn't," she assured. "It's wonderful and – and I want to be with you – to sleep with you, but – I'm Catholic enough that I – I have scruples. Damn! Double damn! I – there is no way I can explain."

He squeezed her reassuringly.

"Give it a try," he suggested. "I let you know how well you do."

"This is so hard – may – may I call you Norbert?"

"If you allow me to call you Yve."

"Do. Please, do."

They remained quiet and motionless until the silence became oppressive.

"Norbert," she began, her voice crackling from an arid throat. "In the Biblical sense, I am a married woman."

She felt him flinch.

"Yve, I'm Catholic in name only," he said, hesitatingly. "I may not understand."

Yvonne took a deep breath. The very thing she avoided sharing with Sister B_____, that dark, horrible – issue -- she could not speak about in the Confessional was about to be made public. She trusted Norbert. If he betrayed that trust – well, at the very least, a betrayal would be something "different." A violation of her confidence, devastating though it might be, would be transitory. Her great burden would be part of her forever. Hopefully, sharing her load would make it a bit lighter.

"When I was young – younger – when I was a – a child, a man – began to – what you are beginning – or what you may be thinking about. Do you know – how frightened I am – about – Well, I feel – you are special – to me, but – this thing – I must have time – to get past this. Perhaps, I never will – get past – it – it is always – there! This – nightmare – is always – *there.*

"Sad eyes," he reflected. "You do have sad eyes."

"You didn't notice at first," she concluded. "That first sketch – I noticed the difference in your second drawing."

"It was bad?"

She shrugged.

"Not at first – the first time, that is. I mean, he didn't – well, not then."

"How long did this go on?"

"Four years – maybe, five."

He bristled.

"I'd like to put this man away."

She ignored that.

"It was – kind of fun – the touching and the – more touching. When it turned ugly – I felt – guilty."

"Guilty? You?"

"Norbert, my feelings are indescribable. *Guilty* is as good as I can do. I just feel so dirty – so wicked. So, if you succeed in – *seducing me,* I'll be blunt: if you do, and I start screaming or going into convulsions – well, I hope that won't happen, but know this: *I'm* the problem – it's not to do with you."

Dark Comedy

He could not see them, but he sensed the tears.

He kissed the top of her head and held her protectively. When he realized she was asleep, he continued to hold her. He hoped that she was enjoying a pleasant dream.

FALSE HARBINGER

Norbert Blumenfeld treated Yvonne Schortmann as she preferred to be treated, with respect and patience. He did not betray her confidence. Further, he treated her and handled her with a respect seldom seen in modern times. He admired her for her values. He was, by his own admission, Catholic in name only; Yvonne, however, was as punctilious as a nun. There were times, to be sure, when the woman infringed on custom, ceremony, and doctrine if she did not completely understand – or if she considered an item merely a survivor of medieval "jiggery-pokery."

She thought for herself. He admired her for that.

After her confession, he handled her delicately. He left her and her belief system in command. He remained eager to get her into bed, but the thought of her becoming hysterical or epileptic kept him in check. There were times – well, two times – when he thought she would seduce him. She was skillful, adventurous, and poised. Alas, these attempts came to naught.

Near misses

Sex aside, they were best friends. They shared a considerable portion of their lives and beliefs. However, there were things about her that Yve kept to herself. She admitted as much. Eventually, this became an issue – a minor one, to be certain, but it began to fester.

The two met twice or thrice during the week. It was either for coffee or a light nosh. They would exchange news of their insular lives and discussed matters of consequence. Saturday evenings found Norbert in his former apartment. It was decorated to fit Yve's taste – that is, the furniture and cooking items were arrayed according to her desires.

She never bought a bed.

"The ones I like, I can't afford," she explained.

She slept on the couch/bed in the big room. Norbert thought this both Spartan and unnecessary. He scolded her mildly.

"At school and in my former digs, I slept in in worse," she reported.

Subject closed.

Occasionally, they would discuss "matters." These were the kinds of matters which were both personal and delicate. Ever free to offer advice – even when it was unsolicited – these "discussions" often became heated.

Whenever they got excited and began raising voices, Yvonne would always call a momentary time out.

"Norbert," she would begin in her soft, little-girl voice. "Promise. When this is over, you will kiss me goodnight."

He never broke that promise..

Yvonne liked kissing. To be exact: she liked kissing Norbert. The caresses they shared, and the warmth of their lips kept her buoyant for days. Her eyes remained sad, but not as pronounced as they once were. Even Mme. Errad and "the girls" noticed that Magic Needle was quicker to smile and capable of producing an occasional laugh – a genuine laugh and not a contrived counterfeit she frequently manufactured.

Life was not exactly *good*, but it had become "comfortable." Having more room in her apartment contributed no small part in the transformation. However, the friendship and understanding of Norbert Blumenfeld constituted the largest factor in promoting her felicity.

The subdued and somewhat prudish Claudia one day looked up from her work. She looked directly at Yvonne.

"You have a man."

Yve, instantly, turned scarlet. The employees, and their boss, offered up a laugh and hearty congratulations.

"Good bless you," Yve said as the others went home to leave her with the tangle and dregs of the day.

They smiled and vacated the shop.

These women did not pump her for details. They did not compose fantastic scenarios. They did not speculate upon the qualities or the physical attributes of "Yve's man." That constituted a monument to their love and respect. They were worthy of a sincere "God bless you."

Such friends were worth more than gold to Yvonne. At that point in her life, she'd have surrendered her life for any of them. She had Norbert, and she had a quartet of peerless

colleagues. Her cup runnith over.

Yvonne did not hear from the Grand Duchess. She did get a three-page questionnaire with her name and the shop's address embossed in large gilt letters atop the cover page. It was not a multiple-guess form. She had to compose her answers. Some questions required only a terse response; other questions left room for more expansive answers. The final page was designed to elicit a brief essay.

The failed nun provided thoughtful responses. Thanks to the demands of her convent-school experience, she avoided triteness. Her responses were carefully considered and succinct. Her "short essay" was thoughtful and polished.

Mme. Errad allowed three days to attend Yvette's wedding. Yvonne posted her completed form on her way to the *Bahnhof*.

The village of D_____ was much the same as it was when she left. The intervening years, however, had not been either kind or prosperous. Many structures, including her childhood home, were denied paint. The few paved roads had sprouted potholes, no few of which were dangerous.

The interior of the Schortmann home, predictably, was a showcase. Floral arrays abounded. The furnishings were all dust-free and polished. Anything that could be cleaned, mended, or refurbished were ready for inspection by any fastidious citizen. The girls' rooms were a tidy summation of the lives of those who grew up in them. Favorite dolls and decorations were tastefully displayed. The bedding consisted of *facsimiles* of the faded and discarded items of their youth. Mother and father brought forth the proverbial fatted calf in honor of the return of the "prodigal" daughters.

Dark Comedy

There were hugs and kisses enough to put other local reunions to shame. Visitors came to offer good wishes and stayed for refreshments and recitations of experiences from beyond the horizon. It was late in the evening when the sisters, at last, had time together.

It was in Yvette's room. The siblings marveled at the spit-and-polish that had never existed when they lived at home. Clean never stood much of a chance when the girls, singly or in concert, frolicked in dirty clothes, shoes, or examined items brought in from the outside – many of which were filthy or, in some cases, a state of decay.

Vet's satin dress was sheathed in clear plastic and hung down from a special fixture, lovingly installed by their proud and loving father. Yvette applauded her sister for producing such a beautiful garment.

"I had a lot of help," the modest Yvonne replied.

Vet rushed to the door and peaked out. She surreptitiously closed it and leaned against it to prevent an unwelcome entrance.

"Vovo, I need your expert help," she whispered.

Sensing something horrible, Yvonne braced herself, figuratively.

"What is it?"

Yvette leaned forward but kept one hand flat against the door.

"Could you let it out? Just a little."

She mouthed the words more than she articulated them.

Yve was vexed. She, and the entire shop, had checked and double checked every measurement. How could they have failed? If the fault were hers or theirs, Yvonne would be most unreasonable upon her return.

"What did we do wrong?" Yve asked, on the verge of panic.

"Nothing," Vet replied.

She motioned for her sister to draw near. Yvonne complied.

"Henri and I – we got a head start on our family –"

An electric current burst from the base of Yvonne's skull and traveled the length of her spine. She felt love and wonderment in every particle of her body. She bounced on her toes and gathered her sister in her arms. The tears – tears of joy – filled her eyes and her heart was bursting with love and wonder.

"Vet! I am so happy! I'm so thrilled!"

"Shush!" Vet screamed – in a breathy whisper. "This is between us. Not even Henri knows yet."

"How could you not tell him?"

Yvonne stepped back and eyed her sister suspiciously.

"Are you afraid he will create a fuss?" she asked.

Vet shook her head emphatically.

"He'll be over the moon," she affirmed. "It's Mama and Papa who might make a fuss."

Might?

In the Schortmann family, there was the right way to do things. Any other option was vehemently opposed. The girls had endured severe punishment for transgressions. Yvonne once had to stand in a corner for three hours because her dish washing did not meet Mama's exacting standards. Similarly, Papa sentenced Yvette to three days of bread and water for being rude to a neighbor boy. These were but two of the punishments meted out over the years. Slothfulness was a sin not tolerated in the Schortmann home; rudeness ran a close second.

Should either parent suspect that Yvette was "carrying a passenger" to her wedding – well, chances were she'd *not* be put on bread and water. Who knew what might happen? Who dared to find out?

"I'll do my best," Yvonne promised.

Yvette breathed easier. Her sister could do no wrong. More importantly, she would take her secret to the grave.

Dark Comedy

LIGHT AND SHADOW

Yvette placed her career on hold. Indeed, she never considered herself on a career track. She did clerical work, gained plaudits for her efforts, and met a man ("the man of my dreams," as she put it). Yvonne had such a brief interaction with him, she was unable to make judgements. Henri seemed intelligent and personable, but one's wedding day seldom provides a satisfactory composite. He was not particularly tall and – in Yve's estimation – not particularly handsome. He had, however, won her sister's heart; that vouched for his character.

The guests swooned over the bride's gown.

Mama employed the word *swoon*. Yve, hardly an impartial judge, was satisfied to report that the women's comments concerning the gown were "effusive." Beyond that adjective, Yvonne was not prepared to venture. She did swell with pride over her part in the gown's creation and assembly, but she fought down her emotions. Pride, of course, is among the *deadly* sins; Yvonne preferred to keep her "effusiveness" in check.

Yvette made the gown look beautiful. The gown made Yvette look beautiful.

After a culinary feast that promised to remain a village legend for eons, the couple decamped on the first stage of their Interlaken honeymoon. Upon their return, Henri would resume his "career" with SNCF. Yvette would settle for the life of a mother. She did, however, inform her sister of her "dream." She wanted to start a small delicatessen or, more accurately, a small restaurant ("only three or four tables") to serve gourmet meals "by appointment only."

"That's for when the children are in school. When I'll have some time to myself."

Children – plural.

"How many do you want?" Yve asked.

"Two would be nice. If Henri insists on more, we can negotiate."

Yvonne took care in preparing the wedding gown for storage.

She spent the evening in a haunted house. Suddenly, she realized that nocturnal noises were rare in her childhood home. Mama liked to lounge in the living room with a book or her darning. She'd listen to music until ready for bed. Papa would, also, read or retire to his den to read, putter with his coin collection, or listen to the radio – that is, when he was not visiting Yvonne in her room.

She half expected Papa to come in and sit next to her on the bed. Her heart raced until she realized he was not coming. He heard Mama come upstairs. Papa came up some minutes later. After that, there was no noise.

Yvonne slept fitfully.

"Can't you stay for a couple days?" Mama asked over breakfast.

"We are swamped with work," Yve replied. "I come in the afternoons and work into the night to keep up. The pantsuit orders exceeded all our expectations. It's hard work to fill orders in a timely manner."

She wandered around on foot to chat and say goodbye to friends and former school chums. Collecting a sandwich Mama made for her, Yve hitched a ride with a local boy, a former classmate, who deposited her at the train station.

It was dark when she arrived in Trier.

How appropriate.

She walked home from a bus stop. It wasn't far and she hadn't much luggage.

Herr Beckmann approached the door to the apartment building seconds before her. He was a man of middle years and of middle girth.

His cheeks were perpetually red. In the dim light of the door lamp, the cheeks seemed to glow. He was the friendly person who lived alone in the capacious top-floor apartment, therefore, he was (relatively speaking) in the chinks.

Herr and Frau Schulz instructed Yvonne to contact them if she experienced problems necessitating monetary dispersals. All questions or concerns about facilities. i.e.: damaged bike rack or malfunctioning washer or dryer or a broken or damaged step or handrail, she was instructed to contact Herr Beckmann. He was the conduit to the building's owner. In short, Herr Beckmann, by virtue of his plush, top-floor apartment was the *Hausmeister* – or the nearest thing to it.

"Your gentleman friend came by the night before last," he reported.

Yve was nonplussed. She told him she'd be away for three or four days. Norbert wasn't daft; he'd remember.

"*Danke,*" she responded.

That didn't seem enough. Though it was no business of Herr Beckmann's, she informed him that she had gone to her sister's wedding, and she was certain she'd told her "gentleman friend."

It is considered imprudent (or outright rude) to bandy names about in Germany. Herr Beckmann, likely, knew Norbert's name – at least his family name.

"Just thought you should know," he said, unlocking the door.

"*Danke.*"

The stairwell lights came on automatically whenever the entry door was accessed. Yvonne followed Herr Beckmann up the stairs. There was no need for either to hurry.

The "mystery" of Norbert's visit did not manifest itself until the following evening when he failed to show. Had it not been so late, Yve would have trundled over to his new digs for, at least, a chin wag and a goodnight kiss. It was, however, late. The harried shop employees were forced to leave a mountain of minor chores for her attention. Rather than add to the backlog, Yve decided to dispatch as many tasks as possible. She exceeded her "authorized" workday, but a three-day absence kept her out of *Schwarz geld* territory.

Since neither Yve nor Norbert had a phone, the couple were forced to rely on face-to-face communication. She knew he left his new "apartment" (two small rooms and a shared bath) early every morning. Regardless, she got out her bike and rode over shortly after breakfast.

After knocking on his door, she slipped a brief missive under his door and commenced to replenish her larder. He would see her note and contact her either in person or by a return message.

Yve checked her mailbox once a week. Save for sporadic messages from her mother and postcards from her sister, it wasn't worth the effort to check more than once a week. However, there were shills roaming town who left unsolicited messages from local tradesmen. It was customary to avoid unsightly trash in one's mailbox, so Yve devoted a few seconds to clean out her repository.

There was a letter from Norbert.

This could not be good.

She waited until she was in the apartment. She put a kettle on the hotplate to make tea. Waiting for the water to boil, she tore open the letter and read.

He'd known for several weeks but declined to inform her since there was little chance he'd be selected. However, he was. He was offered the opportunity to study in Italy. He wanted to tell her in person, but word came the day she left for the wedding.

Norbert was a last-minute substitution, he reported. It hurt to decamp on such short notice and trusted his friends would help settle his local obligations. A pauper student would assume his Spartan "apartment" and take over the rent when it came due. Removing to smaller quarters had been part of his plan; he could save money against the day when his "dream posting" came through. It had. It was his ambition to learn as many Renaissance techniques as the experts could teach him.

Norbert promised to write. He apologized for keeping her in the dark, but he feared that informing friends and colleagues would put a curse on his chances. Even now, he was reluctant to provide many details least his high hopes prove in vain.

He promised his love and would write frequently.

She set the note aside and sighed. She looked forward to future reports, but – no more kisses. How she longed for them.

Perhaps, Yvonne's friendship and respect for Norbert would have morphed into love. She hoped, given time, it would. However, she'd miss his kisses far more than his company. He'd done so much for her, and she was grateful.

Damn!

The blood-pounding joy she felt at her sister's wedding, and the realization that she, Yvonne Schortmann, would soon be someone's aunt had her on emotional peaks for several, delicious hours. Suddenly, she was thrust back into the darkness of – well, deprivation. She could talk with Norbert about ideas and experiences beyond the scope of her Magic Needle world. Her colleagues were precious to her, but they were part of an enclosed realm. Norbert was the passage into another, wider and unknown sphere. Moreover, his kisses had provided her with pleasures and emotions her coworkers could never replicate.

Her world was, once again, dark.

She pulled out her rosary. Since her failure to become a postulant, her use of the relic had become sporadic. That proved that Sister B_____'s doubts were justified. Indeed, there were meditative times when she contemplated leaving the Church. She never got far with such thoughts, but she continued to struggle.

She did believe in God. This belief was unshakable. Beyond that, it was all to play for.

Her faith in the rosary prayers remained perilous. However, they'd become ritual. In the absence of certainty, she would cling to familiar things. Later, she'd offer up a prayer for Norbert. To pray for his swift return – that would mark her as a selfish person. God, or so she reasoned, did not care for selfish people.

Yvonne Schortmann didn't care for selfish people either.

If, she reasoned, Norbert Blumenfeld had the opportunity to become a "Renaissance postulant," who was Yvonne Schortmann stand in his way?

The kettle began singing.

She was dragged back into the secular world.

LOST

No one at "the shop" asked about "Sister's man." They knew the moment she came to work that "it" (whatever *it* may have been) was over. It wasn't that Yvonne was snippy, short-tempered or brusque; she hadn't the stamina. True, she'd be cross from time to time and occasionally uttered oaths not suited to convent life, but the extent of these displays was brief. However, the sad eyes returned. Her bursts of gaiety were brief. She managed to laugh from time to time, but her felicity was decidedly subdued.

It was well that she worked only half a day with her co-workers. They were strained by her faux placidity. When left alone for her "night shift," she worked like a daemon possessed. Frequently, she got so involved in something that she'd work well beyond the agreed hours. Should some judicious official find her laboring late at night, there'd be trouble.

Mme. Errad's only defense would be that she wasn't paying *Schwatzgeld*. That would compound the situation. The shop owner might be charged with using slave labor. Once the bureaucrats got involved, anything Yve said in her employer's defense would be scrupulously ignored.

She was searching for solace or, at the very least, diversion. Norbert's company, and his kisses, kept her in a state of harmony. In his absence, she was adrift. Even when her spiritual waters were calm, there existed a strong undercurrent.

Part of her was relieved over Norbert's departure. The closer their proximity, the greater the risk that he would "insist." The possibility haunted her, but not nearly as much as her crumbling ability to "resist."

Yvette and Henri didn't wait until the formal ceremony to "get married." Despite her arsenal of scruples, Yvonne could not fault them. However, . . .

The Bible is specific. If a man and woman have intercourse, they are man and wife in the eyes of God. The blessed Augustine, however, postulates that when the man "forces" a woman, she is considered chaste still. Yve took solace in that only until she realized, she hadn't been forced. She *was*, but she *wasn't*. Her youth might offer her some defense, but ... Can one expect mercy for being an empty-headed child?

Even should she escape damnation for her behavior, one fact remained: "the act" voided her opportunity to marry "again."

Why didn't God strike her down? Why must she struggle? He'd denied her (quite rightly) the opportunity of taking the vows. Had she succeeded in becoming Sister Mary Mercy, she'd be on the express train to Hell. She'd be a mockery of herself *and* the Church. No amount of contrition or acts of mercy and goodwill could save her.

How would she be better off with Norbert or any other man? She'd make mockery of marriage – and her reservation for the express train to Hell would be writ large.

It is such an advantage to be a pagan! She'd still burn in Hell, but she wouldn't have to wrestle her whole life fretting about it.

"Do you recognize my attempt to become a nun was a sincere attempt to repent and do good works?" she asked of the Deity. "Give me the opportunity to do Your will. Even if I cannot save myself, help me. Help me to make a difference – to do something profound – something good – something right."

Would He give her a sign? Would He present her with some great enterprise? Would He aide her? Could the baren fig tree bring forth fruit?

Amid the tsunami created by doubt and the battle between her selfish interests and religion *and* her growing ambivalence about her religious beliefs, she received a three-page missive from Norbert Blumenfeld.

Dark Comedy

He was in Florance. The letter exploded with an excited recitation about his discoveries, his observations, and the learned people surrounding him. He included three small sketches. One drawing was a detailed study of David's left hand. The second was a miniature of a town square which had once been a Roman circus – the by-standers were represented by origami-like figures with flat blobs representing heads. The third sketch was of a round table – not unlike those in the ice-cream parlor where he'd introduced himself. There were two chairs, just as there had been in Wasserbillig. On the table was an empty cup resting atop a saucer in the company of a small spoon.

Mark L. Williams

WISH YOU WERE HERE

This was scrawled under the table with an arrow pointing at one of the unoccupied chairs.

His excited narrative ended with his "love" and six, emphatic *x*s.

Yvonne was excited. Perhaps, there remained hope that her friend hadn't jilted her. The kisses he included were poignant, but they were symbolic. She lusted after the real thing.

She dedicated her evening to four pages of excited prose in honor of their relationship and how very much she missed him. She refrained from sharing her emotional turmoil. She'd never have hesitated were he with her, but an emotional barrage from long range would gain only a momentary purge. She needed a dialogue. She needed him!

On her way to work, she stopped at the post office and waited in line for some minutes. She bought the required postage and hurried to the shop.

Mme. Errad handed her an official, long envelope with an embossed royal symbol. She set it aside. Yve was already late, she didn't want to fritter away additional time with private concerns. Not until she was at home and had a modest dinner simmering did she open the package.

Someone spent considerable time and money to produce a six-page information booklet. The Government of Luxembourg, at the behest of the Grand Duke and Duchess, would promote an aid package to the M_____ Orphanage and Refugee Mission in N_____ A_____.

Subscriptions were solicited from major businesses and private individuals in the Grand Dutchy. The proceeds would be used for the purchase of food, books, and medical supplies for the children and the support staff of the Mission. A troupe of celebrities would accompany the shipment of supplies to highlight the commitment of Luxembourg to international relief efforts and feeding, clothing, and educating abandoned, abused, and orphaned children in the Sahel.

It was impressive.

The accompanying photos were heartbreaking.

There was a cover letter addressed to Yvonne Schortmann. It was, obviously, not a part of the publicity campaign. It warned her that the area she would enter was not without danger. A military escort would be provided, but the area serviced by the Christian Mission was rife with corrupt officials and no few freebooters. Additionally, there were health risks.

People selected for the mission – part of a publicity campaign to encourage donations – would receive a "stipend." The exact amount had not yet been determined, but an approximation was included.

Further, to be "eligible," the applicant must submit to a physical and be injected and vaccinated against a series of potential hazards.

Yvonne scanned the inoculations required. She had, as a child, been protected against smallpox and polio. The list included a half dozen additional requirements.

Was this what God had in mind for her? If it was, she didn't dare ignore the opportunity. If it wasn't, she'd put life and limb at risk for less money than she'd earn in at the shop during any normal week. However, if something did happen, and she returned in a wooden box, her theological and philosophical struggles would be at an end. If God brought her "home," they could discuss these matters in detail. She'd get *the* Judge's *official* ruling devoid of earthly flimflammery.

She set the medical page aside for the moment and began filling out her application.

After eating and washing up, she wrote another letter to Norbert. She informed him of the application and her desire to participate. She did not ask for either his approval or support, but she hoped he would provide both by return post.

Mme. Errad was not supportive.

"You walk in here like you own the damn place and ask me to hire you," she snorted, as only Mme. Errad can snort. "You help me build up this business. We take photos of you wearing our duds and orders come in. Now, just when I'm getting used to your annoying habits, you're walking out!"

"I have not been selected," Sister emphasized. "Even if I am, it will take me away only for three weeks or so."

"Three weeks of back breaking, finger breaking, damnation when we can barely keep up with business now. People get pissed when we don't deliver in a reasonable time. I must hire two or three people to take your place. We haven't room for three or four people. We're tripping over each other now."

"Mme. Errad, I owe you so much. I'll be in debt to you for the rest of my life," Yve announced. "There are children in need, and I *might* be able to help them."

"And what can you do?"

"Not a damned thing, but my being there might give them some hope."

"And when you're gone and they're no better off than before, they will hate you!"

Yvonne decided that Mme. Errad should have been a tragic actress.

"And when I come back, you will hate me. If I stay, you will tolerate me – and exploit me! I'm not a model, and I cringe whenever you want me to model for you."

"You get paid to have your picture took," Errad fumed.

"Not anywhere near what you'd have to pay a professional. You use me."

"Well, Mademoiselle, you've used me!"

Yvonne decided that Mme. Errad was correct – one hundred percent. Yve came without being asked. She needed to support herself since her chosen vocation had been denied her. This knowledge made their combat pointless. Since the problem defied solution, there was nothing more to do but sigh.

"If I am accepted, I'm going," she announced.

"You might not have a job when you get back," Errad warned.

Yve thought that over for some while.

"Mme. Errad, I must take the risk."

There was nothing more to do or say. It was time to get busy.

MARKING TIME

Yvonne and Norbert exchanged three additional letters. She enjoyed his sketches very much. She saved his missives for the artwork alone. Meanwhile, she framed and made a display on the top of the bookcase of the two sketches he'd made of her: the woman she was and the woman she wanted to become.

She made no mention of her African adventure. He hadn't dropped any hints about his Italian adventure. Perhaps, that was the accepted protocol. Regardless, she'd keep her journey under wraps until she knew for certain she'd been selected.

Having the mornings free allowed her the opportunity to get paperwork and medical documentation together. Since she lived in Germany, she needed documents, both state and local. Because she worked in Luxembourg, she needed more documents, both state and local. Her French passport would expire within the year, so she had to attend to that. The nearest French consulate was nearer than training back home, so she only had to take one day off work.

She was examined and jabbed and poked. Having instructions from the Luxembourg government not only expedited the process but made certain she'd get only the required injections. As expected, everything needed a signature, a date, and a stamp.

Finally, Yve was faced with a work morning when she had no more errands to complete. She made copies of her paperwork before forwarding the originals by courier.

Yvonne had breakfast at "home." She felt as if she were on holiday. She didn't have an appointment; she didn't need to use a pay phone to arrange for an appointment; she didn't have pages of government forms to fill out and sign. Faced with nothing to do and nowhere to go, she went to the basement and muscled her new (used) bike up the steps to the back yard – a tiny plot of grass edged with a flower bed.

Who, she wondered, took care of the flora? Obviously, the lawn and flowers were tended frequently. She made a mental note to ask Herr Beckmann.

Yve didn't enjoy suspense. When she became curious, she wanted answers or, at least, information.

She walked her bike to the street and mounted.

Yvonne rode by the remnants of the largest Roman baths outside Rome itself. Too bad, she thought; if the baths were operational she could exercise there and pamper herself with the invigorating, three-step wash the Romans (and the "civilized" Germans) so enjoyed.

She checked her watch. Only eight minutes had elapsed since leaving her building. Nearly the whole of the morning remained.

She veered left and followed the traffic circle and took the first exit. It was uphill, so she'd get a fair workout. Finding a bike rack, she chained up her conveyance, and walked a few score meters to the *Kasse*. She paid the extortion money and entered what remained of the Roman arena.

The arena itself was defined by the retaining wall. The spectators' stone seats were removed during medieval times and used in construction elsewhere. The subterranean cells and holding pens remained, but she had no interest in them. She settled down on the grassy slope and began to think.

Once upon a time, the arena hosted "sporting" events. On days when there weren't any "games," the structure served as an entry gate. Wagons and visitors would come through the same avenue Yvonne had utilized. People, livestock, and foodstuffs would trundle across the "business portion" of the structure, and pass through a second gate and, thus, into the city proper.

Yve appreciated the irony. She had entered the arena. Was she destined to struggle where wild animals and gladiators once met their fate, or would she pass into the city and resume her life? She had no way of knowing if her paperchase and her series of inoculations would be of any use. She was comfortable with the life she lived, but she feared growing stagnant. Her career in the shop was largely routine. There was no room for advancement.

Was that important?

Mme. Errad put her life into that shop. It provided a good living precisely because she had no ambition to get into the "big time." There was a minimum of stress and worry. Yve was content there. If she worked for a major supplier, she was certain to face tremendous pressure. However, if she remained comfortably ensconced in Wasserbillig, would she catch a "bug," as had Norbert? If she did, and if her yearning remained unfulfilled …

What then?

Her left arm hurt her.

"Are you right-handed?" The doctor (or the doctor's assistant) asked.

"Yes."

"Then, this is going into your left arm. You won't be using it for a couple days."

It hurt still. It made walking miserable and riding the bike intolerable. Nevertheless, she'd asked for it. The pictures of those children were embossed on her brain. There wasn't anything she could do to improve their life chances, but she could – at the very, very, very least – let them know that there was someone who cared for them; someone who would pray for them.

I am, she decided, a spectator. She'd sit in the stands and cheer for the underdog beasts or the underdog gladiator or the unarmed Christian forced to defend his faith against ravenous creatures. No matter the outcome, the spectators would leave and, perhaps, enjoy a bit of running or wrestling in the *palaestra* before entering the baths. Later, at home and over a bowl of figs and slices of cheese, they'd review the highlights of their day at the arena.

Dark Comedy

Yvonne needed to be *in* the arena, not in the viewing stands. She wouldn't stand a chance against the beasts or a man with a sword. Didn't they roast Blandina alive? (very creative, these Roman pagans) Nevertheless, her place was on the ground and in the fray.

What good could she possibly do in Africa?

I come; I see; I go home!

Is this the mission God intended for her? At least Blandina, cooked, had a purpose: she and her fellow martyrs were examples to the people; people who could not help but notice the profound faith they displayed. They refused to deny their God even while enduring the most excruciating pain. The number of people who took up the study of Jesus because of such bravery is known but to God. However, even as the persecutions continued, the power of the Roman pantheon was crumbling, one convert at a time.

The pain in her left arm was excruciating. It brought tears whenever she bumped against something (or someone) or when she rolled onto it while sleeping. It was insufferable. However, it was nothing compared to being roasted alive.

How will this fadge?

If God sends me; I go. If not, there's no point in thinking about it.

Three weeks slid by. The shop was nearly caught up. The pantsuit orders had dwindled to two or three a month allowing Yvonne to work normal hours again. The worker bees at *Errad Creations* were once again enjoying a mid-morning and mid-afternoon break. The experience of chatting over a cup of tea or coffee was intoxicating. They had time to become friends again. Even the heartless task master could relax and reintroduce herself to calm and civility.

"Have you heard?" Carla asked while leisurely stirring her coffee.

Yvonne shook her head.

"I think I've been passed over."

"All that work to get those documents," Marie sighed.

"And those shots," Claudia added with a visible shudder.

"God may be punishing me," Yve replied with practiced calm. "I lied – or as good as lied – when I wanted to become a postulant."

"Stop!"

Mme. Errad, though much more human than she'd been of late, retained a salty tongue and a ridged demeanor.

"If you lied, you have no business as a nun – even a pretend one. If God wants to punish you, He's not going to stop you from going to some African Hell Hole. It would serve you right if He left you there. Somehow, running your legs down to stumps to get all those papers and stamps and seals and fancy signatures ain't punishment – all we powerless peons are punished with that nonsense."

Yvonne smiled politely and averted her eyes.

"You sell yourself short, Sister," Errad continued. "You work hard, and you do it excellently. He brought you here. It seems to me that this is part of your redemption."

The entire shop was Catholic, but Yve was the only one who took it seriously, or so she thought. Suddenly everyone one was talking like a theological student. They admired Yvonne for her faith though they weren't anxious to copy her. They weren't very patient whenever Yve engaged in self-flagellation.

Yvonne was an educated woman with a strong background in the Bible, Augustine of Hippo, and Shakespeare. How strange that she never thought in terms of *redemption*. She was convinced that she'd offended her Maker so completely that she was marked for retribution. Suddenly, she felt that good will and good deeds might pave the way for a second chance.

The following afternoon, Mme. Errad called Yvonne into her office. She was sorting through the mail and segregating it into an immediate-attention pile and a maybe-later pile. The moment Magic Needle entered, the woman fetched a large, bulky envelope from her lap. She threw it onto the upper right corner of her desk.

"For you," she announced.

One look at the return address sent Yve's heart into her throat.

"I – I'm right in the middle of something," she stammered. "I'll open it later."

"I don't care if you eat it!" the boss snorted. "Get the damned thing off my desk."

The employees had neither lockers nor cubbyholes for personal items. They shared the same hall tree for their coats and sweaters, but other personal items were scattered about in or on any available space. The only place to stow the "package" (so it seemed) was to prop it edgewise behind the electric kettle. She placed it so the address and addressee faced the wall. However, such a fancy envelope screamed for attention.

"The royal family beckons," Marie announced while making tea.

All ears were on full alert.

"What does it say?" Claudia demanded.

"I'll open it later," Yve replied from behind gritted teeth.

She shot Marie a withering glance. The flat chested woman merely adjusted her pince-nez and returned to work.

When lunchtime arrived, four people gathered around Sister Yve. They said nothing. They stared at the young woman and issued a silent demand. Magic Needle stood and shared her stormy visage with her audience.

They watched as Yvonne ripped the envelope open. She slowly and carefully lifted the contents and read the cover letter. Her audience slithered expertly behind her so they could read over her shoulder.

"You're going to Africa," Carla announced.

"In two-weeks and two days," Errad snarled. "How can I find a replacement in two weeks and two days? Damn! Sister, I hope you choke on your own spit!"

Yve wanted to eat her sandwich. In truth, she wasn't hungry, but she didn't want to examine the rest of the packet in public. Carefully, to avoid an explosion, Claudia began sliding the pages of the text and the photos included therein.

"That's it?" Errad asked as she grabbed the montage of photos featuring a ramshackle, open-air schoolhouse and ill-feed and ill-clothed black children. "That's where you're going? Dirt streets! Animals roaming around – I hope you have thick soles, Sister. You'll be stepping in shit – and I doubt it will all be from the animals."

"God in Heaven!" Carla gasped. "You *want* to go there? I'd rather be in jail."

"It isn't a vacation!" Yvonne roared.

The commentary stopped, but the crowd continued to look through the materials.

"It won't be a vacation," Marie whispered while backing away. "That's for certain."

According to the information packet, there would be a brief plenary session with Her Royal Highness and such "mission specialists" as she saw fit to include. Yvonne's actual instructions were terse and "idiot proof." She was to come to the city the day before the meeting; she was to inform the Palace (phone number included) of her arrival and place of residence. Have her travel case (see instructions) at the ready. At ten o'clock the following morning, a car will call. She and her personal items will be brought to the session after which the team will be escorted to a military transport.

During her previous visit, Yvonne collected a few informative items from the visitor's bureau adjacent to the train station. She flipped through a list of hostelries and found the one most budget friendly. The following morning, she used Mme. Errad's business phone to arrange for her registration.

"A bed and breakfast," Errad scoffed. "Her Royal Highness will dispatch a state vehicle to pick you up at a flop house?"

"If it were a flop house," Yve countered. "The visitor's bureau would not list it. The government has oversight powers."

Errad was skeptical. However, to argue with her recalcitrant employee would require her to acknowledge her existence. When Madam Errad wore a chip on her shoulder, she did not resort to half measures. She rode Yve mercilessly. The young woman could do nothing right.

"Will I be glad to be rid of you!"

No one in the shop believed there was any substance in Madam's invective. She was upset and disappointed, but the woman was too proud to let Sister go graciously. She couldn't find anyone who was half as skilled as Mlle. Schortmann. This stoked her ire.

Yvonne made certain her financial affairs were in order. She paid for an additional month's rent, but cautioned Herr and Frau Schulz that she would lose her job. Therefore, her subsequent rent payments might be either sporadic or delayed. Despite the veil of secrecy Yve imposed about her mission, word reached the landlords very quickly. They were supportive of their tenant's quest and were prepared to forego the rigors of the law to keep a responsible and respectful occupant. Yvonne took care of her apartment and was assured by Herr Beckmann that the woman did not host all-night raves or, otherwise, disrespect her fellow residents.

Similarly, the seam stitcher made provisions concerning her other financial obligations. She wrote a long letter to Norbert explaining her absence and warning him that he mightn't be receiving further communications for some while.

Was she doing the right thing? It was too late to back out. Indeed, to renegue on the head of state might constitute a criminal offense. She spent considerable time on her knees begging for reassurance. To agree to partake in this mission as an act of vanity was a major sin. However, she didn't feel any affinity for either the orphanage or the children sheltered there. Not caring for children was, also, a sin.

Why, she wondered, did I ever agree? No matter what I do, it is evil.

For the first time in her life, she identified with Pilate. No matter what her final decision, she was knee deep in sin. Washing her hands was analogous to using chewing gum to stench the flow of blood from an amputated limb.

It was her last day. Mme. Errad threatened to replace her, but she had yet to find anyone. Yve suspected she hadn't tried very hard. Maybe, she expected somebody to walk into her shop and audition, as Yve herself once did. She resented Yvonne's abandonment. The woman had no business to banish herself in desert sands for a single hour – never mind several days!

Her attitude toward Sister was brutal. She scolded her for the tiniest transgression and swore incessantly when Yve displeased her – which was most of the time. On that last day, however, she realized her scolding and bullying hadn't put so much as a second thought into the source of her aggravation.

"Get in here!" she barked.

Yvonne looked at her co-workers who looked back. She took a deep breath and trudged into the office. The office consisted of a desk, a phone, a chair, and room enough to close the door. Errad did exactly that – well, not *exactly*. Rather than close the door, she slammed it shut. The trio on the other side of the barrier experienced a momentary shock.

They were practically nose to nose – well, nose to collar. Yvonne forced herself to look down and into the eyes of her tormentor. To her surprise, she found copious tears. Errad was embarrassed, but she remained stubborn.

"I want you back here real quick," she said with a quivering voice.

"I'm not fired?"

"And let you get all that free government money? No, Little Shit, I want you back here so I can kick your sorry ass!"

At that moment, the woman's arms pulled her until their bodies were, practically, melded. Shocked and ill at ease, Yvonne put her arms around the woman who had taken her in.

"Can you manage?" she asked.

"I can lend a hand on the floor," she moaned. "I can fight with the paperwork at night."

"I'll get back without making any detours," Yve promised.

"I can fill in for you, Sister, but I can't replace you. I need you – for more reasons than one. I love you. I will miss you, every minute of every hour."

Yvonne's throat was blocked, again.

"You have a funny way of showing your love," she noted, recalling the verbal torrent of the past several days.

"I tried to hate you. I told myself you are betraying me. I can't do it. I will pray for you every day."

That created a shiver. She was grateful for the promise, but Yve didn't feel worthy.

"You've done so much for me," she moaned. "I owe you more than I can ever repay."

"Get out of here," the boss commanded. "I've got some crying to do."

There was nothing to say, so Yve didn't speak. She released her benefactor and vacated the space. She closed the door quietly behind her and was greeted by six, curious eyes. Her tongue had turned to stone. The only communique she could issue was a shrug.

MYSTERIOUS COMMISSION

Yvonne slept late and didn't arrive in the city until midafternoon. She was under orders, so she looked no different than several hundred rubber-necking tourists.

It was a quarter-hour walk from the station to her bed and breakfast. She checked-in and paid her tariff. She used the desk phone and called the assigned number. She supplied her name and identified the establishment housing her. After these tasks were performed, she retired to her room.

There was nothing pretentious about the place. There was a single bed, a table (no more than a stool) with a fake, lace doily between it and an ashtray. The bathroom was slightly larger than those found on airliners, but it was tiled and sparkling clean.

The "orders" were clear. The "team" was going on a humanitarian mission. There was, of course, a publicity angle, but they were going to the Sahel, not the Palace of Versailles.

NO DRESSES, SKIRTS, HEELS, OR JEWLRY

This reminder appeared in four, conspicuous spaces on their "travel orders." Makeup was discouraged, but the sponsoring agency must have realized that such items can easily be smuggled.

There was one item on her "highly recommended" list which she'd yet to fill. She needed a sun hat. Recklessly, she purchased a baseball cap. Later, she realized that a relentless sun would beat down on the back of her neck. She needed a brim. Her first mission in the city, therefore, was to secure that one, last item.

She didn't bother to cross the gorge and go into the tourist portion of the city. Prices there would be inflated. The shops near the train station were plentiful enough. There must be a plethora of sunhats available.

Indeed, there were. Most, however, featured gaudy symbols and tacky messages. Frustrated by an hour of fruitless searching, she bought a straw (likely imitation) hat with ribbons for securing it in a high wind. Not knowing the wind velocity of their destination, she thought preparedness was in order. The moment she was out of sight of the vendor, she removed the clever little add-ons and deposited them in the nearest dustbin.

She returned to her "hotel" and placed the purchase on her travel bag.

After an afternoon stroll and a modest dinner, she returned to her room and slept.

She woke to darkness. It was early, but not too early. She showered and slipped into her jeans and a plain, roomy top. She slipped on her running shoes but eschewed socks; she would save them for their target venue and didn't want them soiled before time. She had no idea if there were laundry facilities available in the Sahel.

If she'd only brought a book! There was no way to fill the time other than to review, and shudder, over her accumulated sins. At least, she wouldn't lack material.

Breakfast began at seven thirty, but Yvonne was in no hurry.

She washed her face and hands before descending the stairs. A matron brought her a hardboiled egg, a cup, and a saucer. Yve helped herself to some sausages, two croissants, butter, and jams. By the time she returned to her tiny table, matron had deposited an insulated carafe of coffee.

The coffee was rich and steamy. She consumed two cups with delight despite her T.B. (tiny bladder). Hopefully, she'd be near toilet facilities at their assigned rendezvous. Once satiated with coffee and satisfactorily fortified against starvation, she gathered her traps and descended the stairs one last time.

She sat, travel case at her feet and sunhat in hand, on a small luggage rack near the front door.

"May I call you a cab?" the desk attendant asked.

"I should be called for by someone before long," she informed.

It was within two minutes of her promised appointment that a highly polished limo pulled up to the curb. Yvonne didn't believe it. She assumed she would ride in the front seat of a sedan, or a cab would be sent to fetch her. The desk attendant couldn't believe it either. How many patrons of a hole-in-the-wall bed-and-breakfast are whisked away in a limo?

Yve rounded the answer to that question down to the nearest zero, picked up her travel case in one hand, her hat in the other, and hurried out before the uniformed driver could do his duty. She smiled an apology as she got herself and her luggage in unassisted.

"I was ordered to bring very little money," she warned when the driver resumed station.

"No fear, Madam," he assured. "It's all been taken care of."

"Where are we going?" she asked. "Nobody tells me anything."

"The residence, Madam."

That cryptic remark was better left alone. Perhaps, the driver was under mysterious orders as well. She resisted the urge to open her case and make certain her passport and other vital papers were inside. She'd checked three times during the evening and three more times since waking.

It was a long drive. They left the city.

Soon enough, a huge mansion appeared. It grew larger and larger as they approached. The car, driver, and passenger entered a large circle drive and came to a halt at a large portal complete with colonnade. Three uniformed men descended the marble steps toward them.

"Mademoiselle Schortmann," a middle-aged personage of regal bearing and impeccable posture opened the passenger door with aplomb. "Her Royal Highness awaits."

Yvonne was half out of the limo but was arrested by the announcement.

"I'm hardly dressed to appear before the Grand Duchess!"

Her protest had no appreciable affect on the liveried servant.

"Her Highness is aware of your apparel, Mademoiselle," he responded expertly.

What more need be said?

Before Yvonne could regain her balance, the two supernumeraries reached into the vehicle. One emerged with her travel case. The other looked ridiculous handling her cheap, straw chapeau as if were a Faberge Egg.

"Ah –," there was no protocol for this. None that she knew of, anyway.

"These gentlemen will see to your – things."

It was a slang word in the orbit of her escort. She could tell by the way he said *things* that the word, in his personal lexicon, was low, common, and, likely, only a small increment above *poop*. Well, when in Luxembourg do as the Luxembourgian does. If any of her personal items or papers went missing, the royal family would face a damaging scandal.

"This way, Mademoiselle."

She had sense enough to keep behind and a bit to the right of her guide. This was not the result of study, but she surmised that it wasn't proper to march through a castle shoulder-to-shoulder when under escort.

Once beyond the impressive entryway, Yve found herself in a reception hall large enough to host a tennis match and no few spectators. It was empty. The servant's shoes created a faint echo. The woman's athletic shoes remained blissfully silent.

The invited guest gawked at the paintings and statuary she passed while doing her best not to make her gawking obvious. Her "escort" couldn't see her unless he had a set of eyes in the back of his head, but in a "home" this large, a dozen unobserved people might be watching her every move.

They scaled a modern staircase to the first floor. She was led down a long passageway and past several solid, wooden doors, each decorated with carved features marked by the meticulous precision of the craftsmen. They paused a moment at the last door on the left. It was the mirror image of the last door on the right.

The servant knocked once with mighty knuckles sheathed in a white glove. Without waiting for a response, he opened the portal and entered. He kept hold of the door lever and took up a position as if was an extension of the door itself.

"Mademoiselle Schortmann, Your Highness."

Yvonne turned to stone. She knew who was beyond that door. She knew the clothes she was wearing. She was afraid to move. The servant gestured for her to enter. Still, she could not move. He turned his head and gave her a warning scowl worthy of note. This, she did notice.

Which was worse, to enter the presence of the Grand Duchess in a state of seeming nakedness, or to endure another scowl? It was a difficult choice.

Somehow, she entered the room. She didn't recall exactly how. She didn't remember walking in. She didn't remember being dragged in. She didn't remember being pushed. Yet, there she stood.

Yvonne viewed a huge desk to her left. Behind that desk sat the Grand Duchess. She was examining a document and making notes on a notepad. She looked up and spotted the humiliated woman who dared enter her office in the guise of a stable boy. Her Highness gestured toward the collection of overstuffed chairs surrounding a round, highly polished tea table.

"Please, be seated," the august personage invited. "I won't be a moment."

This time she *was* pushed. It was gentle, but it brought her back to consciousness. She took a step forward enough for the servant to close the door.

"Sit down," he whispered, hoarsely into her ear.

Dark Comedy

The young woman was flummoxed. She moved toward the collection of fine furnishings, but – to sit in the proximity of the Grand Duchess? Protocol be damned; some things are not done!

Fortunately, Her Highness was only a moment. She put down her pen and stood.

"A moment, please," she asked of Yve's statue.

He nodded. He exited the room, but Yve surmised he did not get out of shouting range. Moreover, there were bound to be cameras. Armed guards, certainly, were on instant alert.

The Grand Duchess came around the desk in a white pantsuit. It was impossible for Yve not to notice; it was *THE* pantsuit.

She shivered.

The woman recognized Yvonne's reticence. She smiled politely and sat in a chair. Once seated she gestured to her guest to do the same. Slowly, struggling with unresponsive muscles, the interloper settled into a chair so comfortable, she imagined herself back in her mother's arms.

"I wanted to speak with you before we meet with the others," the hostess said. "I have learned about you from people who are most effusive in their recommendations of you."

"Of me, Your Highness?"

The woman smiled. There was no need to respond to such an infantile query; ergo, she didn't.

"I knew when I married my husband what was in store," she began. "When I accepted this job, I surrendered my freedom and much else. Mainly, I miss the freedom do what I want and go where I want. What I wouldn't give to be able to go to some street fair and sample some of the foods. Well, that can't happen. Not anymore."

She settled back in her chair, crossed her legs, and examined Yvonne closely.

"This mission – the one you will visit. It is funded and run by a Protestant organization, so there's been criticism in the press already. However, when I saw those pictures – when I interviewed the people who feed and clothe and educate and protect those children – I cried. The more I learned, the more I cried."

She paused and averted her eyes. Yve thought she observed a chin quivering.

"Not many of those children will live to be twenty. I doubt if any of them know who their parents were or anything about them. In the beginning, they dropped like flies. The survival rate is much better now, but there is much to be done. I want you and the team to deliver the food, medicine, and school supplies we're sending, but I'm counting on you glamour girls to get some press attention. We can exploit you and your activities to encourage people to donate funds. That's why we're sending some press people with you."

"I'll do what I can, Highness."

Highness? Was that right? More importantly, was it inexcusably rude?

The Grand Duchess didn't notice. She lowered her eyes in thought. Judging from her visage, the thoughts were dark.

Suddenly, she refocused on Yve.

"Mademoiselle – may I call you Yvonne?"

"Please."

No more *Highness*. It was too easy to say *Majesty*. That, she was certain, would invite admonishment.

"I initiated this mission. I've worked on it for months. I've been discouraged by everyone in the government. It's been a battle because some Protestant group is heading up the school and the orphanage. What do the children know about that? Why should theological disputes stand in the way of humanity?"

She uncrossed her legs and leaned forward.

"If I had your freedom, Yvonne, I'd have been there a year ago. I would be going with you now. Unfortunately, I'm a prisoner, so, Yvonne, I'm sending you."

"I am here to be sent," she responded, thoughtlessly.

"I want you to know," the Grand Duchess continued. "You are not going to represent me. I command you; if royalty is allowed such powers still: You *are* me! You must be diplomatic. You must not display your temper – even if you're ready to shout *Off with his head!* You listen. You learn. You observe. I'll supply you with notebooks. I will arrange an interview, but that mightn't be scheduled for some weeks after your return. Until that is entered on the calendar, I will read your written report. Are you up to this assignment?"

Yvonne gulped. It may have been audible. Regardless, she felt a responsibility she never knew existed.

"I promise, I will do all that is within my power."

Empty words. What else was there? The Grand Duchess had experienced that place and those kids vicariously. Yvonne knew next to nothing. It isn't often a twentieth-century peasant is summoned to court and given a royal command. Yve was eager to obey and serve, but the responsibility weighed heavy.

The Grand Duchess got to her feet. Yvonne sprang up as if shot from a catapult. One does not sit when the Grand Duchess is not sitting – even then, one must be given permission.

"Come with me, please."

Yvonne padded silently behind. The Grand Duchess circled behind her desk; that was forbidden territory. Yve took up station two steps back and two steps to the side of the royal writing desk. Her host opened the top drawer and withdrew a passport-sized document. The cover was a bold beige. In the center was a rampant red lion silhouetted over a field of white and blue alternating stripes.

"This is a secret," the Grand Duchess informed. "Not even the Americans know about this. It identifies one Yvonne Schortmann as the personal envoy of the Grand Duchess of Luxembourg. Use this only – and I mean *only* when *absolutely, no-choice-left* necessary. It may not carry much weight, but it might tip the scales in your favor. Do not show this to anyone, save in a dire emergency. Don't mention its existence, not even to your mother! If the people who really run this place know of its existence, I will be disciplined, and my husband will be exceedingly angry, embarrassed, and upset."

She extended the secret document. Yve was reluctant to take it but dared not refuse. She could not resist opening the cover. There she found her own picture crimped and wrinkled by an official seal. How did the government secure a photo of Yvonne Schortmann? Perhaps, it was better not to inquire.

Taking her instructions to heart, Yve secreted the document directly over that organ.

"You were serious when you said that I *am* you."

"I want those people to know I'm serious. I will do everything in my power to support the mission, the mission school, and the people who keep it running."

"I promise to do all I can. It's a responsibility I shall not take lightly."

She hoped her presumptuous syntax would not be interpreted as either fatuous or satirical.

"Very good," the stately woman nodded. "The rest of the team will arrive shortly. While we wait – Gunter."

The door may have been substantial, but the dutiful servant responded in an instant. He opened the door and awaited orders. He did not stand at attention as servants do in the movies, but his demeanor made clear the Grand Duchess had his complete attention.

"Refreshments for Mademoiselle."

He nodded obediently and disappeared, closing the door quietly behind him.

THE TEAM

The luncheon was as informal as is likely to be found in a royal residence. The room was originally intended as a recreation retreat. A grand piano had pride of place. Perhaps, other musical instruments, and people who play them, would entertain while the "distinguished" guests attended in the sumptuous splendor of chairs and couches. When "the team," two women and three uniformed commandos, entered, the piano was much in evidence. However, the lounge furniture was replaced by three, highly polished tables with seven, polished wood armchairs.

The "glamor girls" were seated at the south table facing the security team at the north table. The Grand Duchess took position in the single chair on the east table. The open-ended space to the west was reserved for "presenters." These people would not sit; they would stand behind a highly polished, wooden podium draped with a banner of red, white, and blue, ordered as in the flag of the Grand Duchy.

First, the luncheon.

It was blue-plate and extremely modest for a royal residence, but it underscored the theme of informality. In the world of the peasant, the meal would be thought of as sandwiches and crisps. The royal chefs, however, employed several culinary adjustments that made it more substantial and, simultaneously, aesthetic.

No one had to be briefed on meal etiquette. The guests were the first served, and the hostess, the Grand Duchess, last. However, no one dared touch so much as a baby tomato until the Grand Duchess began eating. Drinks were provided by two servers, each armed with highly polished silver ewers. As the duo made the rounds, each person could choose hot coffee, hot tea, iced tea, or iced coffee.

When the meal concluded, the tables were cleared; the presentations began.

Surreptitiously, Yvonne measured the women on each side of her. Dressed, as was she, in desert-ready apparel, they did not look impressive.

Sarah Welter, a singer, sat on Yve's left. She was a bottle blond with bangs and tresses cropped to frame her delicate features. Sara was perky, vivacious, and "entertaining" in every positive sense of the word. The twenty-something woman resembled France Gall of decades past (with whom she was frequently compared). Sarah was a native of France. However, this singer was popular in Luxembourg because she represented the Grand Duchy two years previously in the Eurovision Song Contest.

Charlotte Werner, to Yve's right, was an actress with a regional following. A native of Germany, she made a name for herself in Luxembourg as a dim-witted Tonto figure in a comedy TV series. Presently, she was increasing her popularity and her fan base by playing an enigmatic character in a daily soap. Her alter ego was not exactly evil but far from angelic. The writers kept the audience in a quandary as to the true nature of the character.

As an aside, Charlotte later confessed to Yve that she didn't know if she was a villain or a tarnished goodie-two-shoes. The writers refused to tell her (they mightn't know themselves). However, her portrayal of this mysterious "creature" was the prime draw of the series.

The uniformed security team were, indeed, commandos. They had trained with special forces in Germany, France and America. They prided themselves on being on duty twenty-four hours a day, every day, year-in-and-year-out. Each one was muscular in appearance and extremely courteous to all and sundry. However, they knew how to disarm, neutralize, or kill any potential assailant without hesitation and by using any of a score of different means.

There were (at the time) a dozen or so of these special forces personnel in the Grand Duchy (the actual number remains a closely guarded secret). These men weren't eager to provide security for three, bimbo prima donnas. Their interest piqued, however, when they learned of the vigilante band of ruffians prominent in the "area of operations."

Due to the nature of their business, the exact identities of the trio remained a "state secret." They were known only as Andre, Bruno, and Charles (A, B, and C). One of them was blond; the other two were not. Their close-cropped hair showcased muscular, bull-necks.

The festivities began with the entrance of a key member of the sponsoring organization. He was a balding man who'd seen enough sorrow to make him look ancient, though he informed them he was in his early forties. It's possible he lied. A Protestant reputation is not a resume enhancement in certain parts of Europe.

"When I first visited the Desert Compound – an apt name as you shall see for yourself – it was a rat and roach infested sink hole. It took us over a year of hard work to get the pest situation under control. Since then, we've made progress; progress best measured in baby steps. When we started, six out of every ten children died from hunger or disease. Some died from no physical cause. They died because they simply had no reason to live."

Yvonne cast a furtive glance at the Grand Duchess. Her visage remained stoic, but there was no way to hide the moisture collecting in her eyes.

"We've heard the criticism," he continued. "People are reluctant because we are not a Catholic organization."

All eyes were on the Grand Duchess now. She lifted her chin slightly and displayed a proud calmness. She radiated a bravery that was palpable.

"Keep this in mind: if we do not continue to make progress, most or all of these children will not live long enough to practice any religion."

The Grand Duchess looked directly at Yvonne who, diplomatically, refocused on the man behind the podium.

"This year, three of ten die. We're not proud of that. It's unacceptable. Out of desperation, we turned to Her Highness because she supports many fine, charitable organizations. Thank you, Your Highness. We hope this mission will make people aware of our desperate situation."

The Grand Duchess nodded once – almost imperceptibly and, Yve thought, grudgingly.

"We have beds for a dozen children. At present, there are fourteen boys and girls at the orphanage. When a child dies, a survivor gets their bed. We have a school. It is run by locals who can barely read and write, but it's a start. Our main water supply is a well – a well in the middle of the desert. Without it, there'd be no orphanage, no school, no village, and – obviously – no children.

"We put in electric pump to make it easier to draw water. It was stolen and, presumably, sold. We installed another. It was stolen and, presumably, sold. We went back to drawing water with a bucket. This made the thieves angry. They shoveled animal dung into the well. It was weeks before the water was safe to drink again. Water had to be shipped in. When the government decided it was too expensive, they stopped the water shipments. It was a very near thing and a miracle that only two adults died of dehydration – those two, by the way, refused their daily ration so the children could have it."

The room was filled with incredulous and mournful expressions.

"We have a dispensary – the hospital the locals call it. It has one bed, precious little medicine, and a nurse who is more witch doctor than medico. Quite frankly, our backs are up against the wall. If something doesn't break soon – I can't even think about it."

"Where do these kids come from?"

Yvonne admired Sarah's courage. To speak without being recognized in the home (castle more like) of a royal personage took tremendous fortitude. Perhaps, she was merely clueless.

"We're on a caravan route," Baldy replied. "Well, near enough to say we're on a caravan route. They still have them. If an unwanted child is born en route, it is often left in the desert to die. If an older child becomes a liability, they just leave it behind – to die in the desert."

The eight people in attendance were *not* enjoying one syllable of this.

Dark Comedy

"I haven't been there for over a year. I've been hard at work soliciting funds. The latest reports are encouraging. People are "adopting" some children from afar. Eight hundred dollars will support a child for a year. Nearly all the children have financial support. It has made a world of difference. If your visit will help increase donations, we have a chance – not a good chance, mind you, but – well, a fighting chance. Once the children are taken care of, we can begin improvements in the infrastructure. The buildings, especially the "hospital" are in shocking disrepair."

The theme was clear: life is cheap in the desert waste.

The next invited speaker was from the department responsible for the security of government officials, including figure heads. It was through him that Andre, Bruno, and Charles were assigned. He brought out a map and easel. With a pointer, he indicated their "objective."

"That's where you're going," he informed. "Notice that it is very near an international border. The two countries have a tacit agreement not to send troops into this area. A skirmish between French-speaking forces and Arab-speaking forces has, in the past, led to serious bloodshed. This region is not worth fighting for, so it is, virtually, isolated. Notice, also, there is no symbol on this map. The village is too small to record. The aircraft will land – here. Vehicles will take you and the supplies the rest of the way. Roads in this area are very crude. You will arrive with the aid of the compass and radio direction finders – if the hellions haven't stolen them."

He removed the map and easel. There was nothing further to see.

"The area is lawless. I don't use the term lightly. It is too small and too remote for the government to maintain any presence. There are roaming bands of freebooters and, we are certain, a few of the local *citizens* who work together to steal anything that can be turned into cash, food, water or whatever commodity is in highest demand.

"Three years ago, one of the children wandered off during the night and, apparently, saw and was frightened by three or four thieves. She was found dead the next morning with her throat cut. Do not – I say again – do not leave the compound in the dark. A, B, and C will escort you or stay with you during the day. They will sleep in the same area as you ladies during the night.

"The thieves do not snatch children. They cannot be sold or ransomed. However, young, women, and *white* women in particular, will fetch a lot of goods and a lot of cash. Do not – I say again – do not go anywhere an A, B, C men cannot see you. There are toilet facilities if you can call them that. They will check before you enter and wait until you come out. When you're sleeping, two men will be posted at the most likely entry points. The third will keep watch for two hours before being relieved by one of the others. Don't be afraid to scream. If you're bothered during the night, shout out! If it's a false alarm, you can laugh or argue about it later. Better to be embarrassed than to be missing.

"We have people and aircraft on standby. They will be dispatched if we must search for you, but we'd like to avoid that. If the kidnappers think they're cornered, they don't want to be hobbled by *non-essential baggage* – if you get my drift, and I think you do.

"Finally, the A, B, C men are trained to kill. Do not play jokes on them. They will act first and ask for details later. Don't allow some practical joke to become a tragedy.

"If I am frightening you – good! Be extra cautious. Be aware of your surroundings. If you are suspicious of someone, leave the area and stay as near an A, B, C man as you can get. Being overcautious is a virtue out there."

When this man withdrew and the three women began breathing normally again, the Grand Duchess stood. Because she stood, everyone in the room got to their feet.

"On that cheery note," she began. "I wish you luck, as I wish us, the people who are sending you out there, luck. I want those children to grow up and, at least, have a *chance* at life. The reporters will be there with you. Bullies and cutthroats don't like cameras. That should provide a little extra protection. Know this, I will pray for you – every morning and every night.

Do not – I say again – do not get in trouble out there."

Yvonne couldn't help herself. The idea of the Grand Duchess pretending to be an officious security person made her snicker. The colleagues on both sides of her joined in.

"Your Highness," Andre inserted.

That was as near "permission to speak" as this bull of a man was likely to get.

"Ladies, we will go to the airfield and board the plane," he continued. "When we arrive, I urge you to use the ground facilities. Empty your bowels and your bladders. It will be a long flight, and the only facilities on the aircraft are slop jars. There's very little privacy up there."

That, more than the frightening security briefing, caused visible consternation.

"How do I get out of this chicken outfit?" Charlotte whispered in polished English.

"Too late," Yvonne whispered back.

DARKNESS: PRECURSOR

The Grand Duchess and three members of her entourage escorted the mission participants to the circle drive. There was one military vehicle and one limo. Before anyone was permitted access to their carriage, the Grand Duchess bid them farewell individually. The ABCs were first up. What Her Highness said to them was not in the public domain. However, each received a handshake and a personalized send off. Each, in turn, stood to attention and saluted the Duchess before mounting the vehicle.

This was no time to dawdle. The ABCs were whisked away without further fanfare. The limo pulled forward into that space vacated by the military transport. As a finely togged official opened the rear door of the black monster, the Grand Duchess boldly interceded between the ladies and their transport. She shook hands with Sarah Welter.

"Thank you for your support of the children. God be with you."

Sarah, looking even younger and more innocent than her public persona, was unable to speak. Was she scared, or was she unable to fetch a proper response? She settled for a polite smile and a bob curtsey. When her hand was again her own, she ducked into the vehicle and hastily slid down the seat to settle into that place furthest from the open door.

Sister stepped forward and accepted the extended hand.

"I wish you a safe journey, Mademoiselle Yvonne. Thank you; God be with you. I shall pray for you."

Where did this Mlle. Yvonne come from? Yve was subject to a momentary shock. This was not proper protocol. On the contrary, it was inexcusably familiar. Even in a pretend monarchy, there exists a clear demarcation between the (pretend) ruling class and their (pretend) subjects.

Perhaps, this was a sign of friendship. The Grand Duchess could not be friends with a person she hardly knew. However, she not only offered her a commission, but she also anointed Yvonne the royal *doppelganger*.

After a moment of flurried thought and confusion, Yve cleared her throat.

"Your humble servant," she said while executing a bob curtsy.

She threw herself into the vehicle and pressed against Sarah Welter. She needn't have bothered. There was more than ample room in the spacious limo.

The exchange between Charlotte and the Grand Duchess was lost amid the momentary confusion in the back seat. Soon enough, Charlotte was safely ensconced in the vehicle. The liveried servant closed the door firmly and the trio were secure in a, supposedly, sound-proof chamber.

"You're the model, right?"

Charlotte's question created a spike in Yve's blood pressure.

"My entire modeling career lasted all of a minute and a half!" she snapped.

Charlotte was surprised by the emphatic response, but she was not offended.

"Tell me how you really feel."

There was a moment of thoughtful rumination.

"I'm sorry," Yve announced with sincerity. "I'm overly sensitive about certain things."

"What do you do?" Sarah asked, reasonably.

"Until now, I haven't given it any thought," she mused. "I guess, I'm a dress maker, for want of anything better."

"A designer?" Sarah asked, hopefully.

"I helped design my sister's wedding gown, but that's not my forte. You might say, I put the designs together. The pantsuit the Grand Duchess is wearing; I might have had a hand in that. I'm a seamstress, I suppose."

"Do you think you could make a pantsuit like that for me?" Sarah asked. "It would look so special in a pale blue."

"Let me get you measured when we return," Yve promised. "I'm certain we can satisfy you."

Charlotte would not be put off.

"What's with you?" she demanded. "The Duchess looks at you like you walk on water."

"Well, I don't," Yve asserted. "We met briefly once. She asked after me specifically. I'm as flummoxed as you are. She trusts me. I assume that means she likes me. Beyond that, I'm clueless."

Charlotte sniffed to register her dubiousness.

"You're not jealous of me?" Yve asked in near panic. "Please, don't tell me you are!"

There was a point-blank issue worthy of serious thought.

"I suppose I am, I don't know – *resentful*, maybe. *Envious*, perhaps."

"Don't be. I'm a nobody from nowhere."

Charlotte shook her head thoughtfully.

"The way the Duchess looks at you and speaks to you – no. I don't buy it. You are somebody. What's more, you're somebody important."

Yvonne took a deep breath.

"We're going to be with each other for the better part of two weeks," she began. "I'd feel so much better if we can be friends."

"I don't make friends easily," Sarah pouted.

"We will get along," Charlotte promised. "It's either that or we kill each other."

"I don't think Duchess will be very pleased if we kill each other," Sarah predicted.

"Oh, stuff it! Sing us a song," Charlotte commanded.

"Act out a scene from *Hamlet*," Sarah countered.

"Just to let you know," Yve interrupted. "I can sew your mouths shut. Both of you. I have the skill."

It started as a snicker. Moments later, it became a laugh – a laugh of camaraderie.

Yve shuddered. Did she really diffuse the situation, or did she merely delay it? Would the representatives of the Luxembourg Mission to Africa be at each other's throats for the duration?

The limo deposited them on a military portion of the airport. There were facilities, and the women took advantage. No one was anxious to learn how to operate twelfth century plumbing. There were bottles of water and soda aplenty, but the women declined.

"Maybe later," they promised simultaneously and almost in unison.

Their aircraft was supplied by NATO. It was a huge, American cargo plane. It was equipped with an American crew. Little Luxembourg must have considerably more influence that anyone, hitherto, suspected.

Part of the American contingent occupied themselves with preflight checks. Three men in flight suits were too focused on examining the exterior of the aircraft to notice what exited the limo. A fourth man, tall and thin, had remarkable visual acuity. He studied the three, slovenly dressed women as if looking for defects. The ABCs were nearby, and their eyes were, likewise, critical. One of them must have said something either to the lanky American or loud enough for him to overhear.

"Would you care to board?" he asked excitedly.

"We're waiting for our luggage," Charlotte announced.

"That arrived with these three brutes," he informed, gesturing in the direction of the ABCs. "There wasn't much. You might want to see if it's all there."

The suggestion seemed prudent enough to override their caution concerning a stranger – and an American stranger at that. He guided them to the massive ramp at the rear of the aircraft.

Yvonne's eyes popped. Lodged inside the plane and secured with mighty, thick-linked chains was the biggest truck she'd ever seen. It was painted U.S. Army green with stenciled white markings. To mount the cab of that truck, one required either a rope or ladder.

Compared to the monster inside the plane, the paltry gear of three women was almost invisible. The combined luggage of the trio was secured between the front wheels of the truck. Their sun hats were in a sack of nylon netting dangling from the front fender of the huge truck.

"I ain't never seen nuthin' like that afore!" Charlotte exclaimed in a slangy English that Yve couldn't quite decipher.

"You're American!" The tall blond exclaimed.

Charlotte didn't smile. She was trapped in a mild state of shock.

"Actually, I'm German."

"German? Where'd you learn to talk 'Merican?"

Recovering from her amazement, the woman shrugged.

"I read a lot."

"We're riding in here?" Sarah, with eyes threatening to pop out of her head. "Where do we sit?"

The man smiled at the neophytes.

"I'll be happy to show you, later. If you're flying with us, go ahead and look around, but don't touch anything."

They decided to look around. By law and by right, they should be safe. However, six eyes surveyed their surroundings to make certain the ABCs were within shouting distance.

"It isn't just the truck," Sarah noted. "There's a big trailer attached!"

"Both the trailer and the truck are loaded with wooden boxes," Charlotte noted.

"How can this thing get off the ground?"

Yvonne's question focused all their attention on the single, most critical concern.

As they gawked and wondered, the tall American pushed a pallet of cardboard boxes up the ramp.

"Bottled water," he yelled.

"Can we carry all this stuff?" Charlotte challenged.

"We can carry a lot more than we've got aboard now," the nonchalant Ami replied. "Right now, I've got four more loads of water. It's going to be a pain to lash this stuff down. Stuff packed in cardboard is a bad idea on an airplane."

None of the women were interested to know the nature of his concern. The single thought they shared concerned *not* being in an aircraft that was bursting at the seams. Before they could conference or complain, they were hailed by someone unknown. He, however, knew of them.

"Ladies, would you come out here, please?"

Instinctively, they scanned the area for the ABCs. They saw one. That was all the reassurance they needed. As they approached the ramp, their field of view increased allowing them to see all the security men.

"It's the press," Sarah guessed.

"Show time," Charlotte announced.

"May we ask a few questions?"

It was the man who had hailed them. He appeared to be alone. Who, then, was the missing *we*? There was neither time nor opportunity to speculate. A woman with a microphone attached to a man with a video camera on his shoulder were rushing to the scene.

It was chaos. The two teams competed to get the trio to themselves. Charlotte suggested they split up. She would attend to the man and his missing other, while Sarah and Yve entertained the duo with the camera.

"We're with *Hei Elei, Kuck Elei*," the woman announced.

Sarah had been a featured segment on the program before. Yve didn't watch TV. Her family didn't have one; the dorm didn't have one; Yve didn't have one. She hadn't a clue as to the existence of the popular Luxembourg version of part-news-part-rumor program.

"Are you the reporters who are travelling with us?" Yvonne asked.

The woman thought that hilarious. It was clear she didn't envy Yve and her companions. She wanted all three of them to get "into shot." Charlotte, however, told them essentially to pound sand. She was very polite, but she made it clear that the press had to share.

Questions were asked, video was taken, interviews were conducted, pictures were snapped, and inane questions were hurled. None of the women could recall, precisely, what was asked or what their answers were. The one common theme was that the Grand Duchess had recruited them, and they agreed to go.

Thirty minutes after the assault was initiated, it ended. The ABCs hustled the pests away. They didn't need much hustling. They faced a deadline and had precious little time to punch out their fiction.

For the trio, however, the performance lasted hours.

Yvonne caught her breath and counted to ten. She did not want to provoke her "partners." She sensed that they were one careless syllable from a hair-pulling, face-scratching free for all. Nevertheless, one of the main objectives of their journey was to seduce the press to get them behind the aid program. She wasn't properly trained in kid-gloves techniques, so she said a quick, silent prayer before launching.

"I think we handled that very badly," she began.

She expected a snarky retort. Instead, she gathered questioning looks.

"Remember our objective," she continued. "We want a constant flow of support to these children. I think we need to emphasize that."

No one interrupted, but neither woman joined in the discussion.

"You and Sarah are used to handling the press – or you have people who know how to do it for you. Do you think we could work out a little script?"

That was as far as she intended to go. If the trio was unable to work together, they must discover some way to avoid undue friction. The media would have a field day if the "hand-picked" representatives of the Grand Duchess began brawling. Of course, they'd prefer to have a video for their hungry audiences. However, second-hand reports would allow them tremendous latitude in inventing details.

Charlotte studied Yve carefully before casting a glance at Sarah.

"Let me make a few notes," she concluded. "Let's all make notes on what we should showcase – and how. We can compare and discuss them later."

Sarah nodded.

"That's a good idea," she said.

Yve sent forth another silent prayer.

"Can we adopt a rule?"

"What kind of rule?" Charlotte demanded.

"You won't like it, because it won't apply to me; I have no fish to fry."

"Get to the point," Charlotte insisted, her eyebrows narrowing.

"We avoid any attempt at career enhancement. The children and the school and the facilities should be our primary concern."

Charlotte pursed her lips before directing her attention to the remaining party.

"Sarah?"

The singer did quick calculations.

"I'll agree to that," she concluded.

"Okay," Charlotte nodded. "I'm in."

Yve swallowed with relief.

"You two are experts at playing the media," she noted. "You take the lead and I'll back you in the unlikely event they want my opinion."

"Hardly experts," Sarah objected.

"*Experienced* then," Yvonne amended.

They watched as the cargo capacity of their transport increased.

"We may have plenty of time to do our homework," Sarah suggested. "I don't think this aircraft will get off the ground."

"You better hope it does," Charlotte replied. "Otherwise, we're all human cinders."

DARKNESS DESCENDS

They were kept, so they thought, until the media had an opportunity to talk to and take film and photos of the "Bold Trio." After the locusts fled to more exciting adventures, the women expected an immediate (attempted) take off. When the loading continued and they were not hustled onto the aircraft, they began growing petulant.

Yvonne's first impressions of Charlotte were less than generous. Tact was not a part of the actress's personality. She wanted the same information as Yve and Sarah. She asked the tall Ami who was wrestling additional water aboard.

"I'm not the one who insisted we take more water!" he barked.

Charlotte was ready to author something equally abrupt. To her credit, she hung fire. Yvonne accepted the job to placate on behalf of the team. It wasn't in her job description for there was no job description. The three rather attractive crusaders were expected to focus attention on the plight of children half a world away. Until they reached their destination, there was no reason for them to speak. To complain was to overreach.

"He's pissed," she whispered to Charlotte who hardly needed to be told. "For some reason, he's got his pants in a bunch because the water bottles are in cardboard boxes. Let him do his job and manage his anger."

The actress looked daggers at the officious interloper but held her tongue. She should be enjoying a three-week hiatus from shooting for the soap. Instead, she'd spend half that time away from her husband or her boyfriend – perhaps both. Her impatience was understandable, but she must be made aware that many people were involved.

Moments later, with no help from the women, the tall Ami snapped.

"If we hit major turbulence, these boxes will split, and we will be bombed by a thousand bottles of water!"

The remark, apparently, was aimed at the aircraft commander who was not within Yve's ken. The "load master" (that was the title someone used) was tasked with placing the pallets of water "just so," and secure them to prevent their moving about on the rollers of the aircrafts floor. To be certain "water-bottle" bombs would not become a hazard to either crew or passengers, he must wrap the last-minute in cargo netting.

After this outburst, Charlotte turned to discover Yve examining her. Her visage remained stern, but her eyes appeared apologetic.

"We may want to make one more trip to the head," she said.

Yvonne was unfamiliar with the slang, but she required no translator. Sarah, the most practical of the three, had initiated a saunter in that direction even before the latest delay was announced.

Twenty minutes later, they were seated. Three little monkeys in a row.

There was a bench running the length of the cargo bay on both sides. There were seatbelts galore. These did not snap. The "clasps" were small levers attached to a grooved roller. When the strap was pulled through, the grooves dug into the belt until released. If the grooved rollers were not released, nobody was going to stand up, never mind being thrown about the cargo bay.

Andre sat next to Sarah. Bruno and Charles were to the right of Charlotte. Yvonne was, once again, in the middle. Across from them were supernumeraries. Two reporters huddled together and engaged in a guarded conversation. Periodically, they cast surreptitious glances at the three women. Several spaces away were two uniformed personnel. Yve wasn't familiar with their clothing. They weren't Luxembourg military and, certainly, not German. They might have been French or Belgian.

She'd satiate her curiosity later.

One of the two men was, likely, the driver of the massive truck they carried. She hoped so. If not, someone expected one of the women to steer that monster to its destination.

The tall American was attached to a lengthy chord allowing him access to any spot in the cargo bay. The chord was attached to the blue headphones he wore. There was a movable device, a microphone, which could be swiveled up or down. He kept it near his mouth. When he wished to talk to whoever was on the other end of the "commo system," he'd press a button further down the chord.

He came by with a cardboard box. Charlie reached in and extracted a small cylinder of wax. Bruno followed suit. Charlotte didn't hesitate to grab her cylinder, so Yve unhesitatingly did the same.

Bruno took out a pocketknife and sliced his wax into equal parts. He offered to perform the same service for Charlotte. Before she could notice, Andre had sliced for Sarah and tapped Yve on the arm.

"What's this about?" she asked since no one else would.

"Put these tight in your ears," he advised. "It won't blunt the noise much, but it will prevent damage to the inner ear."

Sarah didn't need to be told twice, but Yve remained skeptical. If the ABCs were advancing a practical joke, her trust in them would terminate. She watched Andre plug his ears. When he looked over to find her earplugs still in her hand, he leaned across Sarah. The poor urchin suspected that he was initiating some kind of unwanted advance, and it showed in her expression.

"When they start up the engines, you will understand," he promised.

He returned to his "zone" much to Sarah's relief and satisfaction. Rather than produce umbrage, Yvonne was grateful to Andre. He'd passed this information in a low voice aimed specifically at her. He could have blurted it out for all and sundry to hear. Sister knew she was ignorant of the military and military aircraft, but no one enjoys being considered a "rookie."

Within minutes, Yvonne knew exactly why ear protection was on the docket. The noisy engines were overpowering. She noticed that when one reporter spoke to his companion the chords in his neck became prominent. To make oneself heard, it would be necessary to be near the person being addressed. Even then, one needed to yell.

Thump – cathump – thump – cathump – thump – cathump

At least they were moving.

Thump – cathump – thump – cathump – thump – cathump

Yvonne became uncertain. Since they were loaded down with cargo, they might thump – cathump all the way to the Med. Does this thing float? She considered the craft better suited to floatation since she doubted its ability to fly.

Maybe, while they were thump-cathumping, she could ask to leave the plane and visit the necessary one last time.

Finally, the behemoth squealed to a stop.

Are we there?

The engines began to roar. They were much louder than before. There was a slight lurch – just enough to press her into Charlotte. She struggled to right herself, but the lurch graduated to a persistent force. She couldn't sit properly; Sarah was leaning against her making it impossible to disengage from Charlotte.

She felt a surg of panic. If she continued to invade Charlotte's space, that bellicose woman might decide to retaliate.

Thump – cathump –thump – cathump – thump

The rhythmic beat began to change tempo.

Thump-cathump-thumpcathump – thumpcathump – thumpcathump –thump –

The roar of the engines continued but the vibrations ceased. Charlotte had yet to launch a protest. Yvonne dared to turn her head slowly, fearing Charlotte's fist might be on the way to greet it. Unexpectedly, she noticed that the woman was leaning against Bruno.

The aircraft was tilted! They had taken off. Yve could hear the whirring of motors as the wheels were retracted. She heard and felt the currrrrrrrrr-thump as they locked into place. She turned all her attention to the filled-to-overflowing truck and its filled-to-overflowing trailer. They hadn't moved.

She took a relieved breath.

The team was on its way.

No fatalities so far.

The tall Ami was up and walking around. He meticulously checked the load. He examined the netted water boxes with particular care. He continued to inspect the load while ignoring the humans.

Gradually, the aircraft leveled. The passengers could, once more, sit upright. Yvonne wanted to apologize to Charlotte for inadvertently shoving her, but she doubted she could yell loud enough to be heard. For her part, Charlotte did not appear resentful.

Charlie untied himself and got up. Andre followed suit. They ambled over to the truck, opened the door, and climbed in. Yvonne could see them talking. She thought it a clever idea. Nothing could block the persistent roar of the engines, but sitting in the cab of the truck would provide an extra layer of insulation. They could chat without straining their voices over much.

Yvonne's primary goal was to avoid provoking Charlotte. She struggled to escape the restriction of her restraining device. She popped up and discovered that standing was not so far removed from her experiences while earth bound.

She was relieved and, unexpectedly, tired. If she could only lay down. Once flat, she could, at least, relax. The engine noise would make sleep impossible, but her taught muscles might slacken enough for her to regain some normality.

There was one place – a nearly perfect flat surface – a siren's song devoid of audible allure but irresistible all the same.

She climbed up the outside of the trailer, grasped the ropes and cables securing its load, and pulled herself up until she was atop the wooden crates. She lay on her back, folded her hands under her head, and rested one cheek upon her arm. Moments later, she closed her eyes.

The ground began to shake.

Her eyes popped open.

Her heart rate spiked. Instantly, she realized she was not on the ground; she was atop a stack of supplies in wooden crates.

She shook her head to clear it. She must have dozed off. There was an eerie illumination inside the aircraft. She searched for the small "port holes" sunk into the fuselage. They were all dark. Yvonne realized that – deafening roar of four aircraft engines aside – she had slept. Not only had she slept, but she'd been dreamless for a considerable while.

She sat up and examined her surroundings. Everyone in the cargo bay was either sleeping or trying to. Only an ABC man (she couldn't identify him) sat alert and ready as advertised. He was entertaining himself by sharpening his this-means-business knife.

Charlotte, following Yve's example, lay sandwiched between two pallets of web-encased water cases. Sarah lay on her side along the bench. Her face was against the fuselage and a protective hand kept the dim light from her eyes. There was no way to know if she was awake or asleep.

Slowly and carefully, Yvonne lowered herself to the floor. She was curious to know if those flying the aircraft were also in repose. With courage she'd never suspected she possessed, she made her way forward. The tall Ami was conspicuous, but he paid her no heed; he was far more interested in checking and rechecking the cargo, the lashings that kept them in place, and referring to the loose-bound military book he carried.

Yve climbed a few steps to find herself in a green glow. Her eyes struggled to readjust. She nearly tripped over something. No one could hear her mishap, but someone was alerted by her struggle to keep herself standing. She'd seen pictures. She identified the pilot. That person in the right seat was, apparently, napping.

"Where are we?" she asked.

This stale question was applied in delf-defense. She wanted some reason to explain her unauthorized intrusion.

"We're either approaching the coast of Africa, or we're just passing Qubec City."

Yvonne decided she didn't care much for the American sense of humor. Without any means to see her reaction physically, the pilot correctly assessed her mood. He threw back the right armrest and unbuckled himself. The co-pilot, whom Yve identified as asleep, was, suddenly, fully alert.

"Maybe, you can get us out of this mess," the pilot said as he extracted himself. "Have you ever flown a plane before?"

"No," she responded.

Whatever his joke, she didn't find this any funnier than the one preceding.

"Then, it's time you learned."

He unceremoniously pressed her aside and squeezed around behind her.

"Sit down," he said.

Was that a suggestion or an order? She decided to call his bluff.

The pilot helped her get into the shoulder straps and instructed her on how to fasten the seat belt. He then stepped back to stretch and reintroduce circulation.

The young man in the right seat was illuminated by an anemic green light. He looked like a twelve-year-old child. To Yve's relief and reassurance, he spoke with a bold baritone. He pointed to key instruments, explaining the purpose of each. He instructed her to rest her feet on the pedals and had her grip the yoke.

"Gently," he urged. "Don't try and use muscle. Just rest on the controls gently."

She suspected a trick. He would instruct her to do something, and a Christmas-cracker pop would precede the appearance of a dancing scarecrow from the control panel. Instead of pinching her or shouting, he settled back into his seat and rested his hands in his lap.

"Okay," he announced. "You're flying the airplane."

Yvonne's palms were instantly wet. This wasn't possible. She had her hands on a vehicle packed to the gills with tons and tons of cargo and a dozen or so people! This must be a trick, but the pilot behind her and the co-pilot at her side remained still and stoic. For two minutes or so, she didn't dare move. She sat and stared out into the blackness. She imagined she saw a star – perhaps, two.

"Look," the co-pilot said, pointing to the display between them. "You're drifting to the left."

She noticed the yellow line on the screen. The top of the line began to "lean" slightly to the right.

"With your right foot, slowly, and gently, press on the … easy. Keep going until that line is pointing straight ahead."

Yve pretended she was teasing a kitten. She wanted to stroke it, not crush it. To her amazement, the line returned as promised.

"Now," the co-pilot said while pointing to another instrument. "You're climbing like a home-sick angel. Stop pulling back on the yoke. Gently push it forward just a tinny bit. A little more. Good, now pull back until that big needle is on the zero. Very good. Now, look here. You're drifting again."

This continued for, perhaps, ten minutes. Her hands were wet, and her throat was parched. The moment she grew used to scanning two instruments, the co-pilot would introduce her to a third, then a fourth. She couldn't keep up. She was trembling and exhausted.

"I think, you'd better do this," she announced.

There was no discussion, and – thank-you, God – no arguing.

"I have the aircraft," the co-pilot assured.

Dark Comedy

With the assistance of the pilot, she was unbelted and unstrapped. It took her a while to extract herself and stand aside. Her knees were jelly.

"Pretty good for the first time," the pilot reported as he resumed his seat. "I'm glad you quit when you did. I was beginning to think I'd be fired."

Yvonne remained where she was until her limbs felt responsive enough to move. She wanted to say something, but words failed her. She wasn't about to thank them for the time she spent in stark terror, but she didn't want to appear rude.

"I feel better as a passenger," she concluded.

"Don't disparage, Ma'am," the pilot replied. "I predict you'd be a damn good pilot if you decide to take it up."

That was a lie, she was certain. Nevertheless, it was wrapped in the form of a complement.

"Thank you," she said.

It was the first time she'd been addressed as a "ma'am" by an Ami. She had, hitherto, considered it a word of derision. The pilot's context implied that it was not.

The Amis remained a queer and unsettling people, she decided, but they were far better than she'd been led to believe. Perhaps, it was their informality and their slang – the one bringing the other into sharp relief. Regardless, her attitude vis à vis Amis would, likely, undergo adjustment.

Her throat hurt. She was so tempted to refresh herself with the bottle of water she'd been issued. If she drank, however, she'd have to pee – eventually. She wasn't anxious to tempt fate.

The tall Ami prowled around constantly, checking and testing every chain and strap which kept the tons of cargo from breaking free. He explained that a sudden shift in the "center of gravity" would seriously influence the aircrafts performance.

"How seriously?" Sarah asked.

Tall Ami responded by clapping his hands together followed by a thumbs down gesture. Following this mimed performance, the female trio took special interest in the security of the cargo and equipment.

No matter where he went or what he did, the load master kept his headphones on. Not only did it retard the roar of the engines, but also kept him in direct contact with the pilot.

Yvonne sat atop the cargo in the trailer. She was debating with herself. Should she return to her comrades, or should she lay back and try to sleep? Tall Ami suddenly sprang from a crouch, stood erect, and pressed his earphones even tighter against his ears. He pressed the button at his side and said something immediately lost in the cacophony. He gestured to Yve.

Slowly, she lowered herself from her perch. She was careful. She didn't know if she would suffer serious injury if she were to tumble onto the floor of the cargo bay, but she was determined to avoid finding out.

"The pilot says we can't get clearance for Algerian airspace. We must take the long way round."

Yvonne's heart sank. She didn't want to be in the cocktail shaker for one minute longer than necessary.

"How long will it take?"

Tall Ami ignored the question.

"We're going to land in Gibraltar and take on fuel. We will land in forty minutes or so. You might want to help me wake up your people and have them strap in."

Instantly, she rushed to Charles. It was his turn to keep an eye on "the girls." He'd witnessed the exchange between Yve and Tall Ami. His expression made clear that he wished to be made privy of their exchange. She barked a synopsis of the adjusted itinerary and moved toward the front of the aircraft.

There were three uniforms in the control area. One sat behind a consol of levers and between the pilot and co-pilot.

"Mind if I watch?" she asked.

"Help yourself," the pilot yelled back. "Hold onto something. Hold on tight!"

There followed a recitation concerning Algerian traffic controllers. It was laced with frosty words and phrases. This tirade was intended for the two uniformed people within earshot, but Yve couldn't help but hear. One of the pilot's tributes struck her as funny. She tucked it away for future use. She was obligated to find out exactly what it meant, however; it wouldn't serve her well should she inadvertently repeat something that was obscene.

She experienced the turns and banks of the aircraft. Tons of material was lashed down in the cargo bay, so the pilots exercised supreme caution. They must avoid sudden turns or drastic adjustment in speed.

Yve saw the rock – little chance of mistaking that feature for anything else. Eventually, she saw the airport. She grew impatient when they did not head directly for the runway. Instead, they flew around the facility twice.

There was a disturbance behind her. Turning, she found Bruno. He was checking up on her.

"They told me I could watch," she yelled.

He nodded. Without any gesture of protest, he returned from whence he came.

This journey was becoming an exciting adventure. However, Yvonne couldn't enjoy it fully. She wondered why she was doing this. What reason could God possibly have for sending her to a remote location? She was bringing aid and comfort to needy children. It was a laudable endeavor and the Christian thing to do – but *why* was He sending *her*? Sarah and Charlotte were the headliners. Yvonne was a seamstress – just as out of place as a puppy in a horse race.

With the engines shut down, the reporters felt this was a good moment to get the feel of their prey. However, first things first, i.e.: a visit to the relief station. Those nearest the parked aircraft were segregated. The women took full advantage of their opportunity.

"If we admit we're nervous about this whole thing," Charlotte began.

"We are," Sarah admitted.

"Good," Yvonne nodded. "Then we won't be lying, but let's not start speculating."

"I like that," Charlotte agreed. "Do not let them lead you into anything. If they start making up situations, just say we will wait until we are there to appraise things."

Realizing they daren't delay too long lest the media reap a harvest of speculation, they got the most of their hurried conference.

Predictably, the "press corps" accosted them at the first possible moment. They adhered to the terms of their treaty.

"Any plans for the near future?"

Yve couldn't help but cringe. Charlotte, however, remained mindful of their agreement.

"You should talk to my husband," she replied. "He's my agent. I don't do anything unless he tells me."

Later, Yvonne congratulated Charlotte on her answer.

"Just between us, though," she prodded. "What are your plans?"

Charlotte, judiciously, surveyed her surroundings. When she responded, she kept her voice as low as the surrounding noise allowed.

"I love theatre," she announced. "I love being on stage. I was in *Midsummer Night* as a fairy for three weeks. It was a hoot! I was Cecily Cardew in *Earnest* for two weeks. My husband thinks I've got a good chance of being Nora in *Doll's House* next summer. If I get that part, I'll know I've arrived! Of course, I must learn how to do that dance, but – man!"

Dark Comedy

Charlotte was excited. There was no room for doubt. Yvonne didn't want to be a wet blanket by informing the actress she hadn't a clue about the plays. She had a nodding acquaintance with Shakespeare, the others were Greek to her.

She filed this precious information for future use. If Charlotte turned belligerent again, a change of topic to live theatre might prove invaluable. Of her two companions, she liked the girlish-looking Sarah more. However, Charlotte had – or seemed to have – an excellent mind. It was too bad she carried a chip on her shoulder.

All too soon, they were inside that noisy cocktail shaker again. Yvonne climbed up onto her "bed," and attempted to sleep some more. It was a waste of effort. With no place to go and nothing to do, Yve just lay and endured.

Why? What am I doing here? What can I possibly do?

They landed in the late afternoon. It was little more than a dirt strip plowed out and leveled during a government campaign to rid the interior of guerilla activity several years before.

There had been a small army base around the airstrip. The mud buildings that remained were crumbling and devoid of any signs of human habitation.

In honor of the European "publicity stunt," a company of mobile army rangers had set up a base camp. There were four canvass tents for the troops, a headquarters tent, two small motor vehicle maintenance facilities of the some-assembly-required variety. There were, also, two "visitor" tents; one for the men, and one for the "not-men." These had wooden (or a wood *fac simile*) sides with a spacious canvass covering.

The pilots didn't like the looks of the place – not even a little bit. Tall Ami and a contingent of six soldiers off-loaded the water pallets. The driver and his assistant drove the huge truck and trailer off and parked it off the runway and near the guest tents.

The aircraft was made ready and took off as soon as possible with an hour or two of daylight left.

Here was a conundrum: The army captain was "at the service" of the "mission commander." The mission commander would be – whom? The press gaggle (both of them) wanted to keep as distant from decision making as possible. The driver and "the *other* driver" had no interest.

"Our job is to get you there, get you back, and make repairs as required," the taller and more rounded of the duo announced.

The ABCs were quasi military. The nature of their job was clandestine, and their actual identities and military rank were not subject to public scrutiny.

Unhesitatingly, Sarah and Charlotte turned toward Yvonne.

She cleared her throat and proceeded to *exaggerate* (her scruples did not allow her to lie).

"I am the appointed representative of my government."

She nearly choked.

"You are a woman," the captain observed.

Am I? I've often wondered!

This was no time to be a smart ass. If this thing went south, all the food and supplies they brought, and the motor vehicle and the heavy-duty trailer would become the property of a foreign government.

"I am Yvonne Schortmann, the appointed representative of my government."

She had her French passport in her tucker bag, her German identity card, and her Luxembourg identity and work permit. There was, also, the document the Grand Duchess had provided her. That was tucked in her bra and would remain there until all options were exhausted.

The round-faced captain didn't like it. He didn't like it one bit. He might have blushed if his skin were a different color. A thousand thoughts cascaded through his military brain. Doubtless, he had instructions of his own. Hopefully, they included "don't botch this mission, or you will be permanent latrine orderly."

It took some while before he reached a decision.

"Please, come with me, Lieutenant."

"*Lieutenant?*" Yvonne croaked.

"I am permitted to deal only with officers."

Andre was on the verge of saying – or, worse, *doing* something.

"Stay with me, sergeant," she said, in what she hoped, was her best command voice.

The captain didn't like this. Not one, little bit. A woman giving a command to a man! Intolerable!

At any rate, the situation stabilized – at least a little. She could hear the captain out and Andre could perform his assigned task without having to resort to violence.

The captain outlined his instructions. He and his company were to provide security for the LZ (landing zone) and provide food, shelter and security for the "guests." The guerrillas had been successfully "eliminated" years prior, but there was always a chance of an upsurge. He would provide an escort only so far. They were bound by treaty not to proceed past a certain point. The "no-man's land," he assured was free of guerrilla activity because of reasons Yvonne neither understood nor believed.

The village Yve and the others had come to visit was very near a caravan route. Some of the orphans were transported thither because their families could not support them. If they didn't get to the orphanage, or they couldn't be properly cared for once they arrived – who'd care?

There were salt "mines" in the area. Nothing compared to the industrial operations further south, but enough to keep jingle in local pockets. Miners used the village as a base of operations. There was gold in nearby hills, but not enough to accommodate commercial mining. Prospectors and their families were subsistence toilers. They'd leave and seek better employment elsewhere except they were too well known to take the chance. They worked too hard to create problems and understood if they drew too much attention to themselves, the government would consider it worth the effort to "eliminate" them.

The main economic activity was trading gold and salt with passing caravans.

The greatest drag on the local economy was having to care for the children the caravans left behind.

The captain and the lieutenant agreed to proceed at nine o'clock the following morning. That seemed very late, but the captain reminded her that preparations would require an hour or two.

Their business concluded, Yvonne replaced her sun hat and prepared to leave. She hesitated while expecting a formal dismissal. The captain remained still with an expression of contempt on his fat face. Recalling her alias, she presented – what she hoped – would be interpreted as a military salute. The captain, reluctantly, returned it.

Yve made haste while trying to make it appear that she was not making haste. "Sergeant" Andre dutifully fell into formation, one step behind and to the right of the "lieutenant."

Bruno, Charles, Sarah, and Charlotte waited nervously near the entrance to the "un-men" tent. Yvonne halted in front of Charlotte.

"You're the actress," Yve reminded, none too amiably.

"Only when I have text," the actress replied meekly. "For *ad lib* work, I suck."

Yve sighed.

"I hope I didn't botch this thing."

DARKER STILL

It gets cold in the desert. Yvonne's concept was based upon excruciating heat, sand, and sand dunes. The area adjacent to the "hard surface" runway was bristling with anemic vegetation. The sun, when it popped up over the horizon, was blinding and unrelenting, but the unnerving cold would linger for some while.

Glad she was to have her sun hat protecting her eyes as she looked east – into the waste they must traverse. Save for the wind, there was no sound. The army camp on the opposite side of the runway had yet to stir. Even the sentries were motionless; either they were asleep or frozen in place.

She heard the tent flap behind her. She shuddered. She knew who it was.

"The world is too much with us," she said, not bothering to whisper. "We lay waste our powers ... little that we see that is ours ..."

"What are you chuntering on about?" Charlotte demanded.

"Wordsworth," Yvonne replied, not bothering to bring the other person into view. "I was mangling one of his poems because I don't remember the – *text* as you would say."

"Any reason?"

"None, other than I felt it was important to say it –."

Yve heard the woman slightly behind her shuffling her feet.

"I woke up twice last night," Charlotte reported. "You were kneeling – both times."

"I had matters to discuss," she replied.

"You were praying."

It was not a question.

"I'm starting to appreciate that you are a hell of a lot more than a dressmaker," Charlotte continued when her declaration went unacknowledged.

"At the moment," Yvonne replied, "I'm not even that."

Charlotte took a long, deep breath.

"Yesterday, I was ready to chuck it in."

"Too late," Yve reminded. "The plane's gone."

"That only added to my shakes. I've never been so scared in my life. I was about to throw up. I might have, too, if I had anything in my stomach."

There followed a long, gaping void.

"I'm feeling better, now," Charlotte confessed. "I didn't get you at all. I thought you were some pretentious prig with considerable suck power; some pain in the ass who had pulled a lot of strings to get this gig. Maybe you did, for all I know. Well, I'm ready now. I'll follow you anywhere, Schortmann."

Yvonne turned to face her compatriot. What she intended to say is known but to her.

"How long have you been there?"

Charlotte turned to find Bruno not three feet behind her.

"I'm doing my job," he replied, softly.

"Thank you," Charlotte responded with an edge in her voice. "There are times when a person wants a private conversation to remain private."

"I hear nothing," he replied. "I remember nothing."

This confrontation might have continued, but the army camp was coming to life. The moment before, all was silence. Suddenly, all was fuss and feathers.

"The slumbering giant awakes," Charlotte concluded.

Dark Comedy

"We probably should tidy things up a bit," Yve suggested.

"Yes, lieutenant," Charlotte replied.

The army allowed the visiting contingent bedding as well as shelter. Each woman was provided with a length of canvass upon which was laid a mattress (by desert standards), a headrest, and two woolen blankets. The men were allotted the same, but not of the same quality as the women received.

Yvonne rolled up the blankets and attempted to bring her "bunk" up to military standards.

Sarah had difficulty getting sleep out of her eyes. She wasn't used to such a Spartan routine. She brought pajamas and slippers. These items were omitted from the travel list issued by the mission planners, but they weren't prohibited, so –

The first agenda item was the venting of the bladder. For such a delicate flower as Sarah, this must have rated five barbaric stars. Yve's heart bled for the girlish-looking woman. If Yvonne and Charlotte were out of place in the desert environment, delicate little Sarah was the equivalent of a princess captured by a heathen band of cutthroats. She gained points with Yve, however, when she spent no time with her hair. Sarah gave it a quick brush and parked her sun hat on it.

"Sleep well?" Yve asked, eventually.

"Much better than I expected," she responded. "I dreamed of my husband. He'll be gratified when I tell him that."

Yvonne fell in love with the diminutive singer at that moment. She was someone she didn't want to see hurt. She was too old and worldly to treat as a child, but she was a sweet, little cherub. She decided to adopt her, surreptitiously at least.

Breakfast was military MREs. The ABCs were most familiar with these ration packages. Andre, who was a bit ahead of his team members in English language proficiency, called them Meals Ready to Excrete. As Yvonne and the others were soon to discover, that designation was exceptionally inaccurate. The rations had taste and texture. They did not, however, contain satisfaction.

The ABCs wolfed down their allotted provisions quickly. They didn't enjoy them, but they realized they were vital to maintaining physical dexterity. The women, however, picked away delicately. Adding water was recommended, and they adhered to the recommendation. Still, eating food that did not have the appearance of food required effort.

Sarah struggled.

Yvonne noticed because she was determined to keep an eye on her.

"Let's try this," she suggested.

She mixed sugar, creamer, and a dash of instant coffee (included with the rations) to the "girl's" entree. Once mixed with the freeze-dried "whatever," it was tame enough for Sarah to ingest.

"I hope we can have some real food before long," the little angle sighed.

Yve hadn't the heart to break Sarah's.

As the "ranking officer," Lieutenant Schortmann rode in the right seat of the huge cargo-carrying truck. She squeezed Sarah in next to her. The singer was compact enough that she did not interfere with the driver who must constantly shift gears.

Because two of the "stars" were in the cab, one of the ABCs was stationed directly behind them. Charlotte rode in an army vehicle with the two reporters. Yvonne trusted Charlotte to keep her word. Indeed, there was little chance for interviews. The road was more imagination than substance. The entire caravan was constantly lurching and bouncing.

They drove over holes, boulders, mounds, and all manner of obstructions. Less than an hour into their journey, Yvonne was exhausted. Twice, she thought Sarah was about to heave. She put her arm around her and held her near to try and provide the singer with a little comfort.

The sadistic captain called a halt and strutted around a bit. He came near the truck as if to examine the load. Yvonne thought it a good idea to check on the condition of the cargo. The captain did not look pleased to see her dismount.

"Is there a problem?" she asked, point blank.

"How are you doing?" he asked.

"Fine," Yve lied. "Is there any reason for our stopping."

"I thought you might like a break."

He was clearly disappointed. If Sarah could have provided a little vomit for him to gloat over, he'd have been satisfied. He didn't like women. He didn't like foreign women. If he could do so without fear of repercussion, he might have ordered them shot. Were it up to Yvonne, the captain would be left by the roadside for the carrion birds to feed upon. Unfortunately, there didn't seem to be any scavengers about.

She checked on the ABCs. They seemed to be bearing up very well. Likewise, the cargo remained secure. She sent a silent prayer of thanks for those unknown people who loaded the truck and trailer with such care and skill.

Just beyond was the vehicle carrying Charlotte and her "escorts."

"Getting a good story?" she asked them.

Both scribes looked as if they were about to plead for mercy. Charlotte appeared annoyed. She was acting. She was putting up that "macho," *I-am-woman; I-can-do-anything* crap. Part of Yvonne wanted to slap her face; the other part wanted to congratulate her for presenting such a bold front.

"Is anything wrong?" Charlotte demanded.

"Between you and me, I think the captain is a little seasick."

"How much further?" she wanted to know.

"His majesty will be along." Yve assured, gesturing with her thumb. "Ask him."

Charlotte didn't care about that. She'd been too scared to speak with him the afternoon prior. She was less anxious to do so during their road march.

Yvonne returned to the cab to find Sarah's gazing at her as with eyes resembling raisins in a half-baked sponge cake.

"Come out, Sarah," she encouraged. "Walk around the truck a couple times and get some air in your lungs."

She was too nauseous to speak, but she forced her limbs to move. Yve thought she needed a drink, but water on a delicate stomach mightn't be a good idea.

"Bruno, have we got anything other than water to give this – woman?"

She nearly said *girl*.

"I'm Charles," he corrected. "Let me look."

He had his own haversack. Doubtless, it was filled with unauthorized materials. If Yve suspected he was carrying booze, she'd have harsh words with him – and his superiors, upon their return.

"Try this."

What did to Yve's amazed eyes did appear but a lime in freefall! She caught it.

"Gotta knife?"

"Silly girl."

From somewhere, he produced a knife that resembled a Saracen sword. Those spacious jackets the ABCs wore certainly made good hiding places. Yvonne had no intention of taking the menacing weapon. Conversely, Bruno had no intention of surrendering it. He made it disappear and, in its place, he provided her with a pocketknife.

Had that officious captain been nearby?

Yvonne didn't bother to look. She made the necessary modifications and sliced the lime in half. After returning the weapon, she ministered to her friend.

"Suck on that for a bit," she advised. "It will get spit back in your mouth."

Dark Comedy

The teen look-alike appeared dubious, but she followed orders. Yve whispered soothing sentiments to aid the healing process. It was too late to turn back, and there was no way they'd leave her where she was. They must proceed together.

Sarah was just beginning to return to life when the captain ordered them forward. If his country ever got a look at this salty soldier in battle, there would be a new stableboy by nightfall.

Yve scolded herself for thinking such things. She needed to reign in her venomous thoughts. Meanwhile, she had another tidbit to add to the ton of misdemeanors she'd acquired. Her next confession would require a tag team.

Onward they went. They travelled slightly too fast, or Yvonne would have suggested she and Sarah walk for a while.

"I feel much better," Sarah said, finishing off the lime.

She leaned up against Yvonne and rested her head on her shoulder. Yve put her arm around her and held her close. Minutes later, she realized the woman was asleep. How it was possible to sleep on a bucking bronco was beyond her understanding, but the miracle precluded another bout of seasickness.

Yvonne was very nearly asleep when the truck lurched to a stop. The captain marched proudly back along the trail and stopped at Yve's inquisitive visage.

"We can go no further," he bellowed. "Treaty line is here. Guerilla danger is behind you, now. We will make sure no one is following on our way back."

"How much further?"

"Two hours. Three. Maybe."

"We will need a guide."

"Stay on road."

Yvonne surveyed the terrain to her front. The road was – well, very subtle. If they got off it, even for a short time, it might take days to find it again.

"Give us a guide," she demanded.

"Soldiers not allowed."

"I'm a soldier," she reminded.

The slimy creep had insisted on her being one. Let him deal with it.

"Not the same," he responded at once. "You're not in their army, or mine. Treaty says our soldiers are not allowed nearer the border."

"If we do not go on, we go back," she insisted. "If we go back, many questions will be asked. Your government might not enjoy answering them."

His expression transmitted his thoughts quite sufficiently.

"Suppose your government begins asking you questions?"

Bull's eye!

The black Napoleon's expression changed considerably. He was between a rock and a woman. Of course, he could shoot her. Yve thought she detected that exact option was alive in his thoughts. He was sorely tempted, but there were too many witnesses. Not everyone would agree that a renegade band of guerillas had done the shooting. Moreover, one of the junior officers might covet his captain's bars and use the incident to take his place and his rank.

Two soldiers, who were guarding the "command vehicle" wandered into the scene.

They took turns speaking. No one spoke French for some while. The rapid-fire exchange went on in an African language. The captain got angrier the longer the conference went on. Finally, the incessant babbling stopped when the captain stomped his foot like some spoiled kid.

"Enough!" he roared.

Dark Comedy

A brief but civil exchange followed, after which the two "volunteers" shed their uniform shirts and service caps.

"If there is trouble," the captain warned, "These men are deserters. If there is no trouble, they must return to camp with you on the agreed day."

"*Oui, mon capitan!*" she replied, rendering a salute from a seated position.

Were soldiers allowed to salute while seated? The captain did not return the salute – pretended not to see it. He spun around on his heel and marched back to his vehicle. Three minutes later, that vehicle trundled off the road and around the truck. The captain rallied the rest of his command and drove on to lead the column back to camp.

"Do you speak French?" she demanded of the "deserters."

"Enough," one of them responded.

"If you get us lost, you know what will happen."

"You won't get lost," the spokesman promised. "The road gets better two or three miles ahead. We know this country."

"Are you teasing me?"

"No, Lieutenant."

They snickered over the title.

"We know you are not an officer," the second man, hitherto silent, explained. "A few days away from Captain D_____ is better than double pay."

"Triple pay," his co-conspirator insisted.

These "irregulars" were hatless and wore only wife-beater undershirts. They were black as coal but exposed to the sun. Sgt. Andre (who may well be a sergeant in real life) was digging through a collection of non-crated items in the bed of the truck. He found a blanket and two castaway scarves that could substitute for hats.

"Let's go," Yve commanded the driver.

It was brutal. For one more, endless hour, the truck followed a faint trace. Not long after Captain Supercilious turned back, the trace became a wheel track. In places it was obvious heavy trucks had bogged down or gotten stuck during a rare, desert deluge. The driver, slowly and cautiously, drove around these "booby traps." Once off the beaten track, progress was very bumpy and very slow.

"I'm starting to sweat fuel," the driver announced.

How, Yvonne wondered, could we use so much fuel when traveling, on average, ten miles an hour? They carried some fuel in the trailer, but not much.

Yvonne began sweating the fuel, also.

Suddenly, they spied something silhouetted against the horizon. It looked like a beehive.

"That's it!"

It was one of the "deserters" who called out. Yve remained dubious. It looked like a beehive, but how many bees are there in that forsaken land? As they grew nearer, it became obvious that the structure was not for bees but for people.

There appeared other "people hives," four more. As they drew even with the first hut, they could see buildings – two of adobe (or the African equivalent), a concrete building, and three amalgamation structures, part concrete, part aluminum, part something else. The road turned into a street – a rutted trackway which went past the "business district." All the buildings were on the northside of the road. A well, a people hive, and a shipping container were off to the right. The two desultory habitations were twenty meters or so off the "road."

There were small plots of land tended by the locals. The crops they grew were few, scrawny, but edible. Water was a problem. With only one well and very little rain during the year, any plant requiring daily watering was likely to be banished by thirsty villagers.

North behind, and well beyond the business district, lay the sand. It was like an ocean of sand with the dunes washing up to within a two hundred or so meters of the village. The community, figuratively, turned its back on the sand. Every doorway faced south.

Beyond the business district was the "slum." The buildings here were made of anything available: wood (imported), aluminum, mud, concrete, corrugated metal, tarp, canvass, disused tires, and (ultimately) anything that could be used or re-used.

This was the orphanage. Only three buildings were recognizable as structures.

The roar of the truck had aroused everyone. The welcoming committee was giddy with excitement. There were five "Mamas," full-figured women with large, sagging breasts. They were back as coal and wore patched and modified dresses that had gone out of fashion in the fifties. There were children, over a dozen, in all shades and sizes. The "caravan rejects" were Arabic bronze; the rest were black as night. The latter may have come with the caravans, or they were shipped in from the south and west. The oldest (and tallest) was eleven or twelve. The youngest, visible, was three or four. There was a child learning to walk which was kept in a "safe area" or in a Mama's arms.

The lethargic and sickly Sarah was as alert and excited as the children. She reached across Yve, opened the door and scrambled out with remarkable haste and dexterity. Yvonne was too amazed by the metamorphosis to be offended by the rough treatment she suffered during Sarah's excited exit.

The reporters were out, each with cameras at the ready. They captured the joyous reception Sarah received. They gathered around her, shouted, bounced on their toes, and touched her as if to prove she was not a desert mirage. She was blond! A blond, white person in that part of the Africa rated celebrity status.

Yvonne dismounted and attempted to get the kinks out of her body. She kept her eyes on the Sarah Welter show, but she remained appraised of other concerns. Which of the Mamas should she approach to establish proper relations. To her left, she noticed a white-haired man approaching. He was advanced in years. His slacks were well worn and in need of darning. His pullover was "air conditioned," and its use in deflecting the cold nights and the morning chill was, likely, psychological. He wore silver, wire-rimed glasses, but walked with the agility of a much younger man. He was thin – disturbingly thin.

He wore a collar.

C. of E., Yve thought. Of all the protestant groups to head up the mission, that denomination was the least propitious for her personally. It was, alas, very clear why any mention of a specific protestant sect was avoided.

Yvonne sent a hasty prayer on its way. The children were *the* issue. This was no time to argue theological disputes.

She forced her legs into motion and attempted to intercept the aging prelate before he could interrupt Sarah and her "congregation."

"I'm Yvonne Schortmann," she announced only as a formality.

The man altered his course and extended his hand.

"Dr. Josiah Evens, interim head of this mission. God bless you and your associates. The supplies you bring, no matter what their nature, are most welcome."

Yve was formulating a reply when she felt a restriction in her sore and quaking legs. She looked down to find a child hugging her knees. She hadn't seen him approach, but the brown-haired boy ignored Sarah completely and picked Yvonne to hug. Despite the child's long sleeves and faded jeans, there was no mistaking his skin color.

"Your grandson?" she asked for want of something better.

The man shook his head.

"He's our newest member," Dr. Evens replied. "He was found three days ago."

"Found?"

Dark Comedy

"No one brought him in – not that we know of. He didn't seem to wander in. He just appeared one morning."

Yvonne gently stroked the young boy's hair and hoped he would release her. Instead, he looked up into her face and smiled. He tightened his grip on her."

"What's your name?"

"The only thing we know is his name. He's Klaus. Beyond that, we know nothing. He speaks only German, and none of us do."

Instantly, Yve thought of Charlotte. She speaks German and could make herself useful. However, Klaus clung to Yve with determination.

"Let me talk to him."

Dr. Evens posed no objections.

She freed herself enough to squat down to his level. Her aching limbs protested mightily. She dropped to her knees. She was still in pain, but it was less acute. She took the boy's hands in her own.

"Klaus, my name is Yvonne."

"Eve Non," he mimicked, unsuccessfully.

"Yve, then. Just call me Yve."

He nodded his head vigorously.

"Yve. I like you, Yve."

"I like you, too. Where did you come from, Klaus?"

He shrugged.

"Where are your mommy and daddy."

He shrugged.

"How did you get here?"

"We came in a big car," he informed. "We stopped. We got out. I went to play. The car left."

"They left you?"

He shrugged.

"Who left you? What were their names?"

He shrugged.

"Did your mother and father leave you?"

"I like you, Yve," he replied. "You're nice."

"I like you too, Klaus. I hope I can help you."

He replied by putting his arms around her neck and hugging her.

Trapped!

The little boy was not about to let her go. She stood and hefted him up in her arms. He wasn't light as a feather, but he was manageable – temporarily.

"Maybe, I can talk to him later and learn something," she hypothesized.

"I'm glad you're here."

Because she could speak German?

She wondered about Charlotte. Where was she? When she turned to look for her, she found Charles just to her right and behind her.

"Where the – where's Charlotte?"

"Not my day to watch her," Charles replied in full automaton mode.

"Would you get the manifest? Dr. Evens should know what he's getting."

"If you come with me," he replied.

With a child in her arms, a counterfeit prelate to her front, and Charlotte wherever the hell she was, Yve's patience was nearing the end of its tether.

Dark Comedy

"The cab is fifteen feet away – if that."

"My job is to be with you," he replied with irritating calm.

"Here?"

"Anywhere, until I am relieved."

She counted to a hundred, by fifties. She didn't want to waste time, and she didn't want to be tethered to Dr. Evens a moment longer than she could help.

"Take him," she ordered in her best this-is-not-an-order tone.

The doctor was willing enough to comply, but the stubborn Klaus made it clear he wouldn't be left behind again. He transformed into a fungus. No matter what she did or said, his arms were around her neck to stay.

"Would you come with me, please?"

She had to be addressing Dr. Evens; Klaus demonstrated he had not the slightest notion of leaving her.

"How old are you Klaus?"

"*Vier.*"

"Now, Klaus – you wouldn't lie to me, would you?"

"*Lie?*"

The interrogation would have to wait.

Yvonne opened the cab and searched for the clipboard. It had rattled and been thrown about the cab for hours. It was Yve's quick reaction which had deflected it on its way to dent the slumbering Sarah's skull. It was on the floor, a safe enough place for it. She fetched it and removed the manifest from its clutches without disturbing Klaus. She turned and presented the document to the doctor.

"If I promised not to go away, would you sit here in the truck?"

"Can I?"

He was very excited.

She hefted him up onto the seat. He grabbed for the wheel instantly and did what most five (or four) year old boys would do in like circumstances. Yve leaned back and crossed one foot over the other. The weight of young Klaus was gone, but the aches of her journey remained. The little boy monitored her closely. He was excited by his new adventure, but he refused to allow the woman any opportunity to escape.

Where the hell is Charlotte?

"Please, when you unload, do not damage the shipping crates," the doctor announced. "We can use the wood for repairs and, perhaps, in construction."

Unload? Unload! There were the ABCs, three women, a driver, a reserve driver, two "deserters," and two camera-brandishing reporters. Nobody, at any time, said they had to unload tons of supplies! Someone omitted that informational tidbit. Was this a pre-planned heist?

It hurt her neck muscles, but she looked up and behind her. Klaus responded to her upturned face. He smiled. An entire company of gleaming white teeth was aimed at her. Was that little urchin in on the "joke?"

Dr. Evans transformed into a child not unlike Klaus. He became more and more euphoric the more he read.

"A sewing machine!" he squeaked. "Three bolts of cloth! Tools! Medicine!"

"Yve, you need to see..."

It was Charlotte. She looked either flustered or distraught. Yvonne wasn't concerned.

"Where in – God's name – have you been?"

Charlotte reverted to her haughty attitude. She snapped to attention and launched a faux salute.

"Private Werner reporting, sir. Permission to speak."

Not even the mesmerized Evens could ignore this explosion. He lost his glee and wondered if he wouldn't be called upon to referee a cat fight. Yvonne's temper flared. Left to her own devices, she'd have taken Charlotte's neck in her hands and squeezed it with all her might. She remembered Klaus. For reasons she couldn't fathom, she did not want him to witness any more of her temper.

"Forgive me, Charlotte," she replied after a quick ten-count. "You were about to say."

Charlotte wasn't in a hurry to dismiss Yve's rudeness. However, the sight of an excited child at the truck driver's station was an effective anodyne.

"I've seen where the children sleep. To call it a dump would be flattery."

Both women turned their attention to Dr. Evans. He felt the heat.

"We do what we can with what we have," he said, meekly.

Yvonne was beginning to come to her senses. She had no use for the C. of E. or any of its officials. However, the object of their mission was the children. Remembering how little Klaus clung to her as if in fear of her abandoning him, she realized her temper was not doing anyone any good.

"Dr. Evans, there is one thing I expected to see here: exploding bellies. The kind of swollen stomachs starving children develop. The absence of that horrible sight is a testament to the love you have for these young people. I'm not prepared to criticize you. I'm certain, Frau Werner did not intend to criticize you; she was merely making an observation."

Either Charlotte Werner was one great actress, or she realized her comment was ill timed.

"I apologize," she said as contrite as a bridesmaid who accidentally stepped on the bride's gown.

Was she acting? Yvonne wished she knew.

"We need to help unload this – stuff. Before we do that, would you review the manifest with Dr. Evens and see if there is anything you can use to make the sleeping room more – salubrious?"

Charlotte nodded.

"Excuse me, Doctor," Yve began. "I'm not at my best today. Dr, Evens, may I introduce Charlotte Werner?"

He turned and, in the old-school-tie tradition, assumed a posture both straight and ridged. He extended his hand. When Charlotte accepted it, he bowed formally.

"Enchante, Mademoiselle."

She balked momentarily.

"A pleasure, sir," she replied in English.

Yvonne cleared her throat. She'd love to keep her oar out, but she sensed Charlotte was a little miffed. No matter her feeling for "the lieutenant," it wouldn't do for the representative of the orphanage to meet with abrasion.

"*Madam* Werner," Yve corrected as delicately as possible.

"Excuse," Dr. Evens apologized.

Charlotte smiled and nodded.

Acting?

"May I accompany you?" he asked.

"Of course."

The three of them retired together: Evans, Werner, and Andre.

Yvonne lifted her eyes heavenward.

"Forgive me, Father; I know not what I do."

She took one step and froze. Turning, she saw Klaus standing on the seat with his arms stretched wide.

"Okay," she nodded.

He leaped from the truck and landed in Yvonne's waiting arms. She was prepared for the impact and succeeded in avoiding a tumble. However, every muscle in her body screamed. She eyed Charles malevolently. He held up his hands as if to announce he had nothing to say.

None that he would verbalize, at least.

She carried Klaus to the congregation, hoping that he would join the others.

Sarah had produced a toy xylophone from her unauthorized tote bag. She was playing her own accompaniment in a round of *Frere Jacques*. Most of the children knew the song. Those who didn't were doing their best to learn. The talented young blond would sing a line and the children were to sing the next line.

Yvonne put Klaus down and knelt beside him.

"Why don't you sing along?"

She stood, half expecting him to join the others or, at least examine the woman and her strange instrument. He stood for a moment as a silent witness. At the end of that time, he took her hand – her forefinger and middle finger to be exact – and held firm.

DEEPER INTO DARKNESS

The sun magnified as it neared the horizon.

There were fatigued women doing their best to "clean up" prior to an exciting MRE dinner. It was not the – ah, *food* – that urged them on. It was the community they would share. The women and the ABCs would bond while reviewing the day's events. The Mamas were sociable to a fault, and the children were delighted with anything the women did or said.

Matting was put down in the empty bed of the truck. Tarp was spread out atop the matting to help keep the chill of the cold desert night away from the bedrolls. There were blankets and packing materials to aid in keeping them warm – or as warm as they were likely to get.

Modesty was forced to take a back seat to necessity. Though the trailer was set up so they had a private bath, there was no way they could all bathe individually before the evening chill turned intolerably cold.

Yvonne shed all modesty during her nocturnal "lessons" in far off France. Charlotte, as in most things, was bold and unashamed to be seen *au natural*, though she turned inexplicably coy when around the children. Sarah, in keeping with her child-like demeanor, was modest beyond reason – or so it seemed to her fellow travelers. She insisted on a modicum of privacy.

Thus, they agreed to share a bucket of hot water "Japanese style."

They knelt with their backs to each other and wiped the dirt and grime off with rags provided by the Mamas. Rags, that is the remains of unserviceable clothing, was the one surplus item on the compound. They would rinse off with the disposable face towels they brought with them.

Charlotte was the first to redress. Thoughtlessly, she turned to find Yvonne reaching for her pullover.

"What's that?" she demanded.

She pointed at the item peeking out of a bra cup.

"Sorry you had to see that. Now, I must kill you."

Sarah could abide by their tacit treaty no further. She had to discover the subject of this exchange.

"What is that?" she asked demurely.

"Dynamite," Yvonne replied, becoming decent once more. "Please, don't ask. It's – call it *secret orders*."

"Dynamite," Charlotte repeated none too civilly.

"Yeah," Sarah piped up. "It comes in small packages."

That initiated a hearty laugh from them all.

"I promise you," Yve said, "When we get home, I will tell you. I'm only allowed to use it when we're out of options. Please, I beg you, don't ask me and don't tell anyone."

Charlotte said nothing. She had a hold on Yvonne if she ever needed one.

The ABCs surrounded the trailer as near as they dared. They were within quick reaction distance should they suspect trouble. They heaved a sigh of relief when their principles emerged. The last thing their careers needed was a complaint about being too hasty in (what Bruno dubbed) a ticklish situation.

From the trailer to their beds was only a few steps. They mounted the makeshift steps one by one followed by Charles. He would bed down nearest the tail gate. Andre and Bruno would alternate as guards like a policeman walking a circular beat. The other would sleep in the cab. Theoretically, he would hear if anyone tried to get to the women by climbing over the front of the vehicle.

Charlotte and Sarah dove into their bedrolls quickly to trap as much of the warm air before the sun disappeared. Yvonne knelt for some while atop her "bed," much to embarrassment of Charles. He didn't care to invade another's privacy. He liked invading a woman's privacy even less, but he had his orders.

Charlotte watched Yvonne from under her blankets. The woman was inexcusably supercilious, but she, grudgingly, admired Yve. She'd often seen her "discussing" things with her Maker and was in awe of her dedication. Her sun hat was beyond reach. Rather than create a disturbance, she unhesitatingly drew her pullover up to cover her head. It was getting cool.

Uncomfortably cool

She won't be discussing very long this night, Charlotte thought.

Alas, Yvonne's "discussion" continued long enough for Charlotte's eyelids to weigh heavy. She was not awake when Yve concluded business and dove into her bedroll.

"Charlie."

He recognized the voice. They had a secret "hot word." If either of the others heard that word, they would draw weapons first and ask questions, much later, and at a review board. *Charlie* was decidedly *not* the hot word.

"What?" he whispered back.

The women were trying to sleep. They didn't need to hear any ABCs chit-chat.

"The kid."

Charles knew instantly.

"Send him away."

"He won't be sent, and I can't leave the perimeter."

"Smack his butt and send him away."

"What?" Yvonne demanded.

It was a long, tiring day. She wasn't worried about getting her beauty sleep; her only focus was on getting *rest* – lots of rest.

"The kid."

"Klaus?"

"He won't go away."

Yve sighed.

"Let him in."

Charles balked. This was not covered in their briefing. Sure, he was just a kid, but the women were to be kept segregated whenever possible, especially at night.

"Let him in!" Yve repeated.

That kid had been a leech on her arm all day. Her patience with him was exhausted. However, she realized that relenting was the least painless solution.

"What is it?" Sarah asked, meekly.

"Yve's boyfriend," Charotte snorted.

The boy climbed up and through the "curtain." Yve held up her hand to identify herself. The boy, trailing a blanket and carrying a pillow, padded over to Yve's side. Moments later, he lay next to her.

"Just my luck," Charlotte moaned. "I'm stuck here with a woman who sleeps around."

"In nine months," Sarah injected, "You might have a lot of explaining to do."

"Shut it," Yvonne snapped.

This concluded the audio portion of the evening.

Yve, as it turned out, was the unexpected beneficiary that night. She and Klaus shared body heat which contributed to their uninterrupted slumber. Charles, Charlotte, and Sarah weren't so fortunate.

Sarah was the first to stir. It was cold. The sun hadn't a chance to begin the transformation of the arctic tundra to the natural frypan of the desert. Charles woke the moment the singer let slip the embrace of her repose. He didn't move, but he was alert.

The woman reached for her ever-ready hairbrush. There was neither the time nor the inclination to groom herself for "her public." She sought only to keep her golden tresses away from her eyes. Her mission accomplished, she stroked away for a few additional moments. When she returned to civilization, she didn't want the professionals thinking she allowed her follicles to go free range. The hair specialists were paid to keep her hair show-time ready, not to begin from scratch.

Once her hairbrush returned to her shoulder bag, Sarah examined the breakfast MREs. As the first to wake, she was the first to choose. She selected the least nauseating package and tore it open.

"Sleep well?" she asked Charles.

Her only purpose was to deflect any thoughts that she was ignoring him.

"When I slept," he informed.

"Would you like some of this – whatever it is?"

"We have our own rations, thank you."

She ate what she could. The remainder would be discarded. She kept the coffee packet, however. Later, she'd empty a bottle of water and heat it up. Instant coffee was better than no coffee. On the desert, it was nothing short of ambrosia.

"We must haul out this trash," she insisted. "This place will be nothing but packaging and plastic bottles if we dump it here. There's no recycling and no proper means of disposal."

Charles remained nonplussed. He was trained to kill in a myriad of ways. His job was to protect the women from any malevolent creatures, human or otherwise. He took this mission as he did any mission he was assigned – *seriously*. Let others deal with the minutia.

"Time for Johnny-dos," she chirped once her breakfast "food" lost its allure.

Charles got up to allow her access to the ground.

Bruno did not need to be alerted. He heard the movement in the truck as well as the muted voices. When Sarah emerged, he was available for escort.

Yvonne woke with the commotion, minimum though it was. When Sarah left, Yve covered her head in her blanket and began her morning "discussion." When Charlotte opened her eyes, he found her thus.

"I gotta go," she growled.

"Just a moment," Charles advised. "Bruno is with Sarah at the moment."

Charlotte pouted. She could complain, but only one person could sit on the pot. In the truck or at the "relief station," she'd have to wait. At least she'd get to select her MRE before *her majesty*. She'd get some pleasure in leaving the least palatable option for Lieutenant Holier-Than-Thou.

The agenda for the day was worked out the evening before.

Sarah's mission was to help with the children. Her singing delighted them. She could teach them new songs and aid the in-over-their-heads Mamas in teaching them basic math, language and spelling. Charlotte would continue improving the children's sleeping quarters. As an interior decorator, Charlotte was a hell of an actress; however, her efforts at improving hygiene in that vital area was a boon to mission morale.

These tasks were not assigned; they were assumed, much to Yvonne's relief. She was uncomfortable making command decisions and averse to giving orders. So long as the others performed useful service, she'd remain hands-off.

Yve's mission objectives were planned within an hour of their arrival. These were delayed by the gargantuan task of unloading and unpacking. Had the ABCs not entered the fray, some (if not) many of the crates would have remained on truck and trailer until a work crew happened by – an eventuality no one expected.

The oldest orphan was twelve or maybe a few months beyond. Her growth spurt left her draped in rags and worn jeans that couldn't be fastened or buttoned at the top. She wandered around with a string run through the belt loops.

Once the sewing machine was ready, Yve made the poor girl a dress she could grow into. Using a foot-powered appliance was a bit tricky, but she soon mastered the skill. Next, she tutored Klaus. He spoke only limited German. The Mamas were forced to rely on hand gestures in communicating with him. That was most inefficient and, frequently, frustrating. Yve, also, taught him a smattering of baby French.

The initial task of the morning, however, was the most distasteful. She prayed hard at night and in the morning. She wanted the children to get all the best she could give, but her bias – nay her bigotry about the Church of England and anyone representing it was a huge failing.

God, please take this sin away.

God's response, apparently, was *do it yourself.*

She couldn't eat, even if there was anything edible. She relied on bottled courage – three, greedy gulps of bottled water. After visiting the necessary, she returned to find Klaus still in repose. When he awoke, the little leech would be distraught until he was with her again. Yve didn't want the poor thing to be frightened or upset, but she could hardly carry him about papoose-style.

If Dr. Evens was a late sleeper, the churning in Yve's stomach might come right up her throat. She couldn't afford that. There was precious little down there. Drinking water might not have been her best option.

Fortunately, the man had just ensconced himself at his breakfast-lunch-dinner table, a scared and discarded wooden end table with one leg shorter than the others. It was placed on the veranda – a width of tightly compacted earth under a tattered tarp. He sat on a folding chair waiting for a Mama to bring him a bowl of gruel.

Yvonne hadn't time to waste. Normally, she'd have enjoyed annoying the man by joining him, uninvited. That, however, was not her intent.

"Dr. Evens," she began, pulling out the second folding chair and seating herself.

"Good morning, Mademoiselle," he chirped. "Would you join me in some breakfast?"

"Thank you, no," she gulped. "I'm here to ask a favor."

"A favor? You bring us food and material, and you bring joy and succor to the children, and you ask for a favor? I won't have it. If there is anything we have that you need or want, it is yours."

The petty side of her scoffed. What did this poverty-stricken dump have that anyone would want?

There it was again! Her heathen emotions raged against her will. She wanted to do the Lord's work, but she was no better than a common *bandito*. She took a deep breath.

"Little Klaus," she began. "When I return home, I want to pay for his care. I want you word that whatever I can send will be specifically channeled to him."

He hesitated.

"I agree," he said. "I will promise to do as you wish, but I cannot guarantee. Should there be an emergency – they don't come often, but when there is an emergency, God tests us mightily. In short, Mademoiselle, my word isn't worth a thing."

Yvonne gulped and fought down the urge to explode. She had money in the bank, but a year's subscription would constitute a major impact on her resources. Should she face an emergency, God would test *her* mightily.

"Shall we say *pledge?*" she asked as would a penitent.

"A pledge is much better," he agreed. "I will agree to assist Klaus with the resources you send us, barring considerable threat to this facility."

She gulped.

"That will have to be good enough," she surrendered.

"Our headquarters are in Brussels. I'll make sure to give you the address – please do not send money to us here. Cash disappears in this country. It is safer to transport goods."

Yvonne nodded, hoping to break freewithout appearing rude.

"We're thinking of moving to Luxembourg City," Dr. Evens volunteered. "The government there is very supportive, and we hope to have lower overhead. We work hard to make sure that as much of our donations go towards operations. Most of our administration is handled by volunteers."

If true, this sounded hopeful.

"Klaus slept with us last night," she informed.

"I'm glad," he replied. "He isn't exactly shunned by the others, but the language problems make it difficult for him to fit in. He can't help but feel alone."

"Does he speak any French?"

"Only words and phrases."

"Let me see what I can do about that," she said, seizing the opportunity to escape.

"God bless you, Mademoiselle."

Does that count?

Her heart assured her that God's blessings are bestowed upon everyone. Her mind, however, insisted that Protestant pleas for blessing upon those of *the* faith might, possibly, constitute blasphemy.

"Who are you to judge?" she muttered to herself.

Leave this to God, she decided.

While questioning her faith and the faith of others (specifically Dr. Evens), she returned to the truck and the one thing she could believe in: Klaus. However, her short journey brought into view the one person she most wanted *not* to see.

"Any orders, sir?"

That snarky little remark landed squarely upon Yvonne's one remaining nerve. Fortunately, for any auditors within ten kilometers, she kept her voice down. However, there could be suppressing her emphatic delivery.

"Will you stop!" she snarled, turning to confront Charlotte full on. "I'm not your commanding freaking officer. How did I get to be a model? The propogandists made me one for the purpose of better copy. At least you're a real actress; Sarah is a real singer. I volunteered to come here, but I didn't come here as a potentate. We are here, Charlotte, to pose for the camera and convince lazy bums – like me – to dig into their pockets and send some money to support people they don't know and don't care to know."

Yvonne was just getting started. The pressure in her boiler had become critical; Charlotte would not be allowed a moment's peace until the venting was finished. She didn't realize the tears were flooding her eyes until she felt them running down her face.

"Look at this place! Is this what you expected? I wouldn't puke in this hole! I'm struggling, Charlotte. I want to be more than just some ignorant schlub off the streets, but what good am I? What can I do for these kids? I don't know about them. I don't even know their names. When I get home, I won't remember what they look like. I don't belong here – or anywhere else, and your sarcastic little remarks make that crystal clear. Now, this is my back."

She reached around with one hand to illustrate.

"My back, Charlotte, and I want you to keep off!"

There was a time to kick chins and throw dirt in someone's face. Charlotte, however, concluded that this was not the time. She feared Yve might turn violent at any move Charlotte made or any word she spoke. The best part of valor was to keep on walking with Charlie close behind.

Andre was leaning up against the bumper of the truck watching the proceedings. He made no move and withheld comment. Yvonne remained where she was until her tears had run their course. She felt the humiliation of someone witnessing her "seizure," but she was too distraught to hide her face. Let her humiliation and frustration be witnessed by the entire world.

She was nearly composed when she noticed Klaus. He'd dismounted the vehicle and showed signs of distress. The moment he saw her, his face beamed. He rushed to her. She knelt to receive him.

Is this why she came?

Dark Comedy

TIME OUT FOR ROUTINE

The dress was hurried and not up to the standards of *Errad Creations*, but it fit the growing child well and left ample room for further growth. She was nearly as tall as Sarah. Too bad she didn't have a voice to match. Her singing hurt the ears, but Sarah praised her to the skies.

Charlotte cleaned out the sleeping quarters until nearly collapsing from exhaustion. When the Mamas introduced new sleeping mats, Yvonne was available to help.

Klaus was never more than an arm's length away from her. He learned French for beginners while kneeling by the sewing machine. The lessons came in fits and starts because Yve couldn't sew and talk at the same time. While refurbishing the sleeping quarters, she explained what she was doing and insisted that Klaus repeat her exposition.

Sarah taught the children three songs. Ones they hadn't heard before. They were nursery songs and easy to learn and easy to sing. Later, she assisted a Mama in teaching basic math. Most of the children could do arithmetic. They were excited when Sarah taught them entry-level algebra.

"If Pierre has three camels, and Henri has twice as many..."

Just wait until they start searching for x, Yve thought.

Charlotte retired to the truck for a rest. It was blistering hot and she sought refuge by crawling under it. She remained hot but was no longer exposed to the sun. She slept for a few minutes and woke up disoriented. Andre helped her to some water and led her over to the "hospital."

The pallets, which once supported cardboard boxes of bottled water, had been modified to provide a second, more spacious bed. Before, there was one in use together with an abused mattress. After the "make over" there was a canvass covering for each bed and homemade pillows stuffed with whatever Yve could find. They were too short for Charlotte who curled up into a fetal position.

She didn't sleep, but she rested. Additionally, she was allowed the hospital's secret weapon: a small serving of apple juice.

An hour later, the doctor Mama released her but insisted the patient avoid work for the rest of the day. This admonition grated on her. She was humiliated when the prying journalist duo snapped photos of her lying under the truck and in the "hospital." Forced idleness added to her disgrace.

She ambled over to the sleeping quarters to find two Mamas and Yve working like galley slaves. Their clothes stuck to the sweat from their bodies.

"Be careful, Yvonne," she croaked. "Slow down. You don't want to end up like I did."

Yve stood up, took a deep breath, and let it out. She wiped her forehead with her forearm. This action did no more than add to the perspiration on her brow. She tried again, using her pullover to wipe away the torrent of sweat, but she fared little better.

"Take a break," Charlotte suggested.

One of the Mamas seconded the motion.

Klaus understood perfectly. He took Yve by the hand and led her out into the open, bake-oven air.

"Come over to the hospital," Charlotte suggested. "It's cooler because there's just a hint of breeze."

With the bunkbed arrangement of the two pallets, Yve had options. She could bend over double on the lower pallet or climb up onto the upper pallet. Yve compromised by sitting on the dirt floor. Klaus wandered away – nearly ten feet! – and returned with an unopened bottle of water.

"*Danke*," she said with labored breath.

"*Merci*," he corrected.

Yvonne was too drained to laugh, but she smiled at him. He swelled up as if he'd conquered the world.

Charlotte attended the entire scene very closely. She didn't understand what was going on, but there was one thing she did understand.

"Yvonne," she announced. "You are *not* just some schlub off the street."

That night, they let Polly Prude bathe alone while Yvonne, Charlotte, Klaus, and Andre kept guard. When Sarah retuned, she stayed with the boy and taught him a child's song in French. He relaxed. He knew where Yve was and what she was doing.

Yvonne and Charlotte "shot the works." They even scrubbed down each other's backs which, considering the amount of water they allotted themselves, was no mean accomplishment.

"I was looking over the medical supplies in the hospital," Yve reported. "I may have a gift for us all tomorrow evening."

"Morphine," Charlotte guessed.

"No. Something a hundred times better."

The following day was less taxing in the physical sense, but attending the children was challenging. Because these orphans were at varied levels, educationally, it was impossible to present lessons in the traditional format. Sarah took the advanced group in French and math. Charlotte taught basic math and French. Yvonne taught entry-level sewing and writing – with Klaus sewing and writing at her side every minute. In turn, the Mamas and children instructed the visiting trio how to wash clothes with very little water. This was a useful skill, but none of the women thought it would be of much use once they returned home.

Klaus felt more comfortable around his fellow orphans. The small amount of French Yve taught him made simple exchanges possible. He was no longer shunned as unintelligible. Toward the end of the day, he was enjoying simple intercourse with three children roughly his age. However, he clung to Yvonne tenaciously.

After their evening MREs, Yvonne produced a small bottle of liquid.

"Sarah, here's something to help with your cramps."

The singer took the dose Dr. Schortmann proscribed.

"Let's wait a few minutes," she suggested.

They were having a quiet, limited conversation with Klaus. After a while, Sarah began fidgeting. Finally ...

"Excuse me a moment," Sarah said.

Quickly she got to her feet and stepped rapidly away.

"What did you give her?" Charlotte asked.

"Ever notice that the MREs are easier to ingest than to get rid of?"

"Oh! Let me have some of that stuff."

Klaus had food made palatable by the Mamas. He didn't need any "medicine." His friends, however, were decidedly more cheerful and relaxed after taking a dram each of the "magic potion."

"When I had an emergency appendectomy, they gave me morphine," Charlotte related with some animation. "I thought that stuff was top drawer. I'd say your medicine is better. It doesn't deaden the discomfort; it removes it."

"Not a word to the scribes," Yvonne suggested. "They'll make this *episode* a page-one story."

"I wonder –"

Charlotte didn't finish. She didn't have to.

"They're on their own. We must leave some for the kids against the day when they really need it."

After the third day, things became routine. Yvonne was making clothes while Charlotte and Sarah were teaching school. They were willing to lend a hand with cooking and cleaning up. However, Yve didn't want them to be near food preparation; the children were well nourished and reasonably healthy. Similarly, their cleaning and washing up built a sense of community.

If it ain't broke, don't fix it. Even the stubborn Charlotte admitted Yve's hands-off policy had merit.

Daily, Yvonne reminded Klaus that she must leave soon. She told him, repeatedly, and in two languages. The Mamas, some of them, told him in the native dialect of the region. It was Greek to Klaus, but there remained no unturned stones. The boy claimed to understand.

For nearly every minute of their visit, he was glued to Yvonne's side. Not once did Yve discourage him. Save for trips to the loo and impromptu bathing, he was seldom more than a meter or two away from her. They slept together. She sat next to him during meals. She taught him French and German. In return, he "taught" her how much he respected her. She seldom scolded; there was seldom any need. When she did admonish him, Klaus was as humble as a bishop's convert.

They held hands, hugged and kissed each other. They laughed together and were sad together. They were the best of friends. When the final day arrived, they were both sick.

He understood and tried to be brave. When they hugged for the last time, they both cried. She waved when they pulled away, but Klaus did not see. He was busy crying into the substantial lap of a Mama.

A SENSE OF NOT BELONGING

There was plenty of room. The bed of the truck and the trailer were empty. Nobody had to be sandwiched between or on top of crates. That did not alleviate the discomfort of that rock garden the locals called a road.

Yvonne did a lot of calculating and recalculating. She could cover the care and maintenance of Klaus for a year, but doing so the following year was problematical. Sarah and Charlotte, also, agreed to make regular payments. The difference was *they* could afford it.

"Call me," Charlotte instructed. "I'll help."

Yve appreciated the offer, but it could only be a loan. That would simply delay the inevitable. Charlotte gave Yve the private number of her home.

"If a man answers, hang up."

Yve wanted to laugh, but she could manage only a smile.

When they reached the "treaty line," Captain Martinet was conspicuously absent. In his place was a real lieutenant who had with him eight men in two vehicles. The two "deserters" made themselves known and were welcomed and congratulated by the officer for their volunteer services.

The lieutenant was not averse to escorting three women. He'd been assigned a task, and he intended to carry it out.

One of the deserters, once again a soldier in good standing, let it be known that the captain was a captain only because his father was a big kabloona in the government. Apparently, the man was as incompetent as he was abrasive. He'd been reassigned to a unit in which he would have the trappings of office, but little actual authority. He verified Yve's hypothesis that he'd been sent to support the charity mission because he was being disciplined.

When they arrived at the "base," it was well into the afternoon. There was no Tall Ami. Indeed, there were no Amis at all. The aircraft was of the same type that brought them, but it had French markings and a French crew. The load master was a gruesome looking woman. She was mission oriented and paid no heed to the passengers. Her job was to load the truck and trailer and secure them for flight. She was something of a bully and vehemently objected to the passengers returning with so many empty water bottles. She insisted they be left by the side of the runway.

This could have gotten ugly. The lieutenant, however, was a reasonable man. He suggested that the bottles could be secured in containers and flown back to Europe where they could be properly disposed of or recycled. The gruff load master would have none of it. The lieutenant threatened to block the runway with his vehicles. The pilots and flight engineer, all officers, conferenced for a few minutes with the African lieutenant. An agreement was reached; an agreement which did not meet with the approval of the load master. She, however, was not an officer.

They took off just before twilight – with water bottles properly secured and stowed.

Sarah and Charlotte sandwiched Yvonne between them and demanded to know about the "dynamite" in her "small package." Yve balked. She knew she promised them, but she had, also, promised the Grand Duchess.

"Be patient," she shouted above the thunder of the engines. "I want permission."

"We mightn't ever see her again," Charlotte scoffed.

(As a scoffer, Charlotte, the actress, was world-class.)

"I don't want to be a liar," Yvonne replied, "Worse, I don't want to be a traitor. I wish you'd never seen the damned thing."

They didn't like it. They pouted for an hour or two, but they tacitly agreed and acquiesced. To betray the confidence of the Grand Duchess was an egregious fault.

They missed sparing with Captain Sexist on their return, but he was represented (or reincarnated) in the form of the bullying load master. She'd lost the Battle of the Bottles. To make up for it, she denied anyone the opportunity to stretch out during the long-duration flight back. They could lie on the seats but must remain belted – a near impossibility. When her back was turned, which was often, people would scatter. Charlotte found refuge under the engine housing of the truck where she was difficult to see except from certain precise angles. Sarah snuck into the cab, slamming the door behind her (who could hear amid all that engine noise?)

The reporters (and their cameras) discovered that the load master arrested only those she caught in the act. Once Charlotte was in her "hiding place," she was not disturbed. Were she caught in the act of changing places, it would initiate an ugly scene.

Yvonne was caught in the act. While she was being blistered verbally, the reporters scurried for the trailer and stretched out. Yve was willing to sacrifice herself and be a diversion. These men, contrary to all expectations, were not constantly in the women's faces. They got some great pictures of them in action, but they seldom bothered the trio. Information they would use in their propaganda pitch was taken from interviews with Dr. Evens, certain of the children, and a couple Mamas. These third-person sources would constitute the bulk of their feature. Perhaps, they avoided face-to-face interviews to avoid being accused of "horn tooting."

Charlotte didn't need to toot her horn. She was known to viewers and consumers of newspapers and magazines. Sarah had a stage persona that didn't fit with her actual gregarious, little-girl personality. The children thought the world of Sarah, her songs, her singing, and her obvious love for them.

Yve had no public image to protect. She resented the notepads and cameras but realized they were an integral part of the mission. Any story about her was unlikely to impact her for either good or ill.

Eventually, Yvonne stretched out on the fuselage-length bench and so threaded herself with straps that she appeared secure. How successful was she? The load master left her alone. Either she was easily fooled or, more likely, she didn't give a damn.

The drivers disappeared. No one knew what happened to them. Either they didn't get on the plane – no one was certain they'd seen them after the truck and trailer were tied down – or they went out for a walk.

In truth, the pair hid under the sacks of empty water bottles. They made excellent pillows and provided satisfactory insulation.

The ABCs kept stations from varied vantage points. Bruno sat alone on the port side while Andre and Charlie sat widely separated on the starboard side. There was no likely threat inside the aircraft. Perhaps, they agreed to "practice." Regardless, they slept sitting up, and one of them, at least, remained awake and alert.

It was a soiled and slovenly trio of women who stepped off the aircraft into a blustery, overcast day. They removed their wax earplugs, but it would be some while before they could talk and hear normally. A van was sent to fetch them. They waited calmly, enjoying the cool air and being outdoors without their ubiquitous sunhats.

Andre was called forward in during the final minutes of the flight and was barely seated and strapped in when the wheels touched down. He herded the women off then, signaling all others to keep back. Finally, he confronted Yvonne.

"Were you given a document – a secret document, before your departure."

There could be only one source of this security breech.

"Yes."

"Did you use it?"

"No."

"Did you examine it?"

"No."

"Do they know?"

He gestured toward Charlotte and Sarah.

"Yes."

Yve was on the spot. She wanted to explain that her possession of the passport-sized item was noticed when they were not quite dressed. Somehow, the circumstances didn't seem to matter.

"Do you know what that document contains?" he asked, looking at the others with a demanding expression.

They said nothing. Their emphatic gestures spoke volumes.

The interrogation was interrupted by large bags containing empty water bottles crashing onto the tarmac directly behind them. The load master refused to have them aboard one second longer.

"Do you want it now?" Yvonne asked, resuming their interrupted interrogation.

"Not only *no*, but *hell* no!" he barked. "It's to be destroyed!"

How? It was, suddenly, very important that Yvonne and the passport *not* to be together. If Andre decided to send a bullet after it, her homecoming would be spoiled. She sacrificed modesty and seized the item with all possible swiftness. She threw it to the ground. Andre quickly smothered it with his boot.

As several witnesses stood by, Andre, after waiting a few uncomfortable minutes, was provided with a pencil-like implement by Bruno. He pulled the cap off this device. When the tip of the pin glowed red, he knelt, removed his boot, and used the tip of his "glow stick" to hold it in place.

Sarah was the one who shrieked. Alternatively, it may have been all three of them. Andre stepped three, very rapid steps back. The flash created instant, and considerable heat, but it dissipated before anyone other than Andre, could react. In the blink of an eye (they ALL blinked) the document vanished. The few remaining ashes were carried away by a gentle breeze.

No one knew the identity of that device. No one wanted to know.

Sarah and Charlotte exhibited no further curiosity about Yvonne's "dynamite."

The van arrived. The women were escorted by the ABCs. Once their "cargo" was delivered, they disappeared, never to be seen again by Charlotte, Sarah, or Yvonne.

One by one, the women were stripped of their clothing, de-loused, de-ticked, sanitized, showered, shampooed, and examined by a hand-picked woman doctor. They were put in slippers and ankle-length "gowns" while their travel clothes were sterilized, washed, and pressed.

When a team of three doctors were satisfied the women were contagion free and in good health, they were allowed to dress and proceed to a public lounge where a government official welcomed them, congratulated them, and presented them with certificates sighed by an impressive array officials representing three countries.

Charlotte and Sarah were led to a van which would take them to the hotel where their husbands would welcome them. Yvonne, the "bachelor girl," would be whisked off to an official residence.

"You have a report to write," she was reminded.

She was up to the task, but she wished she could consult with her fellow aid workers. However, they'd been cloistered for much of the trip and freely shared most of their observations and comments (including copious complaints). Ultimately, Yve felt she could accurately report on behalf of the entire team.

Unknown to her until weeks later, Yve's "official residence" was assigned to important foreign dignitaries, financiers, delegates, and diplomats. She found herself held "prisoner" in a spacious house with the largest bed (and fanciest bedclothes) she'd ever seen. There was a sitting room worthy of a Rothchild, a "study" with a heavy wooden desk so highly polished it hurt her eyes to look at it. There was, also, a dining room capacious enough to accommodate a dozen settings.

It also came with a staff: a manservant and a cook.

She was escorted by a young flunkey who sat in the front seat with the driver while Yvonne sat in the back, imagining that she was royalty. She was thrilled whenever someone pointed at the limo and gawked.

They think I'm somebody!

The young man opened her door and took her hand to "help" her out. It was farce. She was being treated like royalty while dressed as a peasant. However, the farrago continued with the officious air of a certain African captain. The young protocol trainee saw her to the door which was opened by a stately man of mature years. Doubtless, he'd admitted the great and near great during his tenure. Now, he was admitting Yvonne Schortmann, a woman of no accomplishment whatever. This didn't dent his phlegmatic demeanor one iota.

His mission accomplished, the young escort returned to the car. He, the car, and the driver vanished, never to be seen again.

"If Madam requests a word processor," the butler announced, "I'm authorized to secure one for you."

Yvonne wasn't certain how to respond. She didn't know the language of high society. She wanted to play her part for fear of causing distress with those who knew the book of etiquette by heart. Nevertheless, the way the man enunciated *word processor* made her think he'd rather sweep one up and add it to a compost heap than *secure* one.

"I prefer to write in longhand, unless there is a prohibition."

He nodded respectfully. Her response, apparently, met with approval.

"This way."

He led her to the study and the much too large desk. There was a fresh writing blotter and several writing implements placed with exactitude.

Choose your weapon.

"You will find paper in the upper right-hand drawer." The worker bee informed.

"Thank you. I shall start at once."

He cleared his throat.

I've stepped in it! she thought with a rising sense of panic.

"Would Madam prefer to have some food and refreshment first?"

After living on MREs for over a week???? Peel me a grape!

How far could she push this. She would trade everything she owned for roast duck.

"A sandwich, perhaps?"

She loved him for that. Without sounding like a snob, he established the parameters.

"Lovely," she announced. "A sandwich would satisfy me quite well."

"I will inform cook," he nodded. "I shall inform Madam when all is ready."

"Thank you."

How long could she keep this up? Three days prior, she was ingesting dust and sand with every bite. Suddenly, she was participating in an updated version of *Pygmalion*. She was certain to fumble. She'd break the glass slipper and turn into a pumpkin.

A former composition champion in her school days (there wasn't a lot of competition), Yve decided to divide her work into three parts. First, a comprehensive narrative of their life on a desert compound; second, the improvements made as the result of the supplies they brought and the individual efforts of the trio (sewing dresses, providing music lessons, making habitable the sleeping quarters, and other individual accomplishments); and third, a prioritization of items requiring serious, future improvements.

She did not write a linear script. As, for example, she recoded their first impressions of the facility, Yve set those pages aside and began her exposition concerning the improvements they organized and completed during their stay. Inevitably, this brought to the fore some glaring deficiencies in materials and expertise.

"Luncheon is served."

For want of a proper designation and for her own use only, she named the manservant Mr. Butler. She hoped she wouldn't carelessly use the moniker aloud. Regardless, she had the beginning of three separate piles of correspondence in place before she was called away.

The sandwich was on dark bread. It was watercress, cheese, and an unidentified spread which teased her palate in addition to satiating her hunger. There was, also, a cup of soup – navy bean, she suspected with tiny bits of green and red pepper added.

Yvonne did not dally. When she was satisfied, she neatly folded her napkin and placed it delicately where she thought a used napkin should be placed. Rather than wait for Mr. Butler to return, she skulked away and resumed work.

By nine that evening, she was well into her report. She did not hear Mr. Butler, but the coffee he brought prickled her nose and delighted her. She found a porcelain cup and saucer on her right, the heady steam rising into the circulating air of the room. There was a tiny glass bowl containing sugar cubes and a small white container of cream. She eschewed sugar and cream and delighted in the satisfaction of a truly well-made cup of coffee.

"Dinner is served, Madam."

She was well into her work and did not want to sacrifice the flow of her ideas, but her fingers aches and her wrist was becoming stiff. Yve carefully set the pen aside and followed Mr. Butler to the large dining table with a place setting for one.

The appetizer was a cup of Greek salad. It was delicious and more than enough. Yvonne pondered calling a halt and returning to work. However, the cook mightn't be understanding if she walked away without being properly dismissed.

The main course was fish. Belatedly, Yvonne realized that it was Friday. She was so very tempted to announce that, since V2, she was allowed to eat Spam. Her humor, she decided was as bad as her manners. She ate a sumptuous meal, but her pleasure was blunted by her largely satiated appetite.

For afters, there was a single scoop of vanilla ice cream and coffee.

Again, she returned to her work without making a performance.

An hour later, Mr. Butler announced his presence by clearing his throat.

"All work and no play make Jane a dull girl," he stated.

He'd never get away speaking like that to a state visitor. Was he reminding her that she was an unwelcome buttinski, or did he have a genuine regard for her?

"Her Royal Highness wishes this report," she snapped.

"Her Royal Highness is a patient woman," he declared. "She is, also, a very busy woman. If it takes you two or three days, let me remind you, she is, also, a very understanding woman."

Yvonne stood up and rotated her head to wake other parts of her body.

"I don't belong here," she protested. "My being here is depriving some deserving person of your charming company."

He ignored her sarcasm.

"May I remind, Madam, that you are an invited guest? This is not a hotel. You don't need to be out by noon, nor must you leave the curtain in the shower."

This last struck Yvonne as an attempt to put her at ease rather than a snarky effort to put her in her place.

"So," she dared. "What do I do? I left my opera glasses at home. Even if I hadn't, I'd be arrested for walking the streets in this outfit."

"I suspect, Madam, if one cares to look in one's closet, one might find that one has not been forgotten. Her Highness wasn't always a Grand Duchess."

Yvonne's interest was piqued. It was curiosity, *not* her determination to make a liar of Mr. Butler, that she marched into her boudoir. With Mr. Butler, in stately gait, behind her, Yvonne opened wide the double-doored closet. There amid the vacuousness of a space large enough to constitute a separate room, Yve beheld two attractive ensembles. There was a sleeveless shift in the royal colors and a pair of slacks, blouse and jacket – the jacket could be worn with either the slacks or the shift. Beneath the hanging largess were shoes, a pair of stylish pumps and a pair of street loafers.

"I'd be certain to stain or damage these clothes."

"*Your* clothes, Madam."

"M – mine?"

"Partial payment for undertaking an arduous assignment."

"I didn't take this job for payment," she protested.

"Precisely, Madam."

One thing about Mr. Butler, he certainly knew how to end a conversation. Yvonne hesitated to make mention of clean underneaths. She'd taken three pair on her trip, but knowing where she was headed, the items she packed were nearing the end of their utility. She daren't check the pajama drawer with Mr. Butler watching. If there was no lingerie there, he'd make certain there would be by morning.

There is much to be said for hospitality, but there are limits. She imagined Sarah and Charlotte were enjoying new clothes. The royal couple served at the pleasure of the government. The days of kings and queens getting a fifth of all wealth production went the way of the Holy Roman Empire.

Yvonne was beginning to feel like a common grafter. The Grand Duchy asked for volunteers, then heaped upon them payment in kind. A ton of free publicity would serve Charlotte and Sarah well. Yvonne would get the same publicity, but it would in no way advance her career. Beyond the pleasure of serving a worthy cause, Yvonne needed nothing.

"I have clothes," she acknowledged. "I have nowhere to go and no way to get there."

"We can have a car in fifteen minutes," Mr. Butler informed.

Of course! A car with a driver. More money wasted.

"I need to work," she insisted.

Was Mr. Butler under orders? Yve assumed that he was.

"Madam needs her rest," he insisted. "You will do much better work if you begin refreshed."

There was a large screen TV.

She didn't watch TV.

There was a modern audio system.

"What kind of music does that thing play?"

"As Madam desires."

Being addressed in the third person was irksome. Her few remaining nerves were nearing a crisis.

"Madam desires Bach. The Brandenberg Concerti."

It was a dare.

"I shall see to it at once," Mr. Butler replied, pleased to have a mission.

The moment he disappeared, she shed her desert skin and stepped into her new shift. Of course, it was of high-end quality. Of course, the zipper was in the back, but as a single woman and servantless, she knew precisely how to overcome that problem.

She admired herself in the mirror. The sun had left its mark on her, but there was no denying that the dress made her look and feel like a civilized woman once more. She calculated how she could make a copy of the shift in different colors and materials. Hardly had she initiated her calculations before the music began.

"Madam wishes to step out?" Mr. Butler asked, hopefully.

"Is Sir anxious to be rid of Madam?" she dared.

"Not at all."

"Sit there," she dared again.

"It is not my station, Madam."

Yvonne was enjoying this.

"Your station is to please Madam," she reminded. "Madam will be pleased only if Sir sits there – as instructed."

She couldn't detect it, but she was satisfied he was sweating. Reluctantly, and only after assuring himself that there were no witnesses, he obeyed. The way he moved made obvious his discomfort. Once he was sitting, ramrod straight, she settled onto the settee, leaned back, and crossed her legs.

"Suppose – just *suppose* – that I wanted a Wimpy burger for lunch tomorrow. Would Cook give notice? Would she strangle me in my sleep?"

"Cook will insist that it arrive at table aesthetically."

Yvonne smiled. She'd have laughed had she dared.

"Wimpy is near the train station. I've seen it several times. When I was in Africa eating synthetic food, I couldn't think of anything but Wimpy. I've never eaten Wimpey. Suddenly, in the desert, I couldn't think of anything else."

There was nothing for Mr. Butler to say. He took full opportunity not to speak.

"You don't want me to work. I don't watch TV. I don't want to go out. That leaves you. Entertain me."

Mr. Butler stood. He was in full-service mode, but he was confronted with a duty he hadn't anticipated and seldom exercised.

"Does Madam play chess?"

It was Yvonne's turn to stand and act regal.

"Madam does not play chess enough for chess to hurt Madam."

He did his butler bow, head and shoulders only, and retired.

A few minutes later. Mr. Butler returned with a chessboard and pieces arrayed. He set it on the coffee table (or whatever is the royal designation for "coffee table"), and they began moving furniture until they sat comfortably across the table for each other.

It took an hour and forty minutes to finish two games. During that time, they relaxed and enjoyed not working. They spoke sparingly. When they did speak, it was conversational French, *not* the regal French of similar venues.

He was much too good for her. She hardly ever played, but Mr. Butler apparently played often. She was on the defensive from the first moves. Yve was competent enough to detect his plan, but not skilled enough to beat back the attacks.

"You're very good," she congratulated.

"Cook beats me routinely," he responded.

Was he being modest, or was he criticizing her play? She didn't care to know.

"I'll take a shower and go to bed."

That was her subtle way of telling him to leave. Mr. Butler placed the pieces on the board for instant play later.

"Madam will enjoy her Wimpy lunch early," he announced, carefully lifting the chess board. "Madam and the other women will be interviewed for television."

"Sir could have told Madam earlier," she reverted to the third person with ice produced by her extreme vexation.

"Madam needed to relax," he responded with practiced calm. "Madam will think and speak better for having some distraction."

"Madam will make a fool of herself."

"Excuse my being bold, but Madam is no fool."

The comment was appreciated if misplaced.

She should have enjoyed her shower, but she was boiling. She could have (should have) continued working on her manuscript. The following day would take her away from her task. She'd be fortunate to get any work done.

Mark L. Williams

LIGHTING THE WAY TO DARKNESS

There were two interviews with different sets of questioners. These were professional broadcasts, produced, directed, and featuring professional personnel, propaganda experts who insisted that they, and they alone, knew what the public wanted. Had they been proficient and perceptive they would have examined the "campaign" of the Grand Duchess more carefully.

Yvonne didn't watch the news, nor anything else. Therefore, she hadn't grown up with the subtle seduction of the media. Her hackles were up within seconds of meeting the attractive well-groomed, and well-togged media personalities. Save for the languages they spoke, there wasn't any appreciable difference between the German team and the French team.

Yvonne, Charlotte, and Sarah appeared in the attire provided by Her Highness. They looked rather tawdry compared with the "professionals." They were slated to tape two sessions of ninety minutes each. Only forty to forty-five minutes would be aired. Only the "juicy bits" would enter people's living rooms.

They were a quarter hour into the French-language interview when Yvonne got up and stepped out of the brightly lighted area.

"Charlotte. Sarah. We need to conference."

The professionals panicked. They had more important things to do and some prima freaking donna refused to play! Those celeste eyes were the eyes of evil. The professionals barked and demanded the women participate in their carefully scripted exploitation. Yvonne, however, would not be moved. She'd taken command in the desert because she was the only one brave enough step forward. Her "army" consisted of two publicity-hungry entertainers, but they retained considerable loyalty in their "commander." More importantly, they respected her judgement.

"We're here to drum up support for the Mission and the Mission School," she reminded. "These people only want to talk about your careers and career plans. They've asked almost nothing about what we were doing and why we were there."

Charlotte enjoyed talking about her career and putting in a bid for live theatre. Sarah wasn't lobbying for anything, but she appreciated the career boost.

Nevertheless, the trio agreed to focus on their mission. Charlotte and Sarah were anxious to get back to work which financed their elevated lifestyles. A charity gig is fine, but the charity was worthy only for the spotlight. The whole purpose of their sacrifice was to focus attention on the plight of those children and not themselves.

They returned to explain the ground rules. The professionals didn't like it – not one bit. They knew their jobs and they weren't about to be at the beck and call of amateurs.

"Ladies," Yve said with a boldness she did not feel. "I have a report to write."

That was fine with the professionals. She was a nobody. Charlotte and Sarah were somebodies. Unexpectedly, however, Charlotte made a statement.

"Maybe, I can help you."

When she began following Yvonne out of the studio, panic abounded. The want-to-be dictators were suddenly obsessed with covering their asses. The people to whom they reported would ask pointed questions should they return empty handed. Therefore, the professionals, who seldom exercised initiative, joined in an impromptu pact with the "missionaries."

The interviews were shorter than planned because of the unexpected revolt. To make clear their displeasure, they refused to ask any direct questions of Yve – they wanted to freeze her out. This was satisfactory with her. It wasn't satisfactory with Charlotte, however.

"Actually, Yvonne is better qualified to answer that question. Yve, tell us what you remember."

Sarah, unexpectedly, asserted herself in the same way. Anyone watching the interview would realize that Yvonne, the nobody from nowhere, was the leader of the operation.

Yvonne didn't gloat; she wasn't that kind. She was relieved when the ordeal was over and prayed the Grand Duchess would applaud her stand. This was not about the women in the studio; it was all about those children and the mission.

"People who abandon pets are barbarians," she said at one point. "People who abandon children aren't even barbarians."

She wondered if the professionals would edit that out. Yve was rather ashamed of having said it. The object was the children, and she had no right to insert her opinions. Sarah's eyes flashed when she authored the sentiment. Was she amazed that Yve would speak so, or was she in agreement with her assessment?

As they were leaving the venue, Charlotte grabbed Yvonne none too gently and spun her around.

"I will forever remember you as the infected boil on my butt!" she hissed.

"Did you think that up yourself?"

"Someone wrote it. I told you I can't ad lib. I don't know who the hell you think you are, but if I start getting bad press, I will be looking for you."

"I'm sorry, Charlotte. I really am. I don't know if I did the right thing, but I wouldn't do anything to hurt you – not on purpose. We haven't gotten along very well, but I respect you, Charlotte. I mean that."

There followed the proverbial thoughtful pause.

"I respect you as well," Charlotte replied at last. "Sometimes, I want to kill you, but – well, I understand your motives. Don't take this the wrong way, but I hope I never see you again."

"Fair enough," Yve responded. "Meanwhile, I shall pray for you."

Charlotte's eyes widened considerably. This sentiment was one she'd never heard before.

Yvonne returned to the "residence" and tried mightily to finish her report. Despite a sound scolding from Mr. Butler, she was up until her eyes became so tired a blurry that she couldn't see the letters anymore. It was nearly two o'clock when she got to bed.

She worked in her pajamas until Mr. Butler announced breakfast. She ate in her pajamas and promptly returned to work.

"Madam is making my position intolerable," Mr. Butler scolded.

"I suggest that Sir ignore Madam and let Madam finish her work."

"I shall inform Her Highness. That's an obligation. Her Highness holds me responsible. I shall be dismissed."

"Her Highness would never hold you responsible for my misconduct," Yvonne countered.

"You are not employed by Her Highness. Which of us, then, shall be discharged?"

She paused in her scribbling.

"I shall do as you wish, but it will cost you."

"Madam?"

"I couldn't enjoy Wimpy yesterday because that da – uhm – *darn* media circus was hanging over my head."

"Understood, Madam."

"I'll shower and get dressed before returning to work."

"Madam is most gracious."

"Madam wants to get out of this place to find out if Madam still has her job."

"May I warm the water for Madam?"

Message received. Stop work now or the burger lunch is scratched. Yvonne put paper and pen aside. She wanted to make a show of temper, but she couldn't muster the malevolence. Mr. Butler was right. She'd work better and smarter if she took a few minutes to tend to herself.

She sighed when, at last, her work was finished. It was not a sigh of relief. The report, as commissioned was finished. However, Yvonne realized she must add a fourth part to her work. She must include the story of Klaus.

It took her eight pages.

Upon her return, Yvonne unpacked and put things away. She was particularly careful with the newest additions to her wardrobe. She was flattered to have them, but not satisfied that she'd earned them. She wanted to review and edit her work, but her report was forwarded as is – misspellings, lined-through words and whole passages. She'd, also, added snarky asides in the margins. Hopefully, the official scribes would have sense enough to omit these malicious comments.

She dusted, cleaned, scrubbed, and made the apartment habitable once more. She washed and dried the clothes which were left dormant during her absence. She added air to the tires of her bike and set out to reprovision.

That evening, she baked some cookies. She was proud of herself for figuring out how to bake on a hot plate. This was a skill she never studied or read about; she figured it out for herself. Yve was pleased with the results.

She made her bed.

She slept soundly.

The following morning, she trained to Wasserbillig. Filled with trepidation, she entered the shop. Mme. Errad looked sternly over the top of her glasses. Carla, Claudia, and Marie (in the company of a matronly woman) bid her hello but did not interrupt their work.

"Do I still have a job?"

"Part time, if you want," Errad responded.

"I guess – I suppose that will have to do."

"Come in and close the door."

By this time, Yvonne was used to following orders.

"There is a major *KaufHaus* across the river. It has stock that isn't moving. The fashion line it features is – too busy. They fired the buyer, but they're stuck with the merchandise. They need people to modify the inventory. It's temporary work, but – as always – you will meet people who know other people."

"*Schwartz Arbeit.*"

That's dangerous. Yvonne would be subject to fines and, possibly, jail.

"You misunderstand, Sister," Errad continued. "They want to keep the alterations under wraps in case the manufacturer finds out. They might turn nasty. The work itself is legal. It's full-time work – well, until their inventory is modified."

It would buy time. Further, she'd be earning Deutsch Marks.

"Whom do I see?"

Mme. Errad wrote down a person's name and the address of the establishment.

Yvonne received one letter from Norbert during her African tenure. It was shorter than those hitherto and contained only one sketch. Either he was too busy, or he'd met a nice Italian lady who possessed superior charm and personality. It wouldn't take much of either to best Yve.

She replied by appending a brief note to a newspaper clipping of her African excursion. Norbert could read between the lines. If he wanted to break it off (whatever *it* was), this was her tacit permission to go ahead.

The following morning, she signed over much of her savings to provide for the care, feeding, and education of Klaus. She told Frau Schulz what she'd done and warned that it might impact on her rent payments. The gracious lady assured Yvonne that they considered her a good investment. They were willing to carry her for a few months if matters got too bad.

The major department store opened its doors only eight minutes prior to Yvonne's arrival. She checked the store directory and escalated to the fourth floor and women's fashions. She asked a saleswoman for the person Mme. Errad named.

The man who wore the name was tall and bullish. His collar was open to make way for his thick, muscular neck. He was not very attractive, but his slovenly appearance made it clear that he did more than order people about. Here was a man who was eager to get his hands dirty.

Mme. Errad's name was all the references the man required. He hustled her into a white BMW and drove her to the workshop. It was not in the better part of town, but there was a tram line stop near the main entrance. Yve would not be stranded.

"Frau Berghoff, this young lady was sent over by Frau Errad. Would you show her to alterations and get her started."

Berghoff had once been a striker, but her glory days were far behind her. She was still lithe and trim, but the lines around her eyes testified that she and stress were close acquaintances. Yve's chauffeur disappeared with alacrity.

"He's rather brusque," Yvonne observed.

"He doesn't know much about paperwork either," the woman commented. "Let's step in the office here and we will get started with the law."

Dark Comedy

Yvonne felt the welcome breeze of relief. Being employed in Germany, legitimately, is a matter of form. In truth, it's a matter of several forms – all of which must be filled out punctiliously. The government and the tax collectors wanted to know exactly where you are every second of the day.

Yvonne did not begin work until after lunch. After filing a mountain of paper, she was told to watch and listen to the trio who worked like galley slaves to make the design modifications. When, at last, she joined them, it took her most of an hour to complete her first challenge. After that first attempt, she worked much faster. By the end of the day, she was approaching the level of productivity of those who had worked for nearly a week.

It was not hard work, but it was exacting. One of the sewing machines insisted on malfunctioning periodically which produced communal frustration. Yvonne, however, profited from the expansion of her vocabulary. She mightn't use any of it, but she would understand the nuances when others employed certain memorable words and phrases.

During her four-day stint, she worked hard, fast, and efficiently. There was little time for chit-chat, not even during breaks and lunch. She obtained no additional contact names. When she left the facility on her last day, she was presented with a healthy payment.

The following morning, she deposited her wages in her German Sparkasse. She kept another account in Wasserbillig as a hedge. The German government needn't know of her Wasserbillig nest egg, and vice versa.

She grabbed one of the ubiquitous publications specializing in job listings, for rent, for sale, for trade, and similar items. Perhaps, she might get very lucky.

They're writing ads for services, but not for me.

Yvonne realized she was on the road to insanity if mangled song lyrics were marching through her head. She rolled up the paper and tapped it against her thigh as she walked. Her eyes were open, and she remained alert to any opportunity that might present itself.

Focusing on potential job opportunities, she was oblivious to her surroundings. With each step, she was wandering further and further from her digs. Life, it seemed, had led her to a dead end. The money she sent to Klaus would last for the year – then what?

The mission would continue to care for him, she knew, but the quantity and quality of that care was predicated on an influx of donations. If the efforts of the royal family of Luxembourg were successful, the donations would make a huge difference to those African children – and Klaus. However, public support for such programs would wane eventually, if not sooner.

Klaus did not belong there. He wasn't African; he was German. He deserved to be brought up German. If, one day, he wanted to aid those he'd left behind, he could head up a charity drive of his own. Yve hoped he would. Regardless, his life chances in Germany were far better than the chances existing where he was.

She had to get him out. That would cost money. It would require mountains of paperwork. Living in Germany would better both their chances, but the African bureaucracy was bound to be capricious and voluminous. Additionally, there would be the cost. She must travel there to fetch him; she must travel to the mission; she must bring him back to civilization; she must deal with African authorities; she must deal with German authorities; she must secure a passport for him; she must – the list was too lengthy to contemplate.

"Pardon! Fraulein, bitte."

She was awakened by a balding man with a very expensive camera slung around his neck. He looked directly at Yvonne and gestured to her as he approached. She ceased her meandering and braced herself. If this person intended to assault her, she was prepared to make a champion fuss.

This is Germany, Idiot! It isn't Africa!

It made a difference. Assaulting women on crowded German streets would initiate an instant uproar. Before screaming for help, she'd give the man an opportunity to explain himself.

Dark Comedy

"My name is Wiegel. I'm a professional photographer."

He'd done this before. He reached into his shirt pocket and produced a laminated photo ID with his name and a list of organizations he worked for or had worked for. Yvonne recognized several of them.

"I've been commissioned by the tourist board to put together a Trier montage aimed, specifically, at overseas tourists. Normally, I take candid shots of a crowd, but the way you came through the gate struck me as perfect. Could you go back and do it again?"

Yvonne looked over her shoulder. Only then did she realize she had come through the nearly two-thousand-year-old Roman gate – just as several hundreds of thousand of people had been doing since it was erected.

"I'm hardly dressed to have my photo taken," she muttered, struggling to find the best excuse.

He gestured toward the people milling about.

"There doesn't seem to be a wedding party here today," he pointed out, fatuously.

"Why me?"

"Because of the expression on your face just now."

"My expression?"

"I don't know what you were thinking about, but would you mind going back and thinking about it again. I – well, when I require human subjects, I pay. Would you walk through the gate again for twenty-five marks?"

She hesitated.

"You're not a model, are you?"

Again, with the *model* thing!

"It makes a difference?"

"I can't afford professional rates," he explained.

She bit her lip.

"At the moment, twenty-five marks represents a lot of money, but I – I don't think I can give you what you want."

"Try. Please, try. You get the marks regardless – just think, again, about what you were thinking before."

That twenty-five marks was the first money set aside for the Save Klaus project.

She felt she had a mission. Her assignment was to bring Klaus home. That entailed a labyrinth of bureaucratic twists, turns, forms and documents. Being unemployed was an advantage; Yvonne could keep bureaucratic hours and avoid making several trips (by appointment) during business hours. Employers were tolerant about missing work due to government hokey pokey, but tolerance stretched only so far.

Yvonne needed money. She needed a considerable sum of money. Without money, her official paperwork was valueless. There must be something she could do. Waiting table required a bare minimum of skills and requirements, but her earnings would cover her rent and food (provided she kept her diet simple). It would allow precious little for the Klaus Project.

She visited a church once a day and asked if she was doing something wrong. Was she being punished? Why must Klaus suffer for her sins? She trusted in God to be with the boy and watch over him, but that child needed a home. Perhaps, God had selected someone else to be guardian. Perhaps, He'd selected a couple – a husband and a wife – who would love and care for Klaus. Yve hoped so. Simultaneously, she hoped not. Klaus had come to her; he'd hugged her; he remained with her like a loyal puppy.

Was that it? Was she being punished for her selfishness?

If God would send her a sign. If He had other plans for Klaus, Yvonne would step aside, and gladly. Well, not quite "gladly." Klaus had burrowed into her consciousness. Likely, she'd make a poor mother, but she felt that Klaus would do as much for her as she could do for him.

Dear God, talk to me; give me a sign; let me know if I am truly serving You, or has pride seduced me?

Dark Comedy

Eight minutes after leaving the church, Yve experienced a "sign." She was certain that it was a message from "above." As is so often the case, she hadn't a clue. What a curse! She was aware enough to realize this must be a divine communication, but she was too obtuse to interpret it.

"You're wearing clothes today,"

When she turned around, there was fire in her eyes and evil in her heart. To speak to a woman on a public street was transgression enough, but to say such a thing was beyond tolerance.

Alas, the alleyway was devoid of traffic save for the principles. She recognized the camera first. The balding head was too prominent to mistake. Nevertheless, hailing her with such a ribald sentiment was unacceptable. She made certain her visage communicated her message. Instantly, his joviality receded.

"Sorry. Very clumsy of me. I was amazed at how well you look in nice clothes."

She wore the shift seeded to her by, or through, the Grand Duchess. Yvonne thought it attractive, but not superlative.

"Please," he pleaded. "Forgive my thoughtless remark. However, you are rather alluring in that dress."

"Thank you."

This was forced. However, she retreated from her initial hostility.

"I'm on my way to the Babara Baths," he informed.

"You like Roman ruins," she concluded.

"Can't stand them," he insisted. "There is so much gorgeous medieval and eighteenth-century architecture in this city. Next to them, Roman ruins are, alas, ruins. Still, when working for the tourist authorities, one must feature tourist sites. Not so?"

"I suppose."

"Want to earn another fee?"

She was taken, momentarily, by surprise.

"Are you on an expense account?"

"Indeed, I am."

Yvonne agreed. The idea of her posing in an ancient Roman bathhouse was her idea of a lark. Further, it was twenty-five marks into the Klaus fund. She'd need much, much more to accomplish her mission. At least it was a start.

As they walked, she told Herr Wiegel about Klaus and her plan to rescue him from the Sahel. He asked several questions. He surprised her. His queries were not conversational gambits; they indicated his interest. Perhaps, he was merely scouting out, by proxy, a future photo project.

"Surely, he is being well cared for," he suggested.

"So far as the money allows," she replied, not without emotion. "The point is his parents threw him away like a sack of garbage. This is his country. He deserves to live in it until he decides otherwise."

"You don't know they threw him away," he insisted.

That hurt. She'd generated considerable hatred for people she never met. However, what were they doing out there? If it was dangerous for Yvonne and her troop, it would be dangerous for a family traveling alone – but with a child?

"Point taken," she responded.

She had something new to think about. She wanted the man with the camera to know that.

Once upon a time, the Barbara Baths constituted an impressive edifice. People assumed that since the Imperial Baths were so huge, there was no need for another. Likely, Barbara pre-dated the much more grandiose facility. The remains suggested that it was, perhaps, a private bath house attached to the stately home of Mr. and Mrs. Gotrocks. However, that conceit was too outrageous. These baths were substantial and impressive. The pitiful remains could not do them justice.

The remnants were fenced in.

Dark Comedy

"I do not want you to damage that dress," the photographer announced. "We must be careful."

He removed the camera from around his neck and handed it to her. Gingerly, he hoisted himself over the wire fence and stood on the other side.

"Do you have permission?" she asked, expecting to see policemen rushing to the spot with weapons drawn.

"You're holding it," he assured, pointing at the camera she cradled.

No sooner had he made his announcement than he gestured for her to hand over the device. He set it carefully aside and returned to her. He issued instructions. She was ready to flee, but the twenty-five marks prodded her on. If he snapped a photo before the police arrested them, she'd get money.

His concern was for the dress, not for her. He handled her very rudely. In his defense, there was no book of etiquette on trespassing. The dress survived intact. Since she was inside the dress, Yve was, likewise, unharmed.

Obviously, he'd studied the venue prior to their adventure. He knew what he wanted. Now that he had a live model, he placed her where she would serve his purpose best.

"Notice how thick that floor is, and how large this room was," he pointed out as he prepared his instrument. "If you sit with your legs free – yes. Anyone looking at the photo will make you a point of reference. Because of you, the size of the room and the thickness of the floor will be obvious. Imagine how hot the air must have been. It would flow underneath you. It would take tremendous heat to penetrate that floor."

He was very excited. Maybe, Roman ruins left him cold, but amazing engineering brought him to a boil.

Yvonne was not present when the photographer showed his work to the money men. They were impressed with his work and assigned their scribes to create a text, being very careful to include the points of information the tourist board was most anxious to impart.

The photos of Barbara Baths, however, momentarily interrupted the proceedings.

"Who is that woman?"

It was a demand more than a question.

Yvonne never considered herself beautiful. If pressed, she might admit to being attractive – moderately, at least. Her figure was rather – well, linear. Her face was pleasing enough, but hardly one to launch a ship – or even a canoe. However, she was no ogre. When posed by a professional photographer and in the royal shift, Yvonne was attractive – "Who's-that?" attractive.

Yvonne Schortmann is not a fool. She saw herself in her mirror three or four times a day. She realized her face was attractive enough for everyday use, but she was not vain. When people

flattered her, she was instantly alert; when they praised her for her looks, she questioned their judgement. It was well she did not know the chaos created by a twenty-five-mark photoshoot.

Herr Wiegel was under siege. Who is this women? Where does she live? How can we contact her?

The man fulfilled his contract; he was paid for services rendered; he'd left Trier. As a freelancer, he was seldom in his Koblenz studio. His messages were forwarded and, eventually, attended. Her name was Schortmann. In keeping with German custom, she didn't give her forename – they were not friends; they were "business associates."

In a civilized society, that would be the end.

Why, then, was it not?

Yvonne, a woman of faith, could answer that question without the hint of a blush. Her faith, however, could not direct the course of events. Moreover, she hadn't a clue that circumstances effecting her had been set in motion. One over-zealous city employee contacted the *Polizei* demanding (*demanding*, mind you) that they find and produce this Schortmann woman.

Dark Comedy

What began as a simple inquiry ("Who is this woman?") became an obsession. People, who were recognized by friends and co-workers as reasonably sane and rational, made constant enquires. When leaving a restaurant, bar, shop, or other public venue, certain city officials would ask bizarre questions.

"Does anyone named Schortmann work here?"

"Do you know a Frau Schortmann?"

Others employed a more traditional approach. They carried a print of the "Lady in the Bath" with them.

"Have you seen this woman?"

Six weeks passed without a nibble.

Yvonne secured work in a corner bar near the *Bahnhof*. It was a gathering place for mature men, many of whom had little or no surviving family members. They came for the society and the beer – the featured beer was made next door in Luxembourg. Some were war veterans, some were retired laborers, a few were retired fishermen from the north. Few, a very few, were rowdy.

Yve's wages were embarrassing, but the men were generous with their government stipends. Between wages and tips, Yve could cover rent and food expenses. When she needed extra, she tapped her savings.

The work was not very demanding. Indeed, it was rewarding. These men had a thousand stories – each! Of course, the "storyteller" was featured in every story, but, ultimately, each tale was entertaining and edifying. She wondered how many were true or, at least, mostly true. When she could, she engaged in conversation. These men needed a fresh set of ears into which to pour their copious tales of adventure.

Financially, this job would do until she found something better. Emotionally, she became an extremely wealthy woman. Not an evening passed without her inclusion of a blessing upon some aging patron who had touched her heart.

Not an evening passed when she did not pray for an increase in the Save Klaus fund. It was increasing but only in anemic increments. Yvonne should have become morose and sullen. Instead, she reviewed the previous three years: Sister B_____ sent her to Mme. Errad which led her to a Grand Duchess which led her to Africa and Klaus. These events didn't fall into place by chance – every link in this chain of events was planned.

Klaus came to her. Led by pure instinct, he had, literally, attached himself to her. He remained with her every possible moment. She became attached to him. She wanted to bring him home. If that was what God wanted, it would happen. If He had something else planned, He'd make it known in time.

Have faith, she told herself. How her job in a beer bar for geriatrics fit into a "master plan" was beyond her understanding. However, this was where He wanted her. Therefore, she would draw and serve beer, make change, gather up tips, wash and rinse glasses, heft kegs from the storeroom to the taps, keep the bar and table tops clean, tend to the garbage ...

She gave every task her best effort because He expected it.

Two of the regulars were favorites of Yvonne. It took a while to establish a relationship since they were closed-mouthed around strangers. As with all people their age, they had stories that could curl one's hair.

Her boss, as an example, recalled the air raids as a child; he never ceased to be amazed at how his fearless brother and an uncle would rush to the roof of their house – *while the bombs were falling*. If flaming material was deposited on the roof, the uncle and brother would quickly smother it with coats, blankets, anything they could grab. This action saved their house from burning down to the foundations on, at least, two occasions. However, keeping watch on the roof during a bombing was a superlative example of courage – or of faith.

Yve felt ashamed of herself. She had convinced herself from her early days that she had faith in God and His mercy. However, if given the opportunity to replicate the heroism of her boss's brother and uncle, Yve suspected she'd quiver like a coward in the cellar.

Dark Comedy

There was Franz, an arthritic survivor of the vaunted Afrika Korps. He'd been taken prisoner by the Americans in Tunisia. He was shipped to America and spent the remainder of the war in Kansas. There he and several of his mates volunteered to help on surrounding farms.

Labor was a scarce commodity during the war. German prisoners, eager for some meaningful occupation, volunteered to fill the void. They helped with the planting and the harvesting. They ran errands, and repaired farm equipment and barns and houses. They drove tractors and hauled crops and animals to market. Many were invited to sup with the families they served. War rationing kept meals simple, but what the people had, they shared; it was way better than what they were served in the camps.

After the war, Franz married. When their two children were old enough to be aware of their surroundings, the family sailed to America. They visited Kansas. They met many of the people Franz befriended during his imprisonment. This impressed the children so much, they attended American universities, became American citizens, and raised their own American families.

Franz's daughter was a dentist in Omaha. His son owned a retail store in the very town where his father was once a POW.

Yvonne wondered if Franz and his reminiscences were the reason God sent her to work in this hole-in-the-wall beer bar. She treasured his stories and his company, but she did not understand the purpose behind her being there. Perhaps, she was sent as part of a divine mission for someone else. Perhaps Franz, the widower, needed *her*.

Revelation: Why does divine guidance have to be only for me? I might be the agent for someone else!

If her mission was to provide aid and comfort to a lonely old man, she enjoyed the assignment.

Heinz was proud of his English. His idea of a good time was to speak to anyone in English. Not many who frequented the venue could speak conversational English. Yvonne could. Well, she thought she could until she met Heinz.

Heinz often corrected her. He knew, for example, when to use "less" and when to use "fewer." Thanks to his kind corrections, Yve learned much, and her English improved substantially.

Was this why I was sent here? Will I need better English for the task ahead? Maybe, this is just an added benefit of my laboring here.

"Your English is excellent," she gushed one evening. "Did you attend *uni* in England?"

"In a way," he reported. "I was in the *Luftwaffe*. I was shot down in 1940 and spent much of the war as a POW near Peterborough."

As horrible and tragic as the war was, it had profoundly changed the lives of the survivors. Yve was impressed. Still, was she here for insight, or was she here for some other purpose? Would she ever know?

Another feature of the Lux-beer watering hole was the informality. Normally, patrons are *Herr* (females don't, generally, go into such establishments alone) and the waitress was *Frau* (even if she was young and didn't wear a ring). In the Trier hole-in-the-wall tavern, people were either on a first name or nickname basis. Yvonne was "Shorty" because she was tall. Heinz was "Heinzie," and Franz was "Franz." There was an "*Afri*," after a defunct soft drink. There was a "*Graf*," so signified because he, occasionally, put on airs. The owner of the establishment was "*Lefty*," not for favoring his sinister hand, but because he "left" most of the manual labor to the hired help.

With only a few exceptions, the patrons were regulars. They liked to chat, play *Skat* or Cribbage. Mostly, they were lonely men who preferred the company of other lonely men. They told the same stories over and over. Even "Shorty" knew several by heart. The one commonality is that they were lonely. Only two of the regulars had wives still living.

Walter had a nickname. It was "Kinder," because he was barely into his fifties and had some years ahead before retirement. He worked on a loading dock because he was strong and solidly built. He was likely to remain on the loading dock indefinitely since his reading level is best classified as remedial. He possessed modicum intelligence, he just couldn't get the hang of letters and how they are arranged to make words. He was fluent in English; however, his vocabulary was better suited to the bathroom or the arena. Fortunately, he restricted himself to German when conversing over his beer (he never had more than one).

"You know you're a wanted woman?"

As the only female present, Yvonne didn't feel the need to guess. She smiled at the joke only *Kinder* understood. It was her policy to be pleasant even when she "had her nose full."

"I saw your picture," he continued. "I had to look at it for a long time. It didn't look like you. The longer I looked at it, the more sure I was it was you."

"Numbers at the bottom, I suppose."

"No. No. You were wearing a dress and sitting on a concrete slab."

She shrugged. He was either making it up, or he imagined it. Suddenly, however, she recalled the photo Herr Wiegel took of her at the Barbara Baths. The authorities had photographic evidence of trespassing. The local monument preservation society must be in a snit. They were looking for Yvonne so they could put her in the slammer for years – perhaps, decades.

She broke into a cold sweat. Getting caught up in litigation might completely derail her Save Klaus campaign. What if they (whoever *they* were) opted to confiscate her passport? Would Herr Wiegel come to her defense? If he did, would they end up sharing the same cell?

I'm being punished she told herself. I did something I knew was wrong; that's two sins for the price of one. She wasn't worried about Klaus. Someone more worthy would be selected to bring him home. It would happen – of that she was certain. Meanwhile, Yvonne had transgressed one time too many.

She couldn't sleep that night. She shed tears until there was no water left.

Klaus had come to her. He had picked her! Yvonne had betrayed both herself and that sweet, harmless, little child. One foolish little slip –

Well, a sin is a sin. Yvonne Schortmann was turning her back on Catholicism, on her own judgement, and on an innocent party.

This, she thought, was the beginning of perpetual darkness. Yve need not suffer from fire or thirst or torment. The nuns promised all these, and more, for those lost souls who dared to defy God. Yvonne's own conscience would punish her far beyond fire, brimstone, and tortures.

She tried to pray. She wanted to pray for forgiveness. However, that would compound her sin. *Let me be free of this. I will never transgress again!* She couldn't. Yvonne Schortmann knew how she repeatedly begged forgiveness only to surrender to temptation at the first opportunity.

Would she ever know peace again?

Dark Comedy

RECALLED TO LIFE

She showered and mantled herself in jeans, a nice blouse, and her loafers. Yve didn't want to overdress for jail, but she didn't want to look like a street urchin either. She shoved her thin pocketbook in her left, front pocket. She considered taking her passport but dismissed the idea. She carried identification enough in her pocketbook. The fingerprint people and Interpol would have no problem confirming her credentials.

Yvonne wanted to leave a note for her employer notifying him that she might not be at work that evening. If she were allowed a phone call, as in the movies, she would call later and give him the details as required.

She marched into the Presidium and identified herself.

"I was told you were looking for me."

It was news to the office staff.

Yvonne sat patiently in the lobby and waited.

Eventually, a uniformed man appeared and the half dozen people (and Yve) gathered in the waiting area.

"Frau Schortmann."

Yvonne took a deep breath and got to her feet. Her knees quaked. She half walked and half limped toward the young man who'd hailed her. She cleared her throat. It didn't help much. She squeaked when she spoke.

"I'm Frau Schortmann."

She wasn't a *frau*. Under the circumstances, *fraulein* was too informal – childish, actually. She wished to make it clear that she was not hiding behind immaturity. She knew it was wrong; she disobeyed; she'd been caught.

"You claim that we are searching for you."

What's this *we*? Odds are, this is some trainee, a university or trade school student serving a practicum. Despite his impressive uniform, he was no more a police official than Yve herself.

"I was told by a friend that people are showing a picture of me and are trying to find me."

His eyes sparkled.

"What kind of picture?" he asked, hopefully.

"A with-my-clothes-on picture."

She noted the disappointment in his eyes.

"Give me a few minutes," he suggested. "I need to make a couple phone calls."

Yvonne returned to her seat. How long does it take to get arrested in this city?

A few minutes in "bureaucrat" language was thirty-eight minutes in "civilian time." Yvonne knew, because she checked her watch frequently. The young trainee returned with a mature man in mufti. The gray-haired official with damaged veins in his left cheek eyed her suspiciously. Well, at least, he was old enough to have some idea of police procedures. Yve got up and approached cautiously.

"People are showing you picture and asking after you," he stated to avoid superfluous chit-chat.

"Correct."

"You know this how, exactly?"

"A friend," she replied.

"Who is this *friend*?"

"I'm reluctant to state. If the police are looking for me, I'm here to answer for my crime."

"What crime?"

She took a deep breath and counted, quickly, to ten.

"A photographer coerced me into entering the Barbara Baths to pose for a photo. That is the photo which is being shown about."

The man took his time digesting this fatuous story. Was this woman wack-a-doo or was she a reporter attempting to get the police behind the eight ball?

"Coerce how? Did he have a weapon?"

"He paid me twenty-five marks to pose for him. He was taking photos for the tourist board, or something, so he said. He paid me to pose for him at an ancient site."

"He paid you? I mean, once the photo was taken, he gave you the money?"

"He did."

"That's all?"

"Yes."

"Why would the police be asking about you?"

"For trespassing."

He struggled. The man wanted to laugh or, at least, smile. His ruddy complexion reddened slightly more under the labor of self-restraint.

"As far as I know, we have no photo of you; nor has anyone here been looking for you. Leave a contact number and an address with this man," the mature man in the too small suit coat advised, "If anyone in the department wants you, they will call or come to your door. A word of advice: exercise caution. Any person with your photo and asking for you is not a policeman."

Yvonne shuddered.

"A thought does occur," the man continued. "Did this photographer really work for the tourist office? If he did, they would likely have a copy of the photo. Regardless, this is not a police matter. It might be, if we knew the identity of the person or persons who are trying to find you."

Yvonne swallowed hard. She nodded. The mature man retired into the inner sanctum. The "kid" took her name, her workplace, and the work phone; she had no home phone. Her knees quaking and her nerves frayed, she returned to her chair. She needed to recuperate before returning to life.

She wanted to go home and have a good cry. However, someone was looking for her. If he, she, or they were legitimate, Yve wanted to know. If she were being stalked . . .

There is the tourist board known to the public. They have a cubicle in two or three lobbies about town, but the hirelings who man them seldom do more than give directions and hand out literature. One of these stations makes reservations for walking tours and bus tours.

There is the tourist board known to the mayor's office and the publicity agents. This tourist board is not easily found. Yvonne kept looking and asking until it was nearly time to go to work.

"Kinder, did you see that person who was flashing my picture?"

"Ja, I told you."

"I mean, since then."

"Ney."

"If you see him again, bring him in here. I'm counting on you guys to help if there's any funny business."

They agreed readily enough. Most of the patrons were too old to help a "damsel in distress," but they could get in the way. They could, also, create a lot of noise and fuss. She wasn't afraid of some bounder coming into the beer bar. She was frightened of one who might be lurking in the shadows at two in the morning while she made her way home. Maybe, she should call for a cab. The tourist people might – just maybe – have a legitimate reason to contact her. If it wasn't the tourist people . . .

Dark Comedy

After breakfast, she wrote a note to her sister and inquired about how the baby was coming along. It was weeks early yet, but Yve was anxious for some word about the pregnancy and her sister's health. In the parlance of one of the beer-bar patrons, Yvonne could not wait to find out if she was an aunt or an uncle.

There were other considerations, however. Considerations that were less playful. The health and welfare of Yvette was the prime concern. Yvonne did not want to risk being sisterless. If there were problems, Yve would throw up everything and dedicate herself to doing whatever she could for her sibling.

She stopped at a Post and purchased the required stamps. Once the letter was on its way, she had little to do until reporting for work. She bussed into the business district and tried to find the people who were, allegedly, looking for her.

It was a typical bureaucratic office with typical bureaucratic cubicles behind a typical bureaucratic reception desk. These people took no chances. There was a heavy glass barrier between her and the officious, matronly woman whose expression announced that she wasn't here to be bothered by members of the public. Yve leaned over toward the microphone just off to her side. She didn't know how close she must get for the woman opposite to hear her.

"I'm Frau Schortmann. Has someone here been looking for me?"

It sounded silly. Well, it was. However, the reaction was hardly predictable.

The woman gave Yve a resentful glare. Suddenly, her eyes grew large. (Was she reacting to it the celeste eyes?) She turned in her swivel chair and said something Yvonne could not hear. When she turned back around, she knocked over her designer coffee with her elbow. She shifted to full panic mode. Keeping her eyes on Yve as if expecting her to flee, she dabbed at the spill with a paper napkin and a sheet of printed matter. Yvonne could see but not hear the commotion behind the coffee woman.

Two men approached the scene but paid no attention to the coffee tragedy. They stared at Yvonne as if they expected her celeste eyes to strike them dead. After several seconds of study, the younger of the two men gulped and approached the door. He opened it cautiously.

"Come in, please."

She followed instructions.

Yve was inside the soundproof lair. What now?

The older of the two men hurried past a partition and out of her sight. The younger one examined her as if he intended to buy.

"Has anyone here been looking for me?" she asked, realizing she held all the cards. "I think I'm entitled to know."

The coffee carnage was under control, but much remained to be done. The harried woman at the desk rushed off, supposedly in search of proper cleaning materials.

"I – believe – yes."

The young man examined her from top to bottom before repeating the process. Was this, Yvonne wondered, the tourist bureau office or a booking agent for Vaudeville acts? The second and older man returned with a photograph. Together they examined both the photo and Yve. This went on for some while.

"Um – would you – sit down – please?"

He motioned toward a swivel chair. It was the one previously occupied by the older man.

"Have I come at a bad time? All I want to know is have you been trying to locate me? I've been to the police. They're not looking for me. They suggested that I come here."

"The police?" The older man quivered.

"The police," Yve repeated. "They do exist, you know."

Dark Comedy

If this was some practical joke, she vowed to see the police again – and soon.

Both men were flummoxed. How did the police get involved? Did this woman believe she was in danger? Perhaps, they hadn't planned this properly. Perhaps, they hadn't planned it at all. To buy time and give themselves the opportunity to create coherent sentences, they backed away and asked her, again, to be seated. The young man rushed to his cubicle and returned with another photo, an enlargement. He and his older partner examined Yvonne carefully before examining the photo – carefully.

"This is you," the younger man tried to assure her.

"I'm wearing a dress, and I put on a face," she reported. "Yes, that's me."

The older man cleared his throat. They had bungled this every step of the way. Still, he hoped to salvage the situation.

"We want a face – an attractive young woman to promote the city. We thought you would be an excellent choice."

Yvonne couldn't help herself. She was in the driver's seat. She enjoyed watching these men squirm.

"You really think I'm attractive?"

"Well, in this picture – I mean – well –"

"So, if I put on a face, I'm attractive."

The men knew they were in way over their heads. They needed to confer with someone above them on the food chain. Presumably, a person who could form complete sentences.

"Monday. Can you come here Monday morning at ten? We will have all the details to go over with you. You will, of course, be paid. If you wish to bring a lawyer, that would be fine."

"How much would I be paid?"

The two men looked at each other. These people were not authorized to make decisions.

"We can discuss that on Monday," the elder man suggested.

Yvonne didn't say a word. She got up and smiled (she hoped) graciously. She opened the door and returned to the world.

"Forgive me," she muttered, descending the stairs.

She worried herself sick about being banished from God's grace. Still, she took sadistic pleasure in seeing three people virtually at her mercy. That was a sin, she was certain. It would take more than begging forgiveness to save her. She vowed to ask the men's forgiveness on Monday. That would be a start, but it would take hours of prayer and good works to obtain forgiveness for herself.

Yvonne never considered herself a head-turner. Someone, however, did. It was a sure bet that Trier did not want a sexy vixen to bring in the tourist trade. They needed a woman who was attractive and, yet, next-door-neighborish. Since she was not a model, they would be obliged to direct her in how to pose. The money wouldn't be princely, but every pfenning would go into the fund. So long as she kept her job, she'd want nothing more.

She'd have to keep her employment secret. Nobody wants a barmaid to represent their city. Still, she did the publicity work during the day and worked at night. Getting enough sleep might be a problem, but how long would it take to get the pictures they needed?

INTERREGNUM

For eighteen months, Yvonne Schortmann was the anonymous "Face of Trier." Every pamphlet, information packet, folder, and flyer – everything the tourist board created for public consumption – has Yvonne's photo either on the document or appended to it. There was a four- foot cutout image of her propped up in the Bahnhof and another at the center where one booked bus tours and several guided walking tours.

Yve's image was wholesome without being Shirley Tempelish. She was attractive, not vampish or *Vogue*-like. What the directors found in her image was the same many tourists discovered. The visiting public responded well to her image; whenever they spied her, they paused to notice whatever city feature or monument she promoted.

The tourist board hirelings with whom she delt were professional men and women. They bore no resemblance to the clown show of her initial visit. These were the suits, the professional propogandists, the elite who hobnobbed with the city and district fathers and mothers. They loved their city, and they loved promoting it. They treated Yvonne with respect and with professionalism.

One or two of the tourist people chaperoned Yvonne at every photo shoot. They drew up the contract detailing her services. They reviewed it with her, clause by clause. When she wasn't satisfied with something, amendments were made. She didn't sign her name until she was cognizant of every detail, including the "fine print."

While the ink dried, there followed the ubiquitous tax information. There was a secretary well versed in tax documents who graciously filled out all the required information in a neat, precise hand.

"Married?"

"No."

Not, that is, according to secular law. Neither she nor the tax authorities needed to know about that other ... thing.

Miraculously, the suits did not pry. They knew she was French because she had to produce a residency document. They suspected she was Catholic, but they didn't ask. They knew she was a barmaid because she volunteered the information. Beyond that, hers was the face they wished to use in their promotions. It was all very professional and above board.

There was, of course, a clause in her contract. If she did anything "unseemly" that adversely impacted their campaign, the contract was void and she be subject to "redress" and not just her emoluments, but production costs as well.

Yve was paid for every photo taken. Out of the hundreds snapped over the course of a work week, they used eight. They paid her a monthly stipend for the duration of the contract. She had a pass to every tourist attraction requiring paid admission. Best of all, she was omitted from all official fetes. Her image, not her person, was under contract. She'd receive notice of special events and had an open invitation, but she was not required to attend.

Yvonne attended a select few "official" gatherings. She was eager to sample some of the local wines. Another time, she went to the dedication of a newly refurbished public building. A flower show was part of the dedication. She was enticed into mingling with the "honored guests." She was not recognized by anyone at either venue. If she was, those who knew were civil enough to keep her identity to themselves.

The patrons of the beer bar knew who she was. After the initial hazing, they left her alone. None of them ever boasted that the "Trier Tourist Maid" fetched beer for him. Her love for them increased several fold for not complicating her life.

During her tenure as the "Face of the City," she managed a three-day visit with her sister. Yve got to coo over her niece, Lea. She managed only one full day with the family, and Yve made every moment count. In addition to holding and pampering Lea at every opportunity, she got to know her brother-in-law very well. She liked and respected this man because he was kind and gracious to Yvette. It wasn't for show, either; he was one in a million.

Far more important, however, Yvonne got to know her sister so much better. They grew up together, fought (very, very seldom), shared chores and playthings, and exchanged secrets. However, they never really *knew* each other. Once that special rapport was established, their mutual love and respect knew no bounds.

During her stint as the "Face of Trier," Yvonne wrote voluminous letters. She wrote to Norbert, who replied only twice in terse, overly polite notes. She wrote to Yvette twice or thrice a week. She wrote Mama once a week, at least. Lastly, she wrote "notes" to Klaus daily.

Her messages to Klaus had to be simple and brief. It might take several weeks for these notes to reach him. When they did, they would arrive in bulk. She wanted him to know that she kept him in her heart. She dared not inform him of the Save Klaus campaign, since too many things could go wrong.

Shortly after the new year, and with four months to go of her eighteen month "enlistment" as the Face of Trier. Yvonne received a royal summons. She, together with Charlotte Werner, Sarah Walter, two publicists, and the reporters who accompanied the African mission, were to be awarded an Order of Merit. There were several degrees of the award. Yve was unaware of which she'd obtain, but it didn't matter.

She had plenty of time to plan. The beer bar could manage with Franz stepping in as "barmaid." He claimed he needed the money. That was a lie, but Yve and her employer were happy to overlook it. He wanted to help Yvonne. While away for three days, she'd not have to worry about "her boys" suffering under a "newbie" who mightn't understand (or tolerate) their brand of mischief.

Yvonne wanted to wear the shift the Grand Duchess provided her, but that might constitute a *faux pas*. Much against her will, she commissioned a dress from Mme. Errad. She promised to pay in instalments since she did not want to raid the Save Klaus fund. Were it anyone else, the businesswoman would have demanded the final instalment prior to delivery. However, she felt obligated to Sister.

"I know where you live," she growled.

That was a lie. Yve dismissed it. Her former employer clearly trusted her. It was child's play for her to transform the lie into an endearment.

Yvonne pondered an interesting conundrum: is a lie really a lie if the recipient of the lie knows it's a lie? For the sake of her own theological views, Yve decided that lying, in such circumstances, in *not* a sin. Friendship first, last and always –

Mme. Errad did a bit of research. Awards ceremonies were formal affairs. A party shift would not serve. Though the "Face of Trier" would be but one of dozens honored, she'd stand out like an elephant at a weasel race if she didn't go formal. Yvonne required a gown. That guaranteed additional instalments.

Yve sweated. What, she wondered, could she do with a gown? It would take up closet space and, likely, never see service again. Despite Mme. Errad's "rock-bottom price," (she considered Sister as a "most-favored-client") the article would be exorbitant. She had time and opportunity to tender an excuse for not attending. That, she decided, would be a sin. Additionally, she wanted to see Charlotte again if only to get up her nose.

Yvonne did not resent Charlotte as much as the actress seemed to resent her. However, Yve was a prankster, and had been from her early school days. Maybe, since they weren't forced to work together, she and Charlotte could become friends. That would be well worth the price of a gown.

She was eager to see Sarah again, under any circumstances.

Yvonne prayed that Charlotte and Sarah would attend the event. Had she any means to contact them, she would insist they be together one last time. As it was, she could do little more than hope.

Dark Comedy

The publicity campaign, headed up by the lady trio, had produced donations that far exceeded expectations. Not only was the mission on solid financial ground for the next four or five years (at least), there was money enough to make possible infrastructure improvements. A proper dormitory was the first item on the list. Construction was started, but it would be a while. Moving building materials was a major and time-consuming operation.

Mark L. Williams

A BURST OF LIGHT

The ceremony was colorful and well-attended. Yvonne was honored to be included, but it was tooth-achingly dull. The ceremony was preceded by an oration of epic proportions. It was shared by various members of the government, the Grand Duke, and an honored guest Yvonne couldn't identify (she may have dozed off when he was introduced). Each recipient had to be introduced; a short biography came next; a description and history of the award (or title) followed; finally, the service for which he or she was being bestowed must be detailed.

Thankfully, Yvonne, Charlotte, and Sarah were grouped together rather than a recitation (and the tedium) of individual plaudits and biographical details. Their medals and ribbons were not pinned on as in the movies. Rather, they were presented a case with the award, ribbon, and a personalized engraving stating the title of the medal, a brief history of same, and the reason for its presentation.

Everyone assembled, some forty-two recipients, heaved a collective sigh of relief when the interminable ceremony officially closed. There followed a "royal ball." There was live music, refreshments, and dancing galore.

Yvonne hoped she would have a few moments with the Grand Duchess, but she saw her only from afar. This was one occasion when the royal couple remained largely aloof. Being seen in congress with individuals might signal favoritism. In a brutal world where the propaganda industry makes news more often than it reports it, everyone must be very, very careful.

The highlight of the honorarium for Yvonne was a reunion with two people she respected exceedingly.

Dark Comedy

Yvonne was not met at the train station, nor was she whisked off in a chauffeur-driven limo. She hailed a taxi and was carried to the hotel where many of the awardees were cloistered. A liveried attendant took her name and the garment bag containing her gown.

"I will see this to your room, *Frau Schortmann*," he assured.

For all she knew, this young man was a vagrant off the streets, but he looked official. Yve decided that there was security enough for a summit conference and banished her doubts. She turned toward the desk to register and collect her room key when she was tackled by a crazy woman.

It was Charlotte. She threw her arms around Yve's neck and half strangled her as her body pressed hard against her.

"I'm so glad you came!" she gasped. "Oh, God! I'm so happy to see you!"

"The infected boil on your butt?"

Yvonne's voice was strained due to the sudden deprivation of air.

"I read your report," Charlotte announced.

She released Yvonne and stepped back. Charlotte began bouncing on her toes.

"My report?"

"We got here last night," Charlotte explained. "It was in our room. It's in a blood-red binding with a ribbon around it – like something you'd see in a medieval library! I bet there's one in your room too. I started reading, then I began reading it to my husband. They sent copies to the PM's Office, the Chamber of Deputies, and the Council of State. There were other copies sent out to – oh, business leaders and – well, we three get one. I'm so proud of you, I could cry!"

Not only could she, but Charlotte's eyes were decidedly wet.

Yvonne was concerned. She'd lined out so much and had scrawled corrections in the margins. Furthermore, she'd committed egregious spelling errors. She wanted to make a final copy and edit before considering the document finished, but she was summarily dismissed.

"Were there many mistakes?"

"Are you kidding? The Grand Duchess and a team of scholars went through it, I'm certain. Read it! I want you to tell me what parts you wrote."

"I'll do what I can."

During this exchange, there was a handsome, clean-shaven man of medium build and piercing blue eyes standing silently behind and to the side of Charlotte. He held the wrist of the opposite hand in front of him. He watched the exchange with obvious interest.

"Sorry, sorry, sorry!" Charlotte stammered while continuing to bounce on her toes. "Yvonne Schortmann, this is my husband and agent, Rudi Vogel."

Yvonne left no one a chance to be formal. She stuck out her hand and dared the man not to shake it.

"Herr Vogel, I'm pleased to meet you at last."

He accepted the dare. He took her hand firmly, but not too firmly.

"Charlotte has told me so much about you," he confessed.

"Please, don't repeat it," Yve begged.

"I'm glad you were there," he informed. "Charlie can be – well, impetuous. I'm glad you were with her. I shudder to think what might have happened."

If he was sincere, Yvonne would be touched. She'd managed to avoid a few, potentially, ugly scenes.

"My contract is up in four months," Charlotte gushed, still bouncing. "By this time, next year, I should be on stage in *Tartuffe*. Can you believe it? Live theatre!"

"Is she acting?" he asked of her newest acquaintance.

He smiled.

"It's true," he replied, proudly. "It's hard to tell, but I think Bouncing Betty here is a happy woman."

Charlotte took her husband's arm and rested her head on his shoulder. She ceased bouncing, but she continued to bubble.

"He's the greatest agent in the world," she beamed. "As a husband, he's a bust. He doesn't spoil me enough."

"Who has time to spoil you?" he demanded. "Promoting you is no picnic. If I ditch you, I could take up Formula One."

The normally overcautious Yve reached a verdict: Charlotte and Rudi were very much in love.

"Is Sarah here?" she asked.

"She told me they were coming, but I've not seen them. Get your key and we'll go look."

Yvonne begged off. She was anxious to see Sarah again, but she had to review her monograph. She wouldn't have a moment's peace until she assured herself that her snarky asides and crude margin comments had been expunged.

She sighed with relief when she discovered the official document displayed no evidence of misspellings or unedited line throughs. Moreover, the turgid remarks she'd employed to scold herself were similarly absent.

Yve did not read it through completely. She wrote it; she knew what was in it. She was thankful to have a well-manicured version of her report but hadn't a clue what to do with it. Likely, she'd consign it to the closet where it would mildew. Still, it was a reaffirmation of the faith the Grand Duchess had in her.

Sarah and her husband, Jean-Baptiste, came to her room and announced themselves. They made a dinner date.

Jean-Baptiste Jeandel sported a well-manicured beard. Yvonne didn't care for beards. Despite this inauspicious first impression, this man was a good partner. He was not in "the business;" he was an architect with a modest reputation. He was the marital backbone for the shy, modest, and reticent singer. Without his support and love, Sarah would have folded long before.

Over dinner, he shone. There was no doubt that the love he had for his wife ran deep. His duty was to buoy her up and support her in everything. When she opted to write music, his encouragement was superlative. When her efforts were lackluster, he proved a brutal critic. Sarah, therefore, trusted him implicitly. She would feel betrayed if he plied her with false praise and allowed her to embarrass herself in front of an audience. Further, he was her voice. Shy, timid, retiring Sarah could not stand up to the pompous promoters and managers; she'd never stand up for herself or her beliefs; Jean-Baptiste, however, never hesitated to put his wife's delicate, shapely foot down for her.

The man sweated bullets during his wife's African excursion. He demanded a full report when she returned. He breathed easier when he learned that Yvonne Schortmann had taken his songbird under her wing. Had he been aware, he could have forfeited several sleepless nights.

The trio chatted merrily over a light supper.

Over an after-dinner brandy, Yvonne took a chance. She didn't want to be rude or brutal, but she was not well practiced in subtlety.

"M. Jeandel, at the risk of sounding – well, just plain rude, may I have a few minutes alone with your wife?"

Yvonne, unknowingly, had been his substitute during the arduous few days his wife spent in a desert hell. Had Yve asked him to cut off his hand, he'd have asked the waiter for a kitchen knife. Allowing Yve and his wife a few minutes over brandy was no sacrifice.

"I like him," Yvonne told Sarah.

The shy woman's brow wrinkled. She was slightly disturbed over her husband's exile, but more concerned over the reason for it.

"I feel I can speak with you," Yvonne began, cautiously. "I – I'm dealing with a crisis of faith. No! I have faith in God and Jesus and the teaching of the apostles, but – I'm not a good Catholic."

Sarah looked around her suspiciously. She leaned across the table as far as she could.

"I'm not either," she confessed.

"It's too much – ritual. I – I pray and pray and, when things go bad, I don't know what to do. So, I – I fall back on ritual. I go to confession – not often enough, and I – do – other things because – because, it's all I know."

"This is about Klaus?"

"Ultimately."

She leaned back.

"Why me?" Yve demanded. "That little boy doesn't come up to my waist, but he hugged me. Why me? I think God made that happen. Again, why me? I'm a backslider, a doubter. I sin and sin and sin at every chance. I know I'm doing wrong, and I do it! Am I struck down by lightning? Am I punished? The more I sin, the more God does for me."

Sarah made a gesture. It was subtle, according to social etiquette. For meek, retiring Sarah, however, it was monumental. It shocked Yve into silence.

"You stood up to that brute," Sarah reminded. "You got us through. You're the one who got us our awards – or whatever they are."

"That wasn't me!" Yvonne insisted. "I'm not like that. God kicked me in the butt! He gave me voice; He made me do what I did. He made Klaus come to me! So, who wants to bring Klaus home? Is it me? Am I doing this for myself? If I am – that's pride and pride is a sin!"

Sarah considered for a moment.

"You got your job," she reminded. "He sent you to Wasserbillig. He sent you here. He sent you to Africa. Why? He sent you for Klaus. This is your trial, Yvonne. Your mission is to bring Klaus home."

"Why me?" Yve demanded. "There are thousands – hundreds of thousand of people who have more faith, and who are stronger and better suited and – much less sinful."

Sarah thought carefully for a considerable while.

"Would you feel this way if Klaus were black?"

That was a blow. Yvonne reeled. She sat back and labored for beath – if only momentarily.

"I don't know," she admitted. "There – that's another sin. I cannot answer your question."

"You're being tested," Sarah hypothesized.

"If I'm being tested, why is He so good to me? I did nothing to earn the job I have now, but I'm so much richer for it. I did nothing to get the Trier gig …"

"What Tier gig?"

"Never mind. I just don't understand how I can doubt so much and sin so much and God rewards me."

Again, Sarah paused for thought.

"Do you think you're worse than Paul?"

Yvonne blinked.

"He was hunting down Christians," Sarah reminded. "He was, probably, as disgusting a person as you could find in those days. He was selected to preach the gospel and do God's work."

Yvonne blinked again.

"My advice, for what it's worth, is to do what you think is best – even if you think it's a sin. You *sinned* us out of a pack of trouble in Africa. If loving Klaus is a sin, then there is something very wrong somewhere."

Yvonne listened, but her thoughts were racing.

"Why did you want to talk to me?" Sarah asked. "Charlotte is the strong one."

"Can you see me having this discussion with Charlotte?"

Dark Comedy

It was Sarah's turn to think.

"Not really," she admitted.

"Thank you, Sarah. You did a lot for those children, and you've helped me."

Sarah – mousey, timid, shy, reticent Sarah – snorted.

"You don't need my help, Yvonne," she insisted. "You need answers, and I don't have any. Just do what you think is best. If you're on God's side, He will see you through."

That sounded so glib, but it was comforting.

Mark L. Williams

THE LONGEST NIGHT

"If you're on God's side.."

That was an interesting angle. It only complicated matters, however. Yvonne was on Klaus's side and was praying for God to help.

Before they parted the afternoon following the awards ball, Monsieur and Madam Jeandel joined Herr and Frau Vogel in contributing a hefty sum toward the Save Klaus fund. It costs money to travel hither and yon, and to get the bureaucratic papers and documents required when bringing an adopted child into the country. The major confrontation would be the bureaucratic paper and documents required to get an adopted child *out* of a country. Yvonne hoped she could clear most of these obstacles prior to entering the African nation. She'd applied and paid for a visa, but there was no telling how many centuries she'd have to wait to get one.

Finally, there was the cost of transportation to and from the African nation. Once there, she must hire both a vehicle and a driver to get her to the mission. She didn't dare think she could drive all those miles across rocks and sand alone. If anything went wrong, her remains mightn't be discovered for decades. Then, she'd require an exit visa for Klaus. Upon their return, she must pay for his examination by health officials before he'd be released from quarantine.

When she first sat down to estimate the cost of her "adventure," the resulting figure was so daunting she gave up hope before beginning. However, both documents and money began accumulating. She remained a long, long way from her goal. It was no longer "impossible," but what remained was far from "possible."

She considered asking the government to intervene. The child was, certainly, a German citizen despite all attempts to discover his surname.

There was a danger in this. If the government paid, it might well take possession. Even if it did not, Yvonne might be hounded by officious prigs who would demand a part in the child's rearing. This horror would begin with the question "Who is your husband?"

The German authorities made clear their attitude toward a single woman's desire to adopt a child. The fewer government buttinskies, the better in Yvonne's estimation.

Yvonne's participation in a part rescue mission and part publicity stunt was a closely guarded secret in the German media – particularly that portion of the media based in Trier. The picture book for tourists was in all the print stalls and stores. Yvonne's photos, at the Porta Nigra and at the Barbara Baths were prominent. If people recognized the former "Face of Trier," they avoided making mention.

Klaus's letters were four and five to one of those from Norbert. Yve acknowledged after the first year that her romance was confined to the past. Meanwhile, with each communique from Klaus, she would study it carefully before comparing it to his previous notes. She was satisfied with the progress he was making in both printing and language skills. Her responses were voluminous. She congratulated Klaus on his progress, praised his printing, encouraged him to be a good boy and study hard. She, also, reminded him that she loved him and missed him very much.

Serving Luxembourg beer to the patrons of the hole-in-the-wall tavern was an education as well as a vocation. These men, as previously reported, had a thousand stories each. She catalogued them judiciously in her capacious brain. She wrote down a few of the more memorable episodes. After reviewing them with the appropriate people, she would ask permission to submit them. Eight were accepted. She shared half her payments with the storyteller. Her share, between seven and twelve marks, went into the Save Klaus fund.

When flummoxed, she "fell back" on ritual, i.e.: confession, rosery, and morning mass. When particularly depressed, she couldn't wait to get to work. The pathetic men who frequented the place did not have to wait until deep in their cups to make the woman cheerful and renewed.

Suddenly, without any warning signs, Yvonne's father died.

It was very sudden. An aneurism, she was told. She learned, from her patrons, that the condition is often hereditary.

She nearly panicked. Yve had to get Klaus back to Germany before she dropped dead! Meanwhile, she must return home. Mama would need solace. Further, she would require fresh, young legs to handle the myriad of civil and familial obligations.

Yvette, Yvonne, and Lea stood with the widow during the funeral mass and, again, at the graveside. Mama held up magnificently. She was so brave and so resourceful. They had, she said, many wonderful years together. They raised two talented and loving daughters. Her husband had served the family and the community well. She would miss him, but she took comfort in knowing he was with his maker; he'd be waiting for her.

Yvonne bristled. She hoped that it didn't show, but she feared someone would get the right idea. That would be a disaster. Ritual was of no help with this. She spent an hour on her knees – in her room, next to *the* bed.

It was the evening prior to her departure. Vet would remain for another day or an additional week, depending on how well the Widow Schortmann was adjusting to her new life.

Yvonne heard her sister across the way. The door to her room was open. She could hear Vet and Lea playing. Since Lea had yet to take her first unassisted step, the game was very simple.

Yve padded softly from her room into her sister's. Vet flashed a smile before returning to her daughter. Yvonne, slowly and quietly, closed the door behind her. Yvette was alerted. This was not right. They agreed to keep their bedroom doors open in case Mama needed attention.

Yvonne cleared her throat. She was trembling.

"Vet, did – did Papa ever come into your room – ?"

Yvette jumped and stifled a scream. She grabbed her daughter and held her tightly to her breast.

"Not you, too!" she exclaimed, tears running down her face.

Poor Lea was sandwiched between two blubbering women.

"Do you think Mama knew?" Yvette asked after a prolonged silence.

She was sitting on her bed and holding her daughter as if she expected someone to try and rip the girl out of her arms. Yvonne sat with her back against the door.

"If she did, she is the greatest She-Devil alive."

Yvette nodded.

"I don't think she knew."

"Should we tell her?"

That was a question that would require prolonged and serious thought.

"Not now," Yvette advised. "This will be too great a shock. If – if she didn't know, she would begin blaming herself. It will eat her up."

"If she *did* know –"

"Stop, Vovo! Just – just stop! If she knew, I don't ever want to come into this house again. I don't ever want to see her again."

They sat silently. Only baby Lea made noise; it was innocuous but soothing.

"Will you tell your husband?"

"That I can do," Yvette responded instantly. "I trust him. Even if I didn't, he should know. It was different – well, when I thought I was the only one – "

Yvonne cleared her throat.

"I won't tell," she promised.

Yvette shook her head.

"Too late, Vovo. With me – that's bad – very, very, very bad. With two – that makes it a habit. If he did *that* with other girls – sooner or later, someone's going to tell. Mama must be prepared. I'll do it."

"We could both tell her," Yve suggested.

Yvette shook her head.

"You go home. I'll do it. I promise. Before I leave, I'll tell her."

Yvonne closed her eyes and looked heavenward. She breathed deeply for several moments.

"I need to know how she takes it," she concluded. "Write and tell me, but don't –"

"I won't write about this – ever! Nothing in writing. I'll tell you how she takes the news, but – nothing else."

"Understood."

"Dear God, Vovo, I'm so sorry."

"What do you have to be sorry about?"

"I'm the oldest. I should have made a fuss. I hoped – well, I hoped that it was just me, and he would leave you alone."

"I could have said something," Yvonne sniffed.

"If you had told me – then – I'd have screamed my head off."

Prolonged silence

"What good would that have done?" Yve challenged.

Yvette had no idea.

"It would have stopped," she theorized at last.

"Maybe," Yvonne replied. "Would we be any better off?"

INTERREGNUM II

Yvonne's head spun during the return to Trier. Was she, in the Biblical sense, a widow? Could she take a husband, or would that be a bad idea? The correct thing to do would be to discuss these matters with a priest. Could she even do that? She considered herself a lapsed Catholic. She remained a believer, but she was no longer certain the faith in which she'd been raised was the "true" faith.

Was there a "true" faith?

When she grew exhausted with her theological turmoil, she turned her thoughts to Klaus. What right did she have to claim him as her own? He came to *her*. He hugged *her*. He remained wedded to *her* for most of the duration of their stay. He slept with *her*. He talked with *her*.

What if someone, because of the publicity campaign managed – in no small part by the Grand Duchess – to move some kind-hearted family to adopt Klaus? Certainly, the most important consideration was to get the child out of that horrible mission and into a loving home, preferably in the civilized world. This possibility rankled. She considered Klaus to be *hers*. He chose *her*. *She* wanted *him*.

That, for certain, was a sin. It was a whopper! Klaus was the victim. He deserved rescue. Yvonne Schortmann, however, wanted him to remain in that desert hovel until *she* bought him out. That was cruel and inhuman. However, Yve considered Klaus her *only* reason to live. If he was taken from her, there was no excuse for her to be.

That was another sin.

Yvonne did not need confirmation from her sister. Mama's letter arrived first. It was six pages long, with copious tears included on each sheet. She apologized profusely many, many times. She trusted her husband; she trusted him with her life. Discovering, upon his death, that she bore him two "beautiful daughters" for him to despoil and ravage – while she, the mother, *was in the house*! That these crimes continued for years – while stupid, unsuspecting Mama trusted him every moment of those years. It was overwhelming.

"I think Yevette will sleep better tonight."

How brutal those words were when Mama recalled them!

"Yvonne is a happy little girl tonight after story time."

Mama was only one of the community members who looked upon Bernard Schortmann as a leader among men, a diligent and just civil servant, and a fair and honest businessman. To discover that she'd been married to a monster for thirty-seven years ...

Whenever a citizen praised Bernard in her presence, Mama would insist on changing the subject. They thought, of course, that it hurt Paulette Schortmann too much to be reminded of her husband's passing. In truth, it hurt her beyond endurance to realize she loved and lived with a man so evil and depraved. Beyond raising two accomplished daughters, Mama's life was wasted.

Not once did she scold Yvonne for not telling her when the "attacks" began. She should have. In effect, Yvonne aided and abetted her father's conduct. That was a sin – a major sin! She was complicit in unspeakable acts. She had lied to her mother by not mentioning – not even *alluding* to her sexual intercourse with Papa. Lying, through silence, is a sin – greater, even, then lying at the top of her voice.

Why did God bother with her? She was a disgrace to her mother, her sister, and herself. The only talent she possessed was committing sin after sin. She exercised the sin of lying, the sin of pride, the sin of greed, the sin of envy. She suspected the sin of lust – had she not enjoyed those early evenings "in congress" with her father.?

Why did God not smite her? He should have sent her to the eternal fires years ago. Instead, he treats her like a woman of merit. He guides her to Mme. Errad; He throws her into the path of the Grand Duchess of Luxembourg; He appoints her to command a charity assignment; He leads her to Klaus; He makes her a local celebrity, albeit anonymously; He arranges for her to be honored by royalty; He provided sage advice through the unlikely Sarah Welter.

He leadeth her by still waters.

Why?

Of what earthly value was Yvonne? Certainly, she was void of spiritual value.

She could not second-guess God, but she was disturbed by his treatment of her.

There was one thing that rattled about inside her head. It was something Sarah said.

If you're on God's side . . .

Helping Klaus, she was certain, was being on God's side. Was that why she was spared His wrath? She was an unworthy, malevolent sinner. If she were on God's side, he'd make use of her. However, was she more on God's side or more on the side of sin?

Sarah admitted that she didn't have answers.

Neither did Yvonne.

She was a year away from claiming Klaus.

Her job faded away. So very close, but she would soon be denied the opportunity to add to her Save Kalus stash.

Heinz died suddenly.

He drank and played cards and provided more valuable tips to improve Yve's English. The following night, he didn't come in. A disturbing hush dominated the room. The regulars could not feel at ease when one of their members was absent without warning. The few non-regulars who came in for a beer, quickly drank and departed.

The silence was spooky.

The following night, one of the cadre arrived and made the announcement. Heinz died in his sleep shortly after departing the venue.

That was the end.

For years, these veterans gathered to share experiences and laugh at events which, at the time, were terrifying. Heinz was not a particularly prominent member of the retired military alliance, but he was known and liked by all. With his death, the group dynamic changed drastically. It was one thing for a person to fall ill and die after months of false hope, but for a knight to "crossover" without warning was a blunt reminder of their own mortality.

The regular customers became more and more irregular until it was all too clear that Yvonne's services had become a hinderance and a financial liability.

She attended the funeral. Most of the beer-hall regulars were there and a substantial number of his family members. Yve counted eighteen grandchildren; two of them approached Yve in age. When she joined the line of mourners extending sympathy for the bereaved, she was amazed to discover that her reputation preceded her.

"Heinz spoke of you often."

That cliché was expected, and Yvonne paid little heed.

"The Trier girl," one of the prepubescent grandchildren announced.

She was flattered to be recognized, but that could not dent her sense of loss.

"You were one of the women who went to Africa," the aging widow affirmed.

"I'm surprised you knew," Yvonne replied.

"Heinz told me."

"I – I never once mentioned it," the stunned Yve informed.

The widow smiled.

"You didn't have to."

Yvonne would ponder that for months.

The writing was on the wall. It was in capital letters. YOU'RE FIRED!

After Heinz passed, fewer and fewer of the "old guard" returned. The card games stopped. Orders for large, foaming glasses of Luxembourg beer dropped off. The few casual customers who just happened to come in could not take up the slack. The place would soon become a fast-food joint or a vacant building. The proprietor, with a strong sense of loyalty, refused to fire Yvonne.

She quit.

The timing couldn't have been worse.

Without work, without income, Yvonne brooded. The desert mission had two girls who had outgrown the services offered by the mission school. They were sent to boarding school in a more civilized location. That cost money.

Yvonne surmised that one of those girls was the one for whom she made the dress. The poor thing was, practically, bursting through her clothes, serviced by Yvonne — a woman unworthy of such a cherub.

The tariff for schooling abroad was nearly the same as the annual stipend. Without thinking, she submitted the funds Klaus required for the next twelve months *and* the cost of school for one of the two exports.

She'd been so close to having funds enough to fetch Klaus and bring him home. In the blink of an eye, she added – at least – two additional years before "buying" the boy. That's two years *with* an income.

Yvonne had no income.

She attempted to contact Charlotte. The best he could do was wire Rudi. He arranged for a trunk call at a certain time on a certain day. Yvonne bought a phone card – more money taken from the Save Klaus fund.

"Sorry," Rudi told her. "She's at a read through. I thought I could get her out. Sorry"

Yvonne explained the situation. She hoped Charlotte could pay for the second African girl. Perhaps, if they could reach Sarah, the two might go half-and-half. Rudi was amiable and sympathetic, but Charlotte's TV contract had lapsed and playing "supporting roles" in live theatre was hardly princely. He promised to talk it over with "Charlie" and notify Yve by post.

Yvonne did not rely on knowing somebody who knew somebody. That had provided employment opportunities before, but she couldn't depend on it. Her stint as a local barmaid was obtained on her own and out of desperation. She scoured the help-wanted pages and went to the local exchange. A barmaid who could sew was not in high demand. She could and would do menial work. However, she would be paid menial wages. That wouldn't do; either Yve or Klaus must do without. She did not want to be forced into making that choice.

Her former employer – the man who must liquidate his inventory, closed the bar, only to wait three years for his pension to kick in – the very man who hired Yvonne Schortmann on sight – the man who admired her afternoon after afternoon and night after night –

He was no lecher, but he had an aesthetic eye. Yvonne Schortmann lacked the required curves in the required places, but her posture, demeanor, gait, and perky disposition made her every move a study in grace and poise. Despite (or, perhaps, because of) her celeste eyes, she possessed an allure. The clientele joined the business owner in studying Yve's every move. Her "uniform" was a pair of jeans and a T-shirt. On warm or hot days, she wore a shirt and Bermudas; in cold weather it was a sweater and woolen "slacks." Regardless, she made anything look good.

One of the owner's sisters and his brother-in-law owned a clothing "shop" just off the town's medieval square. He suggested Yvonne seek employment there; he'd put in a good word.

"You'd make their merchandise look good."

"I'm *not* a model," she reiterated for the hundredth time.

Dark Comedy

She was. She couldn't help herself. However, as discretion is the better part... etc.

Heinz's sister, at the wake, learned of Yvonne's pending unemployment. She suggested the ex-barmaid speak with her brother-in-law. He had a series of investments. His latest was a book "shop." His business plan was to remain independent of any publishing house. He would purchase and sell volumes of German history, historical fiction, and historical romances. He would also run a second-hand section. He would purchase good-condition books of any genre and sell them from the back room.

Selling books appealed to her, though Yve would make hardly enough to support herself. Still, until she could find something better...

She took the man's name and address but did not examine them until later.

Herr Schulz, her landlord, was the bookstore owner and her new employer. It was ludicrous to accept wages from him when slightly over half would be returned to cover her rent. However, the tax man must be satisfied. Meanwhile, the bar owner persisted. The "clothing shop" was within easy walking distance of the bookshop. A plot was hatched.

Yvonne Schortmann would be paid to "model" shop wares. Prior to opening the bookshop, Yvonne would report to the clothing outlet. She would change into the sale-item-of-the-day and walk to work – through the busy town square. The daily round-trip would earn her a few extra marks a week.

"If someone asks where you got your clothes, direct them to me," the merchant instructed. "You get a commission on any sale you make."

Yvonne didn't sell. It was her job to hand out a business card and instruct the interested party to tell the salesperson from whom she (or he) obtained it.

The clothes Yvonne wore to work were not found in fashion magazines. Some of the outfits were positively gaudy. Still, in a tourist city, and during the summer months, flashy colors and quirky designs sold well.

Perhaps magic was involved. Magic or no, the evaluation of many observers held true: Yvonne looked good in anything she wore. There were days, indeed, entire weeks when Yvonne felt like a refugee from a freak show. Nevertheless, she required a resupply of cards every few days.

She wasn't getting wealthy, but she was earning more than expected. The clothing commissions were embarrassingly hefty. Yvonne felt as if she were participating in a fraud. However, she never failed to show up and change clothes on her way to the bookshop.

There was an ugly scene when the proprietor insisted she wear sandals with a particular ensemble. Yvonne refused to go out in public with her toes "hanging out" – even if it cost her a job. In the end, the proprietor relented. He couldn't afford to replace Yvonne with some busty sex-bomb. Yve was all he could afford. Fortunately for everyone concerned, Yve brought him enough business to keep them all in the chinks.

Periodically, she wondered. Was her good (moderate) fortune a result of pure coincidence, or was there some "guiding hand" at work? There was no way she could chalk up her "modeling" commissions as "luck." If anything, she felt guilty. Women who bought the outfits she wore were either fashion illiterate or didn't realize what they looked like in such attire. It didn't matter how ridiculous Yvonne looked, she'd left most of her vanity at the alter as a child. However, she felt the forces that led others to the "dress shop" might be demonic – and that was in dramatic juxtaposition with her prayers.

The "dress shop" (Yvonne secretly thought of it as "The Chamber of Horrors") opened at nine-thirty for no reason. The custom seldom appeared much before noon.

The bookshop opened at ten o'clock, which Yve thought rather late. Several times she unlocked the door with three or more anxious customers waiting.

She didn't have a proper lunch break, so Yvonne carried a ready-made sandwich with her to gobble when trade was slack. It was sufficient to tide her over. If she felt famished at the end of the day, she'd stop at a nearby fast-food emporium and enjoy a hamburger and a cup of coffee.

Dark Comedy

Meanwhile, she spent most of her day in a shop full of books – most of them history books or fiction based on history. Trier was an historical city. If local propaganda is reliable, it is the oldest city within the current borders. It was the second or third most important city in the Roman Empire – for a while, at least. Constantine was once governor prior to becoming "The Great." People who lived in the city and most of the visitors were anxious to learn about the history of the area.

The shop was stuffed with Travel Bureau literature, pamphlets, and booklets. The more serious-minded people would browse the stacks of those volumes written by professors and experts of select historical periods. Occasionally, Yvonne would be called upon to help locate a specific book or a specific type of book.

In the used book section, she found a copy of *City of God* in German. She commandeered it and read it during her evenings. It renewed much of what she'd learned during her false start as a nun. Next, she read Burckhardt's *Constantine* because – well, because she could.

To keep inside federal law, Frau Schulz would run the shop on Wednesdays. However, Yve was obligated to the shop of horror. She'd change togs in the morning as always, parade to the shop and open it. Until her afternoon "parade," Yvonne had the interim free. Wednesdays was dedicated to planning with an African nation to clear the way for Klaus's eventual release. There

was an African delegation in Berlin, Frankfurt, and Koln. The latter two were useless, or so it seemed to Yvonne. However, there was a flurry of letters and forms exchanged with the Berlin office. Much of the correspondence was both esoteric and specious. However, Yve was determined to leave no stone unturned.

With the onset of winter, flashy, fair-weather tourist-wear was in low demand. This freed Yvonne from the drudgery of her morning and afternoon "parade." Freedom to wear jeans and a sweater was liberating It was tantamount to a restorative vacation. When spring arrived, the other shop owners and employees would make bets on the return of the "funny-clothes woman." Tourists and no few locals would wait in ambush to snap a photo of the street celebrity.

Though Yvonne kept a tight reign on expenditures, she did enjoy exploring the stores and shops. These forays not only constituted a visual treat, but they also allowed her access to circulating *warm* air. She made it a point to keep her apartment temperature as low as prudent during the day to keep expenses down. Therefore, she made a deal with Frau Schultz to have alternating Saturdays off and alternating "long Saturdays," when shops and stores retained their weekday hours.

On the whole, it was a satisfying routine. She was saving up money for the "rescue," and she enjoyed a reasonable *fac simile* of a normal life.

Mme. Errad, after a life of drudgery and minor triumphs, retired. The ladies with whom Yvonne once shared camaraderie and a sense of purpose, scattered to the four winds. None of them remained in Wasserbillig; Yvonne lost contact with them all. That contributed to a growing sense of isolation.

Yvonne Schortmann was satisfied in ways that many people envy. She had a steady job with the envious perk of not having to take work home. She had access to books which cost her not a pfenning to read. Yve was paid to parade in attire of questionable merit. She had a boss and a landlord who was gracious, understanding, and lenient well beyond the norm.

However, Yvonne Schortmann was focused upon a single goal. The moment she obtained the requisite monetary and documentary resources she would, literally, risk her life to save a child she knew for only a few days. The epistles these two people shared constituted a lifeline between them. These too infrequent scribbles were tangible expressions of love. They kept the fire stoked.

Was she doing God's work or was she participating in a greedy, self-serving quest? Without question, Yvonne was engaged in satisfying her own desires. If the Deity disapproved, would she be safe from hindrance, or would she be punished? Perhaps, she was being admonished, but she was too self-serving to notice the signs of His displeasure.

Such thoughts were buried under the myriad of concerns to be meet and conquered.

With the spring, the fashion show resumed. Those merchants, shoppers, and transients who dominated the town square mornings speculated when (or if) the queen of gaudy attire would return. When the day arrived, Yvonne walked purposefully across the square to open the bookshop. There was a (muted) smattering of applause from a few spectators who assumed that spring was *officially* in bloom. Yve paid no heed. She was getting paid and on her way to another paying job.

Fortunately, the house of trendy apparel was at the mercy of their suppliers. Someone, somewhere, decided that the "war on taste" had run its course. Outrageously loud colors remained a staple, but the designs themselves were canted toward sentient-being body shapes. Since this had nothing to do with Yve, she paid no attention. She wore what she was given and returned it at the end of each day.

Yvonne had a small refrigerator in which she stored eggs, milk and (occasionally) cream. Unless her evening meal came from a box or a can, she would visit a small, family-run market on her way home. If she spied vegetables, fruit, or other fresh produce that appealed to her, she'd purchase her evening fare on the spot. If, as often happened, nothing caught her fancy, she'd either snack at night or feast on a jar of cherries or a can of soup.

Someone gave her a radio with the decor of early post-war ugly. She kept it tuned to the American Armed Forces Network. She sharpened her English skills before work by listening to the morning disc jockeys. In the evenings, she enjoyed an hour of music from by-gone days and a replay of old radio shows, mostly comedies. Otherwise, her entertainment was whatever book she'd "borrowed" from the shop that week.

Her sedentary evenings constituted a non-monetary contribution to the Save Klaus fund. If she went to a movie, coffee house, or ate out she'd be "stealing" Klaus's money. On rare occasions, Frau Schulz would drop by. They'd enjoy coffee and a chat for an hour or so. These visits were entertaining because they never talked shop. Herr and Frau Schulz had a half-dozen financial enterprises to keep them occupied, but they discussed business only with each other. Their employees were spared the weariness of tax matters and loan payments.

Norbert's missives dried up. Yve expected at least a card or a sketch for Christmas, but it never appeared. The great romance of her life, thus far, was so innocuous that she seldom gave it a thought. Her initial wistful sighs had faded. She scarcely thought of him, but she treasured the "art works" he left her. The two sketches of her were placed in a special folder and separated by a layer of tissue paper. She continued to examine the "fairy-tale" Yvonne whenever she was in one of her disparaging moods.

The male attention Yvonne received since leaving her Lux-beer comrades consisted of those attracted by (what she called) her *hippy-dippy* wardrobe. For the most part, these admirers were scruffy younger men with unkempt facial hair and snarled tresses – except for those who shaved their heads. They had a penchant for piercings and tattoos. Some of them were, apparently, allergic to soap and water. Their "pick-up lines" were, often, unintelligible. Most were turned off by her job; she was surrounded by books and books contained – you know – (shiver) *words* and ... *ideas*!

Yvonne tried very hard to be polite. In most instances she succeeded. Occasionally, she was confronted by a person who was oblivious to manners and morals. These were awarded *the stare*. She was unaware of what her visage became when she assumed this silent attitude, but it proved most effective.

One day, a teenage boy tried to impress her with his charm and sophistication. It took a superhuman effort on her part to keep from laughing out loud at the antics of the young person (young *man* was much too far a reach). She was tempted to play with him and ply him with her imitation of a film actress of the long ago, but she caught herself. She didn't want to humiliate the boy. Instead, she tactfully reminded him that she was too old for him. Further, he could never be happy; she would treat him like a mother.

He disappeared quickly.

Yvonne thought that, in one very important respect, she would have been a superlative nun: her interest in the male of the species was (very nearly) nil.

Regardless, her obsession for one male was all-consuming.

THE QUEST

She paid, in advance, three months rent. Her plan was to get in, get Klaus, and get out. Her time in Africa must be kept to an absolute minimum. Though she had secured the required paperwork of two nations, she expected a bureaucratic snarl would grab her by the ankles and tie her down to interminable frustrations. Fatuously, she convinced herself that the incalculable "surprises" would prove both minimal and easily surmounted.

She prayed mightily for months in advance.

She touched every conceivable base.

She contacted Charlotte and Sarah – no easy task since they were celebrities and constantly deluged with fan mail, "job" opportunities, and personal- appearance requests. Nevertheless, they responded.

Charlotte sent her a three-page missive wishing her good luck. She also included a bank draft to help defray expenses. It was not a huge donation, but it represented a considerable portion of her "residuals" – payments made for repeat broadcasts of her soap opera episodes. Yve accepted this as emergency funds and banked it away. If she did not need it, she would return it. If she required it . . . well, it might be (literally) a life saver.

Sarah also sent best wishes and a much smaller sum to show her support. None of her records ever topped the charts. Though she was a recording artist and the featured performer in six or seven concerts a year, Sarah and her husband lived in a rather modest home. For her, a "donation" was a much greater sacrifice than it was for Charlotte. Yve banked Sarah's largess as well, determined to return it at the first opportunity.

It was nice to know she had a cushion if she required one. It was better to know she had friends or, at least, acquaintances who believed in her and her mission.

Yvonne, also, had friends in the proverbial "high places." She was contacted by the government of the Grand Duchy. She'd require an escort. One had been assigned. *He* would *escort* her to her destination and remain with her, and Klaus, until they were once more on European soil.

Yve hadn't expected this. She wasn't certain it was necessary. However, since the Grand Duchy was paying for it, she'd be foolish to turn it down. She imagined one of the ABCs would be with her. That settled her nerves somewhat. Though her bodyguards weren't needed during her first trip, they proved a welcome security blanket.

Yvonne reported in for her flight at Frankfurt. She checked her small suitcase through. She placed her claim check in a leather folder along with her passport. It was suspended around her neck by a stout chord.

Quickly, she moved away from the counter. The line behind her was substantial; she didn't want to risk the ire of those patiently waiting by fiddling unnecessarily. She undid the first two buttons of her shirt and placed her documents where they would be most secure. As she rebuttoned her shirt, she heard the announcement.

"Passenger Y. Schortmann: please report to the LuxAir ticket counter."

The message was repeated before being announced twice in French.

The LuxAir counter was shared by three other "lesser" airlines. None of these counters were open. She made her way cautiously through the throng of passengers and potential pick pockets. If foreign fingers attempted to get at her documents, Yve would produce a scene replete with sound effects and the flailing of arms. In Frankfurt, any person seen with a hand inside a woman's shirt would catch the immediate attention of security. However, it wasn't the thought of a physical assault that caused her heart to pound.

When she neared the island where smaller lines and fewer passengers were serviced, there was only one person loitering. Her heart reacted in accordance with the man's appearance. He was black as night and as hulking as an aurochs. Yve's practiced eye realized his suit – indeed, *all* his clothes – must be handmade; the clothing industry did not manufacture anything with such hulking dimensions except by special order.

She approached cautiously. His eyes catalogued every millimeter of her as well as every movement of her body – to include her nervous tics.

"Mademoiselle Schortmann?" his guttural voice asked.

"Dr. Livingston, I presume," she squeaked.

He smiled. His healthy white teeth shone like the morning sun. Perhaps, it only seemed so. White teeth juxtaposed against that sable skin would negate any simile.

"My name is (unpronounceable). I was born in Senegal. His Highness has assigned me the privilege of escorting you."

"His Highness or Her Highness?" she asked boldly.

She didn't feel the least brave. This hulk made her feel as tiny as a church mouse.

"Regardless," he said, holding forth his huge hands as if in supplication. "One serves when one is asked."

His French was cultured but heavily accented. It was a chore for her to understand him.

"Do you know my mission?"

"I was briefed," he replied, noncommittedly.

"I'm grateful to have you along, Monsieur. I am rather timid. To have a man along is reassuring, but you – excuse me please – are three or four men."

He smiled again.

"There are parts of Africa where women, white women particularly, are not – exactly – welcome."

"How do I know you are who you say you are?"

The big man cocked a well-defined eyebrow. He reached into the inner pocket of his suit jacket and pulled out a document. It was not his passport – that would have proved nothing. This was a letter on heavy paper. Yvonne unfolded it and read.

Centered at the top of the paper was the royal crest. The document was recorded in an immaculate hand, a hand Yvonne knew well.

Greetings to my faithful friend and ally Mlle. Y. Schortmann

The text itself introduced a Grand Duchy official who volunteered to escort Yvonne as partial payment for previous and invaluable service. At the bottom appeared a signature she also recognized. Below was an official seal over the familiar blue and white crest.

She folded the paper and returned it to the formidable black man.

"I beg forgiveness," she said. "I am unable to replicate your name. This embarrasses me and, doubtless, will irritate you – or soon shall. May I call you David?"

"David?"

She related her experience the with the ABCs. The letter *D* came next.

"An ancient king," she explained. "You appear rather kingly to me."

He nodded.

"Twenty-eight generations removed from the King of Kings," he noted.

Yvonne was impressed.

"You're a believer?"

He nodded.

"You may call me David," he assured.

"You may call me – well, whatever you wish," she responded.

Yvonne had a bulkhead seat. Ahead of her was first class, beside her was a younger man seeking, she supposed, adventure. He had a tour book of Algeria which he paged through and, frequently, devoured entire segments. He was either French or could read French. He wasn't anxious to chat her up. He did speak infrequently, but the young man limited himself to the basics: excusing himself when squeezing by on the way to the necessary or apologizing if he inadvertently poked or prodded her. He did ask if she'd ever been to Algiers before. When she replied that she had not, their conversation ceased.

Dark Comedy

She spent much of her time leaning back and reviewing Klaus's letters. She kept them in order of receipt. When she re-read them, three or four times a month, she took them in order from first to last. She marveled at how his German improved with each communication. Somehow, he was learning (or being taught) his own language. Her capacious memory devoured these short treatises. During her flight, she delighted in reviewing each of his messages; many of which she recalled word for word.

David was on the flight, but she never saw him. Had she conducted a search, she would have found him easily enough. Security risks on a commercial airliner, however, are minimal. Doubtless, special seating was arranged to accommodate his mass. Doubtless, also, should she yell for help, he would be at her side in seconds.

When she saw him in Algiers, he'd shed his suit. He was dressed in work pants and a sport shirt. A thin jacket was casually thrown over one of his broad shoulders.

"Enjoy the flight?" she asked.

"Acceptable," he replied.

She sat on a bench. He stood just to the left and a foot or two to her front. No one else shared the bench. Few people ambled about; none approached. This was a good time to engage in conversation.

She asked if he had ever been to their destination country.

"No," he reported.

"What do you know about it?"

"I read the briefs. Corruption abounds. Crime is rampant because criminals band together into mobs or gangs. Government ministers get a cut of the action, so prosecutions are rare. Those miscreants who are not members of a gang seldom live long enough to see the inside of a jail. Kidnapping is the main source of foreign currency."

Yvonne shuddered. She'd assumed that the ABCs were dispatched to protect the "virtue" of three, foreign women. Given their destination, that threat seemed slight. As she reviewed her exchanges with the pompous captain, Yvonne was thankful for the ABCs. They may well have averted an ugly outrage.

As a victim of "abuse," she vowed to stay close to David. It was one thing to suffer at the behest of a parent; to suffer at the hands of strangers – who had no concern for her health – was beyond her worst imaginings.

"Don't trust anyone," Yve concluded.

"You can trust me, Sam."

"Sam?"

"You said I could call you whatever I wish. I wish to call you Sam."

"Then, Sam I am."

Likely he didn't get the literary illusion. It didn't matter. Chances were slim that he possessed a keen sense of humor. Even had he, David did not strike her as a person whose laugh was noteworthy.

"I will trust you," she affirmed, "because I trust your boss."

She did not see him on the next flight.

It was a smaller plane. There were fewer seats. Those available were more spacious than those on the larger aircraft. Yvonne had a window seat, but she spent most of her time napping. The person in the aisle seat was a black, matronly woman with grey streaks in her raven hair. She wore glasses and radiated a very serious demeanor. Beyond acknowledging each other's existence, they did not speak.

When they arrived, a slovenly attired man sat at passport control. Nearby were two uniformed thugs.

David came from nowhere to grip Yvonne's arm firmly.

"Let me go first," he ordered. "If there's a tussle, I want this passport business behind me."

He presented his passport. Yve was shocked to see it was American. It certainly caught the attention of Sloppy Joe. The uniformed official straightened up slightly.

"Business or pleasure?" He asked as only a uniformed official can ask.

"Strictly business," David replied.

He kept his voice down, but his massive body created a resonance that was impossible to ignore.

"What is the nature of your business?"

"I am escorting this young woman," he gestured toward her with a fist and thumb.

"What business?" the officious slob demanded.

"You must ask her," David reminded. "I'm her escort, not her travel agent."

The man didn't want to do it, but he didn't dare not do it. He opened the passport, stamped it extra hard with his rubber stamp, then scribbled his initials or something more sinister at the bottom of the red-ink stamp. David took the passport and buried it in the inside pocket of his jacket.

Yve waited for David to step aside. There was no room otherwise.

She presented her German passport. She kept her French passport out of sight; that document was a last resort measure.

"The nature of your business?" the man hissed like a snake.

"I'm here to return a German child to his parents."

The official's eyes danced. He, naturally, assumed that a healthy ransom had been paid. Perhaps, he'd be getting a raise soon.

"You have papers for this – person?"

"I do."

"Let me see them."

David cleared his throat. The official at the desk quaked. The two uniformed robots stiffened. This might get ugly. Judging from the bulk of the "escort," the uniformed goons might not fare well.

"The papers are for the child," David reminded with a tone and volume which echoed in the not-so-crowded concourse. "When the child appears, the papers will appear. Until then, his papers are moot."

The officious official's shoulders sagged a little. He may not know the meaning of the word *moot*. Yvonne could not help thinking that the man didn't know the meaning of a lot of words.

The slovenly "inspector," (perhaps related to a certain army captain) decided that it was not worth a possible "altercation." He stamped Yve's passport as if he intended to destroy it. He scribbled at the bottom of the red-ink seal and slammed it closed. He did not return it.

Let the white bitch pick it up herself.

He didn't say it, but his attitude was unmistakable.

Yvonne gently retrieved the document with all the calm of a seasoned pro.

"Thank you for your service, sir."

There was not so much as the slightest hint of sarcasm in her voice. The winning smile she awarded him was worthy of Charlotte who was well-paid to produce shoe-melting smiles on command.

The poor slob didn't know how to react. He wanted to be indignant – even belligerent, if given half an opportunity. The smile and her honeyed words, however, had him so flummoxed he was denied action. He remained paralyzed until Yve and David were underway.

She sighed.

"That was close," she whispered.

"My apologies," he replied. "I could have ruined everything. I really wanted to bop that punk. We'd both have been deported."

Yvonne thought about that for a moment. Deportation might have been the least of their worries if the government was as corrupt as David believed.

"Thank you, David. Please, keep yourself under control."

"I promise to do my very best, Ma'am."

"*Ma'am?*"

"I'm 'posed to be Merican," he replied.

"Where'd you get that passport?" she demanded.

"In America," he responded. "It's legitimate, I assure you. Having one opens a lot of doors. That's one of the reasons the Grand Duchy was anxious to hire me."

She fanned herself with her passport. It wasn't because of the heat, though it was very warm. She was, suddenly, frightened. This was far riskier than she'd bargained. Not that it made a difference. She *must* free Klaus from the clutches of these creatures. That was worth far more than any risk she must encounter.

Because their stay was to be short duration, both travelers traveled light. Yvonne had two changes of underthings, a spare pullover, and a pair of shorts. A small bottle of hand sanitizer and a tube of sunscreen rounded out her luggage. David's travel items were equally sparse.

The airport crew brought in the luggage on two flatbed carts. Each was human powered.

The passengers resembled a flock of sea birds crowding around a dead carcass. To avoid injury, Yve stood back. David (duty comes first) stayed close. By the time the new arrivals had hustled away with their treasures, there were only two back packs remaining.

A bus would leave in an hour to take them, approximately, halfway to their objective. They purchased two bottles of water each and lounged just outside the airport.

"I dread that road," Yve confided.

She recalled the bone-jarring ride from "base camp" to the mission at four or five miles an hour.

"Arrangements have been made," David promised.

He did not elaborate. Yve did not press.

The bus was crowded. Six hardy souls climbed onto the roof with their luggage. There were luggage rails atop the bus for passengers to cling to, but the relentless sun and the precarious twists and turns of the road placed the "fresh-air" travelers at high risk.

David did not sit at the back of the bus. The only exit was near the driver. If anyone wanted to force Yvonne off the bus, they'd be forced to get past him first.

Good luck!

He stood for a time. The bus stopped at every second or third corner to disgorge people. Few people got on, but the original passengers left in pairs, trios, and quartets until there was plenty of room for everyone to sit.

Once beyond the city boundary, the stops became infrequent. The sun was low in the sky and the evening chill introduced itself when David signaled to Yvonne. The bus squealed to a stop near a dilapidated collection of huts. They were constructed with red bricks made from the plentiful red clay surrounding the pitiful village.

"We must spend the night here," David announced.

Yvonne began to pout. Daylight was not going to make that rock-studded road any shorter. She'd hoped to arrive around dawn, grab Klaus, and be on her way home without delay.

David broke the news as gently as possible.

"Guerilla activity around here ceased five or six years ago, but traveling at night is too tempting. Since I'm charged with your safety, I won't move unless the odds are heavily in my favor."

He handled the arrangements. Yvonne suspected those arrangements were made ahead of time, and in another country. It took only a flash of his passport and a few scraps of paper money to conclude the formalities. There was no receipt, no registration form, no chit-chat. He was handed a key.

A key!

She glared at him. Her expression was NOT felicitous.

"Surprise."

Dark Comedy

She was about to cry. She was too tired to launch a verbal protest and too weak to fight him. Yvonne Schortmann was helpless.

"My mission is to protect you, Sam. If someone wants to carry you off for ransom – or recreation, he must deal with me. Not to put too fine a point on it, I don't want you out of my sight."

She gathered her wits and sent a hasty, if silent, prayer aloft. What was her alternative?

"Lodge a protest with the Luxembourg government when we get back," he suggested. "My instructions are clear: I'm to keep both you and the boy from harm. I take those instructions very, very seriously. Until the two of you are safe on European soil, I carry out the mission *my* way."

Yvonne, she told herself, you don't know what goes on in this country. David probably doesn't either.

It's easy to trust someone when there is no alternative. Yvonne left herself in God's hands.

The room was small. The interior wall was whitewashed. There was a wooden nightmare with a straw mattress, pillow-like "thing," and three wool blankets. Illumination was supplied by three battery-powered lanterns. However, wonder of wonders, there was indoor plumbing.

The sink and toilet were stained mud-clay red, but there was no lingering smell. There was cold and colder running, tinted water.

There was a woven mat on the creaking, wooden floor just inside the door. David took one of the blankets and let it drop onto the mat.

"I'll sleep here," he announced.

There were two small windows – little more than slits – high up on the facing walls. If someone forced an entrance during the night, they'd have to move David to get through the door.

Good luck with that!

Yve flopped down onto the bed, promising to rest her bones for a few minutes before tending to her evening hygiene. Her plan was foiled. She fell asleep almost at once.

QUESTING CONTINUED

Normally a light sleeper, Yvonne had to be prodded several times. She forced her eyes open to find a giant towering over her. She blinked several times before the moisture returned. When it did, she was forced to view her surroundings in a blur for an uncomfortably long while.

"Forgive my liberty, Sam," a deep, resonant voice pounded. "I removed your shoes after you fell asleep."

"Thank you," she said, automatically. "I guess I should get out of these clothes too."

"Most unwise," he replied. "It's morning. If we're to eat something before continuing, we must get a move on."

Yve shot up into a sitting position. Though she could not yet focus, there was no mistaking the laser-beam strands of light pouring through the slit windows.

"I slept through?" she asked incredulously.

"You were tired and stressed," her guardian angel responded. "There will be plenty of time to sleep when we get on the plane. If we don't hurry, we may miss the flight."

She groaned.

"Let me get dressed," she moaned.

"Mademoiselle's shoes are here," he indicated with one foot. "I shall be just outside when mademoiselle is ready."

She moaned. She didn't like that stuffy form or address.

"Sam, I am," she reminded.

"Please, do not tarry."

Dark Comedy

He retired magnanimously leaving the bathroom, such as it was, free of incumbrances and unwanted observation.

They adjourned to a community store, lunch counter, liquor store, hardware outlet, plumbing supply, and sundry items establishment. Using D-Marks, David purchased two brotchen (or items that looked like brotchen), a few slices of (goat?) cheese, and two French candy bars. Additionally, they purchased two more bottles (each) of water.

They were famished. Their victuals were largely consumed before they left the establishment.

"The road is back there," Yvonne reminded.

Her fear of missing a morning bus (if such amenities existed on the savannah) gripped her with passion.

"We shall leave the road for the peons," David replied. "The government had graciously allowed us a generous travel account."

Yvonne followed with impatience. That horrible stretch of rocks, ruts, ditches, and chasms was not getting any nearer by walking south. Had her trust in David been any less, she'd have yelled for him to retire to his future (and eternal) address. Had she the means, she'd have been tempted to help send him there.

"Yea of little faith," he sighed.

That sheathed her tongue, but her impatience continued to rampage.

After a few more frustrating minutes, Yve's attention was captured by the sun reflecting off metal. Seconds later, she recognized an airplane. It was tiny compared to the monsters which had brought them into the country, but the wings and tail fin could not be mistaken for anything other.

David called out at the top of his lungs. Yve suspected that anyone still in bed within a mile of them would no longer be asleep. As they drew closer, the unmistakable form of a man appeared from a small lean-to just ahead.

"Air Service Tonka?" David asked, moodily.

"You're lookin' at me," the thin, dark-skinned figure responded.

Yvonne beheld a partially emasculated figure in kaki pants and shirt. His shoes were ancient. The heels were nearly worn away.

David was not happy.

"This your aircraft?"

He pointed to the small machine at the crest of a small knoll.

"Right again."

David turned around and displayed the full fury in his eyes.

"This will not work," he informed *sotto voce*.

Yvonne continued to walk. She understood why they left the highway. She understood why David insisted that his plan was useless. Nevertheless, the promise of avoiding that never-ending road torture was too intense to be blunted by logic.

"The agreement was that you would fly us to the orphan mission and return here."

"So it was," the scruffy, aging man agreed. "Nobody told me a baby elephant was involved."

David looked as if he were about to explode.

"Can you do it?" Yvonne asked.

"Not if he's going," the man reported, pointing at David.

She turned and looked directly into the flaming eyes of her escort.

"I'm supposed to stay with you," he reminded.

"It's my neck," she reminded.

"Do you own this plane?" David demanded of the man.

There was pride in the peon's face. He could not resist smiling. The act displayed four empty spaces where teeth should have been. Coupled with the better part of a week's beard, the man looked like a barroom regular. The crow's feet, however, suggested he'd seen a lot of sky.

"Indeed, I do."

The implication was clear, even to Yvonne. He'd used this aircraft for drug smuggling and assisting anyone (including guerillas) who offered folding money. Kidnapping a white woman would bring a sizable ransom. Selling her at auction could bring even more. This man didn't pay the asking price of his machine by delivering diapers and groceries.

"We'll need a guarantee," Yvonne insisted.

"Ya hire me, ya gets yer money's worth," he assured immediately.

"Not good enough," David insisted.

The man shrugged. He had them over a barrel, and he knew it.

"Show him the money," Yve commanded.

Reluctantly, David complied.

"When the boy and I return, you get the money," she suggested.

"He could kidnap you or sell you," David warned. "He'd get a lot more than this."

"I keep my word," the man insisted.

"But to whom?" David demanded.

The man shrugged again.

It was another moment. When they came, Yvonne lost her identity and became a stranger to herself. She'd done it when she faced down that contemptable captain. Now, she would face off with a man who presented himself as ambivalent if not artificially casual.

"Show that Ami passport," she said.

It was not a request; it was a command.

David did not take the time to debate. He obeyed.

"If that boy and I do not show up in Frankfurt two days from now, you and this airplane may cease to exist. Did I just say something you don't understand?"

He was amazed at her take-charge attitude. It may have been that more than her threat that impressed him. The way he searched the depths of her celeste eyes suggested he was partially hypnotized.

"I understand," he acknowledged.

"You got a knife?" she asked.

She spoke in English just to make the American connection seem a bit more palpable.

David nodded.

"Give it me!"

There was little hesitation. Because David was such a large man, there existed plenty of space to secret items amid his loose-fitting clothes. The knife he produced was impressive. It had a blade twenty centimeters long. It was awkward for her to handle, but she gripped it firmly.

"I've been mauled by a man before, Mister Pilot," she reported. "It shall not happen again. I can use this on you, or I can use this on me. Either way, your only *guaranteed* payment is with this man here. You won't see any of it until the child and I return. Is my French clear enough? Would you like me to draw pictures?"

"I understand you very well," he replied after swallowing very hard.

"I don't like this," David protested. "I cannot do my job by waiting here."

"This is my decision," she asserted. "Would you like me to write a note absolving you of responsibility should this thing go wrong?"

"You can absolve me only with the government. You cannot absolve me from myself."

"I'm sorry, David. I really am. But if this thing fails, I'm not certain I want to live."

He nodded while thinking very hard.

"I understand you," he concluded. "I do not approve."

"Are you ready?" she demanded of Mr. Pilot.

He nodded and led the way to the aircraft.

"The first thing is to inspect," he told her.

Not only did he inspect the aircraft, he kept her appraised of what exactly he was doing. The pre-flight inspection took a little over five minutes. Clutching the knife, Yvonne climbed into the right seat and slammed the door shut beside her. Mr. Pilot mounted and fastened himself in. Realizing Yve could not use the seat belt with one hand, he slowly and very, very carefully, strapped her down. This was not a catch-and-release mechanism. As on the military transport earlier, the heavy canvass belt must be drawn through a buckle until tight. When the seatbelt was properly positioned, the buckle was pressed down. Serrated edges dug into the strap.

Mr. Pilot motioned for her to put on the headset draped over the control yoke to her front.

This she accomplished without releasing the knife.

"Can you hear me?" he asked once his headset was in place.

She nodded.

"We can talk with this. No need to shout. If you want to say something to me, press this key. Understand?"

She pressed the key.

"Understood."

He nodded.

"This, also, protects your hearing from the engine noise."

She nodded.

A moment later, the engine roared to life.

Yvonne knew she was taking a risk. She felt naked without the hulking David at her side. However, she was determined. She hadn't worked for years for this opportunity only to let it slip through her fingers. If she had to take chances, she would take them.

They bounced along the dirt surface kicking up billows of reddish dust. Mr. Pilot stomped on a pedal with his left foot and aimed the aircraft down a path of compacted dirt. She watched his every move. If something happened and she was forced to defend herself, Yvonne would have precious little time to learn how to fly.

Mr. Pilot pressed a knob slowly forward and the clumsy vehicle began to surge.

"I wouldn't double-cross you, you know," the man's voice crackled in her ear.

"Of course not," Yve agreed. "I'm just helping you avoid temptation."

"I fly things into the orphanage all the time."

"We're indebted to you," she replied.

She held so tightly onto the knife, her fingers and wrist began to ache.

They flew placidly for several minutes. They could have been flying anywhere, but she noticed the terrain just ahead. She recognized it. Though it was blemished with several bushes and a few small, scrawny trees, there could be no mistaking a lengthy runway creeping up on them. The bench on the far side had, once upon a time, played host to the arrogant captain and his troops. The shallow depression on the near side of the runway was where Yvonne, Charlotte, and Sarah, together with the ABCs were housed in heavy canvass tents. There was no sign that anyone had ever been there, but there could be no doubt that they were flying in the right direction.

Several minutes further on, she heard a demanding voice in her ears. Mr. Pilot pressed his button and replied in rapid Arabic – she assumed it was Arabic. He repeated his prepared speech twice. There were two clicks but no further voice communication.

Dark Comedy

Mr. Pilot flipped a switch.

"We're approaching the border," he informed. "The people over there get very nervous when there's air traffic up here. They know me. They just want anyone who might be listening to know that they are alert."

Yvonne nodded.

She maintained her grip on the knife.

Finally, she saw the orphanage. There were more buildings in the tiny village than she recalled. The mission itself hosted two buildings with substantial roofs that had not been there three years prior. One would be the new dormitory.

Mr. Pilot circled the compound once then began flying back the way they had come.

"Talk to me," Yve said with impatience.

"Just bleeding off some altitude," he explained. "When I turn back, we will be lined up with the runway."

Village people watched them closely. Children spilled out of the second new building (the school?). They danced and waved and carried on excitedly. Yve tried to guess which of the children was *hers*.

The landing was rough. In truth, the runway way was rough. The mission people, and some of the older children, had created the "airport" with minimal tools. Two weighted fifty-five-gallon drums were pushed back and forth several times to make it as near level and smooth as possible. It would do for Mr. Pilot's small aircraft, but anything larger might meet with a disastrous landing. If there was serious rain – well, there was seldom serious rain in the desert.

They bounced violently to near the end of the patch of dirt. Mr. Pilot stamped on a pedal and the aircraft spun around completely. He shut down the engine and a sudden peace descended. The ringing in Yvonne's ears remained for some while, but the throbbing of the motor ceased. That was enough to satiate her.

With the aircraft still, the heat shot up dramatically. Yvonne did not need to be instructed. She reached across herself with her left hand and pulled the release. When both doors were open, the temperature dropped, but it was still very hot.

Mr. Pilot had to help her with her seat belt. It was a simple operation, but unfamiliar. She was grateful for his assistance.

What to do with that damned knife?

Quickly, as she dismounted, she shoved the blade carefully down her leg along her hip bone. It was dangerous. She must walk delicately, but only the hilt was visible above her belt.

Nine children rushed toward them along with a pair of Mamas. Trailing far behind was a woman – Yve thought she was a woman, though she wore a man's desert attire.

"Valentin! Valentin!"

The children laughed and shouted the name. They surrounded Mr. Pilot and hugged him. One of the older girls kissed him on the cheek. He responded by hugging each in turn and greeting them with joyful platitudes. All the children – save one.

"Vonnie! Vonnie! Vonnie!"

He was so big! How he'd grown! When he hugged her, his arms coiled tightly around her waist – knife blade and all. The power of his hug amazed her. This child was well fed and well cared for.

"Is that you?" she asked in amazement. "Klaus! You're so – so big!"

He looked up at her and smiled. He was missing a couple of teeth, but he was beautiful.

"Klaus, I've come to take you away."

"I know," he wrinkled his nose.

"Are you excited?"

Dark Comedy

"I'm afraid," he admitted. "I want to be happy. You make me happy. I think I will not be so afraid with you."

She nearly lost it. A woman with a knife had no business drowning in tears.

"Let's hurry, Klaus. We have someone waiting for us, He will be anxious."

"Come," he said, taking her hand. "Let's go to Dr. Judy."

This was no time to ask questions. He led; she followed.

Doctor Judy: that sounded encouraging. Yve wasn't anxious to exercise her C of E bigotry again. Perhaps, this new person shared that persuasion. She offered a quick, silent prayer for help in stifling her base instincts.

Dr. Judy, indeed, wore a collar. She was youngish – as "youngish" as one can look after a few weeks or several months in this insalubrious environment. Yvonne bit her tongue. She'd ask no questions and hoped Dr. Judy would not volunteer anything which might create friction. Even if it did, Yve could not afford to make a new enemy.

Think of Klaus she told herself. *Don't forget Klaus – not for a moment!*

"Miss Schortmann, I'm very happy to meet you at last. Klaus cannot allow the sun to set without his mentioning you several times."

American! Her French was drenched in that unmistakable accent.

The woman extended her hand as if her speech wasn't American enough. Yve seized it and experienced a pleasant handshake.

"You're in charge here?"

The woman did not gush about Yvonne speaking English. That scored her many points.

"For the moment. This is my trial by fire. I'm recently ordained. Until I'm given an assignment, I was placed here. Before called by our Savior, I was a doctor in general practice."

She didn't seem old enough. However, a GP in this wilderness would be – well, a God send.

"Things have improved since I was here," Yvonne said, eager to avoid getting bogged down in an ecclesiastical discussion.

Dr. Judy put her hand on Klaus's shoulder.

"Gather your things, dear. You will be leaving us soon."

The boy nodded and scurried off.

"I was told of your mission," the doctor responded. "The funds you and the others helped to generate have been put to good use. We have plenty of room in the dormitory. We have built up a collection of books and hope to establish a library in the dorm. We plan to build a second dormitory so we can segregate the boys and the girls. However, as you may have noticed, we don't have many children here. Apparently, the caravans don't dump their unwanted children anymore. At least, not here. Until there is another influx, we have put many things on hold. Please, excuse me for going on so, but the money you helped raise is precious. Thank you."

"I – we were – *are* proud to be of service, doctor."

"I'd offer you and Monsieur Ponce some refreshment, but we're tightening our belts a bit. The next supply truck isn't due for three more weeks."

"If I'd known, we could have arranged to bring something."

The doctor smiled. She was rather handsome when she smiled.

"M. Ponce is our life saver," she explained. "He always responds to our emergency calls. If we are in dire need of anything, we radio him, and he flies it in for us – usually the next day."

"Good to know," Yvonne nodded.

Indeed, it was good to know.

"We will miss Klaus very much, but we're very happy for him."

As if on cue, Klaus padded through the dust to rejoin them. He carried a small, well-worn, plastic bag. Once upon a time, it displayed a corporate logo. All that remained were disarticulated red smears.

Dark Comedy

"That's all your taking?" Dr. Judy quizzed.

"Everything I need," he nodded with a smile. "My other under pants and Vonnie's letters."

"Toothbrush?" Yve asked, recalling that he always boasted of brushing twice a day.

He grinned, as broadly as his missing teeth allowed, and pulled open his shirt just enough to display a toothbrush attached to a string around his neck.

Dr. Judy's smile mirrored the young boy's. She, however, had a full complement of teeth.

"Come to my office, please. There are papers to sign."

She saw the "hospital" on the way. There were two proper beds (both empty) and two proper medical cabinets, one of which was padlocked. The area was clean, the bedding fresh and clean under a protective layer of clear plastic. This, even more than the new dormitory, warmed her considerably. She made a mental note to tell Charlotte how the "pigsty," which had so offended her and was the cause of her near exhaustion, had been reduced to a horrible memory.

Prior to departure, Yvonne was introduced to the other children. They bowed or curtsied and recited the brief sentence or two they'd carefully rehearsed, undoubtedly under the tutelage of one of the Mamas. Yve curtsied as well in responding to this unexpected but welcome display. She recognized two of the girls. The other orphans were unknown to her. Sadly, two of the children she'd met on her previous visit, had "passed on:" one died of disease; the second from a freak accident. Their "resting place" was clearly marked by crosses, crafted by professionals and flown in by M. Ponce (Mr. Pilot).

During the paperwork, Yvonne was hampered slightly. Klaus insisted on holding her left hand. When she acknowledged the other children, as they "passed in review" Klaus maintained a firm hold on Yve's hand.

"I may have misjudged you, Mr. Ponce," she said in English, so Klaus needn't be privy. "The doctor swears by you and praises the assistance you have performed on behalf of this place. However, I still have a knife. There is a precious cargo in that back seat. I will protect him to my last breath."

He said nothing, but his visage communicated his understanding quite sufficiently.

Despite everything, Yvonne knew he owned his own plane. Airplanes are expensive. Hauling cargo and ferrying children to hospital does not earn the kind of money required for ownership of an aircraft and the fuel to use it.

Klaus was excited to experience his first airplane ride. However, the moment they were in the air, he leaned forward and took Yve's hand again – her non-knife wielding hand.

Dark Comedy

FIRST PETER 2:13

Pilot Ponce made a slow descent over the Little Village that struggled to become a city. There were three vehicles lined up on the eastbound shoulder of the road. One had a rack of lights which, blissfully, were not flashing. Klaus, still in awe at the magic of wings, whimpered quietly. He'd never looked down on the earth from above prior to that day – not that he recalled. As the earth grew nearer, he felt helpless. Were he the pilot, he would soar above the cursed world until the cloak of night hid it away.

"Did you tell those people about us?" Yve challenged.

The emphasis she placed on *those people* is worthy of an entire treatise.

"You're plugged into com," the pilot responded. "You've heard everything."

He'd not said a word since takeoff.

Klaus, despite the awkwardness of the posture involved, kept hold of Yvonne's hand. She squeezed it reassuringly.

Whatever it takes, she reminded herself. *For Klaus, I will do whatever it takes.*

The landing was punctuated by some teeth rattling. The lumps and dips in the "airport's" hastily leveled and seldom maintained runway were not for the timid. Pilot Ponce swung the craft around toward his homemade tie-down area. Upon reaching his destination, he muscled the aircraft around again until it faced the runway. He shut down the engine.

Yvonne, having mastered the art of disengaging the seat "restraint," undid herself, opened the door until it caught the wing-mounted latch, and dismounted. She reached back and freed Klaus. She assisted him in exiting. Predictably, once the young boy was free of restraint, he clutched his benefactor's hand anew.

David was exactly where he'd been left. He hadn't moved an inch. Perhaps, he was punishing himself for not following orders. It was his job to protect Yvonne Schortmann. To protect her, he must be with her every moment. Circumstances demanded that they be separated for hours. That was a serious breach of orders and worthy of severe disciplinary action. Any punishment he received would be inconsequential to the punishment he'd mete out for himself.

The committee of officials approached. There were eight in the mob; two wore uniforms. They were in no hurry. Their prey had few options. If they attempted to flee, an army of police and military personnel would round them up quickly and whatever awaited them would be compounded exponentially.

"Where's my knife?" David demanded brusquely.

Yvonne patted her right hip.

"Give it to me," he ordered. "Make certain they see it."

Klaus appeared oblivious. It mattered not if Yvonne had a no-nonsense knife. She could spit fire, it wouldn't matter a nit; she was his trusted friend.

"Mlle. Schortmann, I presume."

God, give me strength she thought. Some black man in a black suit was trying to be funny. He held all the cards. Yve didn't know what game they were playing. Unfortunately, she held no cards.

"We understand you want to remove this boy from the country," the officious punk continued when she refused to reply. "You, of course, have papers."

David took two steps to separate himself from the others in his party. He had the immediate and complete attention of three men, the two in uniform and another black man in a black suit. It was clear that the man with the knife was their excuse for escorting their officious punk.

"I, of course, have papers," Yve mimicked.

Dark Comedy

"May I see them – please."

The appended word, when it came, was soaked in sarcasm and authoritarianism.

Yvonne needed both hands. Klaus, not to be deprived of her touch, leaned into her and put his arm around her waist. She produced the required papers, ensconced in an official-looking envelope. She held them up. The pretentious phony extended his hand.

"You asked to see them," she reminded.

"May I examine them?"

If his voice was syrup, it would come out thick and smooth. She held them out. The government goon wouldn't deign to fetch them. He signaled to a stooge who stepped forward and seized them. It took almost three steps to transfer them to the petulant man with illusions of grandeur.

He studied them for longer than necessary. She knew, from his demeanor, that the official language, signatures, stamps, signatures, endorsements, and more signatures were all legitimate and in order. Like the heathen studying the Bible, however, the rude prig was looking for loopholes.

"These might do," he concluded at last. "However, passport control can be so picayune about such as this. It might behoove you to procure a writ of export. Such is often required in the movement of goods, but it also applies to people – unless, of course, the child has a passport."

Yvonne kept her temper by some miracle.

"You know he does not," she responded. "Those papers were issued *in lieu* of a passport."

"Even so, I highly recommend a writ of export."

David made a noise. When Yve turned to investigate, the big man gestured for her to come near. She took Klaus by the hand and took him with her.

"It's a shakedown," David hissed.

"Whatever it takes," Yvonne hissed in return.

"If we don't have what they ask?"

"Then we barter. Whatever it takes, David. I want Klaus out of this place. I want him out now!"

David made another sound. It was soft, but it communicated reticence.

"Whatever it takes!" she reiterated.

David did nothing. He said nothing.

"How do we get such a writ?"

The group of four, that is, the brains of the robber band had a quick conference. It was hushed and in a regional language.

"We can issue such a writ."

"How did I know that?" she muttered.

Then, she addressed the robber band.

"How much?"

There followed another hasty conference.

"One thousand U.S. dollars or four thousand D-Marks."

Yvonne realized that hesitation would doom them.

"For that, we must request an international money transfer. I must contact the American Council-General in _____ so he can arrange it. Klaus has no country and no passport, so someone from the nearest Swiss diplomatic office must be brought in. That will take time – perhaps months. Meanwhile, the governments of Germany and Luxembourg are expecting our return this week. When we fail to do so, questions will be asked."

Dark Comedy

The bullies were shaken. All they wanted was easy money. How did they expect to split a thousand miserable dollars amongst the eight of them? It hardly seemed worth the effort. Suddenly, a nice meal and a night on the town looked as if it would go up the spout. In its place, they might well instigate an international incident. Those higher up in the food chain might not be pleased about that. The county's international reputation was taking a beating. This "situation" might encourage other nations to "take measures." If measures were taken, eight roadside robbers might catch something they weren't chasing.

The next hurried conference lasted two minutes or longer.

"Two thousand D-Marks."

There was no camouflage this time. This was a clear extortion demand.

"Do we have it?"

"Yes," David announced through clinched teeth.

"Whatever it takes, David. Whatever it takes."

He grunted. He didn't like it, but he agreed.

"You prepare the writ," Yvonne announced. "Cash on delivery."

Two of the flunkies were dispatched to the vehicle for the proper forms.

"Monsieur Ponce, we owe you money also. We seem to be in a bind here. Will you take a check on a German *Sparkasse*. It's my personal account. The funds are there, I assure you."

He swallowed hard. This was taking a chance, but Yvonne Schortmann had come into a barbarous country to fetch Klaus. That spoke volumes.

"I trust you," he concluded

I must make certain his trust in me is not misplaced she vowed. This would not be easy. She'd be feeding two people. If she got down on her knees and begged, Family Schulz might advance her some money. The idea frightened her, but . . . Whatever it takes!

What a farrago!

Here was a collection of common thieves, pretending to be government functionaries – or, likely, they were government functionaries pretending to be common thieves – and they wanted to make a Mack Sennett comedy of their inflated self-importance. They brought out one of the smaller vehicles and used the hood as a podium behind which the clown-in-chief could preside. His gang fumbled with a sheaf of papers and tripped over themselves – and everything else available – to make a major production of what should have been a simple task.

The chief executive of this highway robbery barked orders and arranged the players to his liking. Square leg, gully, and mid-on were assigned to act as "witnesses." When his team was properly arrayed, the deal maker designated himself the bowler.

He produced a long sheet of paper folded thrice with unerring precision. He scribbled something at the top of the document and then turned it over to expose the last portion. He ordered Yvonne and her hand holder to approach the wicket – ah, podium. He pointed to a line and had her print her name. In the next indicated spot, she was to print Klaus's name.

Yve was, momentarily, flummoxed. The boy knew his identity only by his first name. He either didn't know or could not remember his surname. That was part of his tragedy. This was no time for Yvonne to balk. With only minor hesitation she printed Klaus Schortmann.

The bowler – uhm, toastmaster – complemented her on her excellent calligraphy and pronounced, aloud, that she'd been a model scholar.

"Yvonne Schortmann," he barked. "In the presence of these witnesses, you will state, so there will be no mistake, that this young man is the subject of export."

Yve cleared her throat.

"I so state."

The bowler – uhm, head gang member – frowned.

"Include his name," he whispered only softly enough for anyone within several dozen meters to hear.

"Klaus – Short – mann."

Dark Comedy

There was a catch in her throat which she could not explain and refused to waste time contemplating.

"Klaus Schortmann: In the presence of these witnesses, you will state, so there will be no mistake, you wish to export with this person."

She coached him in his French. He mangled the pronunciation repeatedly before he could recite the words well enough to be identified.

"I state I willingly export with Yve – Yve –onne Schortmann."

"Sign your name," he ordered.

Yve took the pen and signed.

"Sign your name," he ordered little Klaus in such a way that Yve wanted to clout him.

He did his best. His cursive was fair for an eight-year-old boy, but the ink smeared slightly. Klaus and ink hadn't been properly introduced.

"The witnesses will come forward and sign."

They did; the three unwise men, free from any blemish of respectable, civil service conduct.

The presiding phony cleared his throat.

"The money."

This time he did whisper. Roger Ripoff, for whatever reason, was ashamed to mention (aloud) the purpose of this fraudulent ceremony.

David stepped forward. He would not sully his hands by dealing with the Thief-in-Chief. He counted out the money for Yvonne who laid twenty new one-hundred-mark bills atop the document. The sophomoric dolt greedily swept up his winnings and counted the bills with a satisfied grin.

He slipped the money into the inside pocket of his jacket as if to announce *you didn't see me do that*. He produced a cumbersome seal from – somewhere. With great care, he seeded it near the bottom of the document and crimped the paper expertly. He set the implement aside and took up the pen. He signed and wrote out a seven-digit number.

The curtain came down on the farce. He refolded the document and treated it as if it was the finest Chantilly lace.

"If you have any problems at passport control, just produce this document."

"For two thousand marks, there *will not* be problems," the huge man with the long knife announced.

The presiding thief winced slightly. It was clear that if he and his companions were detained for any reason, a raging bull would be looking for a certain government flunky. He wasn't very afraid, however. He knew there would be no problems. However, he knew the location of secret, underground, hiding places should he require one.

Yvonne disengaged from Klaus long enough to examine the document they'd paid two thousand Dream Makers to obtain. It was written in a language with which she was completely unfamiliar. Could it be a tribal language? There wasn't a word in French, English or German.

She looked down at Klaus. He looked up at her.

"Ever seen anything like this before?"

He shook his head and reached for her hand. The child that had gotten so deeply under Yve's skin was suddenly surrounded by a world he knew only from pictures. He was nervous and excited. He was also afraid. There was one thing that guaranteed security: Yvonne. The only tangible promise he had for happiness was Yvonne. Holding onto her hand made the unfamiliar and inexplicable tolerable.

Were she the principal character in this drama, Yve would have torn up the document and pounded the scraps into the dirt and dust of a country she had grown to hate. She was not, however, a free agent. She was Klaus's life preserver. If they were denied exit, the squiggles and lines on this recycled vegetable bag might prove to be their get-out-of-jail card.

She was afraid to fold it or to roll it into a cylinder. She opened her backpack and carefully shoved it in. Upon completion of her task, she turned to find her knife-wielding bodyguard. He'd been in conference with Mr. Ponce. Business was just concluding. Yve noticed a tidy fold of green bills disappearing in the right front pocket of the pilot's trousers.

"He offered to fly you two to the airport," he reported. "He was willing to attempt it with us all, but it isn't worth the risk."

The human hulk put the fear of the Lord in anyone casting malevolent eyes at Yvonne or Klaus, but he, also, limited their options. David had violated his standing orders once; he refused to take further risks.

"You gave him dollars? I told him I'd write a check."

"As long as it remains possible, we pay as we go."

"This isn't right!"

She stood and, instinctively, offered her hand to the little traveler.

"This was my doing," she proceeded. "I'm spending Lux-government money like I'm on a binge. It will take years for me to pay it all back."

"I doubt the government will seek redress. If it does, it will insist the German government come across. The boy is theirs."

"How do we know? He could be Austrian or Sudeten. He might be Brazilian for that matter. A parrot can learn to speak German. That's hardly proof of citizenship."

"Don't argue with me," he insisted. "I'm on your side."

They decided to go to the local version of the bar and grill, that refuge where they bought their breakfast. They could eat and rehydrate. They could get bus information.

They got much more.

The villagers were in a panic when the "black cars" rolled into their midst. Government cars brought government officials. Government officials brought trouble and torment. Sometimes, they brought murder. The local population was thrilled that the gangsters had gone away without stealing everything in sight and, just for jollies, taking three or four of the "usual suspects" with them. No matter who the big man was, or his sour-faced woman with the curious eyes, or their little brat; the government goons had confronted them and left without extracting a pound of flesh. Were there a committee in place, David, Yve, and Klaus would have been nominated for humanitarians of the century.

"They need transportation to the airport," someone announced.

There followed a serious commotion as to which person would provide the local heroes with a ride to the airport. It nearly turned violent. The owner/proprietor of the establishment called for order and suggested they settle the matter by drawing lots. Anyone with a vehicle capable of driving four people (David counted as two) would print their names on a slip of paper and place it in a hat. Someone who owned no vehicle would draw the "winner."

The matter was quickly and amicably settled. The old-timer who won announced that he had to fuel up. He promised to return in half an hour or less.

As for refreshments – they were on the house. In the estimation of the locals, the trio had saved the community from a looting frenzy. To donate snacks and drinks for three people was far preferable to losing everything.

Yvonne was about to suggest that, but for them, the government goons never would have interrupted their lives and caused panic. She balked. This might be another example of divine intervention. If so, she risked serious consequences for interceding.

"How'd you get that knife into the country?" she asked David while stepping into the bed of a half-century-old pickup.

"I tell you; you tell somebody else; then, I have to kill you," he replied.

He was stoic, but she did not take his threat as genuine. The message, however, was received; there are secrets, and secrets must be kept.

The trip was bumpy, but not anything near what Yvonne had experienced before. The blue smoke, which was expelled at certain intervals, however, caused her concern. Should the relic break down, they'd be worse off than before. Klaus, however, was frightened. He wasn't satisfied with Yve's hand. He snuggled up against her and held onto her. He closed his eyes and waited for the terror to abate. Apparently, it did. After a half-hour, Yvonne felt his drool soaking through her shirt. When his arms no longer threatened to squeeze her breathless, she knew he was asleep.

Dark Comedy

HOME: THE TRIALS

Open tickets are a lifesaver. They are, also, merciless.

David did the leg work. Yvonne and Klaus remained within his line of sight while avoiding becoming a hazard to traffic. When the kinks collected during their ride into the city finally ceased their discomfort, the urge to sit down became merciless.

"Sit on the floor," Yve advised.

Klaus was nonplussed. To sit required releasing Yvonne's comforting hand. He compromised by sitting Indian style with one arm wrapped around one of her legs. This guaranteed a plethora of curious stares.

It took several minutes, which seemed like several hours.

"The plane to Casablanca boards in an hour," David informed. "We must fly to Tunis. From there, we take the red eye to Frankfurt."

Yvonne was anxious to get out of this God-forsaken country, but she nearly burst into tears at the thought of the many hours ahead. Klaus, who had flown in only one airplane, had not a hint of what awaited. He was with Yvonne. So long as he was with her, he could face any eventuality.

Yve took a deep breath to mask both a squelch and a sob.

"How do you plan to get that knife through security?"

The question was inane, but she had to speak to some purpose or initiate a fit of crying.

"I tell you; you tell "

"I know the routine," she interrupted. "Can we find something to eat?"

She was regaining control. Her emotional breakdown was successfully surmounted.

She had no intention of producing their two-thousand-mark get-out-of-purgatory-free card unless circumstances forced her hand. Other than a sneer from the document inspector, there was no problem. He was satisfied with the German certificate stating the boy, Klaus (no surname) was classified a refugee and subject to German law upon arrival.

He didn't sneer at David.

"Two thousand marks for a desk blotter," she muttered.

"If we hadn't paid the bribe, those bullies might have arranged to keep us in the country," David reminded. "As squalid and uncomfortable as this place is, imagine what the inside of their jail is like."

Yvonne didn't want to think about it.

Whatever it takes!

That was her idea. She was responsible.

Her subsequent idea was an obligation to make restitution. Yve wouldn't mention this because David was sure to scold her. He'd argue that he was supplied with emergency funds and, as an agent of the government, he held the power of dispersal. Regardless, it would remain a kidney stone in her brain until reparation removed it.

"What can you tell me about your parents?" she asked.

This was not Yvonne. She would never be so bold as to ask such a brutal question. Her fatigue and disparagement, however, had scrambled her brain.

"Yelling," Klaus responded. "A lot of yelling. I'd just lay down and be small until it stopped."

Yvonne allowed Klause to sit at the window to Casablanca. He was the in-flight entertainment. There wasn't a cloud that went unnoticed, nor a hill, city, village, or lake.

Up from her despondency she came. The boy's excitement buoyed her spirits.

This will work! She told herself.

Yvonne had no idea what *this* was. There existed a myriad of obstacles ahead: Klaus would have to attend remedial school until his German and math were up to par; he'd need a doctor and a dentist; he'd need a last name and a passport; he'd need clothes and a place to store them; he'd need a bed; he'd require patience and understanding. His love for Yvonne was palpable, but Yve wondered if her love was equal to his. Her patience and understanding were certain to be tested – she was no longer working with skilled women who shared a sense of purpose. She would be trapped in a small apartment with a bundle of mischief and energy.

Did she have the required stamina?

Yvonne's future would shine far brighter if the little urchin had not burrowed into her heart. Unfortunately, she realized she couldn't leave him where he was. At least, Yve and Klaus together had a future and the opportunity to exercise considerable control over it.

"Klaus, that first day. Do you remember? You came over and gave me a hug. Why did you do that?"

The boy thought this query was worthy enough to turn away from the window. He looked directly into Yvonne's eyes.

"You looked so scared," he said. "I didn't want you to be scared."

It would take a while to digest this. She pulled on the handle and reclined in her seat.

Was she scared? She didn't recall being scared. Even if she had been, that did not explain why Klaus insisted on being her constant companion. She had many more questions to ask, but she thought it was better to deal with them individually and over time.

Perhaps, she was scared that first day. What she saw of the pitiful orphanage was enough to scare anyone. She remembered being revolted and concerned, but scared …? Klaus was not yet six when he was "dumped" into that miserable existence. He survived long enough to be rescued.

If she was scared during their first meeting, she was petrified now.

How can I do this?

Lord, I need help. I need more help than ever.

For most of her years, Yvonne had stumbled and fallen and stumbled and fallen again. Without divine aid, she'd probably be homeless. Everything she was and everything she had came from a power beyond her understanding. She had faith. She knew that God would be with Klaus always. He would help them both. The problem was that Yve had little trust in herself. If she was used as an agent in managing Klaus, would she understand Him when He called upon her to do His will? Likely, she'd be too obtuse to understand. How could she obey Him if she couldn't understand?

She was even more petrified than before. To fail herself was bad enough, but to ruin Klaus would be unforgivable.

SISYPHUS

There are precious few trials this side of the grave as that of being stranded in the Tunis airport for several hours. The few amenities available were shuttered and locked. The pangs of hunger and the weakness from fatigue tortured them as they waited for their flight, under the watchful eyes of resentful security personnel. The only succor possible, under such a cloud, lay in the hope they would die from hunger and exhaustion in more familiar surroundings.

Klaus was the lucky one. Sleep buried the demands of his stomach. His head used Yve's left thigh as a pillow. When he stirred, the alert woman freed her left arm for instant use should he roll over. There were several false alarms, but the child had yet to take a tumble.

David sat a few meters across from them. He eschewed slumber. The man appeared to have an inexhaustible supply of energy. All his attention was fixed on the study of the security contingent who were equally wary of him. Only if a fellow stranded passenger strayed too near did the hulking David change his focus.

Is this part of my punishment? Yvonne asked herself. She'd been both haughty and abrasive during their mission. Did these sins constitute the grounds for the torture, hunger and lack of sleep?

Whatever it takes!

Brave words when anger and resentment ruled. When fatigue and hunger stood watch, the brave battle cry was impossible to rouse.

"Whatever you're being paid, it isn't enough."

Yvonne spoke in a normal voice. There was little noise, and David was only three meters distant.

"I shouldn't be paid at all," he moaned.

"Nothing happened," she reminded.

"I was assigned to stay with you."

"That wasn't possible in that tiny plane."

"I should have stopped you," he stated without emotion. "Maybe, we could have hired a larger plane. Maybe, we should have hired a vehicle and driven up there."

Yvonne sighed.

"David, I'll not tell a soul."

"You don't have to," he responded, equally devoid of emotion. "*I will remember.*"

This was hopeless. She was so eager to avoid traversing a road where axels go to die that she placed a friend into an untenable position. He could have ordered her not to take the plane, but he lacked official authority. He could have physically restrained her – thankful she was that he hadn't attempted that. She'd have been powerless to escape his meaty hands and his mighty muscle and sinew. She'd have fought – not out of pride but from frustration. She might have put up enough of a fight that he would resort to force and, possibly, break something, such as an arm or a spine.

"I'm sorry."

It was all she could say. It was nothing. It was an empty platitude.

"David, I am, genuinely, sorry. It's my fault. I was at that point where I could only think of Klaus. If I'd thought of myself – or *you* – but that's me, really. I focus on something, and I don't consider anything else."

He cast a glance at her before returning to the suspicious looking security guards who constantly patrolled in pairs.

"I wanted to be a nun."

His eyes snapped back at her but only for a moment.

"That's what I wanted more than anything! I never thought, until almost too late, of anyone or anything else. I even lied – well, not saying – something – that must be said. That's as good as a lie. No, it isn't as good, it *is* a lie."

Klaus selected that moment to move. Yvonne restrained him so gently, he never woke. Only when she was satisfied he was out of danger did she continue.

"Then, I got roped into that charity – publicity – *thing*. I met Klaus. After that, I could think of almost nothing else. It's my irrational, unholy passion for this boy that drove me."

"Would you have knifed that pilot?"

This was so immediate and point blank. She blinked.

"I – really think – I would have murdered the man. I think the rage and frustration –"

He let her stew for a while. For a moment, he thought she was about to cry.

"Without pilot – you could have been killed."

She nodded.

"I could only think of this kid," she said, indicating the boy whose head was on her leg. "If I couldn't get him out of that place – my dying wouldn't matter. I – I – I would have been the worst nun in the history of the church."

David sat up and took a long deep breath. After letting it out, he leaned forward.

"To the worst nun in history from the worst security man in history, I know *exactly* how you feel. *Exactly*."

There was nothing more to say. Ergo, they said nothing.

They kept vigil.

Thankfully, breakfast was served on the Frankfurt flight. It was pleasing but not very filling. As they deplaned, Klaus reported he was hungry. More likely, he was *still* hungry.

Where was David when the announcement was made? As always, he was seated near the rear of the aircraft and remained inconspicuous (as if a man of such stature could be inconspicuous) and incommunicado.

Yvonne produced the documentation issued by the BRD to allow Klaus through passport control. As predicted, and promised by the issuing agency, both Yvonne and Klaus were segregated from the throng and escorted to a waiting room. There was an armed guard at the only entrance and exit. Drawing the obvious conclusion, the pair examined their surroundings. There were three couches, four chairs (one at each corner), and a wall-mounted TV.

The TV was tuned to the ARD, but the sound was muted. There were no visible controls, so changing channels or volume was not in the power of the detainees.

"It's early," Yvonne reminded her ward. "We may be here a while."

He said nothing, but he took her hand. His tacit communication was *I can stand it, if you can.* They sat together on the couch, their meager luggage at their feet.

Twenty minutes later, David appeared. He brought a hamburger and fries (*not* Wimpey's) for Klaus. Yvonne was treated to coffee (black) and a sweet roll.

"Thank you. Are you being detained?"

He shook his head.

"Thank you, David. I hope we shall meet again."

He made a dismissive noise.

"I'm not leaving here until you two are released."

"Who knows how long that will take?"

Dark Comedy

"I left you in the lurch once," he reminded. "I'll not do it again. With my papers, I can come and go. I will be your messenger with the outside world."

She smiled her thanks, but she thought he was behaving foolishly.

"This is soooooooo good!" Klaus exclaimed. "What is it?"

"It's a hamburger, Klaus," Yvonne informed. "German name, but an American invention."

"Super! And these things?"

"*Pomme frites*," she responded.

She didn't feel the urge to explain. He'd lived with the French language long enough to know what a potato was, even if he'd never seen or tasted one.

The boy was as happy as she'd ever seen him. That warmed her. So did the coffee. Despite the hole in her stomach, the sweet roll did not appeal. She set it aside. If Klaus wanted it, he could have it anon.

"I never had the chance to complement you on your German," she announced. "It had improved greatly. Who helped you?"

"Dr. Judy," he replied between gulps.

"She's German? She talked like an Ami."

"I don't know. She would teach me German while the others were having French lessons. She's a very nice woman."

"I'm sorry I didn't have time to get to know her. I'm partial to nice people."

This last was aimed at David who nodded his understanding. They'd both had their fill of corrupt people who are legends only in their own perverted minds.

"She was nice," Klaus seconded. "Dr. Judy is a very nice lady, but not so near as nice as you."

Yvonne was in the process of sipping her coffee. For an instant, she was in danger of it going down the wrong pipe. As much as she treasured the plaudit, she considered it suspect. The interactions she'd had with Klaus thus far seemed so pedestrian.

"Thank you, Klaus," she responded. "I'm honored. I hope I can maintain my standing."

She doubted he understood. It wasn't important; she was addressing herself.

"I hope I can have another hamburger soon," he crowed.

"Man does not live by hamburger alone," Yve cautioned.

Klaus smiled up at her. He, a young child, understood the allusion. He puffed up with pride.

"*There's no fear in love*," he repeated with delight. "That's Peter."

"I know," she responded. "I'm surprised that you knew."

"Dr. Judy," he smiled. "We didn't have any English books, so we read the Bible."

Obviously, there was much more than reading going on. She felt a sharp stab of regret that she didn't have the time – or inclination – to get to know this charitable woman who attended Klaus so wonderfully. She made a mental note: no matter what lay ahead, Yvonne must construct a long message of thanks for Dr. Judy's remarkable tutelage of the young boy.

"Are you in fear, Klaus?"

She had to ask.

"Not as long as you are with me."

Yvonne and David exchanged a peculiar glance.

Despite the modest size of the room, there were two "rest" rooms and a drinking fountain. When he fetched fast food, David eschewed soda water. Klaus might have found it unpleasant. Regardless, David considered it unhealthy. Klaus might enjoy the experience of drinking water that needn't be boiled prior to drinking. He further suspected he'd enjoy acquiring water at the push of a button. The suspicions were justified; Klaus enjoyed the treasure of water on command.

It was nearly three hours before the geese arrived. There were three government men in expensive suits to "honor" the non-virgin Yvonne and "her child." They were not bearing gifts.

"Frau Schortmann?"

She didn't dare correct them. That might initiate procedures best left alone.

"Klaus?"

He nodded his head, but he was suspicious. He didn't know these men.

"And you are?"

Oh, it was pure syrup. However, the expression on the man's face made clear his displeasure with David's presence.

David identified himself and his mission.

"We are in a secure facility," the spokesmen for the crew announced. "It would be more *efficient* if you were not here."

Instantly, David's hackles were up. These men mightn't be as corrupt as the bullies they'd left in Africa, but they were equally officious and pretentious.

"I don't work for you," he reminded, keeping a civil tone. "I work for the Grand Duke."

This surprised and irked the leader of the pack. There were several options for breaking the impasse, but they all required time, phone consultations, and a flurry of diplomatic silly. The man who *thought* he was in charge made a command decision. He ignored David.

"You have the necessary papers?"

Yve couldn't resist. After vowing to be civil, she slipped. Travel weary and fed up with bureaucratic flummery, she was unable to restrain herself. She dug through her pouch and produced the required documents.

"If these papers could not keep us from detention, how necessary can they be?"

The man braced. He wasn't looking for trouble, but he suspected he'd found it. He did not want a confrontation, however.

"This is an extraordinary case," he reminded. "Certain procedures must be observed."

Yve withheld comment and surrendered the Foreign Ministry documents. The man examined them.

"Klaus, would you go with this gentleman? He will take your fingerprints."

"I don't want to leave," he responded.

"You needn't leave the room, young man. However, we don't want ink all over everyone. It's much easier if we have a little room."

"It's okay, Klaus," Yve assure. "David and I are right here."

He bounced off his perch next to Yvonne and followed the designated man to a nearby coffee table.

"You've done this before, right?" The finger-print man asked.

Yve's heart skipped a beat. If he gave the wrong answer, they'd be back to square one.

"Sure," he affirmed. "Dr. Judy took them. She told me I'd have to do it again."

I really must get to know this Dr. Judy, Yvonne thought. *She must be remarkable.*

"Have you managed to find any record of his prints?" she asked.

That was out of bounds. They both knew that. However, the well-togged official was not the sanctimonious prig she'd mistaken him for.

"No," he said, *sotto voce*. "If we knew in what city he was born, we'd have a chance."

"I wish I could help."

That was one wish she genuinely wanted to come true.

"Meanwhile, he will need official identification. What surname does he use?"

"None that I know of," Yve said.

"We used the name Schortmann to get him out of *that* country." David injected.

He, obviously, used the emphasized word in a highly derogatory manner.

"Do you intend to adopt?" the man asked, point blank.

Hitherto, she'd never given it a thought.

"If his parents are still alive – but if they abandoned him – I'm sorry. I haven't thought that far ahead. I just wanted him in his own country."

"Will he live with you?"

"That is my plan."

"Would you object to his taking your name – for identification purposes."

"No objection."

The trio was made up of specialists. The lead man asked the questions, filled out the forms, collected signatures and information, and answered questions with alacrity. The finger-print man, fingerprinted. The fingerprint identification man identified fingerprints.

"Identical," he announced after comparing Klaus's prints with the one's on the official forms Yvonne carried.

"Your address is correct and current?"

Yvonne checked scrupulously.

"It is, and it is," she confirmed.

"Expect the young man's identity document within the month."

She stood. The lead man and she shook hands. The trio departed without further ceremony.

"Wow!" David exclaimed. "That was fast."

"And," Yve reminded, "we didn't have to buy some stupid parchment."

"Did you mention that you're a French citizen?"

"Strange," she grinned, "The subject never came up."

A NEW HOME

They sat together on the train to the *Bahnhof*. David caught an express to Paris. It would get him home faster. Yvonne hugged and thanked him. She promised to testify on his behalf if he got into trouble. He thanked her but didn't think he'd be punished too severely. Regardless, she vowed to write a note to the Grand Duchess, though she made no mention.

The train from Frankfurt to Koblenz was Klaus's second known excursion by rail. The few minutes from the airport to the *Bahnhof* was exciting. However, it was nothing to what awaited him.

"Vonnie, what's that?"

"It's a river," she explained.

"Is that – water?"

"Indeed, it is."

"So – much water! And boats! Look!"

She let him chunter away. It did her no harm. However, Klaus's excited babbling was a manifestation of his unbound excitement.

"The cars! I remember the cars from when I was little! I know the cars!"

Three rivers he saw. Rivers with an unbelievable amount of water.

They had a forty-minute layover in Koblenz. Yve took him out for a brief excursion. There were people – so many people. They walked on paved sidewalks, rode in cars on paved streets, and rode on bikes on paved bike paths. He spied a hamburger emporium and begged Yve to buy him another one – not a double burger or any of the several variations, just a hamburger – one with ketchup and a pickle.

As he chewed slowly to savor every, hidden or disguised flavor, he watched wide-eyed as people went about their business. If anyone noticed a slovenly little boy and his protuberant eyes, they displayed no curiosity.

"Is this Disneyland?" he asked.

"How did you ever hear about Disneyland?" she asked.

"I don't know. It could have been in a book. I remember we talked about it. It was – well, it was like this. I've never seen so many people or so many shops or so many cars."

"Sorry, Klaus. This isn't Disneyland."

Yvonne's heart broke yet again. She understood (all too well) how this deprived child could mistake Koblenz for Disneyland.

They were on another train. This one was not as nice as they others, but – ANOTHER RIVER! How many rivers were there? And boats – big boats, some carrying personal cars of the people who steered the boats! And castles!

Normally, Yvonne got in a nap or two during these sojourns. Klaus made slumber impossible. His excitement was so infectious, she never thought of sleep.

In Trier, they took a bus from the station. They got off and walked two and a half blocks with Klaus's head on a swivel every moment.

"Vonnie, how can Disneyland be better than this?"

She considered that for a moment.

"I suppose, Klaus, because Disneyland is make-believe. This – all of it, is real. You must get used to *real* before you can enjoy make-believe."

He eyed her suspiciously. He never thought she would lie to him, but what she said made no sense.

She took out her key and opened the entry door.

Stairs!

They were imitation marble and had no allure for Yvonne.

"You live in a castle?"

"Hardly."

"Castles have stairs."

Quickly, she collected her mail. There was a letter from Yvette, but the rest was comprised of flyers and other adverts.

"Many places have stairs, Klaus. This building has stairs, but it is not a castle."

Yvonne had so much to learn about the perceptions of a precocious eight-year-old boy who knew nothing but well water and desert heat and cold. His memories were confined to a tiny village and the humdrum of orphanage life.

When they reached the third floor, Klaus was eager to chase the rainbow higher still. She had to call him back. She put the key in her lock.

"What's that?" he asked.

She followed his finger which was directed at a door identical to her own.

"That's the neighbor's apartment. I've never seen it, but I suspect it is exactly like ours, only backwards."

"*Our* apartment? Do you mean . . . I don't live with the other boys and girls?"

For the second time that day, she was ready to burst into tears. She knelt next to him. She held him by the arms and dropped to her knees.

"Klaus, I'm so sorry. I never took the time to explain to you. Poor Klaus, you don't know anything. Let's start with this: very few children here, thank God, live in orphanages. They live with mommies and daddies. It's called a family. Klaus, beginning now, you and I are family. This is where you come to eat and sleep and read and – all the other things. We will get you into a school. When the school day is over, you come home; you don't stay at school; you come home."

Disneyland is nothing like this!

That's what she saw in his eyes. To her shame, she realized he was, in many ways, a baby still. The humdrum of her pedestrian existence was so bizarre and alien that the child had no point of reference. This was another world. Hitherto, she'd never devoted a moment's thought.

She needed a spanking.

"Help me pick up this junk I just dropped.," she requested. "Two things you must know, Klaus. First, we keep the common areas clean and neat. If we track in mud, we clean it up. Second, we must be quiet. Many people live here. They don't want to hear a lot of noise or loud voices. Can you remember that?"

He nodded vigorously.

They gathered up the advertising and entered the "hall" or "entryway." She flipped a switch and a light burst upon them. He jumped and threw his arms around her for protection.

"Lesson two: we don't use battery-powered lanterns or candles here. We have electric lights. The important things here are powered by electricity. When we have more time, I'll explain how electricity is made."

She led him into the living room, flipping a light switch along the way.

"This is where we can do our reading," she reported. "If we like, we can listen to music."

His eyes were popping again. All this room for two people? Unbelievable!

"The kitchen where we store food and prepare it. All we have is this hot plate. If we want something fancy, we can go to a restaurant and eat."

"Hamburgers?" he asked hopefully.

"Klaus, if eat nothing but hamburgers, you will grow tired of them."

"I don't think so."

"Well, we should try and eat things that are healthy as well."

He appeared incredulous.

Dark Comedy

"Here's the bathroom."

"What's this?"

"A bathtub, Klaus. You fill it with water and wash yourself all over."

"You fill it? With water?"

She tried to disguise her delight over his reactions.

"The sink where you brush your teeth. You do brush your teeth?"

"Twice a day," he boasted.

"This is your room, Klaus."

"My – my room? *My room*! This is *my* room? All of this?"

"Remind me to show you how to use the heat, Klaus. Please don't touch this knob until I've explained how to use it. You won't need it tonight."

"Vonnie, where do you sleep?"

"I'll sleep in the living room," she replied.

"Please, no. I want you to sleep here – with me."

Who, she wondered, is training whom?

Mark L. Williams

ADJUSTMENT

Most Germans are very protective of their privacy. Part of this resulted from post-war housing. Apartment buildings became the vogue. The "state" seized large domiciles and turned them into buffet apartments; the owners (those that survived the terrors of war) got an extra government stipend a month for the "seizure" of their property (though, in many cases, it was years before anyone received payment). In the chaos following the war, families were close knit and suspicious of anyone who wasn't a relative. Those, whose families were reduced by the death or disappearance of loved ones, were suspicious of everyone. Some made a vow to find "informers" for purposes of revenge; this contributed to make privacy and aloofness more important.

It was not uncommon for people to live in adjoining apartments and never know each other's first names. Even work colleagues might work next to each other for a decade or longer before becoming familiar enough to employ first names. The notable exception was among veterans. Those whose relationships were forged in war and steeled in hardship and suffering were, forever, on a first-name basis. They might meet as total strangers; once they learned of each other's war service, it was – always and ever – first names.

The younger generation, of course, was first name only. Unfortunately, and as a rule, once one's *Abitur* was behind them, or after graduating from university, it was formal titles and names.

Klaus was familiar with his classmates, and they with him. As a "son," his habit of calling Yvonne "Vonnie" was frowned upon by all and sundry. Yve did not discourage him, however. The alternative was "Mama" or "Mutti," neither of which was proper. She was reduced to explaining, repeatedly, that Klau was "adopted." It was, of course, a lie. However, explaining the actual circumstances would leave her little time for any other conversational gambit.

Dark Comedy

The promised ID arrived three weeks and two days after the fingerprinting. Yvonne immediately got him a passport. This was a "delightful experience" (Yvonne's diction) since her French passport was the topic of several lengthy discussions. The "official documents" should have been able to stand alone, but the bureaucratic powers insisted upon lengthy recitations. Yve could tell that few of the paper pushers believed her, but documents are not easily dismissed. It took much longer than normal, but the young child was awarded important papers.

Vet and Lea visited at the first opportunity. They slept a week in a nice hotel. After work and after school the quartet gathered at "Klaus's home." The boy thought Lea was a treasure and doted over her. He envied her for having a loving mother and father and expressed his desire to meet Lea's *Vati*.

Initial "housekeeping" was interesting. Klaus was so amazed with lights coming on at the flip of a switch that he would pause, momentarily, as if suspecting the lights would fail otherwise. Water, that greatest of all wonders, was the object of his unceasing adoration. He would sneak up on a fixture, as if to take it by surprise. When he attacked and water came out, he shrieked with glee.

"It is plentiful," Yve assured, "but it costs money. You didn't waste water in Africa; don't waste it here."

He tried. Yve had to admit he tried. However, there were moments of silence which were punctuated by a gush of water in the sink.

The first, and for several subsequent nights, the most traumatic issue was the sleeping arrangements. Klaus did not want to sleep alone. Assurances that Yvonne would be only eight or ten feet away were wasted.

"I slept with you down there," he reminded.

"No one had a proper bed *down there*, and it got cold. Here, you have a warm room. You're a big boy, Klaus. It's time to do big-boy things."

It was a struggle. For the first two weeks, he would whimper to secure her sympathy. Eventually, he would fall asleep from exhaustion. She would move his bedtime up an hour to allow for his arguments and protests. Even after she had him "bed trained," she often woke during the night to discover Klaus standing next to the couch.

"I wanted to make sure, you're okay," he muttered timidly.

Those were the times she woke up. The was no way to know how often he checked on her or how many times during any given night.

As it was in the mission orphanage, the nighttime ritual included the saying of prayers. In this, Yvonne readily joined in. However, this became something of an issue.

"Why do you do that?" he asked.

"I'm crossing myself, Klaus. It's what Catholics do."

"We never did that."

Yvonne was caught in a dilemma. She wasn't ready to abandon her rituals completely, and she was unwilling to engage in proselytizing.

"I think that praying to God is more important than how we do it."

He was satisfied. Soon, they would take turns. He would cross himself and pray while she refrained from gesticulation. The following night, they would switch.

Getting to and from school was, at first, a hold-my-hand experience.

They each had bus passes. The first week, she rode with him to school in the morning. He, however, had to ride alone in the afternoon. Klaus was instructed to enter the building (with his own key) and the apartment (with his own key) and do homework or play until Yvonne returned. He was forbidden to turn on the hot plate, run the water unnecessarily, or play with the light switches or any other electrical devices. When the days grew short, he was allowed to turn on the light in his room only.

After the first week, Klaus decided that, if he could ride alone coming *from* school, he was quite capable of going *to* school on his own. In the days before child snatching became a sport, she thought little of his walking to the bus stop alone. The same commuters caught the same morning bus. He felt comfortable being around familiar people even if they never spoke to each other. Yvonne remained skittish. Though Klaus was quite competent to travel on his own, she had a mother's concern that Klaus might meet with an accident or be suddenly taken ill.

Dark Comedy

There was one profound benefit to his traveling independently: he was no longer afraid to sleep alone nights.

Several months elapsed. As the dust settled, Yvonne felt that her mission in life was nearly completed. She had faithfully answered the call from above and extracted Klaus from a dead-end existence. However, she experienced considerable anguish and a few sleepless night when she thought of those poor children left behind. She trusted that God would tap other missionaries to bring those children into the light of day.

Her remaining mission was to bring Klaus to maturity. Once he was educated and (hopefully) well brought up, he would be a credit to himself. The one lingering cloud, however, was his finding someone with whom to share his life.

German law is very strict in matters of marriage. The couple must be able to prove to the government that they are not blood relations. Klaus would be unable to offer proof. His "documented genealogy" began with him. Of course, other European nations were not so picayune about marriage. Perhaps Klaus and Lea might find marital bliss anon. Regardless, there should be ample options when the time came.

The one remaining task on Yve's personal docket was restitution. She owed the Grand Duchy two thousand marks for the purchase of a phony parking ticket – or whatever it was the goons pulled out of their hats. David assured her that such a pin prick would hardly rate a raised eyebrow should they be audited. For Yvonne, however, two thousand marks constituted a substantial sum. What she and Klaus could do with such an amount would fill a wish list several kilometers long.

Yvonne set aside a hundred marks per pay period. This was a substantial sacrifice. That money could make a big difference in their domestic economy; it represented food, clothing, and would contribute to a more enjoyable life. However, Yve's own conscience and her concern for David's fate came first.

She took the two-thousand-mark scrap of brown paper and its attractive calligraphy with her one morning and photocopied the first of the three folds. The copy was dispatched to a linguist at the university. Neither he nor anyone else on staff recognized the language. It became an obsession with the scholars. They could not rest until this hitherto unknown alphabet was examined thoroughly.

Yvonne deposited her one hundred marks in ransom money the second week of every month. Another one hundred marks were deposited at the end of each month. She counted the days until two hundred additional marks became available to "the family."

Trust in God, she thought. My mission continues. He won't let me fail now, stumble though I may. The most important item, bringing Klaus home, was completed. The path ahead would be strewn with obstacles, but the most important part of Yvonne's task was behind her.

Apparently, He was not yet ready to release Yvonne and Son.

The manager of a local shop, renting space in one of the large department stores, grew used to seeing Yvonne parade about the town square in "interesting" fashions, a polite expression used to avoid the more accurate "clown suit." After weeks of witnessing her exhibitions, he followed her as she opened the shop. He was, so she thought, her first customer of the morning.

"I see you most every day," he reported.

Her antenna was up. She'd have been more comfortable were other people in the shop, but she felt ready to handle the situation alone.

"You have an interesting wardrobe."

Thank you, Lord!

Now, she had an opportunity to explain that her wardrobe was hardly as gaudy as the clothes she wore. She explained her "moonlighting" for a local business catering, specifically, to gullible tourists. She was both puzzled and pleased when the strange man's eyes glazed over slightly. He wasn't the least interested in her motivation.

"You are a good model," he proceeded when she offered him a lull.

Dark Comedy

What, she wondered, was this indecipherable obsession with labeling her a "model?" She wasn't and never had been. Despite all her denials, Mme. Errad and the Grand Duchess considered her a model; Sarah and Charlotte made certain remarks about her ability to display wares. Suddenly, a strange man insisted on appending that moniker. Her natural and initial inclination was to deny the charge. Instead, she hung fire.

"Thank you," she said affably. "May I help you select a book?"

He explained who he was and what he wanted. In a nutshell, he wanted her. Would Yvonne be amicable to working in his establishment? She would aid customers and ring up purchases which would require a modicum of training. However, he wanted her to wear the items he sold.

"When a woman sees how well our goods look on you, they will be more inclined to purchase or – at least – try them on. Getting them into our goods is only a step removed from a sale."

She was reticent. Yve had two paying jobs and was skeptical about taking on more work.

"I'm trying to raise a little boy," she explained.

"Let's try this," he suggested. "Work as a model and saleswoman for me on the next long Saturday."

Her long Saturdays were accounted for – that is, they were until he mentioned the per hour emoluments. In addition to the attractive salary, she'd get an extra couple marks (per hour) for modeling the inventory.

Yvonne was not greedy; she was practical. Money for Klaus was vital. They boy, as with most boys, was growing at an alarming rate. Keeping him in clothes would become a challenge.

She took the matter up with her employers who, interestingly, encouraged her to seize this unsolicited opportunity.

There must be an order to these things, she decided. When her bid to become a nun ended in flames, she was *sent* to Mme. Errad. The Grand Duchess selected Yve to head up a mission and write a tome detailing the expedition. She became the "face of Trier" because someone had seen her photo and asked for her specifically. She wanted to bring Klaus back, and both money and opportunity were laid out for her as if by a professional touring firm. She needed a few marks more a month, and an opportunity comes to *her*.

Many people would chalk it up to luck. Yvonne, however, was convinced she knew that each step of her "career" was divine intervention. Not only was she obliged to take this opportunity, refusing might initiate a series of unfortunate events.

Whatever it takes, she reminded herself.

Time was her enemy. The currency would change in a few months, and there was no way to know what the "new order" might bring. Yvonne wanted to be free of those two thousand marks weighing her down.

The first long Saturday was a decided success. Three women liked the dress she wore.

"It one of our items in stock," Yvonne reported.

Two of the women bought the dress.

The following long Saturday, she was recognized by someone who remembered her from her stint with the Tourist Bureau. In great excitement, she called her the "City Vamp." She apologized profusely, but Yvonne enjoyed a rare, uninhibited laugh. The unidentified woman bought a skirt and blouse to assuage her guilt over the thoughtless remark. Additionally, two other women were impressed enough with Yve's "dress of the day" that they bought their own.

The ethereal writing was on the wall. Yvonne would make more money in the women's department of the department store. She felt a pang of betrayal leaving her landlord and landlady and their book emporium. The ever-gracious family Schultz expressed pleasure at her obtaining a higher-paid billet. They did bemoan the two interim replacements prior to their obtaining a scholarly gentleman, a retiree, who loved books and enjoyed the extra income. Overall, both Yvonne and the landlords came out ahead.

Sadly, the modish, warm-weather fashion mongers suffered when they were unable to secure the services of another "live mannequin," but the business was on the skids even before Yve abandoned them. Tacky clothing, even at the worst of times, has limited appeal. They'd have folded their tent eventually, even had Yvonne continued advertising.

Klaus was on his own after school. He could let himself into the building and into the apartment, but he was alone. Yvonne suffered from guilt. She should be there for him. She worried about him.

The child was obedient because of his unbounded respect for his "pretend" mother. If she told him not to use the hotplate in her absence, he obeyed. That, however, could not pacify Yve who feared the boy's insatiable curiosity. He might practice tight-rope walking on their tiny balcony, or play with or carelessly handle the breadknife, or play underwater explorer in the bathtub.

There was no way to be certain about his actual activities, but her heart-throbbing fears dissipated the moment she entered the apartment to find everything serine, neat, and unburned.

She usually found him paging through a picture book, drawing or coloring on their tiny kitchen table, or playing with the few toys he'd accumulated.

Yvonne's fears were renewed one afternoon when she heard the radio. The audio was coming from his bedroom. He'd unplugged the appliance, transferred it to his lair, and plugged it in. The idea of Klaus being so intimate with electricity would feed her daymares for months. She forced herself to say nothing. If, she figured, he wanted the radio in his room, let it be. Should she make it an issue, he might transfer it daily rather than just once.

He liked to listen to AFN because, he said, he liked the music and he liked hearing people speak English. He began using English words and phrases.

"What does *silly* mean?" he asked one afternoon.

"Where did you hear that?"

"On the radio."

Once he knew the meaning, he'd use it – frequently.

There were half-hour recordings of radio shows from days before Yvonne's birth. Many had catch-phrases.

"Hi-yo Silver!" he'd say whenever excited.

"What a revoltin' development this is!"

"I'd better be shoveling off."

Yvonne had to laugh. She devoted several minutes a day to bring his German up to par, but his attention seemed focused on English.

At night, Yve would hear the radio turned low. Klaus would go to sleep listening to a baseball game.

"Why?" she asked at breakfast one morning. "You don't know the game. You can't understand what they're talking about?"

"I don't like quiet at night," he confessed. "In Africa, there were always noises."

Yvonne didn't want to explore for fear it would trigger something unpleasant. Certainly, the children would produce noises even while asleep. Any other possible auditory sources Yve did not care to know about. If Klaus required some background noise to sleep, he had her endorsement.

LIBERATION

Alterations.

Before purchasing, many buyers insisted on alterations. Measurements were made and notes required. The items must be transported to competent hands. Since competent hands are a scarce commodity, backlogs resulted. There was no way to predict exactly when a garment would be returned to the purchaser. The lack of said guarantee translated to fewer sales. Fewer sales resulted in unrealized profit. Unrealized profit resulted in grumpy wholesalers.

The women's clothing emporium rented space in a large department store. Roughly two thirds of that space was dedicated the display floor where racks of garments were kept on public display. The remaining third was devoted to inventory, specifically, arriving garments and unsalable merchandise to be deported and, figuratively, executed.

Yvonne, ever ready to open mouth and insert foot, insisted that if she had the machines, materials, and a part-time assistant, she could do most of the alterations herself. The manager "knew his business." He'd been knowing it for close to two decades. Yve's suggestion was fatuous and unnecessary.

One afternoon, she scanned the items due for shipment. Three of these required only minimal attention. On a whim – one which could have won her instant dismissal – she took these items (a prosecutor would use the term "stole") out of the store.

Frau Schultz, the landlady, had become a close friend. This friend had a garret room in her home containing an impressive array of equipment. Apparently, when not engaged in helping her husband with mercantile concerns and property investments, Frau Schulz enjoyed making clothes for herself.

The following day, the department manager was so hot, he was in danger of bursting an artery.

"There are three items missing from this manifest!" he roared.

"They've been altered," Yve informed half in and half out of the day's featured togs.

"If you notify the customers, they can collect them."

He remained hot. Who did Yvonne think she was? Why hadn't he been informed?

"You would have said *no*," she reminded.

He remained an insufferable bore for three days. However, women came in specifically because alterations did not take a change of seasons. From only three customers, word spread exponentially. The manager, through the employee chain, found himself in an awkward predicament. Much against his will, he conferenced with Yvonne.

"You can increase your volume," she reminded. "Your bosses will be pleased."

He grumbled. He yelled. He fumed.

He relented.

The initial outlay on basic equipment proved a sound investment. Yve would work from ten until two, retire to the "shop," and work on alterations.

Sales increased by eighteen percent because alterations did not take forever.

From three garments and the three purchasers, business boomed.

"You did well," the manager begrudgingly admitted.

She wanted to tell him that it wasn't her, it was divine providence in action. The manager, however, was not particularly keen on theology; Yvonne held her tongue.

Dark Comedy

Holding her tongue plus an increase in pay aided her in closing her account with the Grand Duchy. She secured a bank draft and sent it along with an expository note.

"I hope the security man was not excessively punished for the expenditure. If interest is due, please inform me and restitution shall be forthcoming."

She did not assign a date. Yve did not want to make rash promises.

It was such a glorious feeling to be out of debt. To celebrate, she and Klaus enjoyed a very pleasant (and filling) late lunch at a Greek restaurant one Sunday afternoon. He was attracted to the fish tank and the exotic exhibits it contained. He was, also, delighted with the food.

Food not boiled or fried was both mysterious and refreshing. He took to the side salad with special glee. The main course, baked meat and feta cheese, was so enjoyable, Yve heard of little else for three days.

This, she decided, was the culmination of her life. She had a job for which she was suited. Moreover, the job suited her. She had a modest apartment, but it met her needs and was most comfortable. She had Klaus, who could be a trial, but his affection for her mirrored her feelings for him. It was a joy to help him discover things about his new world. Along the way, Yvonne discovered important things herself.

Alas, the currency switch brought her contentment to an abrupt end.

The formula for converting to the Euro was so simple, even a politician could understand it. One simply replaced the DM sign with the Euro sign, but the numbers remained as before – or so it seemed.

Wages were converted into Euros, but the price of goods went up considerably. There were hard times ahead. Well, "hard times" in modern conditions. The post-war "hard times" were light-years worse. Nevertheless, when belts tightened, public attitudes changed.

The Schortmann economy suffered. Compared with the sacrifices required to face life in the "New Europe," stashing away two hundred marks a pay period was, comparatively, painless.

It might be some while before Yvonne and Klaus would experience better days.

The alteration equipment Yvonne brought into the business was sold to trim expenses. The days of quick alterations were gone. Similarly, the extra money Yve's alterations earned was similarly sliced from the operating budget.

She was stoic. Her faith survived. Perhaps, the Maker was dissatisfied with Yvonne and her money concerns. However, He would never abandon young Klaus. Something was in the offing. She didn't know what, but she was certain that Klaus would be properly attended.

She knew!

CONFUSION

Without extra money and without a debt hanging over her head, Yvonne managed the adjustment to the new economy through the same level of frugal living as before. She ached to get Klaus better clothes and feed him better food, but they were restricted by a myriad of minor sacrifices.

There was considerable grumbling. People who had adjusted to the "new" Germany – that is the post-war Germany – dug themselves out of the ruble. They built a new society and a new, prosperous, nation. To surrender their sovereignty in the interests of the European Union was an afront. Remarkably, there was no threat of violence. People registered their objections verbally.

There were no more long Saturdays. More accurately, every Saturday was a long Saturday. Soon, some shops would begin opening on Sundays. There were limitations on the number of hours a week employees could work. Yvonne was but one of millions to be denied the luxury of a little extra income.

Klaus remained aloof. European politics wasn't any part of his life. He went to school; he ate regularly and healthily; he lived with a roof over his head; he slept in his own bed; he could drink water whenever he wanted; he could bathe regularly. Since he did not connect any of these luxuries with German or European politics, the new rules and regulations were as alien to him as life on Saturn.

There was one remarkable aspect to living in Europe that meant as much as all the other luxuries combined. He was loved. Equally important, he loved someone. Dr. Judy, his fellow orphans, and the mamas were important to him, and he would always regard them as very special people. However, he loved Yvonne. He loved her the moment he saw her and recognized how frightened she was. He took it as *his* mission to let her know that he cared for her as much as he cared for himself.

Life with Yvonne was an adventure. She taught him things he would never learn in school. She always made time for him. She patiently answered his questions. She showed him amazing sights and fed him amazing foods.

Yvonne was also a firm disciplinarian. She never struck him and seldom raised her voice. However, she was adamant about his keeping himself and his room clean and orderly. When he failed her, she would look sad and defeated. That hurt him much more than any traditional form of discipline. He never forgot that she came halfway across the world to bring him into the land of wonder and plenty.

She read to him. She practiced German with him. She taught him rudimentary French and English. She explained things. She helped him with homework. She listened to his problems and concerns. That was, above all, most important: she listened.

Klaus had so much to say – so many things he must express. Yvonne did not always understand, but she made him feel that his concerns were important. If she could not help him with a particular problem, she would find someone who could. Many times, the "someone" was a cleric.

Klaus knew nothing of Catholicism. He'd been raised as a Protestant – insofar as one can be raised in a frontier orphanage. To him, the rituals and adornments were interesting but, often, silly. Yvonne never preached to him. She never insisted that he join her in her rituals.

"Am I doing it wrong?" he asked one rainy afternoon.

"Believe in God," she replied. "Pray to Him. Thank Him. Honor Him. Doing these things is more important than how you go about it."

Yvonne suffered. She did not know if hers was good advice. She, who once longed to be a nun, was not qualified to advise anyone about religion or religious practices.

"I'm trying to locate Dr. Judy," she told him. "She helped you so much. Maybe, she can help me as well."

Dark Comedy

There was one ritual that Klaus prayed he'd never outgrow. When he and Yvonne parted, it was always with a hug. When they came together again, a hug was the first order of business. After prayers, Klaus was not "officially" in bed until he got his goodnight hug. When she woke him in the morning, it was with a hug. If, as often happened on Sundays, he woke up late, he would scamper through the apartment in search of her, so he'd get his good morning hug.

He called her *Vonnie*. Standers by assumed the child was trying to say *Mommy* but suffered from some cerebral impediment.

In Germany, adults and children are expected to be relatively formal in public. In this context *Mommy* or *Mutti* was considered acceptable. Anyone who realized *Vonnie* was a diminutive for *Yvonne*, would consider such familiarity rude and disrespectful.

Neither Yvonne nor Klaus would be bothered by such nineteenth-century attitudes. Yvonne was not Klaus's mother. To pretend she was fell nothing short of fraud. They were more than friends but less than kin.

The government, ever fearful of worker exploitation, severely punished employers who *made* employees work more than a statutory number of hours a week. The fact that some workers desired to work extra hours was too challenging for government underlings (or, even, government overlings) to decipher. Not willing to risk the umbrage of the either the German officials or their Euro masters, the fashion outlet in the big department store refused to consider Yvonne's pleas for mercy. Again, family Schultz came to the rescue.

The person who replaced Yvonne in the bookshop was something of a liability. He was elderly and tired quickly. He didn't need the money, and the daily grind was a bit taxing. Family Schultz opted to provide the man a little relief. How about another day off every week?

Yvonne and Klaus began to think God had abandoned them. They'd become a family through His grace and intercession. Suddenly, they were a few short steps above want, and their prayers went unanswered. They reviewed their every word and action to discover the reason for their punishment. Somehow, they'd fallen out of favor. What could they do to earn it back?

Yvonne arranged to have an antiquated (landline) installed. It was one of the perks she allowed herself during the alteration phase of her workplace. When that extra income evaporated, she considered removing the phone. However, it had become a "necessary luxury."

Except for the bi-monthly call from Yvette and their bi-monthly call to Yvette, the phone was seldom in use. Occasionally, former members of the veterans of the Lux-beer fraternity would call for a nice chat. Those calls came later in the evening – after several elbow bends.

Early one evening, the phone rang. It wasn't late enough for the beer-fraternity to call.

Yvonne picked up reluctantly. She feared her mother had met with some dangerous malady or, worse, that her departed husband had been denounced by some irate citizen who'd held a grudge longer than was healthy.

"Can you open the shop tomorrow?" Frau Schultz asked frantically.

It would be Tuesday, Yvonne's day off.

"I'll come round and pick up the key," she replied.

Klaus eagerly escorted her that evening.

They were euphoric. Eight hours more a week. It seemed so trivial, but it would have such a profound effect on their lives. Better food and better clothes were in the offing! Yve's base pay, plus a tiny commission on items sold, plus a more substantial commission on items she both modeled and sold, plus the bookshop base pay – they'd never live in a condo or a house, but they would be much more content while living in their small apartment.

They celebrated on their return by stopping at an Italian ice cream parlor. Yve ordered a *Kiwi Becher* while Klaus eagerly dispatched a *Spaghetti Eis*. These were small vices, but they were symbols of dreams deferred. They could enjoy life together just a little more.

Herr Schultz presented a used bike to Klaus who once mentioned, in the landlord's presence, that he'd like one. Yvonne didn't know if she should thank Schultz or curse him.

Klaus's unalloyed glee made up her mind for her.

For two weeks, they worked on mastery. Yvonne saved the boy from serious injury several times, but he collected a few scabs all the same. He was eager, however. He'd wipe away the tears of pain and frustration and leap aboard again. The days grew longer, and the incongruous duo would take full advantage.

Klaus tired of riding in circles and being bound by Yve's line of sight. She brought out her bike and increased the boy's riding range. One day, they rode together to Klaus's school and back. He was so proud. He wanted to ride his bike to school rather than the bus. Yvonne vetoed the idea. Klaus sulked.

"If I could ride with you, I'd allow it," she explained. "School gets out while I'm still at work. I don't want you riding home alone."

He brightened somewhat. He wasn't allowed to bike to school, but he realized Yve had confidence in his ability to do so. He enjoyed riding with Yve. She led him through the streets to interesting places. They would rest while Yvonne explained what they were viewing.

How many of Klaus's contemporaries got exercise and history lessons at one go? He was proud of himself and proud of his guardian.

By summer, Yvonne had enough in reserve to buy locks for the bikes. When school let out, Yvonne would bike to work with Klaus in tow. He had the run of the town, well, the market area and surrounding streets, for entertainment. Frequently, he ran into school chums. There were kiddie stations scattered about – swings here, a slide there, monkey bars, etc. – and a couple proper kiddie parks were within easy walking distance of the large department store.

So long as Klaus checked in every ninety minutes or so, he was permitted to go where he wanted and do what he wanted. When the business day ended, they would bike home and plan a meal. Several times, Klaus hinted he knew what he wanted for supper. If they did not have the requisite items at home, they would stop by a shop and purchase what they needed.

It was so nice to have that little bit of extra income.

Yve liked books; she liked aiding people in locating specific works; she liked being friendly with literate people. Most of all, however, she enjoyed the extra money.

Sundays were, at times, a trial.

Yvonne tried to go to Mass at least once a week. She could not, with a clear conscience, "drag" Klaus with her. His entire life as a foundling was devoted to Protestant ceremonies. When he was older, he could choose for himself, but Yve would not be party to "forced worship." Most Sundays, Klaus would attend the Aula – the huge civil hall built and used by Constantine (later "The Great") when tending to official business. It was currently used by the Germans who followed Luther.

Some Sundays, Klaus opted to stay home. When he did worship, Yve knew where he was and was assured that he was properly attended. A squadron of Evangelical families established the tradition of going to lunch after services. This collection included two of Klaus's schoolmates. It wasn't long before he was invited to dine with them. Yvonne was eager to send Klaus off with lunch money, but the families insisted on paying his way.

"You are our guest," they reminded him. "Our guests do not pay."

At first, Yvonne was mortified. After examining her own values and realizing her grip on Catholicism was slipping, she thought better of it. Catholics resisted being obligated to "Luther's mob," but Christian values were, and remain, Christian values. Nomenclature was not nearly as important to Yve as observing civilized behavior. If these Sunday revelers invited Yve to join them for a post-service feed, she would be under obligation. Until then, her conscience would rest.

There were times – seldom but frightening – when Yvonne would wake to sobbing. Instant awake! She'd eschew her slippers – putting them on would delay her by three to five seconds.

"Klaus! What is it, darling?"

After the first two alarms, she knew what was wrong. She asked out of form because she could not find any suitable words.

Klaus did not miss his orphanage friends, but he mourned for them. Here he was in Germany, living in the lap of luxury, attending a real school, possessing three or four changes of clothes, enjoying water from a tap and baths in a tub while those he left behind – friends some of them and acquaintances all – must live in appalling conditions. He cried for the mamas who, from motherlove alone, slaved to keep the children clean and clothed in-so-far as they were able. The mamas, also, provided a shoulder to cry on and an ear to listen.

Klaus and Yvonne shared profound guilt. She brought (*bought*) him out of that dirt patch, but she'd left the others to rot. That hurt. It hurt very deeply. Klaus experienced the guilt of living a new life while those left behind were prisoners – some of them for life. Yvonne's guilt was her inability to rescue them all. However, what chance would black children have in Germany? Despite its liberal policies and mind-set, black people (especially black children) are viewed as curiosities – zoo exhibits. They could live in German society, but they, likely, would never be accepted into German society; they required considerable wealth *and* celebrity status to become anything more than an exhibit.

When Klaus and Yvonne cried themselves dry, they'd grab what sleep they could and stumble through the day. When they sat down to the evening meal, they would try not to talk about it. Invariably, however, they'd sneak a short nap after the dishes were washed. Sometimes, the naps weren't very short. More than occasionally, they would wake in the night long enough to shed their clothes and put on pajamas before going back to sleep.

Klaus is German, Yvonne reminded herself. He deserves to be here.

These platitudes did not alleviate the guilt of the children they left behind.

Belatedly, Yvonne applied for *kinder geld*. There were funds available for single parents. To obtain it, one had to join the bureaucratic circus. First, of course, the government must know the circumstances by which a single woman had a child. It was none of the government's damned business, but the Golden Rule was in play: Those who have the *gold* make the *rules*.

As with all government forms, there is no room for perfectly legitimate reasons. If one is lucky, there is a page-width line. Of course, that is not enough space to explain anything. Therefore, there must be a personal interview by some officious prig who would rather be drinking beer than giving the peons so much as the time of day. Interviews, of course, were during working hours. Employers, of course, do not pay employees to go to interviews – well, why should they?

Was the pitiful amount of *kinder geld* worth the sacrifice in privacy and unpaid time off? Yvonne tried not to think about it.

Yvonne should have predicted trouble ahead. She and Klaus were settled domestically. They were separated by religious dogma, but their tacit "live-and-let live" policy avoided disputes. Financially, they turned the corner. By the end of each month, after all their financial obligations were met and their larder was sufficiently stocked, the Family Schortmann could bank between seventy and ninety Euros.

Destitution was fading.

Then, one dark afternoon, the bell rang.

Klaus, assuming one of the neighbor children had come to call, pushed the release button and rushed down the stairs to greet his visitor. Yvonne, scrubbing the dinner dishes, shared Klaus's assumption and continued her work.

"Vonnie. A man is here."

She could tell by the boy's tone, this was not a neighbor or a friend. The woman quickly wiped her hands and hurried into the living room. From the "hallway" – a two-meter tunnel between Klaus's room on one side and a neighboring apartment on the other – Klaus hurried by her and into his room. Framed in the open doorway was a man of medium height and a businessman's suit. His tie had red and white stripes and appeared to be silk. The genuine nature of the cravat, however, was of no consequence. Clearly, this man was either "money" or represented money.

"Frau Schortmann?" he asked. "Frau Yvonne Schortmann?"

She nodded timidly rather than lie outright.

"This is most irregular," the man announced, uncomfortably. "There are proper channels – *official* channels, but –"

Realizing he'd missed a step, he hesitated a moment prior to producing an official document. He was a junior member of the Luxembourg government – foreign service or whatever the official nomenclature was for the foreign service. There was a name and photo ID included in his credentials, but Yvonne forgot the name the moment she saw it.

Yvonne was at a loss.

"And?"

Recognizing his cue, the man extracted a thick, folded document from his inner jacket pocket. She handed it over. Had Yvonne any sense, she would have refused to touch it before knowing what it was. Yve, however, was neither a diplomat nor a lawyer. The second it was in her possession, the man released it as if it contained a snake.

"A summons," he informed.

Beads of sweat broke out on her brow.

"You are requested to appear on the date appended," he stated.

The "proper channel" insisted that the German *Aus Minister*, or some low-level flunky deliver the document – so the German Government would "co-operate" with its tiny neighbor. Perhaps, the Grand Duchess felt that Yvonne would be more receptive to a gentle nudge rather than being bludgeoned by German official protocol. Alternatively, serving a French citizen residing in Germany might be a little "tricky."

Yvonne unfolded the document and attempted to decipher something cogent. The formal heading was half a page long.

"Can you give me the short version?"

The man cleared his throat. He was the delivery boy; it was not his place to know. However, one needs some diversion when traveling by train. Tedium and lack of other reading material might prove tempting.

"The matter of the two-thousand-mark bribe," he said, between stammers. "The government is launching an investigation."

"What's to investigate?" Yvonne demanded. "We were touched; we paid. It was the Grand Duchy's money. This was a personal matter. As such, I felt obligated to make good the loss."

"Our government may wish to lodge an official protest," he said. "There are certain procedures involved. You are called upon to provide a statement."

"I can do that from here," she reminded.

"An *official* statement," he informed. "In front of council members and witnessed by same."

"I must take off work. I need that money."

"The investigation has begun. You are –"

He was considering his words very carefully.

"You are *requested* to appear and provide testimony – ah *statement* – official. If you decline, the German authorities will be notified and – *compulsory* action may ensue."

Voluntarily forfeit pay or forfeit pay and face judiciary action.

The walls were tumbling down.

I should have kept the money – AND kept my mouth shut!

Lord, is this an example of the wages of virtue?

Worse was to come.

Klaus experienced thunderstorms in the desert. He was deathly afraid of them.

The first rumble was so timid, Yvonne didn't wake. Klaus did! He rushed from his room for protection. He lifted Yvonne's blankets and attempted to find succor. Yve panicked. She thought her father was initiating another "lesson."

She croaked and kicked. Her stomach revolted. She felt partially digested sustenance crawling up her throat. She fled to the bathroom and reached her goal just in time. Klaus, in tears, followed. He knew he had done something very, very wrong, but he had no idea what. Would she punish him? Why was she screaming at the toilet?

"Vonnie! Vonnie! I'm sorry. I'm so sorry! How did I make you sick?"

She collected herself and cleaned up her mess. She did these things with alacrity. Her prime concern was Klaus.

"It's night. Why did you wake me in the middle of the night?"

"I heard thunder. I was scared."

He was nearly unintelligible. His tears were copious. She held him. She held him tight and soothed him.

"I was afraid too," she whispered when he began to calm down. "I was remembering – things. Things that happened in the night, Klaus. Horrible things. I panicked."

The thunder announced itself again. This time, it was not subtle. Yvonne felt the boy's body stiffen and his grip on her became more emphatic.

"We're both scared, Klaus – of different things, but we are both very frightened."

"I'm glad you're here," he sniffed.

"Okay, you can stay with me during the storm, but no funny business."

No funny business?

He had no idea what Yve meant. All he knew was her warmth and touch next to her made his fear manageable.

Yvonne knew exactly what she meant, but it had nothing to do with this child. She remained tense and uneasy until assured he'd gone to sleep. She slept but got little rest. There was a warm body pressed against hers and that churned up fear and revulsion. She'd tolerate Klaus clinging to her, but she wouldn't accept it.

ORDEAL

Yvonne must make several arrangements. Her primary concern was leaving Klaus. She could not take the child with her. Expenses for one person would be exorbitant. Taking Klaus would break their budget beyond repair.

She was nervous about asking for time off from work. The document, EU issued and approved, was official; denying Yvonne time off might cause her employer to suffer serious sanctions. However, Yvonne was the "new kid;" she hadn't worked long enough to justify taking time off. The employer determined eligibility in such matters, and Yve hadn't enough clout to make her own arrangements.

Frau Schultz, however, did not bother about such matters. She trusted Yvonne and was amenable to any reasonable excuse. Yve was her boarder and her employee; she was a friend. Friends are awarded greater tolerance. If Frau Schultz couldn't find a suitable replacement, she'd run the shop herself. One day a week hardly constituted a sacrifice.

Yvonne was to appear on a certain day. That was encouraging. She could take a day for travel, a day to "testify," and a day to return. That was the plan. However, she was annoyed by the bothersome possibility that she might get caught up in unforeseen circumstances.

A family of *Evangelicals* agreed to take in Klaus for the duration of Yvonne's sojourn. The family's two children were close school friends. They got along well. When the proposal was first put forward, by the family *not* Yvonne, the "witness" was gracious but unenthusiastic. When faced with reality, she swallowed hard and accepted the family's offer. It wasn't easy for her, but her attitude *vis* the "Luther lot" was softening.

Klaus didn't want Yvonne to leave – not for three days or, even, three hours.

Dark Comedy

"Dieter and Hildie are your friends," Yve reminded. "You get along so well. When I was your age, I was thrilled to stay with friends."

"You're my friend," he reminded her. "We get along well. I don't want you to go."

"Well, I must go, Klaus. It's the law. If they put me in jail, you will only be able to see me once or twice a week."

He was so frustrated, he started throwing things. He wouldn't eat. He couldn't sleep. Yvonne feared she might be forced to consult a shrink. At the end of her tether, she went on strike.

"Klaus, I love you, but I hate the way you're acting. I give up. If you won't eat, I won't either. If you won't pick up after yourself, I won't either. If you won't bathe, I won't either."

He held out for an entire evening. Early the following morning, Yvonne woke up with the young boy staring at her. Tears filled his eyes and rivulets ran down his cheeks.

"Vonnie, I'm hungry."

She sat up, gathered him in her arms, and hugged him mightily. She kissed his face and hands.

"You get cleaned up, Klaus. I'll fix you a nice breakfast."

One hurdle cleared, but several remained arrayed before them. However, Klaus had conceded the two most important points: she must leave, and he must stay.

That very evening, as she checked the mail, she found an item from the university on official stationery. She opened it.

According to a prestigious professor and scholar at Tubingen, the cover of the document Yve submitted was a certificate of civil marriage.

She laughed. This was hilarious and ironic. No civilized nation on earth would recognize a marriage between a woman and a child. Of course, the issuing government was not civilized. The roadside stooges produced the first available form as camouflage for their extortion.

Moments later, she considered the fact that the document was official. In an African nation, according to barbarian law, Yvonne and Klaus were man and wife.

Only one man in her life had earned her love and respect. Could she have married Norbert? Fortunately, he had never asked. Had he – at the time, she was encumbered by orthodoxy – she was blocked. Since then, her faith in the Church had waned. Further, her "biblical husband" was dead. Did that make her free?

Tucked away in her files of trivia – items kept but eligible to be thrown out or destroyed – there was the record of a marriage. It was fraudulent, but – in one corrupt and backward nation – it was legal.

Was it?

Did the banditti have a record or a copy? If there was anything on file . . .

"Will you marry me?"

Should a man ever ask that question of Yvonne, what would be her response?

"I'm married to a person young enough to be my son. Let's ask him."

"I'm married, but it was never consummated."

"I *might* be legally married in Africa."

The more she thought, the more confused she became. The Luxembourg Government paid two thousand Deutsch Marks for a document that might not stand up in any court in any nation, to include the nation of issuance. However, laws are often very inexact. There was that word: *might*. There was no way to shrug it off and, certainly, no way to expunge it.

Should she tell Klaus? He was, according to an official paper, her husband. He had a right to know. She was his wife; it was her duty to tell him.

Don't rush into this, she told herself. It's a joke. It is the most unfunny joke ever, but it isn't anything more than a two-thousand-mark joke.

Keep telling yourself that.

"Three days," she promised. "You can do three days standing on your head!"

"Vonnie!"

"I love you, Klaus. I promise, I will be back the first moment I can."

She hugged him. Big mistake. He wrapped himself around her. It took the combined efforts of Yve, Dieter, Hildie, and their mother to tear him loose. Yvonne hopped quickly up the vestibule before Klaus had a chance to grab her anew. When the train began to move she waved. Klaus stood as still a statue. His visage radiated his pain; his eyes were flooded.

The woman *he* adopted, the woman who rescued her from dirt floors and tasteless food, the woman who showed him the miracle of instant light and instant water, the woman who fed and clothed him, the woman who helped him explore a world far beyond his early imaginings, the woman who was the most important person in his life was leaving!

He treasured those few days at the mission when he refused to leave her side. She allowed him to sit with her, talk with her, eat with her. The woman came back for him. She allowed him to take over her room and make it his own. She was the beacon in his life.

She was gone.

It hurt.

Yvonne did not read. She did not admire the scenery. She heard nothing. The conductor had to announce himself boldly before she regained normalcy enough to hand him her ticket. He punched it before returning it with a smile and a nod.

He thinks I'm deaf.

Not without cause.

Yvonne leaned against the window, the side of her head resting on the cool glass. She saw nothing and heard nothing. She felt the pain of want. She missed Klaus. Klaus was her friend and her joy. He was also her husband. Someday, he'd have to know that he was a child groom. Someday, he would have to explain to a wife of his own choosing that he'd been married before.

He didn't have to know. Yve didn't have to tell him.

That wouldn't work.

Suppose one of those creatures found Klaus. He (or *it*) could blackmail the blood out of his arteries – or Yve's if they opted to target her. The truth was the best protection, but how could she tell him? It wouldn't be easy; he was too young to understand the implications. Later, when he was old enough to understand …

"By the way, Klaus, I'm your wife. Will you take me out for a nice dinner on our anniversary?"

If it could only be that easy.

She must tell Yvette. Aside from the fact that she was her older sibling, Vet was likely to be the repository of sage advice – particularly in marital matters. In this aspect of life, Yvonne and Klaus were – well, virgins.

An annulment seemed the best course, but how would one go about that? Further, how could it be kept secret? She imagined one of those corrupt civic officials telling all and sundry about a grown woman and a young boy reneguing on their vows. That news would circulate around the world. Some Ami or Aussie tabloid would have their pictures transmitted to every corner of the earth. What a great joke! What sport! Neither Yvonne nor Klaus could draw a fresh breath again.

Step back, she told herself.

You must have faith.

Good advice, even when platitudinous, remained good advice.

Okay, she told herself, *hold fast to faith. Now, how does that help? The problem remains. The darkness remains. The trauma remains. Come on, Faith, how do I cope with this? How can I live with this? How can WE live with this?*

She pulled her roller case down the street and across a thoroughfare to the cheap bed and breakfast of days gone by. Luckily, they had vacant rooms. She parked her "things" and returned to the world. Everyone looked and acted so gay and carefree – or so it seemed to her.

She walked on a pedestrian path halfway across a bridge and lingered for some while, looking down on the miniature residential neighborhood far, far below. For several lingering moments, she contemplated doing a swan dive. It would alleviate so many problems. Alternatively, she could throw herself in front of one of the many cars whizzing past. Maybe a truck would be the better bet.

Neither would serve. Brushing aside the fact that her much vaunted faith wouldn't allow such sinful actions, Klaus would never understand. Yve wanted the tears he shed upon her departure to be in vain.

She wasn't hungry, but she stopped and bought a bread roll for later. She returned to the B & B and looked out the window. She monitored the pedestrian traffic. A girl about Klaus's age was playing a game only she understood while avoiding the sparse automobile traffic. Yve stood sentry for forty minutes and, by her count, noted a dozen foot travelers and four automobiles, each too large for such a narrow street. When the girl skipped up the street and disappeared into a small apartment building, Yvonne retreated to the bed and sat.

Eventually, she showered. She got no pleasure from it.

She put on fresh underthings, banished her dirty things to a plastic bag, and stuffed it into her travel case. She brought no pajamas. There was a clean shirt, a hairbrush, a few cosmetic items, and a plastic sack for dirty items. Yvonne hadn't bothered to bring a change of clothes. Her travel ensemble, dark blue slacks, a red, short-sleeved pulli, and her brown walking shoes would be her entire wardrobe for her stay. She held the shirt in reserve for an emergency.

Yvonne hoped she would tend to all her business in the morning and catch the first available train for Trier. If she required a jacket or a rain hat – well, she'd deal with unforeseen matters as they came.

In her shoulder bag, she had her money, ID, a comb, a tube of lip balm, and the papers which had ordered her hither.

There was nothing to read. There was nothing on TV, but she left it on at low volume just to keep her aloneness at bay. Had Klaus been with her, she'd experience diversion, but her dark mood and the fears she carried were as formidable without Klaus as they'd be with him. In fact, she was "cheating" on her "husband." Her nervousness would rob them of all enjoyment. She might have snapped at him in frustration and fright.

She woke early and brushed her teeth for far longer than necessary. It was something to do.

She took the steps rather than the lift to the ground floor. Yvonne was the first at breakfast. She took a roll, a slice of dark bread, a serving of scrambled eggs, two slices of bacon, two pats of butter, and two servings of preserves. She set her plate at the smallest of the available tables only to return and select a pear from a large fruit bowl.

Yvonne ate slowly. When her plate was cleared, she returned for a cup and saucer. She filled it with coffee, returned to her place, and sipped slowly until the cup was empty. She longed for a second cup, but she didn't want to risk bladder problems.

She and her pear went to her room.

She escorted the pear and her "luggage" to the train station and consigned her things to a locker. Yvonne stood under the rotunda and munched on the pear. After consigning the residuals to a dustbin, she went to the taxi stand.

Yve paid close attention to the route. Taxis were expensive. If it wasn't outrageously far, she'd walk back to the station. If it was, she'd look for a bus stop.

It was early. Her destination was in the guise of a two-story office building, but the wrought-iron fence and the uniformed sentries ruined the illusion. She presented her "credentials" to a uniformed guard wearing a conspicuous side arm. Nearby was a soldier with a rifle. Yve suspected that neither weapon was loaded, but she played the game and behaved as if she knew what she was doing.

The pistol-packing soldier spoke into a microphone.

"Yvonne Schortmann," he announced – that, and nothing more.

There was no verbal reply. There were, however, two audible clicks.

"You will be escorted in, Madam," the serious soldier informed.

Even as he spoke, Yvonne noticed a figure approaching from the double-door portal of the official edifice. He was not exactly portly, but he was hardly lithe and spry. He wore an expensive three-piece suit of bureaucratic gray and the obligatory bureaucratic brown shoes. As he drew near, she noticed he had skin damage on his cheeks and nose. Perhaps, he'd been a mountain climber. Maybe, he was a boozer.

The man introduced himself. Yvonne forgot his name immediately due to his off-putting expression of disapproval. Her clothes were not to his liking.

"You should have worn your Order of Merit," he said, trying hard (and failing) to avoid being a scold.

Weeks prior, Yvonne stood before a mirror and placed her award around her neck just to see herself. It was elegant. However, she'd require a formal gown (perhaps, with a sash) to do it justice. There was a pendant she could wear instead. Likewise, it would require immense vanity on her part to use it. Even if she lived in the Grand Duchy, few people would know what it signified. Of course, when on "official business," one might be required to wear one's honors.

It was too late to go home and fetch it.

"I'm a simple peasant girl from a wide spot in a road in the Alsace," she explained, her umbrage surfacing. "What I know of court procedure wouldn't fill a gnat's navel. I came because I was summoned. Next time, I'll be sure to consult with M. Castiglione."

He grinned. Her subdued display of temper did not discourage him. On the contrary, he was impressed. She may have been a cow-pie kicker from the sticks, but she was well read. Further, her means of self-advocacy appealed to him.

"Your identification, please," he commanded.

She handed over the articles which she hadn't bothered to put away. He examined them carefully, as if looking for spelling errors. When satisfied, he returned the documents.

"After you," he said, gesturing with his right hand.

He could have said "follow me." There was only one entrance visible. Not even a peasant girl would be dense enough to think they'd remain in the courtyard or parade ground or whatever was the correct nomenclature for the fitted stones surrounding the stately building.

As they approached the entrance, he hurried ahead to hold the door open for her. She thanked him. Perhaps her initial evaluation of this man was a bit harsh; there was nothing served by being rude.

He gestured her the way and allowed her to lead. There were no other people in evidence. After two turns, they were confronted by an imposing door. The upper portion of the polished wood device was spoiled by the insertion of a large, translucent glass surface painted white and baring a complicated, multi-colored crest she didn't recognize.

"We are contemplating sending a sharp protest to a certain African government," the man explained in low, measure tones. "As a small entity, it isn't worth the bother. However, as a member of the European Union, we – that is, our government, feels that it has both the right and the backing to respond to disrespectful behavior. You are not on trial here, Mme. Schortmann, although it might seem to you as if you are. These men represent the judiciary and foreign departments. They will ask direct questions. Give direct answers."

She swallowed hard.

"I understand," she affirmed.

"The microphones are necessary because everything in the room is recorded. If you wish to review the transcript of the proceedings, it is your right. A text will be forwarded to you upon request."

"I understand."

He nodded and smiled.

"If you require anything, I am at your service. Shall we go in?"

She nodded.

It was a small room as government offices go. It may have been large enough to contain both her apartment living room and Klaus's bedroom. There was a long wooden bench with impressive and intricate designs masterfully carved into the facing. Peeking over the bench were three headrests of black upholstery.

To her left was a small, wooden (IKEA?) work desk. It contained a microphone stand and a microphone, a carafe of water and an intricately designed crystal goblet. The chair was cushioned and had arm rests, but it was not designed for lengthy occupancy.

To her right was a smaller desk (with microphone) and a folding chair. Granted, it was an expensive and aesthetic furnishing but, alas, a folding chair is, ultimately, a folding chair.

Her "escort" motioned for her to take a seat next to the beautiful crystal wineglass. He, meanwhile, retreated to – what Sister B_____ would call the "discipline table." Commensurate with his gesture, two men entered from a door behind the bench. They wore three-piece suits in bureaucratic, foreign-service black and carried a sheaf of paper each. A third man entered just as Yvonne settled into the "hot seat." This last man wore a brightly colored vest which made him stand out. Yve thought it looked clownish.

She cast a glance at her "escort" who had derided her for her casual clothing.

He either didn't notice or he ignored her.

"For the record," one of the men (she didn't know which), "your name, Madam."

"Yvonne Schortmann."

"Full name, please."

This was the man in the clown vest.

"Yvonne Bibele Schortmann."

The trio nodded approvingly.

"For the record, gentlemen," Mr. Escort inserted quickly. "It should be noted that Madam Schortmann is a Knight in the Order of Merit."

"Thank you, M. (name unintelligible)," one of the "magistrates" nodded appreciatively. "We welcome that information. It is worthy of note."

"Further, under the auspices of the Grand Dutchess, she wrote a narrative of the mission on which she was sent. Copies of said narrative were distributed amongst members of the government."

"We are aware," one of the panel members responded impatiently.

"For the record," Mr. Escort emphasized.

That put a different slant on things. The brusque member cleared his throat while reconsidering his officious attitude.

"Indeed," he concluded. "Such information deserves to be included in the record."

You reside at – etc.

You are employed by – etc.

You traveled to Africa for the purpose – etc.

It was "yes" and "no" time. The members of the tribunal (?) knew all this information. They wanted to make it official (for the record). It seemed to take ages, but less than five minutes transpired before the "hearing" turned serious.

"You caused quite a stir when you sent two thousand marks to our government."

"That was not my intention."

The panel ignored her comment (but it went into the record).

"You informed us that this was recompense for a *bribe*."

"Yes, sir."

She said this in English. It's the sort of thing one says in a formal setting. She was too uncomfortable with French or German formality. Yve thought that might make her appear supercilious. The woman wanted to keep her head down.

"We were told that the money was for an exit visa. *Export writ*, they called it, a *guarantee* we would not be detained at passport control. However, that was donkey muffins. It was a bribe."

Her switching languages in the middle of a sentence did not disturb the proceedings in the least.

Guided by their questions, she went through the entire story. She had to explain "David," since she had no clue as to his polysyllabic moniker, which necessitated explaining the security contingent made up of the ABCs. No one attempted to cut her off. They wanted a complete record. Apparently, this "interview" was not being conducted under a time constraint.

"What motivated you to send in reparations?"

"We – I spent *your* money. I was not authorized to spend that money. I did so in a moment of panic. We – I vowed to get that child out no matter what we must do. When we were safe in Europe, I realized I acted rashly. I participated in an act of extortion. It was my responsibility. It was, therefore, my responsibility to replace the money I had – well, stolen."

"*Stolen* may be too harsh a word," someone suggested.

"For the record," Yvonne reminded. "It may be too harsh, but the word is accurate."

There was a pause. Notably, there was no attempt to amend her original diction.

"You stated before that the money was spent to secure an exit visa."

"Ultimately, yes," she replied.

"What was the nature of this document?"

Her body turned to ice. She had to force the words out of her throat.

"We – I – well, we didn't know. It was a proper, printed document, but it was in an African language. I *assume* that. I don't know."

"There was nothing in French to indicate the nature of the document?"

"It was all in one language – I presume it was in one language. There were no French, English, or German words. I would have recognized them had there been."

"Do you have the document?"

"Not with me."

"That is regrettable. Did you attempt to discover the nature of this document?"

There it was! Right between the eyes! Her body quaked.

"Yeeeeee-es."

She dragged it out because she didn't want to say the word.

"How?"

She explained slowly.

"Have you had a response?"

She sat mute for several seconds. No one attempted to coerce her. They let the silence echo through the room.

"Yeeeeee-es."

"What was the verdict?"

Yvonne was wringing her hands. Tears threatened.

"I don't – want to answer," she began with a quivering voice. "It's hearsay. I only have the word of a scholastic who communicated with another scholastic. I do not, personally, know if either of these people are what they claim. Neither one identified the language. Their conclusion may not be accurate."

"What did they *say* it was?"

Yvonne Schortmann did not display emotional distress before others. She was on the cusp of doing exactly that. She fought down her shame and rage, but she was losing.

"Sirs," she began on the verge of tears. "I do *not* want this in the record. I am ashamed that I paid money for this – this *snake*! The fact that I paid for it with your money – that makes my crime a thousand times worse. I wanted to make good my theft – that was before – before I was told what someone says someone else said it was. It mightn't be true – they might not know what they think they know. I know – I know that I *don't want to know*. I wish I'd never asked for a translation. I acted stupidly during my panic and those – those vipers took advantage. We would have given them the money, but – *no!* They had to go through the pretense of being legitimate when a brainless loon would know they were as crooked as as a land agent selling swamp water. I apologize. I will send you a photocopy of the – *thing* – well the first part, at least. But I can't – I just can't! Please, do not make me tell – not for the record – not even in confidence. I don't want to know what I know, but I cannot make it go away – I can't forget what – I can't!"

She buried her head in her hands and made the world disappear. To their credit, no one attempted to prompt her. Mercifully, no one attempted to pacify her or attempt to sooth her with platitudes. These men seemed to understand. She was beyond human interaction.

When she regained consciousness and wiped her eyes with the palms of her hands, she stared at the empty desk.

"We apologize for upsetting you –"

"*You* aren't the people who upset me," she barked.

"Nevertheless," the man continued. "We wish to file a list of grievances against the government of this nation. International sanctions may be in the offing. There are serious issues to be discussed. By no means are you the only person who had been abused by these people."

"Please," another official inserted. "Send us a copy of the document – or as much as you will allow. However, let us continue. Let's forget this line of questioning for the moment. We would like an account of exactly what you did and where you went."

She forced herself to return to earth. Slowly, in fits and starts, she explained what she and "David" did during their "extraction" mission.

"For the record," she inserted at the proper place. "I take full responsibility. David felt that he failed in his mission, but *I* failed him. I was too eager and too desperate to listen to reason. I'm the one who must be punished. If David was castigated, it was undeserved and unwarranted."

"We will look into the matter," one of the board members promised. "We will find out what, if any, disciplinary action was taken. We will inform you. I promise. *We* promise."

She nodded her thanks.

There was no disguising the awe she produced with her tale of desperation. They wanted to know about the knife and if she would have made good her threat. They wanted to know about Klaus and what motivated her to take such extraordinary actions to "rescue" him. They applauded her for wanting to make good the money she spent, though they clearly questioned her judgement. The government knew full well that providing expense money is always a risk. However, money used in an act of extortion – it was one more item on an ever-expanding list of grievances against a particular African government.

When, after two hours and several minutes, the "examination" concluded, Yvonne was physically and mentally drained. Her escort insisted that she remain for a few minutes more before he accompanied her to the front gate. She was not upset. She welcomed the opportunity to relax and catch her breath. It was a tremendous relief to sit calmly and think of nothing.

It felt so good not to have to speak.

She felt a wave of disappointment when her escort returned.

"Madam, we thank you for your service. We thank you for your cooperation. We appreciate what you have done and are doing. Your carriage awaits."

"My carriage?"

He smiled and guided her out to the entrance gate. They walked through together to the limo parked at the curb, disrupting traffic. He opened the door and ushered her in.

"Take us to the rail station," he told the driver.

"I hadn't expected this," she sighed.

"Perhaps not," he said soothingly. "This is the least we can do."

RESUME SPEED

The train arrived in the late afternoon. Yvonne did not pause to leave her travel case at home. She proceeded directly to Klaus's temporary abode. It was important that she be near him. Klaus was her only tangible link with life. During her absence, he'd become the only purpose for her to live. It stabbed her that some bullying boob decided they should be wed. It made her angry to hear, in her imagination, the raucous laughter of the extortionists as they drank two thousand marks worth of dime-store booze. It stoked a murderous rage within her to think that these belly-crawling thugs considered their "harmless" lark a triumph of ingenuity and comedy.

Once she had Klaus in her arms, she felt whole. They were a team. They would endure the worst the secular world threw at them. Somehow, they would obtain a position in life where they could make a difference – an important difference.

The nature of the *difference* was indeterminate. Yvonne had no goal; she doubted Klaus had none beyond being loved and having a life worth living. They would cling to their respective faiths and trust that God would use them for His purpose.

She sent a photocopy of the cover page to her marriage document as she promised. There was certain to be a gaggle of chuckles and merry coffee-break exchanges in Luxembourg Civil Service circles for months.

Let them, Yve thought. Scoff. Deride. It's such a jolly little lark because you don't have to live with it. Were Yvonne human, she'd join in. It was just a scrap of paper. The monetary value of the document would not fetch twenty eurocents. The legal value of her marriage license wouldn't stand up in a court room long enough to be noticed.

Alas, Yvonne Schortmann was not a human being. She was a low creature who existed to pleasure her father; she attempted to hide her guilt and shame under a nun's habit. She was exploited for commercial purposes by an employer, then by a city. She lived by performing demeaning tasks. Such a scoundrel deserved to be the wife of a foundling child.

How could a fraudulent piece of paper have such a hold on her?

Patience, she told herself.

Yvonne sincerely believed that whatever she had and whatever she'd achieved, whatever "good" she performed, it was because her Maker led her to it. He was the general; she was the soldier in the field. He issued the orders; she carried them out. Beyond this, when she lacked confidence or her courage failed, He was there to guide, cajole, and refresh. Through Him, she had completed tasks, conquered fears, and surmounted obstacles. She paged through a litany of her achievements and realized that Yvonne Schortmann was incapable of such things; she was too reclusive, too incompetent, and too cowardly for anything other than sucking her thumb.

"Okay," she said after an exhausting day's work. "I'm here. Use me."

"Vonnie?"

Of course, radar ears had heard.

"Sorry, Klaus. I was talking to God."

"Oh."

That's it?

She peered into his room. He was sitting on the floor and piecing together a jigsaw puzzle.

"Did you hear what I said?" she asked, tentatively.

"Yes."

"You don't think I'm crazy?"

He looked up at her as if he had serious doubts about her mental acuity.

"No. Why?"

The second word was filled with suspicion.

Boldly, Yve went to his bed, the one she bought especially for Klaus, and sat upon it. From there she had a vantage point to examine the entire room. However, she was focused on Klaus.

"Not many people think it is appropriate to talk to God – as if He were living here."

"*Appropriate*," he repeated. "I think I know what that means – I mean, I know *now*."

He went back to his puzzle.

"Do you think it's okay for me to talk to God?"

"Why not?" he countered. "He lives here. He lives everywhere."

"Did Dr. Judy tell you that?"

He looked up at her anew.

"No," he said cautiously. "Dr. Vonnie told me."

Yvonne got up slowly and padded out of the room and toward the kitchen.

She had some thinking to do. Blessedly, she could cook and think at the same time.

The entire prank was getting up her nose. Every time she convinced herself the marriage document was nothing more than a gangland joke, she'd find herself struggling for breath.

Filling out a job application one afternoon, Yvonne faced a conundrum.

"Are you married?"

To lie was a sin. To promote a lie was a sin. To violate the law was a sin.

"Yes."

A lie – or not a lie – or a "maybe" lie. The paper said she was married. The prissy woman at the counter, however, was not wrestling with the vagaries of caprice.

"Where's your ring?"

"In pawn."

In for a penny...

That *was* a lie. She authored it without any hesitation. Perhaps, she hoped it would gain her a boost if this woman made hiring decisions. Clearly, this applicant was in dire need.

Such a machination not only furthered the lie, it compounded the lie.

Later, in a futile attempt to assuage her sin, she went to a shop and bought a ring. There was a nice diamond for very little. Likely, it was glass. That, however, would not do. To wear a lie was nearly as low as having the power to join two innocent people in matrimony.

She bought a band. It erased one lie, at least. Wearing the band on the culturally accepted finger was – well, people, *unmarried* people, often wore jewelry there.

It hurt.

Sinning is painful. It was to Yvonne, certainly. The band became a scalding hot lump of lead; it tortured her and weighed her down – and it burned her.

"Husband?"

"Yes."

"Children?"

"A boy."

It was a different venue and a different inquisitor. Yve congratulated herself on not lying.

Her victory lasted only a moment. Her answers constituted deception. Deception is the same as lying.

It hurt.

"Vonnie, what's the matter?"

"Why do you think something is the matter?"

"You look so sad," Klaus reported. "I don't like for you to be sad."

"I'm a sinner, Klaus. My sins make me sad."

Klaus was the only one she could speak to thus. She would go to confession, but she didn't count that. Likely, she didn't know the priest personally. She, certainly, didn't live with him. She did live with Klaus, and he was precious to her.

Later, as he exited the bathroom after a surreptitious twist of a faucet, he rushed to his room. Perhaps, he suspected a scolding was in the offing. More likely, he wanted to return to his play.

"God lives here!" he reminded.

It didn't make her feel the least bit better.

Someone else was good at keeping their word. An official envelope arrived from Luxembourg City. It was terse but welcome. The man, Yvone identified as David, had not been subjected to official admonishment. The note included an addendum: David met with a supervisor to explain his actions – or lack thereof. Regardless, he remained in good standing.

That was a welcome relief. It perked her up enough that Klaus no longer complained of her sad look.

Several days later, Yvonne received another letter. This one requested the name (or names) of the officials who signed the document. She reckoned that the authorities had deciphered the African squiggles on the photocopy she sent. They must know it was a marriage agreement. However, they may have concluded that it was Yve and David who were ensnared.

Her "not sad" face went away. Now, the authorities in Luxembourg must think that her emotional outburst was prompted by being "jokingly" married to a black man. It didn't matter if they thought that, but she was petrified they might believe it.

Had she not asked about him? Had she not pleaded on his behalf? Had she not made it clear she didn't want him punished? If she had a phobia concerning black people, why would she be so solicitous? Further, half – or more – of the orphans she tended during her mission were black. Would this evidence be enough to keep important people in high places from thinking ill of her?

She was sinking. Still, she was engaged in a very important mission of properly raising Klaus. That was a heavy responsibility, and she did not want to be weighed down by guilt. Somehow, she had to either shed it or rise above it.

"I'm my husband's mother."

Please, dear God! Do not let me say that in a fit of pique. Her quick remark about the wedding ring being in pawn was atrocious enough.

Don't make the pit any deeper.

How and why a German retailer would stock plastic baseball bats and balls was just one of the many mysteries Yvonne encountered in a life rich in mysteries and felicitous devices. Baseball in Germany was slightly below weasel racing in popularity. Klaus, however, knew of baseball from his late evening AFN radio encounters. He recognized implements he'd never seen. He called Yve's attention to the package but dared not ask for them.

"Klaus, when is your birthday?"

He stared at her blankly. How could he answer?

"Mark this day on the calendar," she advised. "Today, you are ten years old."

He blinked. The normally sedate and pensive woman was speaking in hieroglyphics.

"A birthday boy rates a birthday surprise," she concluded.

She snatched up the bat and ball. They were designed, perhaps, for younger people. However, Klaus had become a baseball fan. He couldn't make up his mind which was his favorite team and only understood one out of every twenty words the announcers offered up, but he deciphered the meaning of certain, reoccurring words and phrase.

Strike, ball, fly, single, double, out, run, base, base hit and a few other miscellaneous terms that served to keep his interest. He would fall asleep during a game, but his dream images were fueled by the descriptions in a foreign tongue. In his dreams, soccer stadiums were the baseball venues and players came out in soccer shirts and shorts and swung bats at sporadic pitches until someone hit a ball and other players rushed to retrieve it. Once awake, Yvonne attempted to explain the game. However, she knew little more than Klaus. All his knowledge, therefore, was predicated on his imagination.

He did know about birthdays. His close friend, Dieter, marked his birthday with a party. Klaus was invited. Yvonne said a gift was traditional and she filched money from the household funds to procure one. Klaus took the gift to the party and enjoyed music, games, and snacks. The greatest "takeaway," however, was the oft repeated phrase "It's *my* birthday, so we do what *I* want."

Yvonne may not have realized the trap she laid for herself, but Klaus was determined to take full advantage.

"Let's go to the arena," he suggested.

"It's nearly dark, Klause."

"It's my birthday," he reminded. "You have to do what I want."

"Why must we go to the arena?" she asked, stalling for time.

"I want to hit a home run."

"What's a home run?"

Dark Comedy

"Where you hit the ball out of the pitch."

This was preposterous but, at the same time, brilliant. The young man knew he couldn't possibly access any of the proper sports venues, but for a nominal charge, the ruins of the Roman amphitheater would serve.

She introduced Klaus to the concept of "compromise." She promised to bike with him to the arena the following day after school. He'd get his birthday wish a day late. Klaus was amenable. It gave him the remainder of the day, all night, and the next day to dream and thrill and anticipate.

After supper, he went to his room and practiced his swing. To ensure both domestic bliss and the preservation of breakable objects, Yvonne kept the ball hostage.

When she returned from work the following day, Klaus was on his bike. Yve, who cycled to and from work when conditions allowed, was slightly miffed. However, she empathized with his excitement.

They made it, almost. They were forced to dismount and walk up the remainder of the hill to the entrance. They secured their mounts at the public bike rack. If the attendant objected to a young man entering with a bat and ball, he kept it to himself.

"What's a home run?" she asked, anew.

"That's when you hit the ball out of the arena."

She calculated that anything short of a rocket engine could not make that dainty plastic ball travel more than a few meters. However, it was his birthday; Yvonne was a mere slave to custom.

It was an educational experience for them both. Yvonne learned how to pitch underhanded. Klaus learned that hitting a moving sphere with a stick was not as easy as he imagined. After twenty or so minutes, he began hitting the ball with regularity. No matter where they went inside the "business area," the ball did not reach the retaining wall – never mind sailing beyond it.

Klaus ran and ran and ran. His intensity was such that he couldn't wait for "slow poky" to fetch the ball. Yve enjoyed watching the eager boy display such energy and determination.

"Let me – catch – my – breath," he pleaded, setting aside the back and heaving mightily.

She took advantage of the respite.

Yvonne looked up at the place where she once sat and contemplated. She recalled thinking of Blandina. It shamed her. That woman was roasted in an arena but refused to renounce her religion. Yvonne had strayed so far from her religion, she no longer considered herself a Catholic. However, she retained faith.

She hung her head. Thinking of Blandina and the physical tortures she endured was painful for her. Yve recalled thinking she belonged in the arena. Here she was, in full view of the dozen or so tourists who viewed the ancient monument with little more than curiosity. To Yvonne, it was a monument to her own worthlessness.

Blandina was cooked over an open fire for the entertainment of the spectators. Yvonne went to pieces over a worthless scrap of paper. Since learning about her "marriage," she'd been wallowing in self-pity and fear of what others might think. How shallow! She didn't deserve to be in the arena. Yve didn't know how to behave.

Quickly, she strode over to one of several recesses where animals were once caged, or attendants found refuge from the wild beasts during a performance. She did not enter, but she paused just outside the archway. She bowed her head and prayed for forgiveness. She confessed her shallowness. She was made a coward by a ridiculous parchment.

"What are you doing?" an impatient Klaus demanded.

"I'm honoring Blandina," she replied boldly.

How brave and committed that martyred woman was! Next to her, Yvonne wasn't worthy to exist.

"What?" Klaus demanded.

Yvonne returned to baseball.

Klaus never did obtain his home run, but he took heart in their being together. For the first time in several days, Yve wasn't pouting. He appreciated what she did for him. Before surrendering to fatigue and hunger, they enjoyed playing together.

RESURGENCE

Yvonne's opprobrious attitude toward certain African pen-pushers remained stoked, but her marriage debacle, once a knife twisting inside her abdomen, was reduced to an occasional pang. Somehow *pang* cannot do justice to the sweat-producing moment when her memory sent voltage up her spine, a surge which rushed through each vertebrae like a bullet. It wasn't debilitating – not exactly. At work, she would be arrested momentarily. Occasionally, while performing a task or helping a potential customer, the "shooting pain" caused her to pause a moment or two. If an associate or customer took notice, she would hastily excuse herself.

"Residuals of malaria," she'd explain.

Another lie.

She found herself living in an enclosure made of sticks – and each stick was a lie. They came one after another. She was addicted to them. She would beg forgiveness on her knees at night, but the sin of piling lie upon lie was considerably less horrifying than the truth.

Blessedly, these impediments were infrequent. Yve no longer wore her shame and torment like a cloak. She might go several days without experiencing a "stroke." When one gripped her, it was only for a moment. Rationality and placidity were quick to escort the ephemeral intruder off the premises.

Were she confined by the restraints of her Catholic heritage, Yvonne would have sought some form of exorcism. Under her more personal and immediate concept of faith, she shrugged these episodes off as reminders that her suffering was metaphysical. Blandina's suffering was excruciatingly real. Yve admired that sainted woman, but she had no wish to emulate her.

Dark Comedy

Her life with Klaus became more "liberated." She was not afraid to touch him or kiss him. She no longer experienced gooseflesh when he touched her unexpectedly or when he took her hand or hugged her. They returned to the relationship they'd enjoyed previously.

"I wish I could take you to a baseball game," she said to him one evening.

He appreciated the sentiment, but it didn't satisfy him.

"Actually," she amended. "I think it's better this way."

Klaus was still adjusting to Vonnie's habit of authoring esoteric asides. He tried to ignore them, but he seldom succeeded.

Catching his eye, she continued.

"What you imagine is, probably, much more exciting than real life."

He didn't snort or scoff – he hadn't yet learned how. This did not, however, prohibit him from rolling his eyes. He loved Yvonne because she loved him. However, she was weird.

That same evening, just before evening prayers, she gripped him at the waist and half-tickled and half squeezed while making a comical sound. He jumped in surprise and attempted to wiggle free. He laughed. This encouraged Yve to redouble her efforts.

When her attack ceased, Klaus sat on the floor and struggled to regain his breath. He looked up at her with sparkling eyes. She'd never done this before. It was scary but fun. He liked to laugh, and Yvonne liked hearing him laugh.

"You're better," he concluded.

"What do you mean?"

"You've been so – I don't know – sad."

"Really?"

"Yeah."

Yet another Americanism!

"Well, if you ever see me sad again, you know what to do."

"What?" he asked.

Her reply was to renew her attack. This time he had to lay flat on the floor before Yve's merciless torment ended. Again, he had to struggle for breath after his involuntary fit of laughter.

The next afternoon, while Yvonne was tending a bubbling sauce on the hot plate, Klaus got behind her and retaliated. Luckily, Yve had the presence of mind to let go of the saucepan. She struggled to free herself of the boy's grip and succeeded. The child's delighted expression was contagious.

"Don't do that when I'm holding something hot," she admonished.

Klaus is not the smartest student in his class, but he was, perhaps, the brightest. He took her warning to heart. It made common sense. However, in the "heat of the moment" (so to speak), they shared a good laugh and enjoyed the latest in their increasing string of memories.

There were bad memories as well. Yvonne hated to punish the boy, but she couldn't allow him to do stupid or dangerous things. She, particularly, would not tolerate rudeness – particularly with people other than herself. Yve never struck him, except playfully. She did, however, find one threat she never had to carry out.

"If you don't behave, I'll take away your radio for a day (or two, or a week)."

That never failed to get both his undivided attention and an immediate change of attitude. He was bright enough to realize she hated discipling him but smart enough to know she would. Fortunately, Yvonne seldom had to threaten. This was fortunate because making her threats good was guaranteed to pain her.

"Do you remember Sarah?" Yvonne asked one afternoon.

"Yeah. The pretty one."

That struck her profoundly. Yes, of the three women who appeared at the desert mission, Sarah was, unquestionably, the most attractive – followed (closely) by Charlotte. It didn't surprise Yvonne that he remembered the woman. She was, however, taken aback by his unsolicited estimation of her.

Dark Comedy

"She wants to visit us sometime soon."

"I thought she was always doing shows and making recordings."

"She's taking a vacation," Yve announced. "She's going to have a baby."

The distance between his room and Yvonne's couch (bed) was not great. Still, the time lapse between her announcement and his appearance was nearly instantaneous.

"Really?"

Yvonne was amazed at how excited he was. If possible, he was more excited than Yve herself.

Klaus was something of an enigma. Many times, Yvonne thought she understood the boy. Many times, she was surprised and, at times, upset when he did or said something completely "out of character." Gradually, she realized that he wasn't the least out of character; she had grossly misjudged his personality.

The little imp had bored a hole right into her heart by hugging her – taking her by surprise. Years later, she discovered that he considered Sarah to be the "prettiest woman ever." Yve could have noticed, had she paid attention, that he was infatuated with Hilde. She, together with Dieter and Klaus, were recognized as the "three musketeers," in terms of their games of pretend. Clearly, he fancied Hildie. They had exchanged first kisses, though neither was yet aware the significance beyond their mutual curiosity.

Klaus lived in Germany. Sarah lived, worked, and had a respectable following in France. Their only common link was Africa. Had he been aware that she was a performer and recording artist, he might have insisted upon Yve buying some of her wares. That would require the purchase of a device to play them. Extravagant purchases were discouraged in the interests of financial security.

Yvonne had seen photos of Sarah in magazines. She did not, herself, purchase such works, but there were plenty scattered around for perusal, particularly in hotels and on trains.

Sarah was very modest for a celebrity. She was very modest for a civilian. The publicity photos of her reflected the singer's reserve. Sarah preferred a fifties-type of dress – skirts and dresses just below or just above the knee. Bare shoulders and midriff were not allowed. She projected the image of a proper young lady with proper young-lady values. Her music, lyrics, and performances were tailored to fit her visual image.

The "suits" were constantly after her to "show off." A hip-high slit in her dress, a low neckline that threatened to fail at any moment would, they promised, increase both her popularity and her bank account. She had the face and figure of a temptress; she should use that, they argued, to her advantage. Sarah, however, would not accede to anything that did not conform with her off-stage persona.

Her following was not nearly as large as those of her "competitors," but she'd carved out a comfortable little niche for herself. Her popularity in Belgium was considerably more effusive than in her native France. She had a good voice; she sang songs devoid of suggestive or racy lyrics; she looked and dressed like the proverbial girl next door; she was never rude to a fan or an interviewer. She was content to *live* in France – not *own* it.

Jean-Baptiste, her husband, was charming, affectionate and loyal. He was not nearly as modest in dress or personality as his wife, but they had enjoyed a decade of marital harmony. Her career had reduced children to their mutual to-do list. However, by accident or intent, she was a proud mother-to-be and her personal appearances could wait a few months. Meanwhile, she was booked for two studio sessions. It was decided to take a brief German vacation between those sessions. Jean-Baptiste had promised a land-and-water journey down the Rhine and a break in personal appearances was an excellent opportunity.

Two nights in Trier was an excellent beginning. From there, they would go down the Mosel in an excursion boat before training to Mainz and continuing up the right bank to Holland. It was a chance to be together, far from the maddening crowd. They would work out the details as they went.

As the hostess, so to speak, it was incumbent upon Yvonne to provide a repast. As much as she desired to make a meal and serve it, it was impossible. Even if she had the requisite number of plates, serving platters and bowls, silverware and tableware, there was no space. The table and hotplate which served Klaus and her so well, were woefully inadequate to accommodate a party of four.

She reserved a table at a favorite Greek restaurant. It would put a huge dent in their budget, but it would not force them into receivership. However, she encouraged Klaus to be frugal. She promised to set a good example.

Sarah Toussaint (her stage name) and Jean-Baptiste Jeandel reserved rooms at a tourist hotel rather than a four-star hostelry. She was reasonably well-known in France, a household "face" in Belgium, but her German reputation was minuscule. However, certain Eurovision fanatics would recall her appearance in the Song Contest years before. Further, there were several Francophones in Trier owing to its location.

She was recognized.

The local authorities felt snubbed while the regional journalists were on high alert. Members of both contingents flocked to the usual venues. When the welcome-wagon retinue and the scandalmongers failed to locate the celebrity, the consensus opinion was her presence was a false alarm. Someone reported, days later, she saw Sarah Toussaint in a Greek eating establishment – would, in fact swear to it. However, since no one made a fuss over the woman's presence, the witness opted to respect the woman's privacy.

Klaus ordered the Greek salad much to Yve's relief. The young man was hardly making a sacrifice. Greens, olives, goat cheese, and additional "magic" ingredients were unknown at the mission. When he noticed hamburgers were not on the bill-of-fare, his preference was both logical and satisfying.

Good food and good conversation made for a most satisfying evening. Unfortunately, there was no opportunity for the former "missionaries" to have a private tete-a-tete. However, Yvette informed the woman when and where she spent her lunch hour (a thirty-five minute "hour"). They agreed to sequester during that period.

After dinner, the party adjourned to the tiny apartment. Jean-Baptiste was nonplussed, but Sarah gushed over the quaint and adequate abode. She was, as her musical selections indicated, a romantic.

"You've gotten fat," Klaus announced to Yve's horror.

"Not *that* fat," Jean-Baptiste inserted quickly, but his visage reflected his appreciation of the young boy's observation.

Sarah smiled. She was just beginning "to show." She wasn't the least inhibited. On the contrary, she was delighted that someone acknowledged what, she hoped, was obvious.

"There's a reason," she sparkled. "There's a baby in there."

Klaus was dumbfounded. Apparently, there was something the omniscient Dr. Judy had neglected to impart to her mission-school students. He wanted to touch and to listen.

Yvonne was horrified and protested emphatically. Sarah, however, was proud and in excellent humor. She not only guided the boy's hand over her protrusion, but she also allowed him to place his ear against it.

"When it grows enough," Sarah explained, "It will come out."

"Today?" the boy asked with high hopes.

"Not for a few more months," Sarah explained. "It has a lot of growing to do first."

"Is it a boy?"

"We don't know," the indefatigable singer replied. "It's too soon to know. There are ways to find out, but Jean and I agree; we want it to be a surprise."

"How did it get in there?"

It was inevitable.

Yvonne's face turned scarlet. She knew it; she could feel it; she imagined she saw a red glow reflecting off the walls.

"Klaus," she began with a catch in her throat. "I will explain it to you later."

He focused on her. He couldn't understand how his friend and benefactor would deny him an explanation. She saw the hurt in his expression.

"Later, Klaus," she insisted. "This isn't because I want to keep it a secret. It is something that is difficult for me to explain. I want us – just you and me – to be alone when we talk about it."

He was satisfied. Yvonne, he knew from experience, kept her promises.

It lasted a bit over thirty minutes. Yvonne thought it was closer to thirty hours. She explained carefully. She spoke of things that she had learned through experience. Yve thought it was better to explain than to demonstrate. She *knew* it was better! Her father's "demonstrations" produced inhibitions that might never recede..

When "it" was over, there followed an extensive question and answer period. For one brief while, Klaus was frightened that Hildie might get pregnant because they touched – a lot – and, he admitted, they'd kissed each other. Yvonne quickly allayed his fears.

"I want you to be much older before you make a baby," she stated. "I want you to make babies only with someone you want to be with forever – like Sarah and Jean are. A baby needs a mommy *and* a daddy to help it grow."

He studied her in silence for a long while.

"When I find the right man," she promised. "He will be your daddy. Until then, I must be both. I'm not very good at it, Klaus. I know I'm not very good at this, but we both have the same Father. He will help, I'm sure."

As always, they said their prayers and went to bed.

Not until the following day did Yvonne realize the radio remained silent the entire night.

There wasn't much time, and only staff were allowed in the employees' "lounge." That suited Yvonne very well. The public venue was much nicer, and one enjoys seeing fresh faces.

Yve bought the coffee and "lunch." In fact, she selected a freshly whipped *quark* to have with her coffee. Sarah opted for a salad and a slice of brown bread. Since Yvonne enjoyed an employee's discount, playing the hostess was not a hardship.

Realizing their private time together was limited, Sarah got to the point.

"How's your crisis of faith coming along?"

"I have no crisis of faith," Yvonne reiterated. "It's my growing ambivalence toward the Catholic dogma. I'm struggling. Klaus was raised by the C. of E., and he attends an Evangelical church. I go to confession once or twice a week, but I seldom attend Mass anymore."

"I can't help you," Sarah announced. "I have issues of my own, but I attend Mass every chance I get. I read the Bible. I'm in constant need. Well, I'm sure you know what I mean. My husband is a big help, both as a husband and a spiritual advisor."

Yve nodded but withheld comment.

"Did you *explain* to Klaus?"

Yve nodded.

"I'm still shaking," she admitted. "That was – uhm – an adventure."

"You're good for him, Yvonne. I'm glad you got him out of there. I don't think he could have a better mother."

Without thinking, she leaned over the table and spoke low.

"He's my husband."

Sarah was in shock.

"In Africa, he's my husband. We got married to expedite getting him out of the country."

"Yvonne! This – can't be."

"It isn't. We had to pay a two-thousand-mark bribe to get out. In return, we got a marriage certificate – or whatever. It's all manure. They were careful to keep us from knowing what they were doing. I didn't know until months later. Lux is launching an official protest. Well, for that and – other things."

Sarah took a deep breath.

"That's so – primitive! No one will ever recognize that – thing."

"Just the same, Sarah. Could we keep this under four eyes?"

"Of course."

"Not even Jean-Baptiste?"

"Especially, not him. He'd raise an army if he knew."

They picked at their food.

"Does Klaus know about this?"

Yvonne shook her head vehemently.

They ate in silence.

"I will pray for you," Sarah announced.

"Thank you. I appreciate that more than you can ever know. Compared to this – *thing*, explaining the facts of life was plumb pudding."